**SUDDENLY TAMARA FELT LIKE
A STRANGER TO HERSELF.**

A DANGEROUS STRANGER

Tamara told herself she was totally in love
with her handsome, gallant husband, Mark
Schofield, the childhood friend who had taught
her what it was to be a woman.

Tamara was sure that only Mark could have
healed the scars of her past . . . that only *his*
kisses and caresses could stir her . . . only *his*
passion give her the ultimate fulfillment.

But now it was not he but reckless adventurer
Roderick Moran who held her in his arms . . .
pressed her against his rock-hard body . . .
crushed his lips down upon hers. . . .

And it was she who was responding like tinder
to a flame. . . .

Tamara

Big Bestsellers from SIGNET

Tamara

ELINOR JONES

Ⓞ

A SIGNET BOOK

NEW AMERICAN LIBRARY

TIMES MIRROR

*In memory of my parents,
the Honorable and Mrs. Truman J. Ruhf
and for my collie, Heidi, who fills
my life with joy.*

1

It was late afternoon. The sun had begun its indolent descent, lengthening shadows, caressing the wide expanse of beach with a soft, warm, golden glow. The crescent-shaped shore merged gently with the placid azure sea. A short distance out, a small white sailboat bobbed leisurely toward Kingston.

A tall black woman trod gracefully through the bleached sand, leaving a zigzagging trail of footprints. Her flawless skin, high cheekbones, full lips, broad straight nose, were marred only by the tiredness in her eyes. She was wearing a loose-fitting white cotton dress and a scarlet bandanna wrapped around her head, tied in back. Her only adornment was gold hoop earrings, which dangled from her pierced ears.

Agilely she balanced a reed basket of ripe mangoes on her head. She stopped to rest, setting the heavy basket down on the sand and kneading the muscles around the nape of her neck with slender fingers. She gazed down at a large sea turtle washed ashore, its head protectively hidden by its shell. As curiosity about the turtle vanished, the Jamaican woman looked up to watch with detached interest the only other figure on the beach, a girl about ten or eleven years old attempting to fly an orange-colored kite. A faint, sympathetic smile appeared on the woman's face when she saw the kite drop into the sand. She returned the cumbersome basket to her head and languorously resumed her trek through the sand, following the contour of the shoreline.

The energetic little girl ran along the shore, tightly clasping a piece of driftwood to which a large ball of twine had been wound. Looking back despairingly at the floundering kite, Tamara paused and glanced upward at the fast-moving clouds. There was a brisk breeze, perfect for kite-flying. Why, then, was she having difficulty getting it into the air? Why did it not soar into the wind like the seagull overhead, which glided and dipped between the clouds?

Tamara's pert little face tilted back. She squinted, holding her hand above her eyes to shield them from the glare of the tropical sun. Baffled, she stared into the translucent sky as if searching for some invisible barrier that had bounced the kite

1

back to earth. Then, standing defiantly with hands on hips, sighing heavily, she made another attempt, her long sunstreaked hair, hinting of red, swirling freely as she ran. The Jamaican sun had turned her fair skin bronze, but today the breeze had added rose to her cheeks.

Tamara wore a royal-blue riding habit her mother had chosen, saying it matched the color of her eyes, so dark a blue as to be almost purple. She had removed the jacket, which was far too warm, draping it over the neck of her horse, tucking the sleeves beneath the saddle so that the expensive garment would not be blown away or drop in the sand. Without it, she was comfortable in her long-sleeved blouse of soft white voile.

As she ran, her long full skirt flopped annoyingly around her legs. If she were not wearing it she could run faster. Her fingers went to the buttons that would release it, then retreated as she glanced warily toward her home on the mountainside overlooking the beach, where her mother or governess might be watching.

Tamara did not find it difficult to play by herself. There were English girls her age in Jamaica, but most of them lived on sugar plantations in the interior of the island. Weeks might go by before she would see them. Sometimes they visited her. Occasionally she went with her parents to visit them. Her closest neighbors were the Schofields, who had one son, Mark, nineteen, with whom she had developed a friendship. Mr. Schofield was away a good deal of the time, but sometimes Tamara spoke to Mrs. Schofield.

With the exception of the lack of numerous playmates her own age, Tamara's growing-up was ideal, a time to play in the sun and fresh air, gentle guidance, fair discipline, exposure to the arts, encouragement to learn and to appreciate beauty. It would be a childhood to look back on someday with fond memories of times with loved parents.

Tamara possessed a great zest for life. She was lighthearted and as uninhibited as the trade breezes. Delightfully impish, her eyes sparkled as mischievously as the crystal ripples on the sea; her fragile appearance belied her tomboyish ways. She much preferred flying kites, sailing, swimming, fishing, climbing trees, and horseback riding to the acceptable activities of a girl her age. The slingshot protruding from her skirt pocket was indicative of her preference in toys.

"She is only ten, my dear," she had overheard her father, Sir Robert Warde say to her concerned mother. "She is like a

2

colt. Just wait. She has all the signs of developing into a beautiful, spirited woman."

Lady Sarah, Tamara's mother, had replied, "You spoil her outrageously, Robert."

Tamara had heard her father laugh. "She is such a doll. 'Tis easy to do. Perhaps it is because I have no son that I enjoy her delight in such activities."

Lightly Lady Sarah had replied, "Soon you will have your son, then what? Tamara is accustomed to getting all our affection. When the baby arrives 'twill be difficult for her."

Sir Robert, the Marquis of Readington, England, had put his arm around his wife comfortingly. "Not if we make sure we continue to show her how much we love her. Adjustments will be necessary for all of us. 'Tis only natural after all these years."

Another determined effort to get the kite into the air failed. Tamara decided she might succeed atop her horse. With the lively recklessness of youth, she mounted Little Lady and urged her into a canter. Obeying her mistress, the mare bounded forward. Tamara released the kite and quickly unwound the string. The kite made one loop and plunged to earth with a thud, tossing a spray of white sand into the air. Tamara looked back disgustedly. "Drat it!" she said aloud with a note of impatience, dismounting and running to retrieve the kite.

As she ran, she recognized the young man on the black stallion galloping toward her, in her eyes looking like a Roman centurion. It was her friend Mark Schofield. She returned his wave.

"Hello beautiful." he called.

"Oh, Mark! You big tease," she answered with exasperation in her youthful voice as he pulled in his reins. It was how he usually greeted her, enjoying her annoyed reaction. When they had first become acquainted, he teased her good-naturedly about her name, calling her Tammy, which she hated.

"I do not wish to be called Tammy," she informed him spunkily. The tone of her voice and tilt of her head made him burst into laughter.

"My parents explained to me that when I was born the tamarind trees were in full bloom. My mother told me that since the blossoms are yellow and red, the color of my hair, they named me Tamara, and that is what I wish to be called." she informed him firmly.

The young man had been amused. An easy camaraderie

3

developed immediately. He, too, was an only child and lacked the companionship of peers, which brought him closer to his little neighbor, Tamara, his affections being those of an older brother. He taught her to swim and fish, took her along with him, helped her build meticulous sand castles.

Tamara looked at her friend.

"I received this kite for my birthday." She wrinkled her nose and cocked her head. "Why do you suppose it will not fly?"

"Let me have a look at it," Mark said as he dismounted.

He examined the kite, then ran down the beach and released it, but he had no more success than Tamara.

"The tail is not long enough. Let's try this," he said, untying the white cravat from his neck and fastening it to the tail of the kite.

"Now try it, Tamara."

She ran swiftly, then released the kite. Immediately it swirled upward. As rapidly as she could, she unwound the string while the kite ascended higher and higher. Tamara giggled with delight watching a curious seagull fly close, then circle it.

"Oh, thank you, Mark," she said gratefully, as he took long strides to catch up to her.

She held the string for a while, then fastened it to a larger piece of driftwood lying in the sand.

"Race you up the beach to that boulder," she challenged, mounting Little Lady.

From previous races, she knew her chestnut mare was no match for Mark's strong stallion, but it was fun to try to beat him. She was therefore surprised when she reached the boulder first, winning handily. For a moment she enjoyed the victory, until she realized he had allowed her to win.

He rode to where she was waiting, laughing.

"Why did you do that, Mark? If I win, it must be fairly, otherwise it is not winning at all!" she said with disappointment in her voice.

For a moment, the young man hedged. "Tamara, I am glad I saw you today. Remember, I told you I would be leaving Jamaica shortly. Well, the time has come. I am going away tomorrow, and I suspect by the time I return, you will be a beautiful lady who will no longer wish to fly kites or race me."

Tamara had known he was leaving, but did not know when. He had told her another day on the beach when they had raced their horses. Mark's father owned a fleet of merchant ships that sailed the trade routes of the world. It was time for him to go to sea.

"I am nineteen," he told Tamara. "My father wants me to go to sea a few years. Thinks it will make a man of me, teach me responsibilities book learning fails to do. He is tired of traveling, of being away from home all the time. Wants me to take over. He believes the personal contact is good for business." Mark laughed. "He told me there is more to the business than what goes on in the office, and more to life than what goes on here in Jamaica."

"Do you want to go?" Tamara asked.

"Of course. I am to be an apprentice to the captain on one of his vessels, one of the new steamers," he said proudly.

"Where will you go?" the child asked curiously.

"When we leave Kingston tomrrow, we will sail down along the coast of South America, then across the Pacific to India and around Africa."

"You are going to sail around the world!" she said with awe in her voice. "If I were only a boy, I would go with you!"

"Would you, now?" Mark teased.

"'Tis not much fun being a girl," she complained, sighing heavily. "I am afraid I am a bit of a problem for my mother and Miss O'Brien, my governess. All day long it is, 'Were you playing in the mud again? Wipe that smudge from your cheek. You forgot to brush your hair. How did you get that grass stain on your new dress? Guests will be arriving soon so try to be on your best behavior. Learn your numerals. Practice your music lesson.' Whew! On and on it goes."

Mark pretended sympathy. "It must be very difficult."

"Oh, if only I could sail with you! I sincerely believe grown-ups do not realize the problems of children."

Mark could not refrain from grinning.

Tamara's large violet eyes darkened as she glanced at him, showing disappointment that, like her parents, he was not more understanding.

"Maybe I could wear some of the clothes you have outgrown and go as your cabin boy."

When Mark realized the child was actually serious, he became so himself. "It is no life for a young girl. I wager you would be homesick the first night out."

"And I wager you will be too, after the second night out," she countered.

"I know I will miss my mother. Your parents would miss you."

"Yours will miss you, I am sure."

Mark shook his head and laughed. "Tamara, you are a tough adversary. I will miss our talks and rides together."

With the candid eyes of a child, she looked across at the good-looking young man. "You will have many adventures to relate when you return, and I will have nothing to tell you," she complained.

"I am sure you will have much to tell me. Would you like me to write to you?"

"Oh, Mark, would you?" she asked excitedly.

"Frankly, I hate writing letters, but since we are friends, occasionally I will send you one."

She looked across at him again, observed his dark features, his smiling green eyes. An expression of sadness entered hers.

"You will change. When you come home, you will not bother with a silly little girl."

"Tamara, I hope you and I will always be friends. Worldly experiences should not change that, should they?"

His words brought a smile to her lips. "I hope not, Mark."

2

Tamara and Mark left the shore, their horses picking their way upward toward the two mansions built on the side of the lush green mountain. They did not live far from each other, but even though the estates adjoined, they seemed at great distance because of the social barriers between them.

Tamara's family was of the English gentry. They had come out to Jamaica to operate a coffee plantation. Sitting before a portrait of the illustrious family patriarch, the first Marquis of Readington, which hung over the mantel in the drawing room, her father had explained her noble heritage as his father had explained it to him.

Family ownership of the land in Jamaica could be traced back to 1655, when Oliver Cromwell in his Western Design against Spain, a plan which included breaking her arrogant monopoly in the West Indies, sent an expedition of conquest commanded by William Penn, Royal Fleet admiral who had been successful in fighting the Dutch. While his sympathies were with the monarch, Charles II, in exile in France, Penn remained active under Cromwell, perhaps secretly hoping to serve his king.

Penn's military colleagues who commanded the army were Field Marshal Robert Warde, Tamara's ancestor, and General Robert Venables. This force was responsible for taking Jamaica from Spain and making it a British possession.

When the fleet landed, the Spanish town was deserted. Thinking the English would soon return to their ships and leave, the inhabitants had carried away and hidden everything of value. Having no force to resist an English attack, Passage Fort, the only fortification, surrendered with little resistance. Admiral Penn, Field Marshal Warde, and General Venables went ashore on May 14, and two days later a treaty was signed.

After Jamaica came under control of the British crown, the first white settlers were the soldiers and military officers, who were given free tracts of land. In recognition of his eminent services, Tamara's ancestor was rewarded with a large land grant in Jamaica and a title, the Marquis of Readington, along with land in England. He was not interested in living in Jamaica, however, nor in developing his land there, preferring instead to retire to his estate in England.

Over the next century and a half, the Marquis of Readington's estate was handed down from one generation to another, including the land in Jamaica, which remained idle, virtually forgotten except for much-needed income derived from its sale. Bit by bit the original land grant was reduced through sales to planters for raising sugarcane. Tamara's grandfather had sold the largest and best tract to pay the increased taxes in England needed to finance the second war with the United States in 1812. By 1840, what was left of the original Cromwell land grant was a stretch of 135 acres along the Blue Mountains between Kingston and Yallahs, rugged land unsuitable for raising sugarcane.

From boyhood Tamara's father had been fascinated with the knowledge that his father owned land on the faraway island of Jamaica. He had studied maps and read all he could find about the island. When he inherited the estate, he decided to do something about it.

Back in 1728, Sir Nicholas Lawes had been successful in introducing the cultivation of coffee on his plantation, Temple Hall, in Liguanae. Since then others had produced coffee for export, finding profits in Jamaica's increased trade. Sir Robert, Tamara's father, had been advised that in proportion to his investment and costs, the profits were greater in

7

coffee than in sugarcane. He named his estate Montjoy—a scenic but rugged tract along the mountain's summit overlooking the Caribbean Sea.

Well suited for the cultivation of coffee, thousands of young saplings were planted along the rich hillsides, in the shade of taller trees. The coffee trees flourished in the high altitude and wholesome air of the Jamaican mountains, where the sunshine warms but does not burn the berries, where there is both a wet and a dry season, the dry extending from December until April, ideal for the coffee trees. Since slavery had been outlawed, Negro workmen were hired to keep the trees pruned low, which increased their productivity and made the berries easier to harvest.

Here Sir Robert Warde, Marquis of Readington brought his beautiful bride, Lady Sarah, and built a spacious mansion. He was prosperous, but had not accumulated the vast wealth he hoped for. British taxes and heavy rains that ruined crops cut into the profits. But they were a happy family. Lord and Lady Warde had one daughter, Tamara, and another child was on the way, hopefully an heir.

Their closest neighbors, the Schofields, were not British aristocracy. Mark's father had not attended Oxford and did not own titles or estates in England. During the war against Napoleon he had been first officer on a privateer whose crew shared the bounty captured from the French. By the time Napoleon was defeated, Thomas Schofield had saved enough to buy his own merchant ship.

The years following the war were a period of intense commercial activity. Europe was starved for goods and shipping interests flourished. It was the right time to accumulate a fortune, and Thomas Schofield took advantage of the opportunity.

A new merchant aristocracy arose. Thomas Schofield became a part of it. A skillful businessman, he was successful in increasing his holdings to a fleet of thirty trading vessels, competing with Samuel Cunard and Fraser, Trenholm and Company. He could not buy land in England, since most of it was owned by the nobility and handed down from one generation to another. Therefore, his investments included land purchases in the British colonies of Barbados, Jamaica, and Trinidad. He had chosen Jamaica to build a home overlooking the Caribbean Sea. Jamaica was the largest island in the West Indies, one of the crossroads of the Western Hemisphere. Although Schofield kept his warehouses and offices in

Portsmouth, Liverpool, and London, he decided to establish a place of business in Kingston as well.

Tamara's parents brought their strict social consciousness with them to Jamaica, the unwritten laws of their rank that had existed for hundreds of years. Sir Robert frowned upon the new rich of England. He complained that along with their wealth, they were gaining more power in Parliament. While he, the Marquis of Readington, struggled on the verge of bankruptcy, upstarts such as Thomas Schofield had become wealthy and influential. He refused to acknowledge nonaristocrats, as did the other members of British aristocracy on the island, remaining clannish among their own kind. The Schofields were as ostracized as the wealthy Jewish merchants. When they met the Wardes, they were greeted, but coolly. Several times they had invited Sir Robert and Lady Sarah to their palatial home, but the invitations were politely refused.

Tamara was remotely aware of her parents' attitude toward the Schofields, but she was a child and didn't understand it. She had never been to England and did not know the fixed lines of convention, the strict propriety of the social classes.

A strange bond existed between Tamara and young Schofield. At that moment she regretted their parting and fought back tears. Oddly, Mark felt that by leaving he was in some way failing her.

Mark reined in his stallion. As he leaned forward, his black leather saddle crunching, he smiled and extended his arm. Tamara slipped her tiny hand into his and tried to return his smile.

"Good-bye, Mark. I wish you a safe journey. I know I shall miss you."

They were the only words the child could think of saying.

"You be a good girl, now. You hear?"

As if acting the roles in a parody, they parted, Tamara to bear to the right, Mark to follow the narrow lane that wound upward and westward. Effortlessly Little Lady knew without urging from her mistress which direction to take. The scarcely used path rose sharply. Tamara rode a short distance up the treacherous trail, then took a shortcut across the sloping field.

Little Lady rustled through the waving sea of tall grass spotted with shadows of clouds. As Tamara neared home, she noticed a freshly trampled path, then three saddled horses fettered lightly to a cluster of bamboo tress. She looked in all directions. The riders were nowhere in sight.

9

3

Abstractedly Tamara wondered who the visitors might be and why they had not taken the lane which led to the guest entrance. It crossed her mind wistfully that her mother would invite them for dinner. Although she liked company, it would mean she would be required to bathe and change into a frilly dress. As she rode past the horses pulling and chewing on the long grass she remembered it was June. The harvesting season had begun and her father was hiring additional workmen for picking the coffee beans. That was the answer. The visitors were men looking for work, Tamara concluded.

When she reached the stable, Lionel, the stableboy, removed Little Lady's saddle and put the mare in its stall, where it began to nibble at the crisp fresh hay in the trough.

Momentarily forgetting the three riderless horses she had seen, Tamara was in no hurry. She stopped and turned around several times, looking down at the rolling hills of the coffee mountain, noticing the workmen picking coffee beans. Each worker had the task of picking three baskets, or thirty pounds, of berries a day. Soon their quotas would be reached and their workday over. In 1838, five years before Tamara was born, slavery had been outlawed throughout the British Empire. Since that time, Negroes were paid wages and at the end of the day went home to their families. They lived in unpainted one-room shacks, remnants of slave days. Sir Robert had ordered all huts in the former slave quarters on his plantation torn down, but a few squatters had carried away pieces of used lumber bit by bit and had rebuilt their homes farther from the mansion, on the edge of the estate, in the cool shade, hidden by trees and underbrush. Sir Robert knew they were there, but as long as they caused no trouble he allowed them to remain.

Tamara greeted the estate manager, Nicholas Harcourt. A short, stocky, jovial man he was friendly with children. Usually he took time for a few words with her, but he was also an efficient employee who took his work seriously. At the moment he was occupied, and ignored Tamara.

Mr. Harcourt was examining baskets of coffee beans to

make sure that only dark red berries had been picked by the workers. If plucked before ripe, the coffee would have a bitter flavor. Where possible, the ground beneath the trees was cleared and the trees shaken. Only the ripe berries dropped, and workers gathered them up in large baskets.

Tamara bent down, picked a handful of berries from the ground, and tossed them in a nearby basket before going on her way. She stopped to talk to Jude, hoeing in the family garden plot. He smiled and returned her pleasantries in a slow West Indian drawl.

Moving on, she headed for the curing sheds where workers sat on the ground in a circle, removing the outer reddish pulp of the coffee beans. Across from them two Negroes raked the tiny beans spread out on long granite drying floors, their strong shoulder muscles stretching easily. The beans were stirred several times a day so that they would dry evenly in the sun. Tamara knew each worker by name and the tasks they performed. They enjoyed her daily visits and watching her grow, had developed a fond affection for the cheerful girl.

Tamara had seen the process often and knew, since it was late afternoon, that the beans were being raked into large piles to be covered with canvas for protection against sudden rainstorms and the moisture of the night air.

Tomorrow the pickers would return early, going over the same trees again, carefully selecting only the dark red berries. The entire process would be repeated.

Tamara paused to listen to the rich voices of another group of Negroes singing folk songs while removing the tough skin from beans that had been dried for several weeks. She had learned the words, and sang along with them as they put the shelled beans into large sacks and piled them in the warehouse, ready to take to Kingston.

Tamara skipped along the brick walk leading to the house, barely missing a green chameleon that scurried across her path and disappeared into the coarse grass. Sometimes she caught the tiny lizards, playing with them, delighting in watching them change color, but this one she ignored. The afternoon was quiet except for the sound of the foamy white mountain water cascading over mossy rocks nearby. Tamara knew the stream well, having crisscrossed it countless times for the sole purpose of trying to do so without getting her boots wet.

The house was two stories, made of mountain stone, with rambling verandas completely encircling it. It commanded a breathtaking vista from every angle. In front, far below, was the broad white beach; beyond it, the blue Caribbean Sea stretched to infinity. Verdant mountains and rolling hills beautified each side, with deep valleys in back. To the west, barely visible, lay Kingston and its broad harbor of ships.

A large piazza in the rear of the house, enclosed on three sides, opened to a magnificent view of the valley. Here the family ate most of its meals, even when there was a downpour, for the roof protected them. When Tamara and her parents sat at the table they could smell the heady scents of oleander, hibiscus, and jasmine and see the cascading stream, rolling hills, and fertile valleys with their orchards of citrus fruit.

Tamara stamped the loose sand from her boots, then entered the rear door. She stood her kite along the wall and went looking for Miss O'Brien, her Irish governess, who was usually there to greet her, sometimes to reprimand her for dallying, especially when it was time for dinner.

Tamara visualized neat, prim Miss O'Brien, liver spots intermingling with freckles. A plain woman, she wore her graying hair in a tight bun at the nape of her neck. When the sun shone on it there were flickering traces of the fiery red it had once been. The hair had dulled, but not Miss O'Brien's sternness.

The dutiful governess disciplined her charge along with teaching her the fundamentals of reading, writing, and numerals. The lessons Tamara liked best were those of the history of her country, Great Britain, and her island home, Jamaica.

Miss O'Brien read to her of Columbus, who came upon Jamaica on his second voyage to the greater Antilles on May 3, 1494; he thought he had discovered one of the islands in the East Indies and described it as by far the most fertile, the most beautiful of the islands he had seen. It was densely populated by amiable, peaceful Indians. Like all the islands he explored, he claimed it for Spain.

A Spanish settlement was started, cotton and sugarcane planted, and cattle imported. Indian villages were laid waste and the Indians enslaved and taken to mines.

Jamaica remained the exclusive property of Spain for more than a hundred years. Until the end of the sixteenth century Spain was the only European country to possess lands in the West Indies. When Great Britain, France, and the Netherlands became aware of their importance, when they saw the islands as a source of wealth for Spain, they began to challenge her hold on them. Whereas Spain claimed ownership by discovery, they claimed it by occupation, establishment of settlements, especially on islands which Spain claimed but had failed to colonize.

The islands of the West Indies, including Jamaica, became desirable for tropical plantation products and as bases for military operations.

Miss O'Brien told Tamara about the great earthquake of 1692 when the town of Port Royal sank into the earth, taking with it three thousand inhabitants. The few who survived had fled to where Kingston now stood.

Jamaica became a rendezvous for buccaneers who were drafted by nations to attack and plunder enemy settlements, a practice which was ended by treaty in 1697.

Jamaica did not develop until after 1763, when it was finally recognized as a British possession. After that the island began to prosper. Settlers included immigrants from Spanish and French settlements, Irish, Scots, Germans, Portuguese, and wealthy English planters from Barbados. Added to these in succeeding years were indentured servants, merchants, professional people, and slaves from Africa, who soon outnumbered whites ten to one.

Tamara went from room to room. Where could Miss O'Brien be? she wondered. The house was filled with ominous quiet. None of the household servants were in sight. Where could they be? Tamara, hearing muffled voices coming from the drawing room, remembered the horses she had seen. Her curiosity about the visitors increased. She paused, debating whether to go to her room or meet her parents' guests. Reaching a decision, she walked down the wide tiled corridor and softly turned the porcelain knob, opening the drawing-room door and slipping inside.

Tamara's eyes widened, the color drained from her face. Instinctively, when the first shock of what she saw passed, she slid behind the huge grandfather clock in the corner.

There were three dirty, rough-looking men with greasy dark beards and uncombed hair, wearing badly soiled clothing. They had tied her father's hands behind his back. One of the men was binding her mother's, while the third held a bulging sack and was stuffing the silver candlesticks into it.

The clock shielded Tamara's small crouched figure. It never entered her mind that her parents' lives might be in danger. She thought they were being robbed, and once the men had all they wanted, they would leave. Her father would go after them and catch them.

13

She noticed the intruders' fierce features and crudity of manner and their slovenly appearance. What a contrast to her father. Sir Robert was a man of good breeding, an aristocrat. Not one of his reddish-blond hairs was out of place, not a piece of lint or spot of grease could be seen on his buff-colored trousers, not a speck of dust on his boots. He held himself tall and erect even though his hands and legs were bound. It was the expression on his face and in his blue eyes that Tamara had never seen before, but she recognized it as anger, loathing, fear for her mother.

A special closeness existed between father and daughter. He was a strong, firm man, but Tamara knew she could wrap him around her little finger. If she wanted something, all she had to do was express her wish, and the next time Sir Robert came back from Kingston, he would have it for her. It was he who had given her the kite. But when it was necessary, he disciplined her. Tamara knew when discipline was needed and respected her father's fairness. She also knew that the measures he took were harder on him than her.

Tamara heard her father speak for the first time since she had entered the room.

"For the love of God, take what you want and get out of here. Do not harm my wife."

The men laughed coarsely.

"Ahhh, we ain't seen the loikes o' 'er for a long time. We be at sea fer two bloody months. Goin' agin ta'morra. Righ' now, she be worth more'n this silver an' gold."

"There is a place in Kingston," Sir Robert said anxiously, "where you can have all the women you want. I will give you money."

The men snickered. One said, "Ye've ne'er 'ad tha pleasure of takin' a woman by force, 'as ye? Thar's a sartin thrill to it." He grinned evilly.

Tamara, peeping around the corner of the clock, noticed that her mother's hair, which was normally coiled neatly and fashionably in a chignon, was loose and untidy, hanging in disarray. Her green eyes were filled with terror.

Slowly a feeling of alarm engulfed Tamara. She remained motionless, listening to her father's pleading.

"I will pay you whatever you demand, but do not touch my wife, please," Sir Robert begged. He struggled with the ropes that tied his wrists and ankles, trying desperately to free himself.

The men had drawn lots.

"Who 'as the honor o' bein' foist?" one of the men asked

eagerly, licking his dry lips. Her mother struggled as she was pushed roughly to the floor. Sir Robert pulled more desperately on the ropes that bound him.

"I beg of you, men, she is with child, as you can see!"

His pleas were ignored. Lady Sarah began to sob. It finally struck Tamara that her parents' lives were in danger. She had to go for help. The workmen were nearby; so was Mr. Harcourt. Quietly she crawled from behind the large clock. She reached the door, squeezed through it slowly so as not to make any noise. But one of the men, seeing a movement from the corner of his eye, turned and spotted her.

"Eh! Stop!" he yelled. "Where ye think yer goin'?"

"Tamara!" her father shouted. "Run!"

4

Run! Run! Her father had commanded her to run. She must save him, her mother. Tamara ran swiftly, the soles of her riding boots clapping on the tile floor. She fled down the hallway toward the rear of the house, occasionally glancing back at the man who pursued her.

"Stay away from me, you filthy pig!" she shouted, running as fast as her legs would carry her. But as she reached the door and was about to scream for help, the man caught her, jerked her backward, and clamped his dirty hand over her open mouth. With a steely arm around her waist he dragged her back to the drawing room. She bit him. Her teeth marks showed in a red semicircle in the fleshy part of his hand, behind his thumb. He cursed and slapped her hard, then gagged her with a greasy red kerchief he took from his neck. Tamara retched, repelled by the stench of it, rank sweat, rum, and tobacco intermingled. Her wrists and legs were hobbled and she was thrown to the floor.

Huffing, the heavyset man walked to the table and picked up a crystal decanter of brandy. Without bothering to pour the spirits into a glass, he lifted the bottle to his mouth, guzzling in long gulps. Holding the bottle in his left hand, he used his right to check behind each painting in the room, looking for a wall safe, leaving greasy finger smudges on walls and gilt frames. When he completed the circle of the room he drank

15

the decanter empty, set it down on the table, then wiped his mouth with his sleeve, which was rolled up to display a tattoo of a sailing ship and anchor on his forearm.

The man's head was shaven, but his beard was thick, black, and bushy, his eyes dark and beady. Tamara watched as he tied a piece of cloth across her father's mouth and fastened it at the back of his head to prevent him from calling for help. She listened to his muffled pleas with an ache in her heart.

"Now, where was we? Aye. Oi be foist," said the bald man, called Wally by the others.

"Matey, save a li'l fer us," chided his partner.

"Ye watch. Oi knows ye'll learn much," jested Wally.

The other two men, named Jack and Pete, laughed crudely. All three wore beards, black and untrimmed. Jack was tall and burly. Pete was of medium height, lean. His left eye was half-closed, the eyelid stationary.

Tamara stared as Wally took a knife and cut through the cloth of her mother's dress, then with his strong hands ripped it open until it fell to the floor in a heap. He pulled off her undergarments, exposing Lady Sarah's huge belly and large swollen breasts, which he gazed at and fondled roughly. He ground her tender nipples between his fingers, causing her to grimace in pain.

Lady Sarah was unable to look at her daughter. She squeezed her eyes tightly closed, pressuring a gush of tears down her face, trying to shut her mind as well. Sir Robert looked helplessly at his wife, then at his young daughter. His face was red with fury, his eyes glaring like a wild animal's.

Then, to Tamara's astonishment, the man opened his trousers and pulled out the ugliest object she had ever seen. It was an appendage, a part of him, hideous and threatening. He threw himself on top of her mother and jammed the object inside her. Lady Sarah's tormented screams were suppressed by the gag, but to Tamara they were the sounds of torture. Lady Sarah tossed and kicked until the man stopped her with his brutal strength.

Perspiration stood thick on Sir Robert's brow. His eyes searched the room, frantically seeking a way to free himself. Trying desperately to save his wife, he lunged forward, bumping into the man named Jack, who lost his balance momentarily, but recovered quickly. Angered, Jack pulled a knife from his belt and plunged it into Sir Robert's chest.

"Blimey! That oughta keep ye still," he said, tossing the knife carelessly on the floor to await his turn.

16

Tamara watched as the blood gushed and her father staggered and crumpled to the floor. For one brief moment her eyes closed to blot out the horror, but she could not keep them closed for long. Terror forced them open. She was powerless to look away. Staring at the incredible scene, she felt as if she would vomit. She saw Jack waiting, licking his thick lips in anticipation, eagerly feeling his member with his dirty fingers.

Tamara lay wide-eyed and trembling. Tears dulled her vision. She held her breath, then started to whimper.

Jack looked at her in annoyance, then kicked her. "Shut up, brat, afore ye gits what's comin' to ya."

Wally grunted on top of Lady Sarah, thrusting until he was spent, and dropped his full weight on her. Tamara could watch no more and closed her eyes tightly. When she opened them, the third man, who was called Pete, was lowering himself on Lady Sarah, who groaned loudly in spite of the gag. Pete punched her in the face. Her head snapped back, banging against the floor. Blood streamed from her nose, down over her lips and chin. She lay motionless, no longer struggling. No moans came from her throat. Pete was about to enter her when he saw a pool of blood showing on the floor between her legs.

"Ye goddamned blokes! She be bleedin'. Oi've no taste fer that."

Pete pulled himself up and stuffed his member back in his trousers while the other two men laughed. Then he turned to look at Tamara. "Aahhh, laugh, does ye! Well, looky whut oi got far meself."

He bent down in front of Tamara.

"Pretty li'l lass, eh?" he said, tickling Tamara under her chin with his soiled fingers. He reeled forward. Tamara shuddered, thinking he would fall on top of her. He stank of sweat and ale, of clothes worn for weeks without being laundered.

Tamara cowered on the parquet floor as the men gaped. The one named Jack, who seemed to be the leader, said, "Ah, ye'll git no satisfaction there, mate. She be a child. See, she has no tits. She be as flat as a boy. Her hole can be no bigger'n a flounder's. Ye'll sartin ne'er git whut ye got in there."

Jack and Wally, who had ravished Lady Sarah, laughed raucously, but Pete, who had been denied, grabbed Tamara and began to remove her blouse.

A faint thudding sound reached the drawing room.

"Shhh! Listen!" cautioned Jack, stopping in his tracks.

17

When he turned, Tamara saw a jagged red scar that ran from his left ear to the tip of his lip. "What be that?" he asked, listening guardedly. "Yer sure ye rounded up all the servants an' tied them in the cellar?" he whispered.

"Aye," answered Pete.

"Maybe one got loose," suggested Wally.

"Naaaay, no chance o' that," Pete said.

"Did ye find any money?" asked Jack.

"Aye, it be in the sack."

Pete's eyes lingered on Tamara; the left one with the immovable lid grew watery.

"C'mon, damn ye," said Jack. "Let's git outa 'ere afore somethin' go awry. Oi don't relish a noose round me neck."

"Best make sure the woman be dead," said Wally.

The three men glanced at Lady Sarah. Blood oozed from the corner of her mouth. Jack drew his pistol, aimed it at Lady Sarah, and fired.

"'Ow 'bout the lass?" asked Pete.

"Naaay, whut the 'ell. She's jest a bratty kid. Let's git goin'."

Tamara watched as the three men scurried from the room, Jack clutching the sack in his left hand while jamming his pistol back in his belt. She worked at her wrists, trying to get them free, twisting until her skin was raw.

In Jamaica the duration of the day and night remains almost the same throughout the year. The sun rises about five o'clock and sets about seven. The red disk of the sun was spreading its last pale rays over the mountains. Twilight sifted meekly through the panes. Shadows disappeared as night's darkness descended. Tree frogs began chirping their nightly melody, sounding morose tonight rather than cheerful. Ten-year-old Tamara found herself alone with the bleeding bodies of her dead parents sprawled on the floor.

Her eyes grew heavy, closed, opened, closed. Exhausted, she dozed, awakened, dozed, waiting for someone to find her.

5

Sometime during the night a flare of lightning veined the sky, followed by a rumble of thunder that volleyed through the mountain range, giving the first warnings of an approaching storm. The wind crooned morosely through the trees. Lying on the floor, her hands and feet bound, the gag still tight at her mouth, Tamara winced as jagged streamers of lightning flitted across the room and thunder crashed all around her.

The rain came in torrents, falling in solid perpendicular lines, lashing against the panes as if possessed by an animated desire to get inside the room. The angry drops searched for a place to enter, while the wind howled and whipped at the wooden shutters.

Tamara's body jolted as a thunderclap cracked loudly. Her heart beat wildly. She trembled uncontrollably. Outside, the earth vibrated beneath the house. Flashes came unremittingly, one after the other, brightening the room, mercilessly enabling her to see her mother and father. As if by magic the lightning made their still bodies appear, disappear, appear.

The furor of the storm continued, uprooting trees, hurling leaves and twigs against the panes, until slowly it moved out across the sea, taking the rain with it, weakening its clamor, stopping as quickly as it began. Outside, except for a loose shutter slapping rhythmically back and forth, stillness returned. Inside, the grandfather clock in the corner ticked loudly, remorsefully chiming two, three, four o'clock.

Shafts of morning sunlight slashed through the windowpanes between the parted drapery, falling on Tamara's tear-stained face, warming her nose, piercing her eyelids. She woke gradually, blinking her eyes dazedly in momentary confusion, at first not knowing where she was, then asking herself: "Why am I lying here on the drawing-room floor instead of in my bed? Awkwardly she levered her body, struggling to sit up, aware now of the gag, the binding of her hands and ankles. The flesh on her cheeks was smeared with dried tears. Turning her head, she saw her parents lying motionless in pools of blood. At first, thinking it all a bad dream, stark re-

19

ality struck her like the sound of the thunderbolt in the night.

Her puffy red eyes spotted the tip of the knife that had been used to stab her father, then carelessly tossed aside. It was sticking out from beneath a chair, blood on the blade having thickened and dried, turned almost black.

Tamara crawled over to the chair, turned over on her back, and struggled to pick up the knife with her fingers. She began to saw at the rope. Working for a long time, she was able to cut through one of the fibers that made up the rope, then another and another, until her wrists were free.

She removed the gag, then untied the rope around her legs. Running to the basement door, she went down the steep steps and saw Miss O'Brien and the three houshold servants tied and gagged. With the knife she freed them. They rubbed their wrists and ankles to encourage circulation. Miss O'Brien opened her arms and gathered Tamara to her bosom.

"Faith an' begorrah you're safe, child! I was so worried about you," she exclaimed in her Irish brogue. Tamara whimpered in the governess's arms. "Hush, Tamara, yer a brave lass and ye'll weep no more." Tamara grabbed Miss O'Brien's hand and pulled her to the steps. The others followed right into the drawing room.

Miss O'Brien let out a terrible scream, then crossed herself. She gasped for breath, pressing her fist to her chest in pain, then collapsed.

When Mr. Harcourt was informed of the murders, he rode to Kingston for the authorities. Tamara ran to the stable, mindless of the condition of her clothes, which were moist from perspiration and the urine that, during the night, she tried but was unable to contain. She was thirsty, but did not stop to change or get a drink of water. She mounted Little Lady bareback and rode toward Schofield Manor for Mark.

A rainbow arched across the early-morning sky, encircling the drenched mountainside. The tall grass was wet, the air freshly cleansed. Trees dripped the storm's moisture.

The Schofields were eating breakfast when Tamara pounded her little fist on the door, screaming for Mark. She was on the verge of hysterics when Arona, the Jamaican maid, calmly opened the door. Mark's father, hearing the screams, came to the entrance. Tamara had seen him only a few times before, but recognized him immediately. His blue eyes were friendly. His thick locks were salt-and-pepper-colored. Of medium height, his body was strongly built. Maintaining a ruddy seafaring look, he was a man who had worked hard for the success he now enjoyed.

20

Mrs. Schofield came up behind him. "Why, Tamara, what on earth is the matter?" she asked.

A dam of tears broke loose, gushing down Tamara's face. She ran to Mrs. Schofield and flung her arms around the kindly woman, clinging to her desperately. Jane Schofield put her arm around Tamara and patted her gently, looking toward her husband. "Something must be wrong over at the Warde plantation."

"I will go over and check, although they probably will not welcome me with open arms," replied Thomas Schofield slowly.

Tamara sobbed hard, unable to speak. She pressed close to Mrs. Schofield, groping for comfort and security.

"Now, now. Everything will be all right," Mrs. Schofield said soothingly. "Come with me. Would you like a glass of milk?"

Tamara shook her head violently. Mrs. Schofield took her hand, and as she did, Tamara cried out in pain. The woman saw the raw circles around the girl's wrists.

"Why, what on earth happened to your wrists? Were you tied?"

Tamara nodded her head. She looked around and finally spoke. "Wh-where is Mark?" she asked between gulping sobs.

"Why, Mark left early this morning. Come along. I think you should lie down."

The girl clung to Mrs. Schofield, who ordered a servant to prepare a bath for her. Tamara screamed when she tried to leave her for a moment. With her arm around Tamara she told one of the manservants to go to Kingston for the doctor. Seeing the girl was too distraught to explain what had happened, she did not question her, but took her to the bedroom, helped her to undress and bathe, then put her to bed.

Mrs. Schofield lay beside Tamara on the bed until she fell into an exhausted sleep. Slowly Mrs. Schofield rose, drew the draperies closed, and sat in a chair nearby in case Tamara awakened.

Thomas Schofield did not return until noon. He motioned for his wife to come out into the hall and explained what had happened.

"Tamara must have witnessed it. The authorities are coming to question her."

"No," insisted Mrs. Schofield. "She is in no condition for that. She is a child. Her whole world has just collapsed. Tom, you must stop them from putting her through any more."

"The authorities theorize that the men were from a mer-

21

chant ship that set sail at dawn. I hope to God it was not one of mine. They will be difficult to trace."

"Then why torture the girl further?"

"Was she . . . was she molested?" asked Tom Schofield.

"I do not know. Dr. Davis has not arrived. The poor child! What can we do?"

"We will keep her here for the time being."

Tamara woke, thinking she was in her own bed at home, imagining she heard the voice of her father. She cried and cried. Condolences were of little help. She did not respond to Tom or Jane Schofield's questions. Most of the time she stared into space. Her bruised wrists healed, but the deep wounds to her emotions did not.

Mrs. Schofield sent Arona to Montjoy with instructions to obtain Tamara's clothing and personal belongings.

"She should not return to her home," was her opinion.

A double funeral was held for Lord and Lady Warde, who were buried in a newly created cemetery on the estate. The Schofields thought it best if Tamara did not attend the burial service. People came from all over the island for the final rites, friends and acquaintances out of respect, strangers out of curiosity. Silently, edgily, they viewed the two closed caskets with the Readington family crest on top of each one. Blacks stood in the background at a distance, weeping.

The day after the funeral, the British military police came to Schofield Manor to question Tamara. She turned white, tears close to the surface of her eyes when asked to recall the scene in detail. Remembering all too clearly, words caught in the child's throat, forcing her to nod or move her head from side to side in reply to their questions.

"Were they Negroes?"

Tamara shook her head no.

"Did they speak English?"

Tamara nodded up and down.

"Can you give us a description of the men? How many were there?"

Tamara's eyes welled with tears. Her fingers trembled, and at first she did not reply.

"If you can help us, it will make it easier to catch them, so they will not commit more crimes," the officer said kindly.

She gave him a brief description of each of the three criminals. She remembered their names: Wally, Jack, and Pete.

Alone now, the only one of the family to survive, Tamara

did not snap back. The tragic loss of her parents' love, their affection, the security of family life, was immeasurable. Weeks went by. The Schofields were worried. Tamara insisted on keeping a lamp burning in her room all night. She had nightmares and screamed in her sleep. "Where is Mommy? . . . Papa, where are you?" She awakened trembling, her hair, nightgown, and pillow moist with perspiration. "Papa . . . I want my papa," she cried pitifully.

She grew pale and lost weight. At night the lovely Jane Schofield sat on her bed and read to her until Tamara was asleep. It was not until a month after the tragedy that the girl showed signs of responding. One evening when Mrs. Schofield was reading to Tamara, resting in the crook of her arm, she announced that they had received a letter from Mark.

Tamara sat up in bed. "Where is he?" she asked softly. "Is he coming home?"

"The letter came from Australia."

"What did he write?"

"Among other things, he asked about you. Since he had not received my letter when he wrote, he did not know what happened to your parents. Would you like me to read it to you?"

"Yes, please."

Tamara watched and listened as Mark's lengthy letter was read. It was mostly about business matters for his father, cargoes, consignments, trade agreements. He was delighted by the beauty of the islands in the South Pacific and quipped about the lovely women and their hospitality.

"If you see my little friend Tamara Warde, tell her I asked about her and will write to her soon."

Tamara smiled and looked at Mrs. Schofield very closely. As the beautiful woman continued to read the letter, Tamara was soothed by the lilt in her voice. She noticed her soft, dark, fashionably arranged hair and her green eyes, which sparkled with tenderness. When Mrs. Schofield had completed the letter, Tamara looked at her and said, "Mark looks like you."

Mrs. Schofield smiled. "So it is said, but he has his father's ways and interests. Would you like to write him a letter? I will give you paper and quill."

Tamara shook her head. Lying back on her pillow, she withdrew again. Thomas Schofield had written to Sir Robert's brother in London informing him of the tragedy. Because communication between England and the West Indies was slow, a reply did not arrive until two months later. Tamara's

23

uncle, Arthur, requested that the Schofields send Tamara on the first steamer to London. She would live with him, his wife, and their twin daughters. He saw no other solution.

When Tamara was told, she screamed and became hysterical. "I want to stay here with you! Do you not want me? Please do not send me to London," she begged pathetically.

"Of course we want you, Tamara," Mrs. Schofield said in her soft voice. "We always wished for a daughter, a sister for Mark. We want you to stay with us, but it is not for us to decide. Your uncle is your guardian now."

"Tamara," added Tom Schofield, "I will write to your uncle and ask him whether you can remain at Schofield Manor. How is that?"

"Oh, would you, sir? I am certain Uncle Arthur will not object as long as he knows I have a good home."

Mrs. Schofield took the girl in her arms, hugging her tightly. She gave her husband a wary glance and turned her face from Tamara, trying to hide the plaguing doubt expressed in her eyes.

6

Tamara was wrong, as Mrs. Schofield had feared. Sir Arthur's reply was firm. She was to live in London with his family. He was responsible for her upbringing, and he wanted to do his duty. Since he had read reluctance between the lines, he would come for her himself.

Mrs. Schofield attempted to comfort the girl. "It will not be all that bad, Tamara. There are many interesting places to see in London. You will make new friends. You like animals and can go to the London Zoo, where they have tigers and elephants. Wouldn't you like that? The dressmakers in London are outstanding. I am sure your aunt will see to it that you have pretty dresses. You will meet your two cousins. Here there are no girls your age with whom to play."

The sweet woman's efforts were fruitless. Tamara whimpered. Her eyes welled with tears. "Please. I want to stay with you."

Mrs. Schofield was so distraught she went to her room, not wishing to show Tamara how upset she was.

"Now, now, do not fret, my dear," her husband said, trying to console her. "Perhaps when Sir Arthur arrives and sees
how much Tamara wants to stay with us, he will change his
mind. I will do everything I can to persuade him to allow her
to remain here. Since Mark left, I know it has been lonely for
you. I have become very fond of Tamara, too."

Jane Schofield sniffed and wiped her nose. "I cannot bear
to give her up. To think she wants to live with us and that
dreadful man will not allow it. She was born in Jamaica. She
is accustomed to the mountain air and the shore. I would not
tell her, but I know she will be totally unhappy living in
London."

"Maybe not. Children have a way of adapting," Tom
mused.

Tamara had never met her uncle. He was younger than her
father and had now inherited the family title and estates in
England. According to her father's will, investments and the
coffee plantation were put in trust for Tamara.

She built up a hatred toward her uncle, envisioning him as
an ogre who was coming to steal her away and imprison her
for life. When he arrived she was surprised, almost disappointed, that he was not the beast she anticipated, but a kindly
man. She had prepared to spit at him, stick her tongue out,
kick him if necessary. Hopefully, if he thought her a trou-
blesome brat, he would not want her. But the man looked
very much like her father. He took her in his arms, spoke to
her gently, offered her sympathy.

He was tall and stately, with reddish-blond hair exactly like
her father's. Even the tone of his voice was familiarly like Sir
Robert's.

She knew she had no choice; nevertheless, it was with reluctance that she agreed to go with him. Only after the
Schofields promised to visit her, and her uncle agreed that she
could visit them, did she weaken.

When the day arrived for her to leave Jamaica, hesitantly
Tamara boarded the vessel in Kingston. One of the largest
harbors in the world. it was picturesque, majestic. Rigged and
clipper ships, schooners and vessels powered by steam lay at
anchor, ships which had docked in ports around the globe.

The aquamarine water swished softly against the vessels as
rough-tongued seamen returning from a night of women and
drinking in Kingston bragged of their conquests. Some spoke
English, others Spanish, French, Portuguese. Tamara's eyes
scanned the decks of the ships, looking for the men who had

killed her parents, a gesture which would become a habit, a never-ending search which would ever haunt her. If she saw them, she would recognize them. She would never forget their faces and what they had done.

Although Tamara hated to leave, she was excited by the prospect of her first sea voyage, glad to be sailing on one of Mr. Schofield's steamers. Its black hull sank deep into the water from the weight of its cargo stored in the holds, sacks of coffee beans and hogsheads of sugar and molasses. Smoke belched from its stacks, a signal that the ship was ready for departure.

Tamara heard the water lap at the ship's hull as she stood at the railing of the main deck, resigned to leaving the island and the people she loved. The aroma of saline air reached her. The tropical sun ignited sparks on the bay. Squinting, her eyes moved across the wharf and up along the range of tree-covered mountains, impressing them in her memory so that she would never forget their beauty. Someday. Someday she would return to Jamaica, she vowed.

Waving weakly to Mr. and Mrs. Schofield standing on the quay, Tamara noticed Mrs. Schofield was weeping, dabbing her eyes, and she, too, began to sob. She wanted to climb over the railing and run to her arms.

Seamen toiled with heavy moorings. The anchor was raised. The ship began to move slowly, tooting its whistle as a departure signal.

A seagull swooped low over the water, then perched on one of the railings, proudly flapping its wings.

He is free to come and go as he pleases, Tamara thought, watching the bird. I wish I were a seagull. Then I could stay here. She frowned as the bird ascended, heading back toward shore.

As the ship glided smoothly out of the harbor, Tamara left her childhood behind, happy family life as she knew it, the joys of the beach, the pleasures of living on the coffee mountain. Problems which to her had been serious no longer mattered: the inability to fly a kite, a stain on her dress, succeeding in crossing a stream, all became a part of her past. Tamara stared at the vessel's white, bubbly wake; then, as they passed the tip of Port Royal, she glanced at the British flag fluttering in the trade wind. Still dazed by the loss of her parents, forlornly she looked back at the island one more time. Jamaica became a blur.

When a dark cloud overhead released a spatter of rain, her

uncle put his arm around her. "Come along, Tamara. I will take you to your cabin."

Tamara was the only child on board, Sir Arthur the only adult passenger. They ate their meals with the captain, James Cunningham, a cherubic-looking middle-aged Englishman who had spent his life at sea. As he held his knife and fork, Tamara noticed his chubby fingers, which reminded her of a baby's hand. The sun and salt air had turned his complexion mahogany-colored and streaked his hair blond. His mutton-chop whiskers were fluffed and mixed with gray. His pudginess was emphasized by his white uniform, which obviously had fit when new, but had grown tighter as he gained weight. The cloth of his jacket stretched precariously where the buttons were fastened.

Captain Cunningham was aware that his passengers were very important to the ship's owner and did everything he could to make their voyage a pleasant one. Extra rations of water, meat, fruits, vegetables, and the best wines were added to the ordinary stores of ship's supplies. Thomas Schofield himself had seen them off and instructed him to do whatever he could to make them comfortable.

The first night out, Tamara picked at her food. She had very little to say, and her elders made no effort to draw her into their conversation. She retired early. Sir Arthur went with her to her cabin. He sat down on a straight chair, reluctant to leave her alone but at a loss as to what to say to her.

She longed for her parents. She missed the Schofields. Surrounded by those who loved her since birth, then being suddenly taken away, was a frightening experience, leaving her lonely and insecure.

"Who will take care of Little Lady?" she asked.

"Schofield will keep her at his stables."

Tamara smiled weakly. "Oh, I am very glad to hear that."

"The other horses were sold."

"What about my governess, Miss O'Brien?"

Sir Arthur rubbed his hands together nervously. "You will not be needing her in London."

"But what will happen to her? She is getting old."

"She has retired. I have made provisions for her. All the other workers were discharged."

"I did not even say good-bye to Miss O'Brien."

"She was ill after . . . after your parents . . . died. 'Tis easier this way, Tamara. I am sure you will like your new home and your cousins. They will become the sisters you

27

never had. You will see. We have a home in the country, too, where you will be able to ride."

Tamara glanced at her uncle pleadingly. "You could not ship Little Lady over for me, could you?"

"I am afraid not, Tamara. That is out of the question. We have a stable full of thoroughbreds."

He waited a few moments longer until she settled beneath the covers.

"Now, do you think you will be all right? My cabin is right next door. If you want me, tap on my door."

In her bunk, she tried to keep her eyes open, because whenever she closed them she had visions of her father being stabbed and her mother raped. Sir Arthur had turned down the oil lamp when he left the cabin. She rose, turned the knob that lengthened the flame. Staring at the brass lamp swaying back and forth, her eyes grew heavy. The flickering light danced on the ceiling, made moving circles on the floor.

Tamara dozed fitfully. When she slept she dreamed of the three men who had murdered her parents. The scene returned to her time and time again. Her own screams wakened her. Sir Arthur heard them and rushed into her cabin. He sat down on the edge of her bunk and held her close.

"In time you will forget," he said gently. "Death is something each of us must face sooner or later. It lies in ambush until the Lord beckons." His words were small comfort for the bewildered child.

Endless days at sea were monotonous for Tamara. There was nothing for her to do. Her uncle slept a great deal of the time. She sensed Captain Cunningham was a man uncomfortable around children, so she stayed out of his way.

After two weeks, storm clouds gathered and the ocean turned rough. The ship rolled, dipped, and heeled. Tamara welcomed the change, which she found exciting. Strong winds rocked the vessel, and whitecaps rolled across the quarterdeck. Tamara proved to be a good sailor and did not get seasick, as did her uncle.

The brunt of the storm bypassed them. After two days the sea returned to rocking the ship cradlelike. The sun turned bright, hidden scantily by white, slow-moving clouds. The English coastline came into view. When the ship sailed up the Thames to London and prepared for anchoring, Tamara resolutely prepared herself for her new home.

7

When the ship docked in London, Tamara could not believe the damp climate that greeted her. More like a late-December day than early October. The cold pierced her flesh. All her clothing was suitable only for tropical weather, including the thin yellow voile dress she wore. A chill shook her tiny body, a chill caused by more than the light weight of her clothing.

Sir Arthur's luxurious barouche with liveried footmen was waiting at the wharf. The trunks and portmanteaus were placed in a second carriage, and soon they were speeding through the streets of London toward her uncle's townhouse.

Tamara was astounded by the large number of people. And never had she seen so many buildings, warehouses and homes close together. The streets were thronged with carriages. She never dreamed there could be so many in the whole world, all sizes and models, from elaborate coaches-and-six to the little rattly milk cart drawn by a rundown nag they passed.

The air reeked of unfamiliar odors. Alien, clattering noises deluged her. They were not the sounds of Jamaica, birds singing, musical wind, splashing waves. With an ache in her heart, Tamara remembered the clean, fresh air, the sand and warm sun, the loveliness of her home nestled on the mountainside.

Sir Arthur pulled back his shoulders and pushed his chest forward. "Tamara, this is the hub of the empire," he said proudly. "When you are settled in, I shall arrange to take you on a tour of London. I am sure you will enjoy seeing the changing of the guard, Westminster, Madame Tussaud's Wax Museum. There are literally thousands of fascinating places to see. You might even have an opportunity to see Queen Victoria." He turned his head to look at Tamara. "Would that not be thrilling?" he said excitedly.

Tamara was not impressed by what she saw, not until they left the area of the docks and warehouses. The carriage moved sedately across town. It entered St. James's, where the streets were wider and lined with statuesque elms whose leaves had turned bright orange and red. Gray-uniformed nannies pushing fancy perambulators proudly paraded up and down brick sidewalks thick with fallen leaves. They passed St. James's Park, colorful with autumn-blooming red sage and yellow chrysanthemums, crossed Piccadilly, and turned onto Park Lane directly across from Hyde Park.

When the barouche stopped at the curb on exclusive Park Lane, an elderly butler limped from the stately house to greet Sir Arthur. "Welcome home, your lordship."

"Thank you, Watkins," said Sir Arthur, handing the butler his hat and cane.

Tamara glanced upward, saw the lace curtain move at one of the long windows protected by a black wrought-iron railing. She flinched when she saw the grotesque gargoyles along the roof gutter looking down, scrutinizing her forebodingly. Shyly she followed her uncle up the front marble steps, sliding her hand along the polished brass handrail.

A massive woman wearing a purple silk mobcap shuffled toward them. She stretched her heavy arms and flung them around Sir Arthur's neck. He colored and looked embarrassed.

Tamara stared impolitely, for the woman had the most elongated face, the longest chin she had ever seen. She watched as her uncle reached back, took the woman's chubby hands from his neck.

Sir Arthur cleared his throat. "My dear. This is little Tamara. Lady Alma."

Tamara curtsied. "Your ladyship," she said softly, as the woman scrutinized her with the same expression as the gargoyles.

Lady Alma looked at Tamara coldly. "How do you do, Tamara," she replied in a shrill, high-pitched voice. "Watkins will show you to your chamber."

As Tamara followed Watkins up the winding staircase with its dark mahogany balustrade, she heard Sir Arthur say, "A wearisome voyage, my dear. 'Tis a good thing you did not accompany me. Where are Beverly and Valerie?"

"They are at the puppet show."

Walking slowly with a limp caused by lumbago, Watkins preceded Tamara down the bleak upstairs hall. A stout man with thick white hair, he stopped, opened a door with his knobby, arthritic fingers, and gestured for her to enter the gloomy room. His face was expressionless.

"Miss, this is to be your room. I hope everything will be to your satisfaction. Your trunks will be brought up shortly."

He bowed stiffly and left her, closing the door behind him.

30

Feeling utterly alone, Tamara sat on the edge of the massive black oak bed, her legs dangling. She removed her bonnet and laid it aside. With trembling fingers she wiped the tears from her cheeks.

Looking around the room, which was damp and smelled of mildew, she sighed heavily, contemplating the new life that had been thrust upon her. The room was elaborate to the point of being grotesque; dreary, not bright and cheerful like her room at home. She gazed at the dust floating through a slit of sunlight piercing the window. Hanging on the walls were faded, dusty tapestries with scenes of ancient battles. The draperies were a heavy, bilious green. Tamara suspected that if she shook them, clouds of dust would balloon into the air. She sneezed thinking about it. Alone with her fears, she let herself fall back on the bed, weeping until she fell asleep.

A light tap on her door wakened her. A small, fragile, gray-haired maidservant wearing a black dress with a white apron and cap entered the room.

"Miss, oi'm Ruth," she whispered, walking to the bed, fluffing the pillows, fixing the spread. "Oi'm supposed ta unpack fer ye, oi am, an' 'elp ye dress fer dinner."

Tamara did not look forward to going down to dinner. She had the impression that Lady Alma did not really want her, and feared her cousins would feel the same way.

When Tamara was introduced to Beverly and Valerie, she curtsied slightly, eyeing them cautiously, as they did her. She was conscious of her light summer frock compared to their soft, dark woolens in red and green.

The dining room was drafty and as oppressively bleak and cold-feeling as her bedroom. Woodwork was stained almost black. Sconces on the walls and candles on the table flickered the only brightness.

Tamara was seated next to Lady Alma and across from her cousins. She was quiet throughout the meal, wondering how she could endure living in this household.

Beverly and Valerie were identical twins two years older than Tamara. Their mousy brown hair was arranged in rag curls, their brown eyes matching the dullness of the hair. They had inherited their mother's long chin and chubby figure. Cursed with buck teeth, they appeared to be smiling when they were not, for Beverly and Valerie rarely smiled or laughed.

Tamara listened quietly as they told their parents of their visit to the puppet show and their experiences of the afternoon. When one spoke, the other nodded her head in agreement.

"I have never seen a puppet show," Tamara proffered.

Her twin cousins looked at each other and sniggered maliciously.

Lady Alma seemed to have difficulty speaking directly to Tamara. She looked at Sir Arthur and spoke to him. "Arthur, the child is not eating," she snapped.

"She is probably tired from the crossing. 'Twas a tedious journey for an adult, let alone a child. And no doubt she is homesick. Be patient, Alma."

"I hope she is not going to be difficult, Arthur," Lady Alma commented inhospitably. They continued to speak of her as if she were not present. Tamara could barely wait to escape to her room.

But once there, she found little comfort. She peered out the window. Most of the leaves had fallen from the trees surrounding the house. Tamara had never seen barren trees before. She undressed and slipped into bed. The sheets did not smell fresh and clean like at home. Their odor was distasteful. They smelled of strong soap and a staleness from being folded in a drawer for a long time. Tamara pinched her nose closed with her fingers. The heavy quilts made of dark-colored velvet patches smelled moldy and weighed her down.

Moonlight entered the window. Eerie shadows scaled the walls around the bedchamber. Frightened, she huddled beneath the covers in spite of their foul odor. She could not stop shivering. She imagined someone with a bushy black beard was hiding behind the massive furniture. The moonlight itself looked cold, not warm and friendly like at home in Jamaica.

During the night she had a nightmare, hearing her mother's tortured screams. Tamara screamed.

Ruth came running into her room. "Sh! Sh! Miss. If ye wakes the leidy o' the 'ouse, ye be in trouble fer sure," she warned.

Tamara trembled. "I would like the lamp turned up, please."

The flame was enlarged, and eventually she fell asleep.

8

Tamara's mind refused to accept the fact that she would never see her parents again. The transition from her world in Jamaica to London was difficult. She did not adjust easily to her new home and family. Her cousins were not the least bit friendly. They were inseparable and treated her like an intruder. Refusing to accept her on equal grounds, they did not invite her to join them in games they played or in girlish confidences. Sir Arthur had said they would be like sisters, but Tamara found this impossible. In the presence of their parents Beverly and Valerie behaved civilly toward her, but when they were alone, if they did not ignore her entirely, they bullied her, teased her about her name, and made fun of the fact that she was an orphan. One would whisper in the other's ear so that Tamara could not hear what was being said; then they would look at her and giggle.

Tamara thought they were childish and spoiled.

Since they did not want her, she would run away, hide on a ship, and go back to the Schofields in Jamaica. She knew they wanted her, and it was where she longed to be.

At first Tamara was hurt and confused. She decided until she could return to Jamaica and the Schofields, she would fight back. She resorted to mischievous pranks.

Catching a mouse in a box, she released it under Valerie's bedcovers. When the frightened mouse scurried up Valerie's leg, she became hysterical.

If only I had a chameleon, Tamara thought. That would really scare her.

Tamara was joyously surprised when Lady Alma took her to her seamstress on Bond Street to have long-sleeved flannel nightgowns and warm dresses made as well as a heavy pelisse with fur muff and bonnet. She wondered why she would be needing woolen stockings, mittens, and boots until she experienced her first frigid ice storm, which struck London the first week in December.

She was agog a week later when she saw snow for the first time. She stood at the parlor window and watched heavy clouds give up their moisture. Snowflakes, large and star-

33

shaped, floated from the sky. She watched with awe as the windswept snow continued to swirl and accumulate on trees and lawn. She wanted to thrust open the window and touch it as it piled on the windowsill.

It snowed for twenty-four hours, and it was not until the next day that Tamara and her cousins ventured outdoors. Filled with fascination, she bent down and touched the crystals, gathered a handful, and examined it closely. She watched as Beverly and Valerie took turns rolling a snowball across the white-covered grass. She laughed as it grew larger and larger. They made another like it and put it on top of the first one, then made a third, which was smaller. Tamara wondered what they were up to but was determined not to ask. When she realized they had made a snowman, since they had not invited her to help she decided to make one of her own. She delighted in watching her snowball enlarge and the snowman take shape. She used pebbles for the eyes, nose, and mouth, and when it was completed she stood back and giggled with joy. It was the happiest moment, the first pleasurable afternoon since her arrival in London.

Throughout the winter the girls were kept busy. Every Tuesday they were given piano lessons. They spent three hours each morning in the schoolroom on the second floor with their tutor, Mr. Arnold Matson, a studious young man of thirty, an age which seemed ancient to the girls. They were taught penmanship, grammar, literature, French, and sketching.

Arnold Matson was spare, frail-looking, and scholarly. His coat was mended with large oval patches over each threadbare elbow. He had come to Lady Alma highly recommended, and displayed an eagerness to instruct his charges. He praised them and gave rewards where and when they were justified and offered constructive criticism and encouragement when they were not. His patience was limitless as Beverly and Valerie fidgeted, sighed, and daydreamed, paying little attention to his teaching and his efforts to enrich their lives through his knowledge of art, literature, and history.

Mr. Matson found Tamara to be the brightest of the three girls. He wrote complimentary phrases on her papers and encouraged her to continue her good work. Beverly and Valerie mimicked him behind his back. They grew jealous of his praise for Tamara and accused him of favoritism. One day when the girls were supposed to be sketching an urn and bowl of apples Mr. Matson had arranged on the table, he discovered Valerie had drawn a funny face with large ears and nose. It had been labeled "Arnie." He scolded her severely, which brought her to tears.

When Beverly and Valerie received failing marks on a French test which Tamara passed formidably, an indignant Lady Alma dismissed him. He was a kindly man, sincere in his profession. Tamara was sorry to see him leave.

In his place Lady Alma hired Jeremy Weatherly, an older man, wiser in his knowledge of people, apparently realizing who paid his salary and who would fire him if he did not do well. Although Tamara's work was better, it was her cousins who received the higher grades and compliments. "Good work" and "Interesting" were written across their sloppy papers.

Beverly and Valerie used every opportunity to cast up to Tamara the praises they received. Grabbing Tamara's paper, Beverly asked snickeringly what Mr. Weatherly had written on it. Before Beverly had time to read it, Tamara answered, "That I can do better, which is true."

The tutor was a big-boned man with large hands and feet, long arms and legs. His presence in the classroom was overpowering. Out of fear, there would be no drawing funny faces of this man.

For Tamara, time had no meaning. Winter passed. Spring arrived early. On the family's first outing of the season, she stuck a caterpillar into Beverly's cream-filled scone. Beverly was about to take a bite, when the caterpillar stuck its head through the whipped cream. The girl screamed and dropped it.

The inseparable twins' names were usually spoken as one, Beverly and Valerie, never Valerie and Beverly. Beverly and Valerie spent much time in the garden in the rear of their house embroidering or playing with their dolls. Each had an expensive wax doll with real hair and blue glass eyes. The dolls were outfitted with exquisite wardrobes, jewelry, brushes, and combs. The twins sat for hours dressing and redressing them and arranging their hair in the latest style.

Tamara would accompany them, taking a book or paper and quill to practice her penmanship, sitting by herself. Sometimes she made dissected puzzles. She was not invited to join the twins, but she was not interested in dolls anyway.

One afternoon Tamara's cousins were particularly cruel, chiding her and chanting "Clammy Tammy." Look at Clammy Tammy. Ha ha! Clammy Tammy the orphan." Tamara fought back with spirit. "Beverly, you are the one who is clammy. You still wet your bed."

Humiliated that Tamara knew, Beverly burst into tears.

Tamara tried to concentrate on her book, not letting the girls see she held a long ground worm in her hand that she had found in one of the flowerbeds and saved for the right moment. When neither twin was looking, she put the worm on Valerie's head. It wiggled its way into the thick mass of lackluster curls without her feelng it or knowing it was there. Tamara chuckled to herself, but finally could withhold it no longer.

"Ugh!" She pretended being revolted. "You are wormy, Valerie!"

"What do you mean, brat?"

"Look at your head. Ugh! There are worms crawling."

Valerie put her plump fingers to her head and felt the worm. Imagining there were millions of them, she began to scream and pull at the slimy, crawling creature, but it was entangled in her curls. She shrieked as she ran to the house for her mother.

Tamara returned to her reading. It was difficult, but she managed to maintain a look of innocence when an indignant Lady Alma waddled toward her, glaring angrily.

"You naughty child! You did that deliberately."

"What, ma'am? I do not know of what you are speaking," Tamara answered sweetly.

"You put that worm in Valerie's hair," Lady Alma accused crossly.

"Why would I do that? Did Valerie tell you, ma'am?" she asked with a note of surprise in her voice.

"Tsk! Of course she did, and Valerie never lies."

Lady Alma glanced down and gasped in horror. Tamara had removed her shoes and stockings and was barefoot. She liked the feel of the soft cool grass on her toes and the bottom of her feet. Lady Alma put her hands on her hips. "What can one expect, raised like a savage in the jungles? Go to your chamber at once."

Tamara rose, picked up her shoes and stockings, curtsied politely, and headed for her bedroom, which had become a sanctuary. Lady Alma followed close behind, cuffing her on the back of the head, causing her to stumble forward. She dropped one of her shoes, and when she bent to retrieve it, Lady Alma kicked her.

When Tamara reached her room, she locked her door so that no one could enter, then plopped on her bed. She de-

36

cided she would not dress and go down for dinner. Even the tempting aroma of pound cake baking in the kitchen oven could not lure her from her self-imposed prison. She did not want any food, let alone to sit at the table with her horrible cousins. She would stay in her room forever!

At dinnertime her uncle rapped on her door and tried the knob. "Tamara, open this door immediately! You are not too old for a good spanking."

"Yes, sir." Reluctantly Tamara opened the door, and her uncle entered.

"Tamara, what is all this about? Lady Alma is right. After all I have tried to do for you, your behavior is most provoking."

Grabbing the corners of his gold brocade vest, he pulled them down with a jerk, a habit he had whenever he was annoyed.

"I insist you come down and sit at the table with the family."

That night Tamara had another nightmare. She screamed, sat up in bed with a start, believing someone was in the room. Her heart pounded wildly. Pulling the covers up in front of her, she squinted to check every corner of the bedchamber. No one was there. Cautiously she lay down again, double-checking with her eyes, afraid to close them.

Lady Alma flung open her door and bounded into the room. From her haste in reaching Tamara, her robe askew, nightcap sitting crookedly on her head, she looked as if she had miraculously survived a hurricane. Tamara took one look and tried hard not to giggle. "Oh, why is it, she asked herself, when one is not supposed to laugh, 'tis more difficult to refrain from doing so?

Standing arms akimbo, Lady Alma snapped, "We simply have to do something about your screaming in the middle of the night, you tiresome child. You awaken the entire household. You frighten poor Beverly and Valerie."

"I am sorry, but I cannot help it," Tamara said apologetically.

Lady Alma left in a huff. After she had closed the door, Tamara slid from her bed and bent down on her knees, lifting the dust ruffle, checking to be sure no one was hiding beneath it.

Tamara's only friends were Ruth and the butler, Watkins. They were kind to her. Although their positions in the household made it impossible for them to express their thoughts, they recognized her plight and in little ways let her know. Grateful for the least show of understanding, she began to confide more in Ruth and spoke less in front of Lord and Lady Warde.

She did not eavesdrop, but one evening she accidentally overheard a conversation between Sir Arthur and his wife.

Lady Alma said sharply, "I knew it was a mistake to bring that tiresome child here. I told you, but you insisted." She never used Tamara's name, but always referred to her as "that tiresome child." "Tsk! She is nothing but a nuisance in this household. She is a bad influence on my girls."

"But, madam, what else could I do?"

"There are orphanages for such children."

"Alma, dear," he protested, "she is my brother's child. How could I? Her rightful place is with us."

Lady Alma shrugged her broad shoulders. "You could have left well enough alone," she chirped. "Those people in Jamaica said they would keep her, but ooooh, noooo! You had to play the good Samaritan. Now I have the trouble with her."

"But they are not nobility, my dear."

"Hmph!" There was a pause in the conversation before Lady Alma continued. "Since she is here, I think she should be sent away to school, a select school, of course. Look into it, Arthur," she commanded. "Find out the name of a good finishing school." Sir Arthur's wife, always concerned about what people said and thought of her, added, "We would not be criticized for that, and she would be out from under my feet. 'Twould be best for all of us."

Arthur grunted his consent. Lady Alma goaded her husband inexhaustibly. She was more adept in needling him than her tapestry.

Tamara knew she was about to be sent away. Fretfully she returned to the gloom of her bedchamber and gazed out the window. Uncle Arthur resembles my father in appearance, but he is not at all like him, she mused. My father was sweet and kind, but a man. Uncle Arthur is no man. His heart is made of wood. He is Lady Alma's puppet, and as petty as she. She can wheedle him into thinking and doing anything she wants.

Tamara was not surprised when her uncle tapped on her door. He entered unceremoniously, followed by Lady Alma.

"It seems you cannot get along with your dear cousins. A pity. There is only one alternative. You are to be sent away to school."

Lady Alma peeped from behind his shoulder. "Tsk! Mayhaps there you will learn to get along with your peers and mind your elders," she said snidely.

Tamara lowered her head and did not reply. She was tempted to tell Lady Alma she was relieved to be getting away from her ugly brats, but she was afraid of being slapped.

Sir Arthur added, "You will leave next week if I can arrange it. My patience is at an end. I want peace and quiet in this home."

He turned abruptly and left the room. Lady Alma followed, closing the door triumphantly.

9

Tamara was sent to Lady Bedford's school, southeast of London, in Kent, between Faversham and Canterbury. The ancient, stately stone mansion was Lady Bedford's ancestral home. The last of her family, the pious gray-haired woman of sixty had converted it into a finishing school. Lady Bedford, a spinster, was firm but fair with her charges. The girls knew beneath the authoritarian facade was a heart of gold. She had dedicated her life to the education of young women at a time when book learning for ladies was considered a waste of time. Emphasis was placed on preparing them to be proper wives of noblemen, including how to handle large numbers of servants and entertaining. They were taught a woman's objective in life was to be submissive to her husband and to devote her life to promote his happiness.

The days were pleasant in the gentle English countryside. Tamara developed close friendships with several girls her own age who were also members of the aristocracy.

The rules were strict, but Tamara was happier than she had been living with her relations. During her years at Lady Bedford's she was taught the social graces contained in *Etiquette for Ladies*, a popular book that included instructions on how to carve, how to pour tea, when to wear gloves, the proper time to pay calls. *Mongnall's Questions* was also required study. She excelled in her lessons, which included sketching, fancy work, French, and geography. Appreciation of the arts was encouraged, particularly the works of Renaissance painters, poets, and composers.

She was deeply interested in geography. Looking at a globe in her classroom, she studied the trade routes of the world and wondered where her friend Mark Schofield was and why he had not written. When she was living with her uncle, she had sent a letter to Mrs. Schofield, but had not received a reply. Unknown to her, Lady Alma read, then destroyed all Tamara's correspondence, for reasons known only to herself.

Tamara played the piano, practiced her lessons diligently, and also enjoyed riding. She joined the other girls in hikes, picnics, and social affairs sponsored by the school, getting along much better with her classmates than she did with her cousins. Outwardly she had all the appearances of a well-adjusted girl, but the emotional wounds remained unhealed.

Holidays were spent with Sir Arthur's family, with whom she never felt comfortable. She enjoyed the Christmas festivities at school several days before closing time. Traditionally the girls went into the village nearby and distributed mittens they had knit for needy children. That same night, holding candles, they sang Christmas carols in the snow beneath Lady Bedford's window. When they ended the last carol, she came out and gave the girls little packages of sweetmeats.

Getting away from school for a short time was a welcome change, but Tamara was always glad when it was time to return. Some of her friends threw tantrums, not wanting to go back, but not Tamara. She was almost lighthearted when the holiday ended.

Sex was prudishly banned from conversation as if it did not exist. Even uttering the word in front of young ladies was unthinkable. Tamara received her knowledge of it the same way the other girls did, secretly, speculating and discussing it among themselves—except that she had the experience of witnessing her mother's rape, a scene that was branded on her memory.

The other girls, not knowing of Tamara's dreadful experience, attributed her behavior around boys to shyness, which in reality was mostly fear. Boys from a nearby military academy were invited to parties, picnics, and balls, and in turn, the girls were invited to social functions at the academy. It was part of their education in learning the social graces. After such events, the girls spoke excitedly of their experiences, of the boys they had met and danced with.

One of Lady Bedford's rules was that meals were to be eaten in complete silence. Conversation at the table was forbidden. Once in their dormitory, when all lamps were dimmed, the girls sat on their beds in long-sleeved flannel nighties, laughing and chattering about clothes, menstrual cycles, and boys. Sometimes Tamara giggled along with the others when her friends good-naturedly imitated their teachers' and Lady Bedford's eccentricities.

Tamara, who was now eleven, was among the youngest of the group who naively speculated about what boys looked like beneath their trousers. In the dormitorylike room, there was a precocious girl of fifteen, Mary Elizabeth, who was a great authority on the subject.

"Boys are different," said Sally, one of Tamara's best friends.

"You silly goose," said Mary Elizabeth, "did you never see your brothers naked when you were little? 'Tis called a penis."

Innocently, little Sally corrected her. "My brother calls it his peepy, not penis."

"I do not have brothers, only two sisters," added Ellen.

The girls giggled gleefully. Mary Elizabeth would not allow the subject to be dropped. She frowned, annoyed by the ignorance of her friends.

"Well, then," she continued, "did you never look at that chestnut stallion in yonder field? I watched him mate the sorrel mare." The girls inched closer. "He was at least this long," she exclaimed, holding her hands fifteen inches apart. "He came up from behind and mounted her, ramming it into her."

"Why did you not call us?" asked Ellen. "What did the mare do? Do you think she liked it?"

Mary Elizabeth turned serious. "It gave me the strangest feeling watching. I could not tell whether the mare liked it. Her coat turned glossy with sweat. Her eyes bulged as if they would pop right out of her head." Mary Elizabeth, having captured the attention of all the girls in the dormitory, enjoyed her newfound importance.

"My friend at the academy has shown me . . . everything," she bragged. "Last week when the cadets were here, Eddie Wittcomb took me out into the gardens, behind the gazebo, and kissed me."

The girls, sitting cross-legged on their beds, rocked back and forth, gurgling with laughter. "Did you know that when a boy is attracted to a girl, his penis swells?" she asked, getting bolder.

Her friends looked at her and gasped.

"How do you know this?" asked Ellen, the little freckle-faced girl whose red hair was braided in one large pigtail weighing heavily down the center of her back.

"Because Cadet Wittcomb did not have the bulge in his trousers when we first went strolling. It was not until he slipped his hand into my bodice that I noticed it."

"Mary Elizabeth! You did not allow him to do that!" Sally exclaimed with shock in her voice.

"Of course I did. He did before," said Mary Elizabeth, poking her chin into the air. "'Tis what grown-ups do, and I am grown-up. You would not understand. You are too young."

"I know that for some strange reason men like to peep at ladies' ankles," Ellen said softly, almost to herself, "but . . ."

All the girls' eyes were fixed on Mary Elizabeth, waiting for what mystery she would reveal next.

"He lifted my skirts and put his hand between my legs."

The girls looked at each other. Tamara did not like the turn in the conversation. It was opening the wound. She lay down, nestling beneath her comforter, pretending sleep. Once again she relived the scene in the drawing room of her home in Jamaica. She could tell her friends, she thought. She could tell them what horrible things men did to women. How could they speak of it as if they looked forward to it! Never would she allow a boy to come near her, touch her. She pondered whether to warn her friends what would happen to them, but was afraid they would question her, so she remained silent.

Mary Elizabeth, however, sat on the bed next to Tamara, so she could not avoid hearing the rest of the tale. Spellbound, the girls listened as Mary Elizabeth continued brazenly. "We fell into each other's arms in the grass, and . . . well . . . you can imagine what happened," Mary Elizabeth boasted. "It did not hurt this time."

Again the girls looked at each other aghast.

"Mary Elizabeth, you mean it has happened before?" Sally asked, astounded.

Mary Elizabeth smiled at the expression on all their faces. Little Ellen, who had begun to unbraid her hair for the night, said, "That is very sinful, Mary Elizabeth. My mother told me never to let a boy near me until I am married."

"You will get a bad disease," added Sally.

"Really, Sally," Mary Elizabeth said tartly.

"And I have heard that is how babies are made," retorted Ellen.

"No, you must be wrong," countered Sally, looking

puzzled. "They are brought to the house by an angel. My mother told me that is where I came from. My mother and father would not commit a sin. They are good, religious people. They go to church every Sunday."

"Are you adopted?" Mary Elizabeth asked with a note of sarcasm.

"No, of course not," replied Sally, at first not following the older girl's motive for the question.

"Well, then, how do you think you were made? Not by an angel, I can tell you that."

The question left the girls round-eyed. It triggered each to thinking about her parents and what they did beneath the bedcovers in the privacy of their rooms.

Sally mused, "Well, if they do it, it cannot be all that bad."

"Look at her Majesty, Queen Victoria. She and Prince Albert have one baby after another. So far, there are eight, and who knows when it will stop," commented Mary Elizabeth.

"Not the queen!" gasped Ellen incredulously.

The girls giggled again.

"I have seen my mother and father sneak kisses, but to think that my papa would do . . . that to my mama! You must be mistaken. My mama would not permit it!" concluded Sally.

"No, I am not," insisted Mary Elizabeth. She had completed brushing her long blond hair and laid the brush aside before she continued. "That is how all of us were . . ." She paused, trying to think of the correct word. "Conceived," she added.

Ellen asked, "How does a lady know when she is going to have a baby?"

Mary Elizabeth supplied the answer. "When her monthly flow stops."

"Her flow," repeated Ellen. "Mine has not even started. Does that mean I cannot have a baby?"

Mary Elizabeth scratched her head, mulling the question. "I do not think so, but I am not sure."

Tamara cowered beneath the blankets. The discussion aroused memories of her parents and their loving embraces. She remembered her mother was expecting a baby when she was killed. The brutality of what she had actually witnessed must be far different from when two people love each other. Her father would never hurt her mother. What a husband and wife in love did must be something mystical, unknown until after the wedding ceremony. Marriage and love must make the difference, she thought. She could hear her mother's sweet voice, could recall the affectionate hugs and kisses her mother gave her father and her father's pleased, deep laughter.

Mary Elizabeth made one last statement before snuggling under her covers. "Reverend and Mrs. Pudd have three children, a fourth on the way. They must do it."

At the mention of the prudish little bespectacled vicar all the girls laughed heartily, each trying to envision him in bed with his obese, constantly nagging wife.

The dormitory grew quiet, until the girls heard Mary Elizabeth giggle.

"What is so funny?" Ellen asked.

"Do you think Lady Bedford ever did it?"

Girlish guffaws rang through the room.

Not long after this conversation, Tamara awakened in the middle of the night to hear whimpering from the next bed. She rose and went to the girl's bed, sitting down on the edge.

"Mary Elizabeth," she whispered, "why are you crying?"

Mary Elizabeth blew her nose. "I am not supposed to tell anyone, but tomorrow my parents are taking me away. I know you can keep a secret, Tamara. I think you are very nice."

"Why would they do that?"

Mary Elizabeth sobbed harder. "I am going to have a baby. Please do not tell the others."

"I promise. I am sorry you are leaving, Mary Elizabeth."

Tamara was silent as the girl continued to weep. Not knowing what else to say, she crept back to her own bed. The next night, Mary Elizabeth was conspicuously absent from her bed. The girls wondered what had happened to her, but Tamara kept her secret.

Tamara remained at Lady Bedford's school for six years. As she grew older, her hair turned from sun-streaked blond to copper. When the sun shone on it, it was the color of her father's, both gold and red struggling for dominance. Her lashes were long and dark, the blue of her eyes deepened, and depending on the light, sometimes turned the color of violets.

The years passed. Unknown to Tamara, one of the reasons Lady Alma had resented her presence was Tamara's striking beauty and natural grace. By comparison, Beverly and Valerie looked colorless and homely. It was not until suitable husbands had been found for his daughters that Sir Arthur wrote to Tamara and told her that he was coming for her, that her education was completed, that other arrangements would be made for her.

Lady Bedford's school closed over Christmas, and the girls went home until the end of January. Tamara said good-bye to her friends, knowing she would not be returning.

Before she left, Lady Bedford called Tamara into her office. The woman watched as Tamara approached, holding her head with regal poise. An expression of pride crossed Lady Bedford's face. Tamara had been one of her best girls, and she credited herself with the successful results appearing before her.

"Tamara. You walk very gracefully. If only you would smile more often, show those beautiful teeth and dimples. I am sure young men would find you quite charming."

"Thank you, Lady Bedford, but I do not wish young or old men to find me charming or anything else," she said quietly.

Lady Bedford looked over the rim of her pince-nez and frowned. She cleared her throat, hugged Tamara, and wished her happiness.

10

The Tuesday before Christmas, Sir Arthur came to Lady Bedford's for Tamara in his coach-and-four. It was a raw day when they started out for London. Tamara wrapped the heavy blue carriage rug snugly around her legs and tucked it in tightly at her ankles.

Saying good-bye to her friends had upset her. As she stared moodily out the carriage window, the sun peeped between gathering clouds. She felt its subtle warmth on her face, shadows of her extravagant lashes touching her cheeks. She was apprehensive about her future, fearing she would be introduced into society. No doubt a search had already begun for a husband.

Tamara and Sir Arthur rode in silence. She suspected he was struggling to find the best way to announce his plans for her, which, she was certain, were Lady Alma's plans, whatever they were.

Staring at his fingernails, at last Sir Arthur broke the

silence. "Do not worry, Tamara. I will arrange a suitable marriage for you."

"Uncle Arthur, I have no wish to marry—ever. Is there not something else I could do?"

"Bah, what nonsense!"

He looked at her in annoyance. The carriage wheels clacked across the planks of a bridge.

"Do not be ridiculous. You are sixteen, going on seventeen. 'Tis time you marry. Beverly and Valerie are both married. Every girl wants to wed. That is that!"

"But I am different," she protested, looking at him warily. "Men do not attract me," she replied plaintively.

Sir Arthur had not failed to notice the change in Tamara since he had first taken her to Lady Bedford. She was no longer a child, but a provocatively beautiful young woman.

"But I am certain you will attract them. With your looks and poise I am afraid we will have a hard time keeping suitors away from my door. Lady Alma says it must be done properly. You will be formally introduced next month. Lady Alma will assist us."

Tamara startled her uncle when suddenly she stamped her feet on the floor of the carriage, causing the rug to fall from her legs.

"No. No! I refuse to be put on display like a horse for sale!"

She lifted her face in the cold air of the carriage. Pointing her finger, she mimicked an auctioneer. "Here, here. Looky here. Who will start the bidding at one thousand pounds? Silence. Come, come. Do I hear a thousand pounds? This is an untouched damsel—one with a title and a dowry. Silence. You, sir, was that a bid or did you just scratch your head? Ah, gentlemen—sorry—only dukes, marquises, and earls may offer."

"Good God, Tamara, that is quite enough!" Sir Arthur commanded vehemently, reaching beneath his heavy black cape and pulling down his waistcoat with a jerk. He shook his head in disgust. "It is obvious Lady Bedford has failed to temper that streak of stubborn arrogance in you."

The carriage grew quiet. The weather worsened abruptly. The sun disappeared completely, the sky turning murky gray. Dark, racing clouds dimmed the range of mountains to the west.

Tamara sat glumly. They had not journeyed far when it began to drizzle, a fine mist that shortly turned to freezing rain. The pelting sleet tapped against the windows of the carriage and thumped noisily on its roof. Horses' hooves splattered and carriage wheels churned through icy slush. Rain crystallized on barren trees, forming a thick coat of cold glass on their branches. Pointed icicles clung to the tails of the horses and along the bridles.

The moisture on the gravel road hardened. The carriage moved slower, its wheels crunching along the rutted main highway to London. Cows hovered beneath trees which offered little protection, and a herd of sheep bleated sadly in the corner of a stone fence that enclosed their pasture.

The sound of ice against the panes increased alarmingly, penetrating the silence inside the carriage. Sir Arthur pulled the collar of his cape up tightly around his neck and arranged the rug snugly around his legs. Now edgy, he glanced from the carriage window apprehensively. Sleet and bitter cold wind whipped across the countryside.

"We are thirty miles from London."

Tamara said nothing, but tucked her dainty hands into her fur muff. She stared blankly out the window. There was an awesome beauty in the frozen wonderland, but she did not enjoy it. She had never become acclimated to the cold, damp climate and continually longed for the warm days and balmy nights she had known as a child. She thought of Montjoy, the Jamaican sunshine, and palm trees that would never feel the weight of ice.

Her uncle broke into her thoughts when he leaned forward, pulled the blue velvet curtain back, and peered out, assessing the condition of the ice-shrouded road. "I am afraid we cannot proceed to London as I had planned. Trees might have fallen across the road, and if we are stranded, we could freeze to death."

He sat back on the seat beside Tamara, letting the curtain swing forward into place. He had made up his mind. "It will be wise to stop at the inn just beyond this hamlet and wait out this blasted ice storm. Let us hope accommodations are available."

Tamara watched as the sleet turned to snow. The carriage turned, leaving the highway, swaying as the horses came to a halt in front of the inn. Ice clinging to fetlocks and manes, they pranced restlessly, gray clouds puffing around their nostrils from harsh breathing in the cold air.

Tamara alighted from the carriage, stepping into the heavily falling snow, careful not to slip on the snow-covered ice. Large star-shaped flakes touched her cheeks and nose. She lifted her head to look at her surroundings, but visibility was poor, as bleak and obscure as her future. She shuddered as the cold penetrated her body. Stuffing her hands farther into her muff, she hastened toward the entrance.

The ancient inn was built of fieldstone. Warm, welcoming light glowed through its misted windows. A weatherbeaten sign, THE CROWN INN, with a gold crown drawn above the name, screeched as the wind swung it back and forth.

They entered the common room, leaving a trail of snowy footprints behind them on the wooden floor, even though they had stamped their booted feet outside the door. The crowded inn looked warm and friendly. Sir Arthur succeeded in renting the last two first-class rooms. As he stood making arrangements for his men and horses with the proprietor, Tamara walked to the large fireplace, where flames crackled. She slipped her hands from the white fur muff and took off her mulberry-colored pelisse, which was lined and trimmed with white fur. Removing the matching bonnet, she shook and fluffed her hair, wiping away ice crystals that had clung to curls not protected by it.

Standing in front of the open fire, she stretched her hands toward the warmth of the logs burning on the grate. She rubbed her hands together and stamped one foot, then the other on the bare oak floor to encourage circulation.

Staring at the leaping flames, she experienced an eerie feeling of being watched. She turned. The room was crowded. Everyone was chattering about the storm and the disruption of his travels. No one paid any attention to her, as far as she could tell.

She glanced through the wide door leading to the dining room and noticed a large, overpowering man in rich attire. Their eyes met. Quickly Tamara looked away, but did not fail to notice he was a man in his sixties with a thick black beard with blotches of gray, professionally trimmed. His facial features were harsh, autocratic.

Fear swept through her. She checked to be sure her uncle was close at hand. Feeling stifled, smothered, claustrophobic, if it had not been sleeting she would have run out into the fresh air. She moved a few steps to the right, until the man could no longer see her.

Sir Arthur completed the transactions with the proprietor and came to Tamara. "Let us proceed to the dining room. I think it best we dine before they run out of food."

"I am not hungry."

"You must eat something, if only a nourishing bowl of hot soup," he insisted.

Sir Arthur led her through the door to the dining room. As they entered, the man who had been eyeing Tamara rose.

"Good heavens! Sir Arthur! Fancy meeting you here."

"Upon my word! Lord Sheldon! So the storm has detained you, too."

"I was on my way to my country estate to spend Christmas."

He stared at Tamara's face, noting her beauty and innocent look; then his eyes slid down and lingered on her round breasts, the curving-in of her slim waist, and her provocatively rounded hips.

He looked at Sir Arthur, a twinkle entering his eyes. " 'Twill be a cold night, but you will not know it, however cold it gets, eh? You lucky devil . . . what a way to be stranded!" He winked.

Sir Arthur's face turned pepper red. "Oh, excuse me, Sheldon. I should have introduced you to my niece. The Duke of Lyndenhurst, my niece, Lady Tamara Warde."

Tamara curtsied politely, with her lashes lowered so that she would not have to look at him, not realizing it made her look seductive and increased the duke's interest in her.

"This is Robert's daughter. She has completed her education at Lady Bedford's, and I am taking her back to London to live with us."

Tamara smiled wintrily. Lord Lyndenhurst gave her hand a tug, then lifted it to his dry lips. "Enchanted," he said, nodding and never taking his eyes from her. "I was enjoying a glass of port and was about to order dinner. Will you and your niece be kind enough to join me?"

He drawled his words irritatingly. Tamara hoped her uncle would refuse the invitation, but there were no vacant tables, and to her dismay, Sir Arthur accepted.

"Splendid! Splendid!" responded Lord Sheldon. "What a bit of luck to run into you."

He sneezed and blew his nose.

"Dash it all! I am coming down with a head cold from this beastly weather."

11

They had settled at the duke's large round table near the fire-place when Tamara noticed a somber-looking man wearing black, severely plain attire enter the dining room. With a note of sarcasm, under his breath Sir Arthur looked at the duke and said, "The great Lord Shaftesbury is looking for a table. Shall we invite him to join us?"

The duke shrugged. "Why not? It might be amusing. We may disagree with him, but differences should be forgotten in a storm. Let us hope he is not in one of his despondent moods." The duke turned, raised his hand, and motioned for the man to join them. "You are welcome to dine with us, old chap," greeted the duke.

"Thank you, I believe I will."

Tamara was introduced to Anthony Ashley Cooper, the seventh Earl of Shaftesbury, a tall man approaching sixty with reproachful, defiant-looking, walnut-colored eyes. His dark hair, touched with gray, was fluffed above his ears, and his side whiskers extended to the edge of his jaw. His lips were full, his straight nose prominent.

Before 1851, he had been known as Lord Ashley. Serving in the House of Commons, he had devoted his energies to labor legislation, limiting working hours for children and women in factories. In 1851 he had inherited the earldom and begun his tenure in the House of Lords, continuing his efforts for humane causes.

After a brief comment on the weather, Sir Arthur and the duke chided him about his nickname, "Pope of the Low Church." They were members of the high church in the Anglican religion, believing in the strict observance of traditional rites and continued connection with Catholicism, which Lord Shaftesbury fought to abolish through evangelical reforms. A serious man, he did not take their bantering lightly. For a moment the air was strained. He looked at Sir Sheldon with a frown.

"I have just been to Canterbury to speak to the archbishop. I told him the rites of your high church are showy and not needed, but prayer, moral conduct, and strict observance of

50

the Sabbath are important," he snapped, abruptly dismissing the subject by looking at Tamara, who sat quietly listening to the men.

"I say, my lady, you are a beauty. You remind me of my wife, Min, when she was your age. What are you doing traveling with these old scoundrels on a night like this?"

Tamara explained to his lordship her return to London, and was shocked by his frankness.

"You should marry. Marriage is a state appointed by God, to which we must all submit."

The Duke of Lyndenhurst nodded in agreement and added, "Lady Tamara, I am sure you have not heard about Lord Shaftesbury's speeches on the plight of women when he was in Commons. He believes a woman's place is in the home. He was responsible for the bill that prohibits women from working in the mines. He would rather see them stay home and starve."

The Earl of Shaftesbury stiffened and lifted his head. "Listen, gentlemen. Has either of you seen conditions in our mines? They are not fit for men, let alone women and children. I might add, that does not only apply to mines. What I have seen in the textile mills is not much better. When I first started to work on labor legislation, children started in the mills when they were five years of age, working fourteen, sometimes sixteen hours a day. There were and still are far too many accidents around machinery. Too many children have rickets and tuberculosis. Illiteracy is rampant. 'Tis a national disgrace, and I for one cannot turn my head as if these conditions did not exist."

He looked at the duke. "Pardon my saying so, but I wager that these conditions prevail in the mills on your estates."

The duke looked irritated by his accusation, but without hesitation Sir Arthur admitted, "I must give you credit, Ashley. Because of your efforts the lot of the working class in this country is much better today than forty years ago."

"But where will it all end?" asked Lord Sheldon.

Anthony Ashley Cooper arched his brows and looked at Sir Arthur with brooding dark eyes. "I am presently concentrating most of my efforts on the children, but I must say, 'tis a difficult road. There are too many milksops in the House of Lords," he said solemnly. With a challenging expression in his eyes, he looked at his two colleagues.

"One day, instead of strolling through Hyde Park, I suggest you tour the slums of South London and the East End. Children beg in the streets, steal, sleep under arches of bridges.

51

But you do not even have to go to the East End to see poverty. When you are in Westminster or Mayfair, open your eyes. It exists at your very doorsteps, and you ignore it."

The duke put up his hands in protest. "Now, now, Shaftesbury. Do not be too hard on us. After all, both of us voted for the labor bills you fought for, and the appropriations for your Ragged Schools."

A slight smile bent Lord Shaftesbury's lips. "Thank you for that much, gentlemen. Can I count on your support for more funds this year for the Ragged Schools?"

The two members of the House of Lords chuckled. Tamara, who had remained quiet up to this point, asked about the Ragged Schools. Lord Shaftesbury explained, "Throughout London, schools have been established for outcasts, waifs, urchins, to get them off the streets, especially in the slums. They are taught morals and the three R's. We are sending some of the promising pupils to Canada and Australia to get a new start away from the crimes of the streets."

"Champion of the Factory Children," said Sir Sheldon acidly, sipping his claret.

The menu dwindled as hungry travelers came into the dining room, ate, and left. The serving wench who stood before them announced they were out of roast beef and pork pie. Tamara did not like pickled whelks or pig trotters. She was undecided between rabbit or mutton, finally ordered the mutton. Lord Shaftesbury hesitated too, saying he was suffering from another bout of dyspepsia. He ordered chicken broth and a glass of goat's milk.

"When I served in the House of Commons I introduced and fought for the Ten Hours' Bill to put a stop to women and children working nights in the mills. Factory Acts passed before 1830 were ineffective because there was no way of enforcing them, no system of inspection or checking up on millowners . . . ah . . . such as in your mills, Sheldon."

Sir Arthur laughed, but the duke was beginning to feel as if he were being pricked by a needle. There was a pause as their food was served and wine poured, much to Tamara's relief.

"And are your philanthropic endeavors appreciated?" Sir Sheldon asked sneeringly, showing ancient yellow teeth. "Do the downtrodden thank you? The lunatics in our asylums, the miners, the children of the streets? And now I understand you have taken on a new crusade, the fight against slavery in the United States. What next, Shaftesbury? What you need is a young woman to distract you from all these things."

Sir Ashley looked at him, a serious expression on his face. "I will leave the dallying to such as you." He frowned. "Why should I not be interested in slavery in the United States? Most of the cotton that comes to our mills comes from South Carolina through the port of Charleston. The first Earl of Shaftesbury was one of the founders of the Carolina colony and Charleston. As long as there is injustice anywhere, I shall fight it. I have devoted my life to fighting it." A faint smile parted his lips. "My wife complains I drive myself too hard. She thinks 'tis the cause of my tinnitus, but my nature is such that I cannot help it."

"Do you have children of your own, m'lord?" Tamara asked quietly.

"Aye, child, but sadly, two of my sons have died. Francis died while at Harrow and our son Maurice died four years ago in Lausanne. We had sent him there to be cured of epilepsy. Our three daughters are lovely, and we have our eldest son, Ashley. I certainly would not want my daughters working in the mills," he said reflectively. "I am sure every father must feel the same."

He looked at the duke. "I know why you millowners prefer to hire women. They work for lower wages and are less likely to organize to protest for better pay and working conditions. You do not realize that the structure of the family, the foundation of this country, is in jeopardy with mothers working long hours."

Neither gentleman commented on this. Tamara sat quietly. She had never seen a coal mine or textile mill and had never met a woman who worked in one. She had never thought about poverty and misery before. The conversation left her much to ponder. She admired the awe-inspiring Earl of Shaftesbury, and did not fail to notice the difference between him and the Duke of Lyndenhurst, whose motives concerning women were to win them for his own pleasures, otherwise ignore them. It struck her that here, sitting across from her, was a man of greatness, and she was privileged to meet him.

The earl's hand went to his stomach as if he were in pain. He faltered before he continued. "The State should control conditions in mines and factories through legislation regulating working conditions and the length of the working day." He cleared his throat. "As members of the nobility we have the responsibility for the welfare of all the people. May I quote Tom Hood's 'The Song of the Shirt'?" He did not wait for approval, but began to recite:

O! men with sisters dear,
O! men with mothers and wives!
It is not linen you're wearing out,
But human creatures' lives!"

Lord Sheldon and Tamara's uncle looked at each other in dismay. "You are not blaming us for all of Britain's social ills, are you, Ashley?" the duke asked with a note of irritation in his voice.

"I have one more suggestion for you, gentlemen, then I must be excused. I am not feeling well. Thank you for inviting me to join you." He turned to Tamara. "'Tis a pleasure meeting you, Lady Tamara." He turned to the men and rose to leave. "My suggestion is this. The law shortens the working day in the cotton mills to ten hours, with seven and one-half on Saturdays. I suggest you give up one of your numerous hunting expeditions and work in a mill for a week." He nodded politely. "Good night, gentlemen. Lady Tamara."

Lord Shaftesbury's rebuke made Tamara feel good inside. He was right, her uncle and the duke wrong.

"The fellow is a fool—ruining his health, and for what?" the duke said. "He seems to get perverse satisfaction dwelling on misery."

"I hear he is in financial straits," proffered Sir Arthur. "Was forced to close his home at St. Giles for lack of funds."

As they completed the meal, the two men engaged in conversation on a variety of current topics. Tamara found the roast mutton tasty. She drank two cups of tea and remained dutifully quiet. She had the impression the duke was trying to claim her attention, but her thoughts were on the ideas raised by Lord Shaftesbury.

She heard the duke say, "I read in the *Illustrated London News* that Richard Burton and Speke are quarreling. Both claim credit for discovering the source of the Nile."

"Aye." Sir Arthur nodded. Exploring is an interesting hobby. Egypt has always fascinated me."

The duke took a sip of wine before he replied. "I am a member of the Royal Geographical Society, which sponsored Burton's and Speke's expedition in Africa." He looked at Tamara to see whether this impressed her.

She lowered her eyes as he continued. "At the Society's last meeting, Francis Frith showed his photographs of Egypt. Fascinating. Simply fascinating. His photographs of the Colossus of Thebes made me want to go there and see for myself."

"I would find it quite thrilling to be an explorer," Tamara said excitedly.

"You, a woman—what nonsense." The duke's glance lingered on her face, then dropped to her bosom. Then he said, "There are many facets which would be thrilling to explore besides rivers and continents."

Tamara blushed. Sir Arthur cleared his throat nervously, squirmed in his seat, and changed the subject. "Have you read about the strikes spreading across Europe? Why is it whenever the country is not at war the do-gooders like Shaftesbury turn their efforts to social reform? Why can't they let well enough alone?"

Tamara listened, wishing to express her views, but since it was unthinkable for a woman to do so, she remained silent.

"Have you read Marx and Engel, *The Communist Manifesto?*" asked Sir Sheldon. "Rubbish, that is what it is!" he added sourly.

"Rubbish or not, the workers are inspired. They are organizing, demanding certain wages and hours, and if employers do not meet their demands, they refuse to work," countered Sir Arthur.

"Humph!" The duke waved his hands in the air. "Good God! 'Tis a horrible thought. This country is going to ruin," he expressed with contempt.

They had finished dining. The duke looked at Tamara, then pulled his gold watch from his waistcoat pocket. He pressed a button and the lid flew open. He checked the time, squinting to read the numbers, then snapped the lid closed.

"Dear, dear. I am afraid we are boring your niece to distraction. We should be discussing the latest London amusements."

Sir Arthur turned his head to look at Tamara as if he had forgotten she was there. Tamara's eyes flashed from one man to the other, infuriated that because she was a female they refused to treat her as an intellectual equal. To them she was a body without a brain.

"You will be surprised, sir, but I find the conversation quite interesting—not that I agree with all you have said."

Lord Lyndenhurst was taken aback, but Tamara continued. "I, too, read the *Illustrated London News.*" A tone of flippancy touched her voice. She had taken an instant dislike to the duke. To him a woman was only a decorative possession to satisfy not only his lust but also his very large ego.

Aloud she said, "I do not wish to shock you, my lords, but

I have even read Dickens, Matthew Arnold, and Thomas Huxley." She lifted her chin proudly, almost defiantly.

Both men looked dumbfounded; then the duke's lips curled at the edges as he stuffed the watch back into its nesting place. His smile grooved his cheeks until he chuckled.

Tamara stood up, pushed back her chair with a jerk, dipped a curtsy, and excused herself. Sir Arthur and the duke rose promptly, waiting until she left the table, then sat down again to finish their brandy. As she turned to escape to her room, she heard Lord Sheldon ask testily, "Do I have your permission to call on your niece when I return to London?"

12

When Tamara had first come to live with Sir Arthur and Lady Alma, she suspected her aunt deliberately chose clothes for her that made her look ugly, colors that were unbecoming, frocks that made her look dumpy. No one could have such poor taste, thought Tamara. She does it on purpose. When Tamara returned from Lady Bedford's she feared this would happen again, but now she was permitted to choose her own clothes, with the help of the designers and seamstresses.

Tamara speculated there were reasons for this change of heart. Now that Lady Alma's own daughters were safely married, Tamara was no longer a threat. Since a wealthy husband was being sought, the more beautiful she looked, the better the match.

Lady Alma took her to the House of Worth and to dressmakers on Oxford and Regent streets. Having outgrown most of her clothes, Tamara spent several days with her aunt selecting a complete new wardrobe, daytime frocks, ball gowns, feminine blouses, ankle-length drawers with lace trimmings, petticoats, bonnets, riding clothes, lace shawls, small-heeled slippers in silk and kid, and Balmoral shoes that laced up the front. Tamara found it exciting to choose beautiful taffeta and satin dresses with layers of ruffles and crinoline.

Two weeks after Christmas the Duke of Lyndenhurst returned to London from his country estate and made his first call. Lady Alma was delighted, but as the evening progressed, she became visibly annoyed with Tamara, who made no effort to converse with the duke, but sat sullen-faced. Sir Arthur and the duke engaged in conversation, and after an hour the duke excused himself, but not before he asked whether he might not be permitted to call again. The young lady had conducted herself as he expected a well-bred woman to behave, listening and not speaking unless spoken to.

The following week Lord and Lady Warde took Tamara to her first ball at Almack's on King Street in St. James's. She wore one of her new gowns, a sapphire-blue chiffon with full, flowing skirt and layers of petticoats and crinoline. Her hair was arranged with corkscrew curls framing her face. Around her throat she wore a dainty necklace of sapphires that had been her mother's.

It turned out to be a long, torturous evening. Much to Tamara's dismay she found her program filled for every dance, and Lord Sheldon's name appeared several times. The tips of her blue satin slippers peeked prettily from beneath the hem of her flowing gown, but her feet hurt as she was twirled around the glittering ballroom by one attentive man after another. Shortly after her arrival, the Duke of Lyndenhurst came and took her hand.

"Lovely, lovely," he said expressively. A sinister smile crossed his face.

She tried to avoid him, but he persisted. She felt his smoldering eyes on her all evening. Whenever she turned, he was there, a paper-width distance away. He did not stand erect, but tilted forward, trying to conceal his arousal bulging his tight breeches.

He offered to get her punch, and suggested a walk in the gardens, but she said, "No, thank you, sir," to whatever he proposed, which made him all the more determined to win her attention.

Lord Sheldon was a man not familiar with the word "no." Ladies hovered around him and did his bidding. Since the death of his third wife, he was considered one of the most eligible men in England.

Not wanting to be rude, but not knowing quite how to handle him, Tamara struggled to be polite. It was when his hand crept up and rested familiarly on her buttocks that she stepped back and glared, showing him his conduct displeased her.

The next evening, Lord and Lady Warde and Tamara were in the drawing room. Sir Arthur pulled the bell rope, and Watkins hobbled into the room.

"Are there calling cards, Watkins?" asked Sir Arthur.

"Yes sir," replied the butler.

"Bring them," ordered Sir Arthur.

Watkins brought a small circular silver salver piled with calling cards and dinner invitations. Sir Arthur shuffled through them, relishing the distinguished names on the cards, while Tamara watched with disgust in her heart.

"I am not interested in seeing any of them," she said determinedly.

Sir Arthur ignored her. His attention was held by one of the engraved cards.

"By Jove! It seems Lord Sheldon is smitten. 'Twas sheer luck we met him at the Crown Inn. I insist you receive him, Tamara, when he comes to call tomorrow evening!"

"I refuse to be subjected to his company again."

Snappily, Lady Alma picked up her needlework. She stuck the needle through the material, pulling the long thread with such a jerk the needle came unthreaded. Taking the tip of the floss, Lady Alma put it in her mouth to moisten it, then attempted to stick it through the small eye of the needle.

"You ungrateful girl," the big-bosomed woman snapped sharply, pinching one eye closed, attempting to thread the needle. "He is extremely wealthy. Owns several of the most palatial residences in England, a luxurious yacht, and stables full of thoroughbreds."

Tamara's eyes glared, mirroring her emotions. "He is old and ugly."

Lady Alma stiffened and straightened her shoulders. She dipped her hand into the red velvet needlework box beside her, looking for her gilded scissors. Finding it, she snipped the end of the thread soggy with her saliva and tried again to push it through the minute eye of the needle.

"What matter his age?" she said. "Tsk! You will be a duchess."

Tamara stamped her foot. "He is a buffoon!"

"Silence!" bellowed Sir Arthur.

"Your insolence is dreadful, simply dreadful," cried Lady Alma.

Tamara shut her eyes and gritted her teeth.

The following week the Duke of Lydenhurst asked Sir Arthur's permission to marry Tamara. When told, she burst into tears.

"Please do not accept. Can you not understand? I cannot do this! 'Twould be cruel. Please! Please! Please!" she begged, wringing her hands.

Tamara remembered his beady eyes pressing her. She was

repelled by the foul odor of rotten teeth and pipe tobacco that came from his mouth.

Lady Alma jerked her head from side to side, shaking the loose sack of flesh beneath her chin. "You ungrateful girl," she repeated. "All we have done for you."

Tamara lifted her chin defiantly. "He repels me."

"Your attitude is shocking, to say the least," said Sir Arthur.

Tamara always slept with the lamp burning, but the nightmares persisted. They were no longer of her mother being raped; she herself was the one who was violated, the same scene appearing over and over. She dreamed Lord Sheldon was standing at her bed looking down at her, ready to pounce. She screamed, then awakened, cold perspiration covering her flesh like a veil. Her heart thumped wildly, until she felt ill.

The Duke of Lyndenhurst called for tea. Coolly, his eyes swept over Tamara as she poured. When she offered him a tray of crumpets and currant-filled scones, he gazed at her delicate fingers. Tamara swallowed hard, masking the inner feeling of disgust she felt for all men.

Before he left, the duke invited Sir Arthur and his family to spend the weekend at Lyndenhurst, his country estate. Sir Arthur graciously accepted. Lady Alma was delighted by the much-sought invitation and the prospect of telling her friends.

Tamara felt differently.

"I will not go! I loathe him!" she cried. This was followed by another rebuke from milady. Tamara's complexion turned florid. She dipped a quick curtsy and fled to her room.

Sir Arthur insisted she accompany them. Ruth was ordered to pack Tamara's pale blue velvet riding habit, Balmorals, dressing gowns for five-o'clock tea, a wrap, and a London ball gown for dinner.

Silence reigned in the carriage. During the two-hour drive Tamara stared straight ahead. The carriage crossed a stone-arched bridge spanning a willow-lined stream, turned into a winding gravel lane, stopping before a pair of high wrought-iron gates. An arch bridged the gates with the name of the estate, Lyndenhurst, in wrought iron. Beneath it was the Lyndenhurst family crest. A gateman in crimson livery stepped from the stone gatehouse and swung the portals wide.

The duke's country home was exactly what Tamara expected, imposing, a four-story Gothic palace with turrets and towers. The house and furnishings were a step back into his

59

country's and his family's medieval history. The mullioned windows were arched, the ceilings vaulted. At the curve of the hand-carved oak staircase a Gothic tracery mottled the sun's rays. Prized family heirlooms were in evidence everywhere. A long gallery exhibited priceless objets d'art and ancestral portraits in massive gilt frames. Walls were of richly carved paneling and decorated with tapestries and armorial crests. Statues in plate armor filled the corners.

Antiquity dominated the residence, except for the latest innovation in lighting. Gas lamps had been installed in all the rooms, one of the first mansions in England to be so equipped.

Lord Sheldon kept a large, sparingly paid staff of liveried servants who waited on the guests diligently. He was able to enjoy his lavish life-style and maintain his vast estates, which included thirty-three tenant farms, innumerable hamlets and villages, by grudgingly paying minimum wages and selfishly extracting from his servants, farmers, textile-mill workers, and villagers all he could without thought to their welfare. In spite of his wealth, he was persistently miserly, collecting rents, fees, and income as greedily as a chipmunk gathers crocus bulbs in autumn. Even when wheat and corn crops failed, he refused to reduce his rents. When tenants fell behind in their payments, he evicted them mercilessly.

The duke, as Tamara feared, followed her everywhere, never allowing her to escape his presence. The graze of his hand on her arm sent chills of revulsion through her.

"My, I have not seen such a shy bloom in a long while. You are extraordinary . . . quite charming, my dear," he whispered.

"Thank you, m'lord," Tamara replied coldly, irritated by the platitudes that came from his lecherous mouth.

He was attentive in spite of her obvious attempts to avoid him. He touched her at every opportunity, his hands feeling disgustingly hot, and in addition, she was subjected to hearing a detailed account of his last wife's long-suffering illness and death.

When it was time to retire, Tamara made certain all doors and hand-leaded windows to her bedchamber were locked securely, but in spite of these precautions, she was jittery. She stared at the gigantic bouquet of freshly cut flowers from his lordship's greenhouses with a card signed "Lord Sheldon."

Thinking of marriage to him left Tamara panic-stricken. She tossed in the tester bed with its luxurious rose-colored damask canopy. Lying on her back, then her left side, then the right, then sliding her head beneath her pillow, she finally fell asleep on her stomach.

Having slept fitfully, she remained in bed until midmorning, then went down to the dining room to eat a breakfast of toasted muffins, eggs, and cold sliced beef. The men were occupied with falconry, which gave her a welcome respite from Lord Sheldon, but left her to listen to women's gossip. Saturday evening a lavish dinner was served at the thirty-foot-long table in the feudal banquet hall, while a band played on the terrace, but Tamara looked forward to the ride scheduled for Sunday.

Not all the guests were interested, but at noon a dozen colorfully attired riders mounted the duke's thoroughbreds to canter across his gently sloped fields varicolored with blooming wildflowers. Hooves pounded clover, mint herbs, and wild orange-colored columbine, wafting their scents to mix in the breezes that rippled the grass and pink-blooming sweet william. Hares scurried, and startled quail took to the air.

As Lord Sheldon led the group to his deer forest, Tamara marveled at the height of the lofty white oaks. Looking heavenward, she saw a blue jay sitting on a bough as if he were overseeing his domain from a mighy throne.

The riders followed a bridle path through silver birches and dogwoods, seeing spotted deer scamper. Leaving their tracks in the duff, their mounts heedlessly trampled wild mushrooms, truffles, ferns, and lady's slippers freckled by sunlight. The air was cool, damp, and smelled of peat. They forded a shallow stream lined with watercress. The clear water rolled sluggishly over mossy rocks where minnows wiggled away from wide-mouthed trout.

Tamara glanced back at the duke, who sat potbellied on his horse. She wished it would throw him. The vision of him landing on his behind in the middle of the stream brought a sparkle to her eyes and a smile to her face.

Lord Sheldon came up beside her. "Lady Tamara, I am pleased to see my home and estate bring you so much pleasure."

She chuckled inwardly, but was relieved by his words, which assured her he did not know what she was thinking. She was forced to admit it was lovely. She surmised it was an enticement he hoped would win her consent. 'Twould be easy to be snared in a false paradise, which I am sure would be just that, she thought to herself.

The duke handled his spirited horse expertly, holding the reins with gloved fingers heavy with rings. He turned his head toward her, looking at her with severe eyes. "My lady," everything in sight belongs to me," he boasted, "even that tomtit on the willow bough. 'Tis lacking only one treasure I am hoping to acquire," he added dolefully, his left cheek puffy from an infected tooth. He flicked a speck of lint from the sleeve of his black riding jacket.

"Your Grace, Lyndenhurst is perfect as it is. It lacks nothing," Tamara answered.

The duke leaned over and tweaked her cheek. "Ah, but my dear, I daresay, you are wrong," he countered. "I have servants galore to attend to all my needs . . . except one. Will you do me the honor of . . . ?" His steely eyes flickered down to her breasts. Tamara felt disgust and was grateful that the other riders had come nearer so that he could not continue with his proposal. The thought of marriage to him, the awful, terrible things he would do to her, what he expected of her, made her feel sick to her stomach.

Upon arrival home, Sir Arthur sent for Tamara. Immediately she went to him in the drawing room.

"You wish to speak to me, Uncle Arthur?"

"Yes, yes. Do not stand there like an oaf. Sit."

Tamara seated herself on the edge of the crimson armchair.

"I have wonderful news," he said proudly, informing her he had accepted the duke's proposal. "Your Aunt Alma will begin preparations immediately. The duke, for sentimental reasons, insists the wedding take place in the chapel at Lyndenhurst."

"I suppose because all his other marriages took place there," Tamara blurted, before the enormity of her predicament struck her. "Oooooh, noooo!" she moaned. "How could you do such a thing! He has children older than I. Grandchildren."

"You will do as I say. I know what is best for you."

Tamara suspected that her uncle's finances were not very secure. He was a heavy gambler, losing large amounts at the tables. She narrowed her eyes and asked boldly, "How much is he paying you?"

Sir Arthur was taken aback by her insolence and glanced about to make certain none of the servants had heard her.

"Hold your tongue! How dare you speak to me that way? As I told you before, you are a wealthy woman in your own right. Your parents left you the estate in Jamaica in trust until you are twenty-one or marry. You need a husband to handle your affairs. And . . . I might add, *my* finances are none of your business."

She wanted to strike out at him. "You must have paid a fortune to get Beverly and Valerie married."

"Good God! That is none of your business!"

"'Tis!" She stamped her foot. "You are selling me, as if I were a slave!"

Sir Arthur stood up and jerked his vest. "Silence! The matter is settled. You are affianced to the Duke of Lyndenhurst."

Tamara turned abruptly, her skirts swishing briskly as she ran to her room. She flung herself on her bed and wept. There was only one recourse. She had to escape. The time had come for her to run away.

13

Having made up her mind, Tamara gathered a few belongings, stuffing as much as she could into her portmanteau. She pinned a bag of coins and bills beneath her skirt and put the rest of her money in her reticule to hold her over until she found employment or passage back to Jamaica. The thought of living by her wits terrified her, but she had to try to fend for herself; trying, she had to succeed.

She confided in Ruth. "Ruth, you must help me. How do I go about seeking employment?"

"Thar be an agency at Langham Place. 'Ire a 'ackney ta take ye thar. An' God bless ye, Lady Tamara."

Tamara rode through cobbled streets to the business center of London. The driver knew the location of the agency and drew the carriage to the curb.

"What can ye do?" the woman in charge asked.

Tamara hesitated. "I am afraid my education has not prepared me to earn a living."

"Do ye 'ave references?"

"No, I am afraid not."

"'Ow 'bout experience?"

"No, ma'am. This will be my first job."

The woman shook her head. "Sorry, miss. Oi ain't got nothin' now. Come back tamorrow. Maybe somethin' will turn up."

Tamara found a room three flights up near the agency and returned the next day and the next without success. On the fourth day, while she was there a man entered the office and asked for a companion for his bedridden wife, one who could read and write.

The employment agent, Mrs. Hawkins, introduced him to Tamara. The man looked her up and down from the top of her bonnet to her slippers. Without comment he hired her.

Tamara found herself seated opposite Lord Richard Foxcomb, accompanying him to his estate twenty miles southwest of London in Surrey, not far from Epsom. At first, alone, unescorted, in the seclusion of the closed carriage with the stranger, she felt uncomfortable, aware it was the first time she was with a man without a chaperon, knowing she had little choice.

When he looked out the window, she scrutinized him closely, relieved to note his innocuous appearance. He seemed harmless enough, a man of importance, but she trusted no man. Tall, with long slender legs, he had sharp features and blond hair. She guessed his age to be somewhere near thirty. He was richly attired, his carriage was luxurious, the horses a team of matched bays. He was ostensibly a man of great wealth. Tamara wondered with all his worldly possessions why his expression was sad one moment, cynical the next.

Lord Foxcomb turned his head, looking directly into Tamara's eyes. "Do you approve?" he asked lightly.

Tamara blushed and swallowed hard. "I am sorry," she said quietly.

He lifted his hand to wave away her apology. "I highly approve of you."

"I . . . I need the job badly and will do my best."

Lord Foxcomb smiled. "I am sure you will, or I would not have hired you."

As they sped along the Coach Road, she was uncomfortably aware of his appraisal of her from beneath half-closed eyes, but when she stopped to consider, she felt he had the right. He had hired her without references. Not knowing anything about her, he had employed her to be a companion to his ill wife. He trusted her.

The carriage drew into a long serpentine driveway and came to a stop before rounded marble steps and a three-story sprawling brick mansion.

"Oh! What a beautiful home!" exclaimed Tamara unthinkingly, before she remembered she was not a guest, but an employee. Ashamed of her outburst, she assumed a ludicrous expression that caused the marquis to throw back his head and laugh.

"At Foxcomb Manor you are free to express yourself."

Servants scurried to wait on him, taking his hat and gloves. His majordomo greeted him with a polite "Sir," bowing and smiling to his employer.

"George, I have found someone for Lady Foxcomb. This is Miss Ellen Birch." He spoke the name she had given Mrs. Hawkins at the employment agency.

When George, who was a man about the same age as Lord Foxcomb, looked at Tamara, his face was expressionless, but she caught a fleeting man-to-man gleam of amusement in his eyes when he glanced back at Lord Foxcomb.

"Is this the only luggage you brought, Miss Birch?" George Ashworth asked sarcastically.

"Yes, sir."

Sir Foxcomb looked at the valise and then at Tamara. "I will send for a dressmaker. You will need proper clothes, since I expect you to dine with me."

"But . . ." said Tamara, about to protest.

He entered the house and turned. "Do not flatter yourself. I simply want someone to talk to while I am dining. My wife no longer joins me," he replied gruffly.

Tamara was shown her room, conveniently located next to Lady Foxcomb's so that she would be available at a moment's notice. It was small but lovely, no doubt a nursery at one time.

Tamara freshened herself before meeting Lady Foxcomb. When she entered the woman's bedchamber, she saw her sprawled on the high canopied bed. She was noticeably overweight, with fleshy arms sticking from under the pink satin bedcovers. Her head rested on a pile of white lace-trimmed pillows, and she was reading a novel. A large box of chocolates lay beside her, within reach. Tamara surmised she was older than her husband by at least ten years, unless her illness made her appear older. A pink ribbon decorated her black hair. Tamara thought she looked like a doll that had grown old and fat.

Lady Foxcomb waved for her to be seated. "Where are your paper and quill? I wish to send a letter to a friend of mine in Paris."

A maidservant handed Tamara what she needed, and she began to write what Lady Foxcomb dictated. The woman had not as much as asked her name. When the letter was completed, she told Tamara to leave, stating she wished to go to sleep. She rolled over, as if the correspondence had exhausted her.

Tamara's feelings about her beauty were contradictory. Sometimes she loathed her looks and the effect she had on men. It would have been better if she was plain and dowdy like her cousins, Beverly and Valerie, but when she thought of them, she shuddered and thanked God for her attributes. Women who dressed tastelessly repelled her. Paradoxically, desirous of looking her best, she liked fashionable clothes and knew which colors and styles enhanced her beauty, never imagining her good taste added to her difficulties. It was as if she dressed beautifully for her own pleasure, and not for others.

She bathed and donned the pink mousseline brought from Sir Arthur's, knowing it was too luxurious and highly inappropriate for an employee, a companion, but it was the only dinner frock she had brought with her.

She met Lord Foxcomb on the stairs, and they walked to the dining room together. He had changed to evening attire, a long black broadcloth frock coat with velvet collar, tight-fitting striped trousers.

Seated near him at the long candlelit table, Tamara was quiet, but answered his questions politely. When the meal ended, after they had eaten a custard dessert, Sir Richard placed his white linen napkin on the table and rose.

"You will come with me to the drawing room and pour my brandy, Miss Ellen Birch, which, I am certain, is not your real name. It does not suit you in the least."

His dark brooding eyes held hers. He smiled arrogantly. Tamara made no response other than to follow him and do as she was told. As he sipped his brandy, he gestured for her to be seated in the crimson damask wing chair, then sat opposite her. He crossed his legs casually.

"Now, tell me who you are. Obviously you are an educated woman of good breeding. What is your predicament?"

Tamara hedged and cast a cautious glance at him. "I would rather not discuss my private life, m'lord."

Lord Foxcomb smirked. "I am certain there is a man involved and you have escaped him. He must be a fool to let an enchanting creature like you slip through his fingers."

Tamara felt ill-at-ease. She asked to be excused so that she could retire to her room.

"How thoughtless of me. You must have had a trying time of it. Of course you are excused . . . for now."

As the time they spent together passed, Tamara remained on guard, attempting to maintain a distance between them as was proper between employer and employee, although he did not treat her as an employee, but as a guest. His behavior was that of a gentleman. His manners were impeccable. He did not appear devious. She began to relax. Tamara, naive in the plots of the male species thought of him as a lonely man seeking companionship. To a degree this was true.

Mornings, when Lady Foxcomb slept late or had no need for her, Tamara joined Sir Richard to ride across his vast estate. In the wide-open, gently contoured fields, she urged the chestnut gelding into a canter, as she had done along the beach in Jamaica. Looking handsome in his scarlet riding jacket, his lordship marveled at her horsemanship. It pleased him to see the added beauty the excitement of the ride brought to her face. Her cheeks flushed and her eyes sparkled, putting a fresh glow to her countenance.

Evenings at dinner she was a delightful companion, and surprised him with her knowledge of many subjects. She amused Sir Richard with expressive gestures when she spoke. She listened with interest to whatever he said, which was often praise for Foxcomb Manor. She smiled fetchingly and sometimes laughed heartily when he told of his amusing experiences in making the grand tour of the continent.

June burst into bloom. Unknown to Tamara, Lord Foxcomb watched her from the library window as she strolled through his sunny gardens of trimmed boxwoods and arborvitae. She fancied the rose gardens, particularly the beds of white roses, stopping daily, usually in the late afternoon when Lady Foxcomb was taking a nap. She watched as the buds developed, then opened one by one. She bent to touch them softly. Closing her eyes, she sniffed their fragrance.

Then one afternoon Tamara came to the bed of white roses to find that all of them had been picked. She stood for a moment dumbfounded.

"What a cruel thing for someone to do!" she said aloud. "Who could have stolen the roses?"

She went to her room to change for dinner. As she entered, the fragrance of white roses reached her before she saw them. On the table beside her bed was the most beautiful bouquet she had ever seen.

When she passed the chambermaid on her way down to dinner, Tamara asked her who had ordered the roses to be cut from the garden.

"His lordship, ma'am."

"Oh," was all Tamara could say. It had not been the answer she anticipated, although she did not know what answer she had expected.

At the table she gave Lord Foxcomb an uncertain glance, wondering whether she should acknowledge the roses. It would be rude of her not to do so, but she was annoyed that they had been cut.

"The white roses in my room are lovely, but they should not have been cut," she said frankly.

Lord Foxcomb shrugged his shoulders. "Why not?"

"They last longer on the stem, and everyone could enjoy them in the garden."

"You are the only one who admired them," he said quietly.

Tamara smiled, knowing that was sadly true. "Did you know that the white are much more fragrant than the red?" Her eyes lit up as she spoke.

Lord Foxcomb was amused at this startling revelation. "Really?" he teased.

"Oh, yes, indeed, m'lord. It seems nature puts all the strength in the color of the red roses, but in the delicate white she adds a lovely fragrance."

"I assumed all roses smelled alike," he retorted prosaically. "Can you prove it, Miss Birch?" he challenged.

Tamara swallowed her food quickly so she could reply. "Yes, m'lord."

Lord Foxcomb smiled. "There could be a scientific explanation. Bees might be attracted to the bright color. To lure them to the white, nature has added a stronger scent," he speculated. "'Tis important for pollination."

She looked at him wide-eyed. "How clever of you! Then you believe me, and we do not have to make the test."

"Oh, I did not say that. I demand final proof, Miss Birch. I am not convinced," he said lightly.

How could he pass up this opportunity? Several times after dinner he had requested she join him in a walk through his gardens, but she had always refused. He was tempted to order her to accompany him, but he decided against it, not wishing to impose his will upon her by force.

Fear of being alone with him away from the security of servants in the night's darkness, and thinking it an impropriety to stroll with the master of Foxcomb Manor in his gardens at night, Tamara had declined his invitations. Now she frowned, remembering there were no more white roses in the garden.

"With your permission I will go to my room for a blossom, and you can compare them yourself," she replied excitedly. Taking no heed of her previous reluctance, she raced to her room.

Lord Foxcomb was waiting for her when she returned breathless and smiling, holding a long-stemmed white rosebud. He gazed not at the flower, but at her, entranced by the vision of loveliness before him, vowing that before the night was over he would make her his mistress. He had been patient long enough.

They stepped from the door and proceeded toward the garden. The moon, luminous in the midst of its nightly journey, cast a silver light across the well-manicured lawn. They walked side by side, their silhouettes moving down the path in front of them, passing marble statues of nymphs and Greek gods. Tamara, her pink skirt with its triple flounce at the hem swishing, clutched the stem in her fingers and waved the bud beneath her nose. The scent of roses was heavy in the night air.

"Miss Birch. Oh, Miss Birch," Marie, Lady Foxcomb's maid called as she walked rapidly toward them. Tamara and Lord Foxcomb stopped and turned.

"Yes, what is it, Marie?" Tamara asked expectantly.

"Lady Foxcomb wants you to come to her immediately. She cannot sleep and would like you to read to her."

"Yes, of course."

"She sleeps all day, how the devil *can* she sleep at night!" snapped Sir Richard with irritation in his voice.

Swiftly Tamara curtsied. "Excuse me, m'lord," she said. "Lady Foxcomb wishes me to finish reading Charlotte Brontë's *Villette*. She pushed the rose into his hand and rushed to Lady Pamela's bedchamber.

Lord Foxcomb swore under his breath. Wistfully he watched her go, holding the rose to his nostrils. Although he had lost interest in the test, he headed toward the rosebed, speaking the words of the poet Thomas Moore:

> No rosebud is nigh
> To reflect back her blushes,
> Or give sigh for sigh.

14

Sir Richard left on a business trip to Paris and was gone three weeks. Tamara was relieved that his majordomo, George Ashworth, accompanied him. She did not like the man and took flight whenever he approached. When he confronted her, he smirked obscenely, making her feel wicked. She construed the expression on his face as a deliberate attempt to tell her he thought Lord Foxcomb was bedding her, or if not, would be soon.

Tamara spent most of her time carrying out Lady Pamela's whims, reading silly novels and completing her correspondence. She learned from maidservants that the Foxcomb marriage was a marriage of convenience. Sir Richard needed money to maintain his estates. Lady Pamela was wealthy, but not very attractive. No man would marry her for love. She suffered a terminal heart ailment and was not expected to live much longer. Lord Foxcomb had given orders to the servants to cater to her, carry out all her wishes, but he spent very little time with her himself. It was customary for husbands and wives to have separate bedchambers, but not once while she was there had Tamara seen him enter Lady Pamela's room and inquire how she felt. Tamara could not help but feel sorry for the woman.

Tamara liked Foxcomb Manor. It was like living in a world of enchantment far removed from reality. The brick house of fine Georgian architecture had been built during the mid-eighteenth century and recently had been richly refurbished.

Tapestries, draperies, and upholstering were bright and clean, smelling new and fresh. The walls had recently been papered, the superbly crafted woodwork painted. Waterford-crystal chandeliers sparkled immaculately, and the Italian marble fireplace in each room gleamed.

Tamara enjoyed the pale green sitting room, which was handsomely furnished in simple elegance. She particularly liked the green velvet deep-buttoned sofa, the delicate porcelain game birds on the mantel, and the three-sided bay window with a lovely view of the gardens. She spent most of her spare time in the cozy room playing the piano or reading, and often thought what a pity it was that Foxcomb Manor was not a happy home. How tragic it was there were no sons to inherit it or Lord Foxcomb's title.

Tamara was not aware of Sir Richard's return from Paris. Night had crept softly over the estate, and burnishing candlelight danced across her bosom as she played the piano. Lost in the melody, she glanced up at the convex Regency mirror on the opposite wall, seeing Lord Foxcomb's reflection. He leaned against the pillared door frame watching her closely, holding a mountain of boxes in his arms. Their eyes met in the mirror.

Disconcerted, Tamara flushed when she realized he was staring at her. She stopped playing, rose from the piano stool, and gracefully dipped a curtsy.

"I . . . I hope you do not mind," she stammered.

"Mind? You are absurdly lovely. If I did not know better, I would swear this room was designed especially for you," he said quietly.

Tamara continued to blush.

"Come over here and sit down. These are for you," he said more lightly, handing her the boxes.

They contained gowns, nightgowns, peignoirs, and lacy undergarments, which made her blush deeper.

"M'lord, I do not want to appear ungrateful, but I cannot accept these magnificent gifts."

His hands swept through the air. "Do not flatter yourself. They are not gifts. I want you to wear them for my own selfish enjoyment. You are a woman of quality, are you not?"

Tamara sighed deeply and hesitated. "My father was a marquis," she admitted.

"By George! I thought so. Your heritage alone compels me to help you. I insist you take these and wear them with my compliments."

Tamara spent most of the next day with Lady Foxcomb and did not see Sir Richard until dinnertime. They dined alone. Tamara was edgy, certain of what the servants thought and gossiped. They were trained to be tight-lipped before the master, but out of his sight their tongues let loose.

She looked exceptionally beautiful in a pale blue gown his lordship had brought from Paris. It fit her perfectly. Its neckline was lower than any she had ever worn.

Enticingly the candlelight flashed on her cheeks, its intangible fingers seductively caressing her creamy flesh. The flickering brightness intensified the copper hue in her long hair, which was formally pinned up with clusters of curls on the crown of her head. Her eyes sparkled in the light of the flames.

Masculine approval flashed in Lord Foxcomb's eyes. His intense stare lingered caressingly on her delicate features. In the eyes of men she possessed the infallible indicators of a sensuously feminine woman, all of which belied her frigidity. He was no different from other men who mistook her bashful behavior for the innocence of a maiden untouched. She would blossom when he had his way with her, when he would awaken her to the delights of his lovemaking. She would resist at first, as a lady should, but then . . .

He was aware of her limpid violet eyes, not the turmoil hidden behind them. It was impossible for him to see into the murky depths of her despair. He saw not a vestige of her fears, but only her curvaceous body made for love, with soft tender lips to be kissed with trembling passion. Her full, up-thrust breasts were created to be admired and caressed, tantalizing hips, slender legs, slim ankles that stirred a man with the least provocation. Since she maintained the illusion of being born to laugh and love, Lord Foxcomb did not realize that a cruel twist of fate had denied Tamara the capability to know the pleasures of passion and its fulfillment. Somewhere deep inside, a scar had to heal before the willingness of her mind would permit her repressed desires to burst forth.

Quietly she avoided his gaze, looking down at her plate instead of at him.

"Drink your wine, madam. I brought it from France. I thought it possessed the flavor you would enjoy."

Mechanically she sipped the vintage French wine, the color of rubies, clear, not sweet, not too dry. When the meal ended, Tamara asked to be excused.

His dark eyes narrowed to slits. He viewed her closely. "Before you go, I would ask one favor of you."

"What is it?"

"Will you play the piano for me?"

Tamara hedged, feeling self-conscious, but had he not been kind to her? It was little in return for what he did for her. There could be no harm in it. She would play one or two numbers, then retire to her room.

Sir Richard sat in the wing chair facing her, swishing brandy in his crystal goblet. He regarded her appreciatively. His half-closed eyes kissed her soft, expressive mouth, then, longingly, slid downward to linger on her breasts.

Over the years he had had more than his share of women, but he had had his fill of the coarse, wanton courtesans in Paris, who blatantly were his for the taking, free or in return for baubles, women who thrust their hips violently to please him, yawning as they did whatever he directed, with no thought of being pleasured in return. He had enjoyed their expertise. It was why he went to Paris, what he had craved, but this trip he had found them crude. He had a need for something entirely different. Everywhere he went he was reminded of the young woman at Foxcomb Manor. Everything about Tamara suggested delicacy, sweet tenderness which aroused and nurtured Lord Foxcomb's masculinity.

He clutched the stem of the goblet between his fingers, resting its foot on the arm of the chair. Leaning back, he closed his eyes, deriving sensual pleasure from the sounds of the soft melody she played. The soothing music transported him into a fantasy of holding Tamara in his arms, a dream in which she responded shyly, tenderly. He imagined himself on top of her, entering her, the first man to do so, thrilling, pleasing her as well as himself. He could almost feel her eager lips, hear her soft, pleading, sweet moans of ecstasy.

The blood ran hot in Lord Foxcomb's veins. His desire was building. He did not open his eyes until she stopped playing. For a few moments they were silent.

"There is a mystery about you that intrigues me," he said at last. "Will you not tell me your real name?" he queried hoarsely. "I would like to help you. I have been trying to place your accent. At times there is a hint of West Indian in it."

"No, m'lord," she replied most emphatically, shaking her head as she spoke, causing the neatly placed corkscrew curls on her cheeks to disarrange. "I am sorry to be insubordinate, but I do not wish to do so. If you know who I am, you will send me back."

"Back where?"

Irritation flashed from her eyes. "I have told you before, I do not wish to discuss my personal life."

The tone of her voice brought Lord Foxcomb back to his senses, and he burst into laughter. "By God, you are charming. I wish you would keep me company a little while longer. I promise not to question you. You see, I am quite lonely," he said beseechingly with a tone of sadness entering his voice. He felt her hesitation. "However, if you wish to retire, you are free to do so."

73

She responded with pity, as he had hoped, and sat down across from him.

"What do you wish to talk about?" she asked softly.

"Anything . . . or nothing," he answered as he gazed at her. "Tell me what you wish from life and I will put it at your feet," he added.

For the first time in his life, Lord Foxcomb was at a loss as to how to win a woman he desired, and this one he desired more than any other he had known. His instincts told him to move cautiously, patiently. She was a woman who had to be wooed gently to be won. This was contrary to the rush of his growing passion, and he had difficulty keeping his emotions under control.

He concluded he had to win her pity first. He would tell her of his loveless marriage, the failure of his wife to present him with an heir to his estates, which he treasured above all else. He would gain her confidence with kindness, like an offering of a saucer of milk to a hungry kitten.

Sir Richard rose and walked to her, taking her hands and pulling her to her feet. He kissed each palm. Tamara withdrew her hands. The color drained from her face. He grasped a long strand of her hair from her shoulder and coiled it around his forefinger until it reached her ear. Pulling gently, he encouraged her to take a step closer to him, then rubbed the lobe of her ear with his thumb.

"Please," she whispered, "I do not like to be touched."

"But I want to touch you more than anything in the world," he replied hoarsely. "My fingers and lips ache to touch every spot of you."

Silence filled the room. He saw immediately his words frightened her, and regretted them. The muscle in his cheek twitched. He cleared his throat and turned away from her, crossing his wrists at his lower back.

"If you wish to retire, you are excused," he replied, curtly, a bitter note entering his voice.

"Thank you, m'lord." He nodded. "Good night, m'lord," she responded quietly. She curtsied and left, knowing his eyes followed her, touched her everywhere.

15

Tamara knew it was only a matter of time until she would have to leave, and frugally saved her wages, keeping them hidden. Over the next few weeks she tried to avoid Lord Foxcomb, but this was difficult, particularly at dinnertime. He was serving in the House of Lords, but Parliament was not in session and would not convene for another month. She hoped it would be necessary for him to make another business trip, but he remained at Foxcomb Manor, spending most of his time during the day riding, hunting, and fishing, and in the evening reading in his library.

The time for her to leave came sooner than she expected. One evening, preparing to retire, she slipped into the pink lace-trimmed nightgown his lordship had brought from Paris. After brushing her hair vigorously, she checked the doors and windows, a nightly ritual. They were locked. The flames burned dimly in the globe-covered lamp. She fluffed the white cambric lace-edged pillow and slid beneath the bedcovers. Eyes heavy, she glanced around the lovely room. The silk papering was the color of cream with blue delphiniums. The doors and woodwork were painted Wedgewood blue, and the cornice was hand-carved honeysuckles.

She relaxed and slid her hands back beneath the pillow. Her bed was a Sheraton four-poster with a delicate white crocheted canopy. Her eyes followed its edge of tassels, then closed. She yawned sleepily, longing for nights such as she enjoyed but had taken for granted as a child, going to bed early, sleeping undisturbed for fourteen hours.

Tamara fell asleep but woke suddenly. A slight noise alarmed her. She had been living at Foxcomb Manor long enough not to be frightened by familiar sounds, but this was in the hall, near her room. Alerted, she sat up with a start. Someone was outside her door. She slipped from her bed, tiptoed to the door, checking the latch again.

"Who is there?" She held her breath and listened. "Is someone there?" She waited and listened, feeling relief until she heard a key rattling in the lock.

Fear enveloped her. She held her breath. Paralyzed into

immobility, she watched the door open slowly. Lord Foxcomb entered the room, then closed the door softly behind him. He put his finger to his lips, indicating she was to remain silent. She could not have screamed if she tried. So terrified was she that she gave no heed to her appearance, forgetting she was wearing only the thin nightgown that clung provocatively to her figure and barely concealed her nipples.

Lord Foxcomb pushed both hands into the air as if she were a thief pointing a pistol at him. "Please, do not be frightened," he begged, making a not-too-steady leg in her direction, listing from side to side. He wore a robe of dark green velvet. A belt of the same material tied loosely at the waist held it together.

"M'lord! Has something happened to Lady Foxcomb?"

He looked at her divine figure showing clearly through the diaphanous gown. He had longed to see her hair hang loose as it did now. The vision made him breathless. Desire filled his eyes. In his inebriated state he staggered toward her. Tamara eluded him.

"This is your home . . . but you do not have the right to intrude upon my privacy," Tamara gasped, trying to compose herself. "Please, sir, leave at once. You have had too much to drink, and tomorrow you will regret your behavior. You are intoxicated and should go to your room."

Lord Foxcomb, propping his elbow against the bedroom wall to steady himself, undignifiedly attempted to cross his tottering legs.

"Aye . . . dizzy from your beauty," said he with a thick tongue, regurgitating sour fluid that burned his throat. He swallowed hard. "How utterly delectable you are! More exquisite than I e . . . e . . . imagined," he whispered, obliquely hanging against the wall. He reached out to touch her hair. "I had planned to wa . . . wait until my wife's demise, then ask you to . . . to marry me, but I can wait no longer for you. Let me have you now," he pleaded unsteadily.

She became uncomfortably aware of the scantiness of her attire. Cold perspiration trickled down her back. Feeling faint, she began to tremble. Her mind leaped. Dear God, she thought, my nightmare is coming true!

"Remove that garment."

She backed away from him. He pursued her. A hand on each of her shoulders moved swiftly in unison, slipping the lace straps from their resting place, causing the gown to drop to her ankles. Lord Foxcomb reeled backward, catching his balance with difficulty. An impish grin crossed his face.

"Ha, the sight of your naked body staggers me."

Desperately Tamara's arms moved up and down in front of her in an attempt to hide her body. Having regained his equilibrium, he moved toward her again. His flittering hands reached for her bare breasts, trying to cling to the firm mounds of satiny flesh. His fingers grazed, soft, puffy nipples. Tamara was too scared to react.

"Do not scream, lovely one," he warned. "Give yourself willingly. I swear 'twill be the most delightful experience of your life. I will give you anything your heart desires. I am at your mercy," he pleaded, thereupon going down on one knee falteringly, awkwardly bracing himself by firmly clamping a hand to the floor. Waveringly, to prevent himself from falling, he brought his left knee down to join the other on the carpet. Thus the nobleman humbled himself on both knees before the maiden, pale with fright.

She clasped her hands to her mouth, continuing to back away from him until she bumped into the bureau.

"Please, sir," she gasped, "your wife is in bed in the next room."

In his befuddled condition Lord Foxcomb's thinking was cloudy. He mistook her meaning.

"Paah! How can I crawl into bed with that bit of obesity, when your loveliness shines before me?" he asked petulantly.

Seeing his noble gestures were for naught, clumsily he stood up, reeling toward her again. His arms encircled her waist, hands sliding down her back, cupping her firm buttocks, jerking her close against his body.

"You have tantalized me day and night. I will not be refused."

She was certain his intentions were to hurt her, although she could not understand why he would wish to do so. He bent his head to grasp a nipple to his mouth. That she shrank from the touch of his lips against her flesh sent him into a rage. His patience at an end, he mumbled curse words, his eyes flaring.

Groping, she reached back and grabbed a brass candlestick from the bureau top. Her arm came down as quickly as a striking snake. With a dull thud, the candlestick smote the crown of his head. For a moment nothing happened. They stared at each other. Then Sir Richard's eyes went out of focus and closed. His knees buckled under him, and gracefully he dropped to the floor in a state of total insensibility.

16

"Oh, Lord, help me," Tamara panted aloud. "I pray he is not dead! Oooohhh! Me, who has boasted of not being able to kill a fly! . . . And in my private bedchamber . . . and in his nightclothes," she sobbed, wringing her hands, confused as to what she should do.

Sir Richard moved, fluttering his eyelids. With a sigh of relief and her hand clamped over her open mouth, she watched him regain consciousness. Anxious to cover her nakedness, she fumbled into her robe while hastily going to the washstand, pouring water from the blue porcelain pitcher into the matching bowl. With a moist cloth she rinsed the blood from m'lord's injured skull.

Lord Foxcomb sat up and puked. The sour-smelling mess plopped out of his mouth onto his velvet robe. He was deathly pale. Tamara went down on her knees. "Ooooohhh! I am sorry, m'lord," she choked remorsefully as she dabbed the bloody wound.

The thwack on his head had sobered him, subdued his passion. "I asked for it," he said heavily, sitting on the floor with his legs spread wide to balance himself, his dignity more shattered than the flesh on his scalp. Automatically his hand went up to his head. "Ouch! Aaaahh, my head," he groaned.

"Please, m'lord. Do not touch it. 'Tis bleeding. If you please, hold this wet cloth to the wound." Mumbling beneath his breath, clutching the towel to his head, Sir Richard struggled to rise. Tamara extended a hand to help him. He shrugged her away, brusquely. Tottering to the door, he opened it, then looked back. "Sorry." He turned to leave, and bumped smack into Lady Pamela, wearing a bright red nightgown.

"Piff, piff, Richard, such stirring oooohhs and aaahs of passion I heard coming from this room, then silence. I feared the maiden had swooned from your lovemaking," she said glibly.

It was the first time Tamara had ever seen Lady Foxcomb out of bed. She had no waistline. Her large bosoms hung low, resting on a roll of fat above her round stomach. Mortified, innocent Tamara gulped hard as Sir Richard closed her door;

hence all she could hear was irritated mumbling. Tamara locked the door and crawled back to bed. Unable to sleep, she tossed and turned, getting herself entangled in the bed-covers. Toward morning she made her decision. When the faintness of dawn showed along the edge of the mountains, she packed her belongings, the ones she had brought with her, leaving behind the pretty gowns and undergarments Lord Foxcomb had given her. Stealthily, with only the thought of escape, she made her way to the stables, assuming the groom would be sleeping in one of the empty stalls. The smell of fresh fodder, hay, and horseflesh hovered in the thick air. The weak morning light had not penetrated the stable. She groped her way through the straw-cluttered aisle, checking each stall. One horse whinnied, pawing nervously with his right front foot. Another, ready for his morning oats, snorted and bobbed his head up and down.

She came to a pen which she thought empty, but the horse was lying down and rose slowly, first on his forelegs, then his hind. She glanced in the tack room, where walls were lined with pegs from which hung reins, bridles, harnesses, and saddles of all sizes, but there was no sigh of humans. Perhaps the grooms slept in the hayloft, she speculated. Clambering between bales of straw, she headed toward the ladder. Coming upon a stall that she had thought vacant, she heard muffled groans. Looking down, she spotted two booted legs, ankles pointed upward toward the low wooden ceiling of cob-webs speckled with dead flies and bugs.

Her first thought was that someone was injured or ill. The legs changed position slightly. Something did not seem quite right. Tamara bent over and squinted in the dim light for a better look. Another pair of booted legs stretched in the op-posite direction. Tamara gasped as she saw the two grooms, each having the other's phallus deep in his mouth, sucking fiercely. Repulsed, shocked, she stepped back, knocking over a pitchfork, which banged to the floor. The two men emptied their mouths and bolted to a sitting position.

"Lordy, we got's a spectator!" grumbled the groom she knew as Willy. He stood up, turned his back to Tamara, and buttoned his pants while the other lad rolled facedown fum-bling beneath himself to fasten his breeches. Straw clung to his shirt and the back of his pants.

"I . . . I . . . must leave for Lon . . . London immediately, Willy," Tamara stammered. "Sa-saddle the gray gelding."

Willy, who was shorter than Tamara by two inches, brushed the straw from his shirt sleeve, then folded his arms on his chest defiantly. "No' 'til ye promises no' ta tell his lordship whut ye seen."

"Aye." Tamara nodded. "I pr-promise. I will . . . I will not see Lord Foxcomb again. Use . . . use the lady's saddle, she ordered. Will yawned and stretched, then obeyed.

On the way to London Tamara thought about the scene in the stable, tried to expel it from her mind. She was not aware of such practices between men. All the discussions at school involved relations between men and women. Tamara tried to erase the scene from her consciousness. She had too many problems of her own to dwell on it. She would try to get her room back at the boardinghouse where she had stayed previously. She would not return to her uncle.

In London she found a livery and paid a boy, giving him instructions for returning the horse to Foxcomb Manor. She went to the same boardinghouse and began daily visits to the employment agency. Weeks went by. She failed to find work. Her situation was desperate.

"Is there not a job for even a scullery maid?" she asked despairingly. Though frugal, she saw her funds dwindle until she was afraid she no longer had enough to pay the rent collected each Saturday. She had heard of a refuge for the homeless located on Upper Ogle Street, where she could stay for one or two nights, but the thought repelled her. She could not accept charity. If only she had brought her mother's jewels with her. She could pawn them. Cutting down on food, she lost weight and grew hungry. She could not beg or steal. Out of respect for the memory of her parents, to wind up in debtors' prison was unthinkable. She must never do anything for which they would not be proud of her.

17

In desperation Tamara returned once again to Langham Place, where a number of women were applying for positions, several others making arrangements to be transported to other parts of the empire for employment. She paused, asking herself whether she should fill out immigration papers for Australia.

Mrs. Hawkins, an efficient-looking woman with a middle-age figure, graying hair, and a brown wart above her left eyebrow, recognized Tamara, who begged, "Is there no need for even a chambermaid . . . anything?"

"Whut 'appened to yer job at Foxcomb Manor?"

Tamara looked at the woman skeptically. "'Twas necessary for me to leave."

Mrs. Hawkins frowned and nodded knowingly. She lifted her spectacles to her nose and looked over her list of jobs.

"Holloway and Company's factory 'as twenty women 'ired who operate steam-driven sewing machines. Oi've 'eard one o' the girls is pregnant an' asked to leave in a month."

"Mrs. Hawkins, I cannot wait that long," Tamara answered nervously. "I am running out of funds."

Mrs. Hawkins, noting the frightened expression on Tamara's face, rechecked her listings. "This is a good year fer the cotton mills. The whole world is demandin' cotton goods. The mills are lookin' fer children over nine an' young women, but ye don' look strong 'nough fer that," mused the agent.

"I will try," Tamara answered hopefully, whereupon Mrs. Hawkins wrote down the address of the Tufnell Cotton Mill on Prescott Street in Whitechapel and gave it to Tamara with instructions to ask for Mr. Beales.

"Ye can thank Lord Shaftesbury. 'Tis only ten hours a day, cut down from twelve . . . only sixty hours a week. Used to be sixteen a day afore he got the Labor Act through Parliament. The pay is two shillings a day, twelve a week."

Tamara folded the paper and tucked it safely in her reticule. "When shall I go there?"

"Six in the mornin'. An', girl, don' be late. Ten after, the gates are locked."

The job was a godsend. Tamara felt much lighter when she left Langham Place, as if a great weight had been lifted from her. Most of the cotton mills of England were located in the so-called cotton districts of Lancashire and Yorkshire. However, several had sprung up in London. The Tufnell Cotton Mill was located close to the railway and not far from the wharf, near warehouses where bales of cotton were stored, shipped from ports in the southern United States.

She took the omnibus to Whitechapel and searched for a room close to the mill, finding the residential area overcrowded and depressing, inhabited by poor workers, including many Irish immigrants. It was Tamara's first real contact with poverty, and it struck her hard.

She passed narrow, sleazy alleys with noxious smells from open sewerage and garbage strewn in the gutters. She walked past rows of ill-kept boardinghouses with broken windows stuffed with dirty rags or covered with brown cardboard. Houses in disrepair were being torn down to make room for additional cotton and tobacco warehouses and for the extension of the railway. The demolition increased overcrowding. The only rooms available were those already occupied by five or six people.

After looking at several places, she decided on a furnished garret room six blocks from the mill on Lambeth Street, where the houses were somewhat better than in the immediate vicinity of the mill. The rent was four shillings a week. The small, shabby room had a narrow bed, a small wooden table, and a rickety chair. In the corner was a gas burner on which she could make tea. There were several pots and pans for cooking stew. A privy and common tap for cold water in the back court was used by everyone in the tenement, but she was grateful that she did not have to share her room with anyone.

To move her belongings, since it was cheaper than a hackney, she took the omnibus back to her room near Langham Place, where the rent had been much higher and the distance too far for her to walk to the mill.

Morning dawned, caught in a silken web of fog. Tamara rose at five, prepared tea, and ate a stale biscuit. She left her dingy room, making her way through the dense low-lying earth-cloud which shrouded her, welcoming it as a protective mantle that shielded her against the dangers lurking in the streets, but so thick was it she had difficulty breathing. Terrified, she hurried on, feeling the mist on her face, clutching her shawl more securely around her shoulders, groping her way to Tufnell Mill.

She arrived at the dreary-looking building fifteen minutes early, watching with grim fascination as the lean, scrofulous children sluggishly entered the cotton mill. She noticed the rachitic effects from poor diet, the deformities, knees bent inward, ankles swollen, expressions of stupefaction on their pale faces.

Without wavering, Tamara resolutely joined the mass of workers and entered the factory, clutching the paper Mrs. Hawkins had given her. At the stroke of six the whistle shrilled. Tamara watched as the overlooker, holding his fine book, checked the names of the workers as they passed, handing bate tickets to those who entered after the whistle had sounded. She waited until the last had entered before she approached the overlooker and asked if he were Mr. Beales.

"Aye," he answered, taking the paper Tamara handed him. Although pallid, compared to the other workers Mr. Beales was a burly man, looking well-fed, with a globelike pouch below his thick waist, which had been created by the large quantities of ale he consumed. His unruly red hair matched the color of his Dundreary whiskers, which almost met in the middle of his chin. Mr. Beales looked her over skeptically with blue eyes cold and hard as ice.

"Oi'm sartin ye've ne'er worked in a cotton mill afore," he commented while unthinkingly scratching his crotch.

"No, sir, I have not, but I am most willing to learn."

The cold meanness emanating from his face caused Tamara to shiver.

"Then ye cannot start on the looms. Ye'll be a carder. T'ain't always whut ye loikes. Ye'll 'ave ta start in the cardin' room. The 'ours be six to six, Saturdays six ta two with 'alf 'our fer breakfast, an 'our fer dinner, startin' at twelve. Yer pay is two shillings a day. Payday is Saturday."

Mr. Beales rattled off the rules rotelike, without expression. He had full power to discharge her without notice if she neglected or spoiled her work. He would fine her threepence if she was a minute late, fire her after ten minutes. She would be fined one shilling for leaving work when she should have been working. For each fine, she would receive a bate ticket. All fines would be deducted from her pay. Wages would be paid in the countinghouse every Saturday at two. He concluded with a bit of advice. "There be a sayin', 'One who is slothful in 'is woik is extravagant in the use o' time.' 'Member that."

Mr. Beales proceeded to tell Tamara how much improved the working conditions were at Tufnell Mill.

"Some millowners cheat their woikers by slowin' down the clocks or cuttin' back on their breaks. T'inks they're woikin' ten, when they's woikin' eleven hours. Not 'ere. Ye should be thankful oi'm 'iring ye."

Tufnell Mill, Mr. Beales went on to explain, abides by the law, according to the Factory Act of 1850. Working hours were limited to sixty per week, with seven and one half hours on Saturdays, plus one-half hour for breakfast.

"Ye should be 'appy 'ere," Mr. Beales said. "Now, come with me. Oi'll show ye ware yer woikin'."

With a sadistic expression on his face, his bulbous eyes

staring at her for a moment, he picked up the leather whipping strap he always carried with him while walking through the mill. He led her to the carding room, using the strap as they passed workers standing at their looms.

"Whut is done in this mill be simple," he said firmly. "We transforms bales o' cotton into textiles."

He led the way, slapping the strap lightly on the side of his leg. Tamara was agog, viewing the inside of a world she did not know existed. It was nothing like she expected, a world far removed from the one she was accustomed to living in. The rooms were poorly ventilated, and the strong smell of machine oil reached her nostrils. The wooden floors were covered with it.

Tamara noticed several girls, no more than fifteen, in the last stages of pregnancy, standing before looms. She wondered how they would be able to work until six o'clock. Children not older than twelve strained to do the work required of doffers, mounting the machines and taking down bobbins.

She was reminded of a poem she was required to learn at Lady Bedford's school. At the time it meant nothing to her except required reading. Now she realized what Elizabeth Barrett Browning meant in "The Cry of the Children": "They look up with their pale and somber faces. And their looks are sad to see."

Tamara felt the vibration on the floor as rollers and spindles whirled. The workers were not permitted to talk, and it would have been impossible to hear above the noise of the machinery. But from the corner of their eyes they did not miss Mr. Beales's efforts to impress the pretty new worker with his authority, knowledge of the mill, and good standing with the millowner. Tamara doubted he took this much time with every new employee, and the workers knew it, too.

He explained how the work was divided, starting from the beginning with the slashing of the bales, followed by mixing various grades of the thickly matted cotton, then, using the scutching process, cleaning the dirt and seeds from the fibers of the raw cotton.

Impulsively, Tamara scooped up a handful of the cotton and squeezed it into a fluffy ball in the palm of her hand. Mr. Beales took the cotton from her hand and threw it back on the pile. "Mr. Beales, where is all this cotton grown?"

"Southern United States. Place called South Carolina."

Tamara watched as the cleaned cotton was spread flat and put through a "lapper," which flattened it into sheets and wound it around cylinders. From there the flattened cotton was sent to the carding room, where it was passed through a carding machine. The teeth in sets of rollers raked the fibers parallel to each other, taking out the tangles and knots. This was where Tamara was going to work. She breathed the itchy lint floating in the air. Her eyes began to water, irritated by it.

The fibers were brought together and twisted in a drawing frame into a "roving," which was again wrapped on cylinders. Tamara watched as the cardings were sent to piercers to supply the spindles in the spinning room, where the cotton was drawn into strands and twisted into thread, which was wound on spindles and sent to the weaving room.

"'Eh! Eddie!" shouted Mr. Beales above the noise of the machinery. "Ye shews this new gel 'ow ta scutch an' put the cotton through the cardin' machine," he ordered, nervously scratching between his legs again and pulling his trousers away from his flesh.

18

Tamara had stripped her plainest dress of all ribbons and frills, but it was still elegant in comparison to the faded, patched, threadbare garments worn by the other women. Her shoes were shiny black, theirs scuffed, with soles full of holes, which barely covered mended hose.

After taking in every detail of her appearance, the mill women suspected she was a spy for the owner or Mr. Beales. They viewed her with contempt and made sneering remarks.

"Humph! Look a' the loikes o' 'er, would ye. A damned blue blood in our midst. Wata' she want? Eddie, ask 'er if she know'd Lord Shaftesbury," chided one of the toothless, uncombed women, named Mabel. She was hard of hearing, caused by the noise of machinery, and spoke loudly.

Lord Shaftesbury was the workers' hero. Everyone knew of his efforts on their behalf and thought of him as mystical rather than human. Wishing to be accepted, innocently Tamara replied, "Aye, I have met the Earl of Shaftesbury. He is a fine gentleman."

The women howled with coarse laughter, not believing her.

Tamara cringed. Nothing in her life had prepared her for

this. Lady Alma was malicious in her own way, but Tamara had never dealt with women like Mabel.

"Speaks loike a swell, she does." Mabel snickered.

Eddie was more compassionate. Between immovable lips he said in a low, warning voice, "Brace yerself. The old fart be 'eadin' yer way."

The women grew quiet, not failing to notice that when Beales stopped to check Tamara's work, he put his hand familiarly on her waist. The women, not seeing Tamara cringe, resented it. They vied for his attention, hoping to receive an easier job, less cruel treatment, avoid the feel of his strap or the kick of his boot. For their favors after working hours the reward was sugar, potatoes, or bacon. Tamara learned that when he looked with favor on one of the girls, it was practically an order for her to comply, out of fear of being mistreated or fired.

Beales had thick red eyebrows, and beneath them, sinister blue eyes. He sucked on his pipe whether lit or not. As he stood beside Tamara, the pipe glowed and he puffed clouds of smoke around her. Her stomach was empty. The smoke made her dizzy.

Eddie, a youth who looked older than his thirteen years, instructed her. Wheezing, he breathed asthmatically, coughing and spitting blood into a cloth. Tamara gagged.

The carding room was not large, and the workers were crowded into close contact. Stale odors of sweat exuding from the women permeated the air, filled with fibrous dust. The heat of the room, Eddie's spitting blood, the asthmatic coughing, the odors of machine oil, sweat, and pipe smoke, the fiber-filled air, reeled upon her, spreading a wave of nauseousness through her. She felt relief when Mr. Beales left the room.

"Pooph! Guess we knows w'o 'e's sleepin' with tonight," commented Mabel, the smell of whiskey fresh on her breath from a night of drinking. Tamara could not fail to notice the undisguised contempt in the woman's voice. She tried to ignore the remark, whereupon the woman kicked her in back of each knee, causing them to buckle.

"Blockhead, ain't ye got a tongue?" She kicked Tamara again. "Haven't ye got menners?"

Tamara winced. The floor spun dizzying circles. She wanted to be accepted, but felt like a deer ruthlessly ostracized by the rest of the herd. Never had she heard the indecent language that came from the foul mouths of the women in the carding room. Much of it she did not understand. Their insults were more painful than the gnawing emptiness of her stomach. They did not trust her, resented her intrusion into their world, such as it was. Before she had arrived, they spoke openly among themselves, when Mr. Beales was out of earshot, about strikes, refusing to work until their wages increased. With Tamara near, they were either tight-lipped or resorted to whispering plans for their secret meetings and joining the London Trades Council, a multitrade organization.

At twelve o'clock the workers left their looms and positions, gathering in corners on the floor where the machine oil had not spread to eat their meager lunches brought from home. On nice days they were permitted outdoors in the fenced-in mill yard.

Hunger pains gnawed in Tamara's stomach. She had not thought of bringing lunch. She glanced at Mabel, who sat poking her finger in her nose. The frowsy women repelled her. She sat back against the wall and closed her eyes. Flies buzzed around her face. An elbow nudged her arm. It was Agnes, a frail woman whose face was withered and unsmiling and who wore a scarf around her neck to try to hide a melon-size goiter. She had broken a piece of bread into two parts and offered one to Tamara.

"'Ere, dearie," said the sickly-looking woman hoarsely. "Oi ain't 'ungry." When Agnes saw how grateful Tamara was, she gave her half an apple. Although it was covered with brown spots, Tamara gulped it down.

Agnes worked at a spindle for the wet spinning of linen yarn. Water splashed over her continuously, so that the front of her dress was always soaked. Her shoes were wet from standing in water that flooded the floor in front of her machine. She complained to Tamara that her throat hurt, and she looked feverish.

Agnes, taking a liking to Tamara, wanted to befriend her. She pitied her for the harsh manner in which the other workers treated her.

"Gel, wheer ye cum from besides yer mother's womb? 'Ow'd ye wind ap 'ere?" Before Tamara could reply, the woman continued. "Ye didn't oughta, ye knows. Not with yer looks. Ye could do batter woikin' the streets," she advised.

"Doing what?" Tamara asked naively, flicking away a fly hovering around her face. She watched as one of the women shared her bread and cheese with a tiger cat that slunk close to her legs. Tamara swallowed hard, longing for the bits of food, slapping at the fly that landed boldly on her arm.

87

A large gray rat scuttered across the floor. The tiger cat leaped after it. Tamara's eyes widened, while the others laughed at the race, a form of amusement during their lunch break.

At first Tamara was clumsy with the work assigned to her, but it did not take long before she learned to move her fingers swiftly. That afternoon she grew weary from the dull routine of the work. She stopped a moment to stretch her back, which ached more and more as the day dragged on. As she moved her shoulders, which had stiffened, the scutching machine began to make an odd noise. Tamara was almost glad for the change.

"Eh, Ellen," shouted Eddie above the noise. "Go to the storage room an' git me a can o' oil."

"She dursn't leave 'er place," commented one of the women waspishly.

"If'n oi orders 'er to, she can. Oi can't leave the machinery."

Tamara left her post and went to the room where supplies were stored. She opened the door, to find the room in complete darkness. Waiting until her eyes grew accustomed to the dim light, she looked around for the oil. Taking a can, she was about to leave when she heard someone moaning. She stepped past the piles of crates and boxes to see a man and woman on the floor. There was no mistaking the identity of the man on top. His hair was red and bushy. Tamara recognized the woman by her dress, which was above her waist, her legs wrapped around Beales. It was Mabel.

Aghast, thinking he was raping her, Tamara almost screamed for help. Then she heard Mabel begging for more, speaking loudly, as a deaf person does. "Faster, faster. Ahhh, 'ell, t'ain't big enough. Yer goin' limp agin," she complained between gasps. "It slipped out," she announced.

Tamara was paralyzed.

"Hush! Not so damned loud, ye hot bitch. Stop yer complaining." He sneered. "Oi tol' ye ta put it in yer mouth foist." He grunted, pumping faster, deeper. "Bloody hag! Yer wrinkled body ain't appealin' to me. Oi don't know why the 'ell oi'm servicin' *you*. Should be the other way round. Ye knows oi loikes it in yer mouth, 'cause ye ain't got teeth." He grunted, continuing to pump. "Old fool! If ye gives me the clap, oi'll not only fire ye, oi'll skin yer wrinkled ass, oi will."

Tamara's mouth widened into a big O.

Mabel panted. "Tamorra, Mr. Beales. Lemme 'ave me way t'day."

"Rut. Always in heat. Ye needs a bull. Yer the only one who does it without 'spectin' somethin' in return."

"Aaaaah, Mr. Beales, oi loves ye, oi does."

"Ye loves what oi got in ye."

Beales's appendage was deep inside, out of sight. His body moved frantically. Listening to the grunts, groans, and bumps on the floor, staring at his bare, rotund behind humping in the rhythm of his mating, Tamara forgot to breathe. She backed toward the door, closing it softly, returning to the carding room with the can of oil clutched in her trembling hands.

"Eh! Are ye sick or somethin'?" asked Eddie. "What ails ye? Yer as white as the cotton."

"Noth . . . nothing. I am all right," Tamara stammered.

Eddie took the can and proceeded to oil the machinery. Suddenly Tamara heard him scream, an agonizing, suffering scream. She opened her mouth, yelled soundlessly. He was caught in the scutcher, and she watched helplessly as he was pulled around and around. Someone shouted, "Shut off the bloody machine." The switch was reached. The machinery stopped. Eddie's head was bleeding, his legs were bruised, his darned shirt ripped to expose a badly crushed right arm.

Tamara felt faint. It was the longest, most grueling day of her life except the day her parents were murdered. At leaving-off time, which was six o'clock, she left the mill with the others. When she reached the pavement beyond the gates, she dusted the lint and cotton fibers from her dress and hair. Deeply depressed, she prayed for enough strength to get back to her room. She stopped to buy two muffins from the muffin man at the street corner, and a piece of fried mackerel from the fishmonger. She purchased two apples from the coster-monger for her lunch the next day.

Trying to figure out what they were doing, she paused to watch a group of boys. A piece of meat had been tied to the top of a pole before it was greased. Each boy paid the owner a halfpenny to try to climb the slippery shaft to retrieve the meat.

Tamara shoved on. Her legs hurt, her fingers were sore, her eyes irritated red, her nose and lungs full of fibrous dust from the raw cotton. Weakly she struggled to mount the flights of wooden steps to the garret. At least the room was high above the noise of the street and the sour smell of the garbage carts. She picked up the wooden pail that caught rainwater dripping from the ceiling, tossed the water out the window, stood the bucket back in place. Not bothering to undress, she fell on her hard, narrow bed. She must not think of the cockroaches, the rainwater dripping through the ceiling ... or tomorrow. Merciful sleep came quickly.

The next morning Tamara woke with severe menstrual pains. She knew if she stayed home, missed work, she would lose her job. Sheer willpower and determination motivated her to rise from the uncomfortable cot. She drank a cup of hot tea and made her way to the mill. Pressing onward, she glanced at a stoop-shouldered beggar selling shoe strings. His right arm was amputated several inches below the elbow, and she knew it was from an accident at the mill. His price of survival was the inability to return to work. A shabbily dressed young man sitting with his back against a building held his tin cup in Tamara's direction. Was this what Agnes had meant by working the streets?

During the morning break, workers collected a few shillings for Eddie, who would not be able to return to the mill. Tamara could spare no money, but promised to make a donation on Saturday when she received her wages.

The days that followed became routine. Arriving when it was still dark in the morning, she left the mill at six, when night covered the streets. She passed a bakery, sniffing the delicious odors of baking dough, but dared not stop. She had to eat her stale loaf at home first and try to hold out until she received her pay on Saturday. All her movements were geared toward Saturday.

She was about to pass the Ragged School a block from the mill when she spotted Lord Shaftesbury standing in front of the school surrounded by babbling children. She ducked into a doorway. She was not sure whether he would recognize her if he saw her, but she could take no chances. He would certainly question her, possibly tell her uncle. She waited a few minutes, then peeped around the corner. He was gone. She sighed relief and continued on her way along the poorly lit street.

By sheer will she made it through the week. It was Saturday. She would be required to work only until two o'clock; then she would receive her pay. Never had money seemed so precious. Plans of how she would spend it tumbled through her mind. One more hour, and she had made it through her first week.

An agonizing scream came from the weaving room. The other workers knew what had happened. It occurred frequently. Saturdays the machinery was cleaned, lint picked out, rollers wiped while in operation. A workman had caught his hand in the machinery. The man staggered past the carding room, blood pouring from his fingerless right hand.

Beales, standing cross-legged at the door, picking at a tooth, noticed Tamara turn white. He shook his head.

" 'E was reckless . . . 'urrying . . . careless. So 'e must suffer the consequences," he muttered unsympathetically, shrugging his shoulders. "Ye'll git used to it. 'Appens all the time."

At two o'clock the factory whistle blasted. In reality its tone was always the same, but it affected the conditioned workers differently at different times. At six in the morning it was a loud, morose shrill, at the end of the day a welcome lullaby of dismissal. At two o'clock on Saturdays it burst joyously toward the heavens, a jubilee of sounds rivaling the end of the week chatter of the workers who flocked to the countinghouse to collect their pay. Mr. Beales motioned for Tamara to come into his office.

"Ye did real fine the foist week. Maybe oi can arrange ta put ye at a loom . . . git ye out o' that cardin' room. Un'ealthy in there. Ye'd git three shillings a day 'stead o' two." Mr. Beales watched Tamara as he spoke. She was too tired to react.

"Luv, whare d'ye live?"

"On Lambeth Street," she blurted, too fatigued to think.

"Oi'm comin' ta see ye tonight. We'll talk 'bout it."

His words brought her out of her lethargy.

"Oh, but, Mr. Beales, you cannot do that. I live alone."

Mr. Beales smiled evilly, showing a mouth with wide gaps between his remaining teeth. "We'll see about that," he said, swirling his tongue around dry lips.

Tamara collected her pay and left the mill, clutching her twelve shillings in her hand, guarding them closely against thieves and purse snatchers who, knowing it was payday, lurked in the area. Dispirited, she scarcely knew the right direction to take, moving with the straggling, pathetic mass of humanity struggling against starvation and misery. Weariness showed in the slump of the workers' shoulders and the slow shuffling of their feet, a look of escape on their faces. Many of them suffered from a lung disease caused by the cotton dust and lint in the air. They wheezed and coughed and were short of breath as they walked.

Tamara reached back to rub the small of her back, which ached, then stretched her shoulders, thinking about the fruit and vegetables she would buy from the costermonger on the corner, the cheese, bacon, and soup bone. She needed four shillings for her rent. She would spend four on food, donate one for Eddie, and save the remaining three. She planned to buy milk from the roundsman who passed the tenement twice a day.

It was raining. Pulling her shawl around her, she lowered her head to prevent the rain from hitting her face. Exhausted from the grueling week, faint from hunger, she forged onward, afraid she would collapse before she reached her room. Many workers, including children, stopped at the pub on the corner, where they would remain until drunk, trying to escape the unendurable agonies of their lives. Some of the men disappeared at the brothel half a block from the mill.

As Tamara trod on she wondered what the outcome of her life would be. The more she thought about it, the more determined she became to return to Montjoy, the home of her childhood. The thought gave her a new spurt of energy, and she walked a little faster. Gradually the mass of workers dwindled. She felt less secure. The streets were not safe even in daylight. After two more blocks alone, she walked waveringly. She heard footsteps behind her. Someone was following her, going to steal her money. Frantically she hurried on. Faster. Faster. The footsteps increased their pace with hers. A man's voice called, "Ellen . . . Ellen," but it meant nothing to her. Her mind was fixed on escaping, saving her money, getting food, reaching home so that she could eat and rest in preparation for the next week. She must earn money enough for her passage to Jamaica.

Strong hands grabbed her shoulders and spun her around. She opened her mouth to scream, but nothing came out. In her debilitated state she turned with very little effort, seeing a well-tailored navy-blue raglan cape. Numbly her eyes moved upward until they reached the man's face.

"Lord Foxcomb!" she cried with relief, then collapsed in his strong arms.

19

Lord Foxcomb lifted Tamara gently. As he carried her back to his carriage, garbage—a mixture of potato peels, coffee grounds, and eggshells—tossed from the tenement window above splattered in the gutter in front of him, followed by a splash of greasy dishwater. He muttered a volley of oaths, followed by, "How the devil did you wind up in this hellhole of the world?"

He set her down in the corner facing him, mindless of the water drenching his plush red-velvet seats. She blinked as rain dripped from her lashes. He stared at her, then tenderly dabbed the beads of rain from her face with his white lawn handkerchief, repeating:

> How many times do I love again?
> Tell me how many beads there are
> In a silver chain of evening rain?

Tamara smiled. "So you like the poems of Thomas Lovell Beddoes, too."

"Do you read poetry?" he asked softly, continuing to dry the rain from her cheeks.

" 'Twas required at Lady Bedford's school.'

Lord Foxcomb sighed heavily. "I hoped to find you here. I have searched everywhere. Then I went to the employment agent. The woman told me where you were working." He paused. "I could not believe it. By God, do you prefer this to me? I am not flattered, but I must commend you for your virtue and courage." To Tamara it did not sound like a compliment, but rather a scolding. He wiped a smudge from her chin. Tamara moved weakly.

"When have you last eaten? he asked solicitously. Concern showed in his eyes.

Tamara bowed her head.

"Answer me," he demanded.

She looked across to him in half-dazed weariness.

"A piece of bread and an apple yesterday," she replied limply.

Lord Foxcomb frowned. "And today? I will hazard a guess you have had nothing at all."

Tamara shook her head. Sir Richard's forehead creased, his shoulders dropped. Moments elapsed before he ordered his driver to take them to the nearest eating establishment.

"You will at least allow me to buy you something to eat and take you home," he said firmly.

Tamara closed her eyes and swayed dizzily. When the carriage stopped, Lord Foxcomb helped her to get out. "This looks to be a chophouse. 'Tis not a suitable place for a lady,

93

but there is little choice. I know of no other except the taverns. Do you?" Tamara shook her head.

Inside, he removed her wet shawl. They sat at a small table near the window. When the serving wench came and stood before them, Lord Foxcomb ordered. "The young lady will have a large bowl of your best stew. Put plenty of meat in it. Bring a tureen in case she wants more, also an order of lamb chops, a loaf of bread, cheese, and a bottle of your best wine."

He watched her intently as she ate. Even though she was ravenous and wanted to gulp the soup as soon as it was placed before her, she picked up the spoon gracefully, dipping it away from her into the hot broth, thick with meat and vegetables, as she had been taught at Lady Bedford's school. She lifted it slowly to her mouth with the dignity born to her.

Lord Foxcomb poured himself a glass of wine and nibbled on a piece of cheese. He sliced the loaf of bread and handed her a piece.

"First, I must apologize for my inexcusable conduct at Foxcomb Manor. I shall regret it the rest of my life."

Tamara looked up from her bowl of stew. "You were not ... responsible."

"Ah, but I was," he said pointedly. "A man must always be responsible for his conduct. A gentleman must accept the consequences of his actions. The question is ... can you forgive me?"

Tamara looked into his eyes. He had changed. The lines around his mouth had softened. The harshness in his eyes had disappeared.

"Yes, of course I forgive you. I am sorry I ... hit you."

She broke a piece of bread, dabbing it with strawberry jam. Watching the expression on her face, he regarded her closely.

"And if I swear it will not happen again, will you come back with me? You cannot continue to live like this. I will not permit it."

He noticed her hesitation.

"Will you not at least tell me your true name?"

She looked across the table to him. "Tamara. It is Tamara," she said numbly.

A smile curled at the corner of his mouth, and he nodded. "Aye," he said, sitting back. "That would be your name. Tamara," he repeated. "Tamara." he pronounced her name slowly, caressingly. "Your parents did right," he continued in a voice that was almost a whisper. For the moment he decided not to question her further, but she proffered additional information about her family.

"Sir Arthur Warde, the Marquis of Readington, is my guardian. His brother, Robert, was my father."

He looked at her with surprise in his eyes. "You are Sir Robert Warde's daughter?"

"Yes. My parents were killed when I was ten."

"Aye," he said slowly. "I recall hearing it. I knew your father quite well, and your uncle. But why did you seek employment?"

Sir Richard sipped his wine as Tamara told him the rest of her story, explaining why she had run away. He listened attentively until she had finished.

"In some cases arranged marriages work out. In your case . . . 'tis doubtful. You are a woman who cannot give herself to a man unless she is in love with him. Of course, it depends a great deal on the man. Who is he?"

"The Duke of Lyndenhurst."

"Lord Sheldon! That deuced jackanapes. Good God, Tamara! I do not blame you for running away. Why did you not tell me all this before?"

He noticed her soup bowl was empty. "Do you think you can eat more? Drink a little wine."

Tamara shook her head. "I could not possibly eat more."

The serving wench said there was green-apple tart and egg custard. Lord Foxcomb looked at Tamara, waiting for her choice.

"Egg custard, please, and . . . I would like a cup of tea, please."

Lord Foxcomb nodded his approval to the woman and waited until she could not hear. He cleared his throat before he spoke. "Tamara, ladies do not work. It is not proper for a woman of your station," he said slowly and firmly. "I might have been drunk, but I was sincere when I said I wished to marry you. Innocently, you wheedled your way into my heart. I am convinced you were created to be mistress of my estates. 'Tis simply a matter of a short time before you will become my wife."

Tamara shook her head.

" 'Tis too indecent . . . too callous to think about, let alone consider. You are asking me to wait with you until your wife dies."

Her words brought a hurt look to his face. The hard lines reappeared at his mouth.

"You think me a scoundrel," he accused sadly. "Tamara,

for God's sake, do you not realize I am in love with you? Do you think I wanted that to happen? What else can I do?" He swung his hands in the air. "What does a rational man do when someone stands in the way of love?"

"You must let me go. 'Twould be better for both of us."

Sir Richard reached across the table and took her hand. "You cannot be serious! What would you have me do? Poison her to hasten her death?"

Tamara cringed visibly. He put his hand up.

"Do not be alarmed," he continued. "I assure you, murder is not my nature."

He hesitated before he continued, looking at her closely. "But you do have some feeling for me. Tell me," he demanded.

" 'Tis all wrong," was her answer. The truth of the matter was that she did not know how she felt about Lord Foxcomb.

"My sweet. You have not yet learned to accept life as it is. My wife is going to die. She accepts her fate. I accept it."

"I wonder how I would wish to spend the last days of my life if I knew I was going to die soon," she mused.

"I am certain you would wish to spend a part of each day in the gardens, enjoying their beauty, not lying in bed all day stuffing yourself with sweetmeats," he said with a note of disgust. "Tamara, I inherited Foxcomb Manor from my father without enough funds to perpetuate it. I would have done anything not to lose it. Lady Pamela understood perfectly. 'Twas her illness I did not know about. I found out after we were married that she had not been well since birth. Because of it, she was spoiled and pampered. In that sense, I, too, was cheated." He struggled. "She has everything she wants, a maid, a nurse, rich foods, books. She spends far more time in bed than need be. 'Tis the way she wants to live."

He glanced at Tamara before he went on.

"I am a man with needs. She has never been interested in her wifely duties. I seek my diversions by visits to Paris every few months. There the women are willing enough to fulfill my needs."

Tamara shuddered noticeably. As she moved her legs, her shoes squished noisily. Lord Foxcomb looked at her with alarm. "You will catch your death of cold."

Tamara sipped her tea.

"Where are you staying? I must take you there immediately so that you can get out of those wet clothes."

" 'Tis only a few blocks from here. I can walk."

Exasperation swept across his face. "The devil you can.

Tamara, why must you be so obstinate! The streets are filled with cutpurses and rapists!"

Tamara smiled weakly.

Lord Foxcomb grew very quiet. Finally he spoke with a tender voice. "You and I are very much alike, Tamara. Our lives are loveless. If you will not come with me, at least allow me to help you, if only with advice."

He emptied the last of the wine from the bottle into his glass.

"Do not let life pass you by. If you continue on your present course, it will destroy you. Without true love, life has no meaning. It is the essence of life and happiness. You have been unfortunate in losing your loved ones at a very tender age. You must find a man who will take their place, be all things to you, lover, husband, father, provider, father of your children. Any man looking at you knows that you are . . . ripe for love and . . . motherhood. It is what you need. You must become part of a family again . . . your own family."

He reached across the table and grasped her hand.

"You poor darling. You are so confused you do not know what you need to make you happy. Come back to Foxcomb Manor with me . . . under any terms you set," he pleaded.

When he had first seen her, talking to Mrs. Hawkins, he was struck by her beauty. He had hired her, determined to take her to Foxcomb Manor and seduce her. Almost immediately he saw she was an exceptional woman of good breeding, different from other women he had known, a lady not to trifle with lightly. She aroused his curiosity as well as his senses. There was something intriguingly mysterious about her.

At Foxcomb Manor he had deliberately tried to win her affections through sympathy. He did not wish to force himself on her, but wanted her to surrender to him willingly . . . until he could wait no longer and went to her when he was intoxicated. To win her sympathy now was farthest from his mind. He was a man in love. His motive was to help her regardless of the consequences. What he did not realize was that he almost succeeded in getting Tamara to return with him. She was touched by his sincerity. A wave of pity swept through her.

Both of us are lost souls, she thought to herself. He is right. There is no love in either of our lives, but mine has been by choice. My life is empty, meaningless. It has no purpose, no direction. I am floundering through life like a ship in a gale.

She was grateful to him for the food, the words of advice, his concern. It was the second time he had rescued her. First when she so desperately needed a job, and now, when she thought it impossible to go on, he had given her not only food but also encouragement. As if he sensed her thoughts, a woebegone expression entered his eyes. He slammed one fist into the palm of his other hand.

"If I were free, do you think I would allow you to go out of my life? There would be no question whatsoever. The thought of you in another man's arms drives me to distraction. That I am not free to wed you at once is tearing me apart." He captured her eyes with his.

"Your amethyst eyes are constantly before me." He looked closer. "I have noticed their darkness is dependent more upon your mood than the light." He smiled faintly. "When you are angry or emotional, they turn the deepest shade of purple."

She looked into his eyes. "And what are they now?"

"Deep violet."

"It is not from anger, but . . ."

"Love? No, but strong liking, eh?" He squeezed her hands tightly in his. "Listen to me, please, Tamara. Take the advice of a man who loves you. This is what I think you should do."

20

Tamara hesitated at the double teakwood door. For reassurance, she looked back at Lord Foxcomb sitting in his carriage at the curb. He nodded and pushed his hand into the air, a gesture of encouragement. Conjuring up enough fortitude, she tapped the brass lion-head knocker lightly, as if wishing it would not be heard inside. She waited, staring at the shiny brass plate beneath the knocker with the inscription "The Marquis of Readington. Eight Park Lane."

Chagrined, Tamara found it irksome to face defeat, but worse to face frumpish Lady Alma's tirades, which she knew were forthcoming. She was relieved to know her dull-witted cousins were living with their husbands and not at home to taunt her.

Watkins opened the door. The stone-faced butler's eyes lit up, then a smile crossed his face. He stood back to allow her to enter. Before he closed the door, Tamara turned and waved to the man in the carriage, then stepped inside.

Night had descended early. Lord Foxcomb had insisted on bringing her to her uncle's house. He had taken her first to her room, where he waited for her in his carriage while she changed into dry clothes and packed her few belongings. Back in his carriage, he advised her to return to her uncle and try to work matters out. All along, deep down, she had known this was what she would have to do. It was Lord Foxcomb who persuaded her.

"Tell your uncle you wish to return to Jamaica, if that is what you want. Give it time," he advised. "If it does not work out, you are always welcome at Foxcomb Manor . . . under any conditions you choose." They had ridden beside each other in silence until they arrived in St. James's and stopped at the entrance to Sir Arthur's establishment across from Hyde Park. Lord Foxcomb looked at her longingly, taking both her hands in his.

"From the moment I saw you at Langham Place, I knew you were different from any woman I had ever encountered. One day, when I am free, I will search for you, and if you are still unmarried, I will compel you to marry me."

Tamara smiled weakly. Lord Foxcomb frowned.

"Promise me you will not return to the mill."

When she was silent, he grabbed her shoulders and shook her.

"Tamara, I demand a promise or I will not leave you. I must be assured of your welfare. At your uncle's, at least you will have his protection."

He waited. "Tamara?" he commanded firmly. "Promise."

"I promise you, Lord Foxcomb, that I will not return to the mill." Filled with heartfelt gratitude for his concern, she paused before she continued. "I am very grateful to you, m'lord," she said emotionally. A wave of tenderness for Sir Richard engulfed her. She leaned forward, and her lips touched his cheek.

"There," she said, "I have given you my first kiss."

Lord Foxcomb smiled. If any of his women acquaintances had called that a kiss he would have burst into laughter, but from Tamara it was sweet and touching. He held her hands, squeezing them tightly, staring into her expressive eyes. He kissed one cheek, then the other. He wanted to sweep her into his arms, but sat stiffly, reluctant to let her leave his carriage. Then with superhuman force he released her hands, leaned over, and opened the carriage door. He looked grim.

"Go. Off with you!" he ordered. "Get out of here before I change my mind."

When she had stepped from the carriage with the help of his footman, she looked back and smiled. Lord Foxcomb nodded. "I will be at my club, White's, not far from here, in St. James's, if you need me."

"Who is there, Watkins?" called the familiar voice of Sir Arthur. Silently Tamara walked into the drawing room.

"Tamara! Where in God's name have you been for the last two and one-half months!" her uncle asked, obviously much provoked. But when she opened her mouth to explain, he interrupted, getting up and turning his back. "Spare me the details," he scoffed.

Lady Alma, rapidly shuffling her large feet, jowls swinging, confronted Tamara at the same time, disgust expressed on her face, from her glaring eyes to the tight muscles in her cheeks to the strong, protruding chin.

"Saints preserve us! You wretched girl," she yelled in a grating voice. " 'Tis an outrage you have committed! You have embarrassed your uncle and me. Oooooooh! 'Tis scandalous!" she whimpered, wringing her hands. "If society snubs me, 'twill be your fault. It has begun already. I was not invited to Lady Holland's tea."

A sound escaped the woman's throat that sounded like a wolf howling in the middle of the night. Sir Arthur looked at his wife, momentarily seeming more annoyed with her than with his niece. "Egad, madam, collect yourself!"

Tamara dropped a curtsy, turned, and went to her room without saying a word. She slipped into the tub of hot water Ruth prepared for her and covered herself from head to toe with suds, as if attempting to soak away the experiences of the past week as well as Lord and Lady Warde's irritation. When finished with her bath, she brushed her hair until it was dry and put on a pretty cream-colored frock. Resolutely she went to the drawing room to speak to her uncle, encouraged by the advice Lord Foxcomb had given her.

"I am almost eighteen. I would like your permission to return to Jamaica, the home of my parents."

"No! Absolutely not." Sir Arthur twitched his lips nervously. "Forsooth! What would you do on that godforsaken island? You are my ward until twenty-one or married. As your guardian, I decide what is best for you," he thundered. "I accepted the marriage proposal of a duke, and you ruined it. After jilting a duke, 'twill be difficult, but I am determined to find someone suitable."

Tamara's endeavors to get Sir Arthur's permission for her return to Jamaica failed. The rounds of cotillions and innumerable balls and parties began again, and it was not long before the Earl of Darrington became a suitor, and not long after, Sir Arthur accepted his proposal. She was forced to agree that the Earl of Darrington was an improvement over the Duke of Lyndenhurst. Not exactly handsome, he was, she admitted to herself, masculinely distinguished-looking, with dark hair touched with gray in his side whiskers. Athletically built, he was quite tall, broad-shouldered, slender at the waist. His brown eyes exuded warmth and merriment. Important to Tamara, he was clean-shaven, for she avoided men with dark beards. Every instinct told her to beware of the brutality of men, especially those with beards. In their faces she saw Jack, the man who had murdered her mother and father. Memories of him were still vivid in her mind, a man she had seen only a brief moment in the span of her life, but whose actions, voice, and appearance continued to obsess her like a demon, awake and in her dreams, always worse when she was alone in the dark.

It was Lord Jeffrey Darrington's personality that attracted women. Self-assuredly composed, he was not easily flustered or riled. Tamara got the impression that he was fun-loving, but he did not have the lecherous countenance of Lord Sheldon, which had repulsed her. Not gushy, he was pleasantly attentive, and when she grew to know him better, her impressions proved correct.

"He has the reputation of a dandy . . . spends his time pursuing pleasure, but his father is pressuring him to settle down, marry, and produce an heir. I am certain you will be able to tame him," Sir Arthur informed her.

Tamara squeezed her fists tightly, her knuckles turning white. She sighed deeply and tried to accept her fate. Sir Arthur looked at her hesitantly, expecting opposition.

"I hope you realize I have always tried to do what is best for your welfare, Tamara."

He drew a handkerchief from his pocket and dabbed his brow.

"I will be relieved when you are married and someone else's responsibility," he concluded.

Tamara's life reverted to that of a lady of nobility who was about to be married. The earl courted her in patient, gentlemanly fashion. There were horseback rides in the Row, carriage drives through Hyde Park in his luxurious equipage, accompanied by Ruth or Lady Alma, tea to meet his parents and grandmother, the theater at Covent Garden for the performance of *King Richard II* and *Music Hath No Charms*. There were dinner parties with friends. The Earl of Darrington enjoyed boating and took Tamara on a pleasure ride up the Thames, looking quite handsome in his yachting jacket. He escorted her to the Opera House in the Haymarket, the National Gallery in Trafalgar Square, and museums. They went to Cremorne Gardens in Chelsea to watch balloon ascents, and the circus at Astley's Amphitheater.

Lord Darrington kept her in a dizzy whirl of activities. One afternoon, as had become their custom on Thursdays, he called for her at two, to promenade in the mall at St. James's Park. Looking particularly beautiful, she carried an orchid lace *en-tout-cas* to protect her face from the bright rays of the sun. Her dress was a delicate shade of lilac in mousseline, its bell-shaped skirt puffing over layers of petticoats and crinoline and trimmed with fluted ruffles at the hemline. Her bonnet was pansy-colored light velvet with artificial pink roses and green velvet leaves, a frill of white lace edging the brim. There were two sets of ribbon drawn under her chin, orchid and purple velvet, fastened in a bow at her cheek.

The attractive couple listened to the band, then strolled through the park. Men turned and tipped their hats. Lord Darrington puffed his chest, feeling as proud as a peacock and tempted to whistle.

Tamara delighted in watching the luxurious carriages with liveries and beautiful ladies in expensive riding habits. It was like a colorful parade. Lord Darrington remained close to her while she rested her hand lightly on his arm. Ruth walked on the other side, two paces behind. Tamara much preferred the maid to Lady Alma, and was in a lighthearted mood. Sir Jeffrey knew many people and doffed his black bowler hat politely, until a woman ran to him and, beaming, curtsied low before him.

"Sir Jeffrey, where have you been?" she asked breathlessly. "It has been weeks!" She completely ignored Tamara, focusing her eyes on Lord Darrington. Tamara scrutinized the woman as she had never done before, noticing her doll-like face and her hourglass figure, suffering her first pangs of jealousy.

Sir Jeffrey appeared embarrassed. "I am sorry, but I have been busy of late," he said to the beautiful woman.

"When will you visit me?"

"I . . . ah . . . doubt that will happen," said Sir Jeffrey, glancing warily at Tamara, who remained quiet. "This is my fiancée, Lady Tamara Warde. Catherine Walters."

The two women looked at each other; then Catherine Walters curtsied and departed noncommittally.

"Who is Catherine Walters?" Tamara asked curiously.

"Ah . . . she is a famous woman . . . in some circles."

"She is very beautiful, sophisticated," Tamara mused, realizing that he had known her on a personal basis, as he must have known many women.

Lord Darrington looked at her and smiled pleasantly, obviously wishing to forget the incident and Catherine Walters.

"I believe I am the envy of everyone in St. James's this afternoon," he said proudly. "Have you decided when you would like the marriage to take place?"

Tamara returned his smile charmingly, but ignored his question. Her hand came up and touched his arm, signaling him to stop walking, her attention caught by a squirrel scaling the trunk of a tree.

21

Lord Darrington was quite dashing. Tamara found herself looking forward to his company, but was glad propriety demanded that they not be alone. At a glance, her emotional injuries were undetectable, but unremittingly the tragic experience of her childhood continued to haunt her, influencing her thoughts and behavior. Fear and distrust of men persisting, she found it impossible not to feel threatened, not to be on guard. Even when chaperoned, however, Lord Darrington tried to hold her hand, resorted to friendly overtures, and on several occasions attempted to kiss her. She found it impossible to reciprocate.

Each rejection of his advances increased his desire. It was a refreshing change from women like Catherine Walters, from the constant barrage of flattery and trappings of the women in his life. He found himself thinking of Tamara constantly, her exquisite figure, her sweet innocence, the frightened look when he came close to her. How he longed to change that expression of fear to desire! He brought her little gifts. He sat near her in his carriage, with Ruth sitting opposite them. Schemes to get her alone failed. One afternoon while driving through the park, he went so far as to try to bribe Ruth into taking a stroll. Ruth would have gladly done so if she had not known her mistress did not wish to be alone with him.

In honor of the betrothed couple, the earl's friends the Duke and Duchess of Elmston gave a dinner party. First, the guests were to attend the ballet at the Alhambra, where the duke and duchess owned a private box next to Queen Victoria's. It was planned that afterward they would dine at the luxurious residence of the host and hostess near Chelsea Square.

The earl called for Tamara promptly at seven-thirty in his expensive barouche drawn by four matching bays. In the carriage Lord Darrington took Tamara's hand, looking at her caressingly.

"Madam, I have never seen anyone look quite as lovely as you do this evening. I want you to know I am very proud to be your escort, proud that you will be my wife."

"Thank you, Sir Jeffrey," Tamara answered softly, withdrawing her gloved hand. A gurgling sound escaped Lady Alma's throat. She and Sir Arthur sat opposite them, watching and listening.

"'Tis very exciting planning Lady Tamara's wedding," Lady Alma said gleefully, while her husband remained cautiously silent. As they rode in the plush carriage toward the Alhambra, Tamara watched Sir Jeffrey from the corner of her eye. He really was very nice, she thought. She felt comparatively safe with him, if only she could relax. Her uncle could have chosen much worse.

She was wearing one of her new gowns from the House of Worth, a Eugénie blue satin which left her shoulders bare and her upthrust breasts tantalizingly in evidence. As she sat beside Sir Jeffrey, her skirt spread out around her, covered with layers of ruffles from hem to waist and fluffed by crinolines underneath, her only adornment was a lavaliere of pearls and fine diamonds on a gold chain, which rested in the crevice between her breasts.

Tamara's spirits improved at the plush theater. She smiled and chatted gaily with the guests until the performance began. She and Sir Jeffrey sat in the front row of the box, which commanded an excellent view of the stage as well as the audience below.

When the orchestra began to play, the lights dimmed and the heavy gold-colored curtain parted. As she watched the graceful ballerina Emma Livry, Tamara was drawn into the fantasy world created before her. The ballet was *La Sylphide*. Magnificent Miss Livry, in the lead role, wore a white flowing net costume.

Tamara envisioned herself in the role of the forest sprite, performing arabesque poses, difficult fouette's, and graceful floating leaps, pirouetting, gliding across the stage on her toes, whirling into the arms of the handsome Scottish youth who loved her.

Tamara blinked her eyes and returned to reality when the curtain closed at intermission. The earl left her to go with the other men to smoke and drink champagne. He seemed reluctant to leave her.

"Would you care for champagne, my dear?" he asked, bending close.

"No, thank you, m'lord," she replied formally.

Tamara listened to the buzzing of voices and musicians in the pit tuning their violins and cellos. She lifted her lorgnette to her eyes and scanned the audience, admiring their finery, the sparkling jewelry, beautiful gowns, and lavish hairstyles. She looked at the men, thinking Lord Foxcomb might be present, but she did not see him.

Moving her head slightly to the left, she noticed through her opera glasses a strikingly beautiful woman seated in the next box, a small crown of diamonds sparkling on her titian hair. Tamara knew it was not Queen Victoria and wondered who she was. She turned slightly, adjusting the glasses. A man came into focus in her lorgnette. She was immediately struck by his handsome features. He had a mop of dark hair, laughing green eyes, and a stern square chin. He was clean-shaven except for a dark mustache and long side whiskers. He was elegant in formal attire, his white ruffled shirt enhancing his sun-bronzed complexion.

The man had the look of command, or was it arrogant confidence? she wondered. He was the picture of success, a man who had everything he wanted, including the beautiful woman beside him who looked at him adoringly, but . . . Tamara thought he looked bored.

She was about to return the opera glasses to her lap when she stared again, taking a second look at the man. Could it be possible? She thought she recognized him. Older now, but no question of his identity. It was Mark Schofield, her friend when she was a child in Jamaica. Her fascination for him had lingered. She had thought of him many times, wondering where he was, what he was doing. As the years had gone by and her childhood memory of what he looked like blurred, warped, she had constructed an imagery of an exceedingly handsome man, the man she was staring at through her opera glasses.

22

Tamara was eighteen, which, she figured, meant that Mark was twenty-seven. She had never seen him in evening clothes, and his handsomeness awed her. Dishearteningly, she thought it unlikely he would recognize or remember her.

Instantly she became disconcerted, realizing he was looking straight at her. Her hand holding the lorgnette froze. He grinned rakishly, flashing white teeth. He winked. Embarrassed, Tamara dropped the lorgnette into her lap. She blushed hotly, not daring to look across at him directly. But he must have recognized her or he would not have winked. Or would he? She reasoned if he had not known her, he would no longer be looking. She simply had to know.

Slowly she turned her head and found him still watching her. His eyes, striking, glittering green, elicited hers. A bewildering feeling flowed through her. She could not look away. He nodded. She smiled uncertainly, which brightened the sparkle in his eyes, but there was no sign of recognition. His eyes glided over her slowly, mentally stripping her of her clothes.

Oh! He was flirting with her. What insolence! Tamara's face flushed deeper. As if he could not help himself, he laughed. His companion looked at him questioningly.

Quickly Tamara looked away, but she could feel his compelling eyes upon her.

At that moment the Earl of Darrington returned to the box. Looking up at him, Tamara said nervously, "I think I will have champagne after all, if it is not too much trouble."

"No, of course not. If you will excuse me, my dear, I will order it for you. I think I shall have another glass myself."

Flustered, knowing her cheeks were unusually pink, Tamara was thankful when the house lights dimmed, but the relief she hoped for failed to come. She was upset and had difficulty enjoying the ballet. Her breath came quickly. She did not know whether it was due to the earl sitting close, watching the rise and fall of her breasts, or because Mark was in the next box and she did not know what to do.

The earl interpreted it as his effect on her. He took her hand and squeezed it gently. He leaned close, his warm breath touching her cheek, his lips displacing a curl at her ear. He whispered, "Soon, my love, soon."

Absently her trembling fingers clutched the lavaliere. She slipped the chain over her chin, then dropped it once again to the cleavage of her bosom. The earl watched as it fell back into place in the valley between her uptilted breasts.

She fidgeted and patted her forehead with her lace handkerchief. The earl's expression changed to concern.

"What is wrong, my dear? Are you unwell? Something has upset you."

"No, no. Everything is fine. 'Tis just a little stifling in here. I will be all right when I get out in the fresh air," she whispered, not wishing to annoy the others in the box.

"Do you want me to take you outdoors?"

Tamara felt as if everything was closing in on her. "I do feel a trifle dizzy, but then you will miss the second half of the ballet."

"No matter. You do look flushed. A bit of fresh air will be good for you," he said, looking worried.

The earl explained to their host, placed Tamara's opera cloak around her shoulders, and led her out of the box, down the thickly carpeted staircase. A uniformed doorman held the door for them.

Concern in his eyes, Sir Jeffrey watched her closely. Gallantly cupping her elbow with his hand, unhurriedly he led her along the marble piazza.

"I am sorry to be such a nuisance," she said apologetically, looking into his eyes.

They walked a short distance in the darkness, then stopped.

"Do you feel better? Mayhaps I should find a physician."

"I feel much better, thank you."

God, she is sweet, thought the earl, fighting to prevent himself from taking her into his arms. He had the greatest desire to protect her, to do what he could to take away that frightened look in her eyes. Ostensibly, she had strong emotions. He had learned women of her sensitivity were responsively passionate. Marriage to her was going to be a delight. He realized he had fallen in love, and would do everything he could to make his beloved respond to him. Once she had overcome her shyness, she would be a tender, passionate lover. He was certain it it.

The earl began to breathe heavily as he envisioned taking Tamara to his bed. He forgot himself and abruptly pulled her to him. Tamara steeled herself against his attempts to kiss her. Violently she struggled to free herself. He released her immediately, looking dejected.

"Tamara! Am I that repulsive to you?"

Her eyes softened. " 'Tis not that, Sir. You do not understand. No one understands."

"If you will explain to me, I will certainly try," he said quietly.

Their host came toward them with a worried expression on his face.

"Jeffrey, Sir Arthur sent me. Is she all right?"

"Yes, I think so. She needed fresh air. 'Twas quite warm in that box."

"Lady Tamara, would you like to go on ahead to our house? We will join you there later," said the Duke of Elmston.

"That might be best," mused Sir Jeffrey.

"I will explain to Sir Arthur," the duke replied.

Sir Jeffrey called for his carriage. His liveried footman opened the door, and Tamara entered, followed by the earl, who slid close beside her. He laid his gloves and black opera hat on the seat opposite them. It was dark. Tamara felt anxious in the intimacy of the plush carriage. He unbuttoned his black cloak with shoulder cape lined in red satin. Putting his arm around her shoulder, he drew her close.

Lightly he pressed Tamara's head against the black velvet collar of his cloak. The carriage proceeded down Charles Street, the gas lamps casting a swath of light on Tamara's face. Lord Darrington's eyes fell on the outline of dark, thick lashes around her eyes. He drank in her coloring and features, a rare combination which made her strikingly beautiful.

Then the carriage plunged into darkness again. As their bodies swayed in unison, he placed his fingers beneath her chin and raised her face toward his.

"Lady Tamara, I know 'tis improper for us to be alone, but let us not waste this rare opportunity," he whispered thickly as he sought her lips. She turned her head.

"You are lovely. How long are you going to resist me, my bride-to-be? Please. Please let me kiss you."

Tamara lowered her lashes. "You should not take advantage of our being alone," she reprimanded.

He sighed heavily, pulling her closer. " 'Twould take a man far less than I not to do so. I cannot wait much longer. My nights of late are very restless thinking of you. Your shyness thrills me now, but when you are my wife, 'twill be different."

His voice was throaty as he continued. "When we are married, I will teach you the way a woman should respond to her husband."

Recognizing the fierce passion in his voice, Tamara stiffened.

He kissed her fingers. "Tell your uncle I will call on him tomorrow evening to set the date for our wedding. It must be soon."

23

Tamara spent a restless night. "I do not wish to hurt Lord Darrington," she said aloud as she lay sleepless. "He has been very kind. I do like him . . . very much . . . but . . . I do not love him." She sighed deeply. "I have seen women flirt with him. He can have any woman he wants. I know I could never make him happy. 'Twould be unfair to marry a man I have no wish to be intimate with for the rest of my life. I would not be good for him. Our marriage would be a mockery. I must go away . . . and this time I will never come back. I am going home to Jamaica."

Devising a plan, she put on her robe. Sitting at the small writing desk in her room, turning up the lamp, she began to write a farewell note to Sir Jeffrey, begging his forgiveness and wishing him happiness.

In the morning she would take Ruth into her confidence. The maid would help her escape. When she had made her decision and finalized the scheme in her mind, she was then able to fall asleep.

By ten o'clock the next morning Ruth had helped Tamara pack a few gowns and personal items into her valise. She ate breakfast with the family as if nothing was amiss. She gave the note to Ruth with instructions to hand it to Sir Jeffrey personally the moment he arrived that evening.

Midmorning, Lady Warde met Beverly and Valerie at the dressmaker on Bond Street. It was after she had departed that Watkins hailed a hackney for Tamara and she bid him and Ruth good-bye.

The aged hackney left that part of London where the nobility dwell and headed for the West India Docks, careening through a maze of narrow cobblestoned streets, jostling Tamara this way and that on the dusty, spotted seat as she tried to brace herself by holding onto the strap with both hands.

They entered the slums of Whitechapel, which she would have known even if she had not been peering from the windows. Harsh noises and the redolent air of the streets was too recent a memory. Tamara wrinkled her nose as she smelled the stench that filtered into the carriage, horse droppings buzzing with flies, human excrement, and rotting garbage.

The squalor appeared worse than when she had lived there. She saw dirty children, street urchins with pale faces, bulging eyes and stomachs, digging through garbage piles like starving mongrels, snatching bits of nourishment. A surge of pity swept through her. She was moved to tears.

I have escaped all this, she thought, but this is their whole world. They will never venture beyond a few blocks. In order to survive, they learn to steal as soon as they are able to walk. At that moment she thought of Lord Shaftesbury and his interest in the children of the streets. She had not fully realized the importance of his efforts.

This was so different from Park Lane. She might have been in a different country, another world. London is an archipelago, she mused, where the genteel live surrounded by a sea of slums of which they are oblivious. She looked at a man sprawled on the broken pavement in a drunken stupor. Uncombed, shabbily dressed women made advances to men passing. The hackney splashed through stagnant puddles of rainwater. A wheel struck a pothole and nearly knocked Tamara off her seat. As they neared the Tufnell Cotton Mill she observed an unusually large number of people walking briskly, all headed in the same direction. She pressed her face against the pane to get a better look. As she came closer to the mill, the people became a solid mass. A throng had gathered along the iron fence around the building. Stones were hurled over it. When they hit their target, shattering windows, a loud cheer went up from the crowd, which surged forward as one. The building was pelted with rock missiles. A cordon of bobbies swung clubs, trying to disperse the mob. The dirty carriage window misted her view. Annoyed, she rubbed her fingers back and forth, erasing enough grime to see more clearly. From her peephole Tamara scanned the scene looking for Agnes or Mabel or other workers she knew. Empathy enveloped her. They had nothing to look forward to, an hour or two less work, a few more shillings at the end of the week. For this they had turned into wild animals, but who could blame them? She felt sick in the pit of her stomach.

Violence begets violence, she mused, recalling the conversation of Lord Shaftesbury at the Crown Inn. Her uncle and the Duke of Lyndenhurst had called him a fool, and men who were trying to help the workers, madmen. If they would only put themselves in the place of a carder or miner, they would think differently. If she had not spent a week working in the textile mill, possibly her views would be no different, she thought. She wondered if she were still working in the mill whether she would be among the strikers.

In 1860, laborers in the building trades had swept London with riots. Cotton-mill workers joined the London Trades Council and met to give aid to the strikers. Violence had now spread to the cotton mills as well.

The morbid scene disheartened her. She closed her eyes and moved away from the window. How could she be so ungrateful? Lady Warde was right. She had a home, food, lovely clothes, the zealous attention of men whom other women would have welcomed, and still she was unhappy. A wave of guilt swept through her.

Once again she glanced out the carriage window. London is a city of contrasts, she mused. She had seen and lived at each end of the social scale, from the great splendor of Park Lane among the nobility to the slums of Whitechapel. She was relieved when the carriage in which she was riding found Commercial Road and sped past Limehouse to the West India Docks near the Isle of Dogs.

The mud-spattered, antiquated coach came to a halt. Tamara's head throbbed from the bumpy ride. The cabman climbed down from the box, opened the door, and stretched out his palm for his fare. Tamara stepped down without his help and paid him.

"Thar be the place yer lookin' fer ma'am," the driver said, pointing to a large three-story warehouse a short distance along the quay. He checked his fare and tip. "Thank'ee, ma'am," he said politely, looking as bedraggled as the coach.

A jumble of tall masts speared the sky. Steamship stacks puffed black coal smoke. Rusted anchors lay along the docks. Tamara lifted her skirt to her ankles and stepped over thick hemp ropes. Several seamen passed and made ribald remarks, their crude humor causing her to wince with dismay and hurry along. Carrying her valise, she headed for a flight of wooden steps that led to the shipping-company office.

When she entered, a pale thin man sitting on a stool in front of a slanted desk looked up from his ledgers.

"Ma'am?"

"I wish to speak to Mr. Schofield, please. Mark Schofield. I am at the right place, am I not? He is here?"

24

"Aye, ma'am," said the spindly clerk, looking over his wire-rimmed spectacles. "One moment, please. If you will be seated." He gestured toward a straight wooden chair. "Mr. Schofield is out on his ship."

Tamara sat down and waited, putting the valise beside her, her two feet together, hands folded on her lap. She went over in her mind what she would ask him, and refused to think about what she would do if he rejected her request. She felt a twinge of nervousness at the prospect of meeting face to face the man she had carried in her memory since childhood. Maybe he had changed.

Mark entered the office with a quizzical expression on his face. He looked more handsome than he had in evening clothes. He was wearing snug-fitting beige breeches that displayed strong, well-formed thighs. His long-sleeved white shirt was casually open at the throat. Black shiny boots reached to his knees. His air of confidence, his controlled, easy manner, bemused Tamara. He was not a member of the aristocracy, but he possessed traits they lacked, an appearance of healthy virility created by hard work. He looked supremely fit, over six feet tall she was sure. His shoulders were broad, his hips narrow, his legs long and firm. An unruly mass of thick dark hair fluffed on his head, with locks covering his suntanned brow. He was not the youth Tamara remembered. He moved toward her with the self-assurance of a worldly man, strong, more attractive than in his youth. With aplomb, he bowed deep. "Your servant, madam," he said in a rich, deep voice.

A pair of expectant eyes lifted to his. Tamara knew instantly that he did not recognize her. She felt disappointed.

"'Tis unlikely you remember me," she said hesitantly, shyly.

"Not so. Of course I remember you." He flashed a jaunty smile. There was a glint in his green eyes. "You are the lady in the theater box at the Alhambra," he said smilingly.

His friendly directness made Tamara return the smile. "The one you flirted with so outrageously."

His smile disappeared. "I did not intend to upset you, and for that I apologize. But could any man not flirt with the most beautiful woman in the theater?"

Tamara was pleased, and laughed spontaneously. If any other man had spoken those words, she would have considered them a threat rather than a compliment. He gave the impression of honesty, a man who could never be deceitful or dishonest. He instilled immediate trust.

"No, no, Mark, before that!" she blurted.

A faint smile crossed his face. "Ah, I see you are at an unfair advantage. You know my name."

A playful smile twitched at the corners of Tamara's mouth. "And you know mine," she teased.

"Oh, indeed? I am positive we have never met. I would have remembered." He wrinkled his brow. "But on the other hand, there is something vaguely familiar about you. Have we a common acquaintance?"

Tamara enjoyed the little game, and laughed. "Nooooooo," she said pertly. "We went riding together."

Mark tilted his head back, trying to recall where they had met.

"How about flying kites?" she hinted.

Mark leveled his head and stared at her momentarily. "You are not . . . Tamara?"

"Yes, Mark," she said laughingly.

"Bless my soul!"

Immediately his formal behavior changed. Laughing heartily, he grasped her hands and pulled her to her feet, lifting her, swinging her around, causing the blue osprey plumes in her bonnet to bounce and twirl.

Pink brushed Tamara's cheeks. Her protesting fists thumped lightly against his muscular shoulders.

"Ooooohhh, put me down you brazen rogue!"

Impulsively he threw back his head and laughed, obeying her, then affectionately wrapping his arms around her, hugging her as a brother would a sister he had not seen for a very long time. His mustache tickled her cheek. He stepped back and spun her around, regarding her fondly, whistling his approval.

"I knew you would grow into a beauty, but this is ridiculous. God, 'tis good to see you!" He nodded his head. "I should have known, but the color of your hair has changed . . . and the violet in your eyes has deepened," he chattered on, assaying her closely. He cocked his head. "But it is not only your appearance that has altered. You have changed, Tamara."

"I am no longer a child."

"That, my dear, dear friend, is quite obvious, but . . . 'tis more than that . . . something I sense but cannot put my finger on. For one, the mischievous twinkle in your eyes has disappeared."

"You are taller," she countered, looking up at him.

He glanced around. "What are you up to? You have not come here to the wharf alone, have you? 'Tis quite unsafe for any woman, let alone one as lovely as you."

Tamara blushed from head to toe. "Yes, I came alone."

"And . . . was the man you were with at the ballet your . . . husband?"

"No. Oh, no. He is . . . was . . . the man I was engaged to marry."

Mark raised his brows. "Is? Was?"

"I will explain later, Mark. I have come here to ask a favor of you."

She licked her dry lips nervously.

"What is it?"

"I want to go home to Montjoy. I have not been back since my parents' demise."

"My mother wrote to me about the disaster that befell your family," he said quietly. "A tragic loss for one so young. I am sorry, Tamara."

" 'Twas a long time ago."

"I wrote to you, you know. Why did you not answer my letters? My mother wrote, too."

"Letters? Because I did not receive them, Mark. After my parents' death, I came to London to live with my uncle. Then I was sent away to school.

"Aye. The letters were sent in care of your Uncle Arthur."

114

"Lady Alma probably destroyed them."

He looked puzzled. "And why does your uncle not make the arrangements for your passage? I do not understand why he allows you to roam unescorted. 'Tis not safe."

Tamara looked at him skeptically, not certain whether she could tell him the truth. She had confided in him when she was a child getting into scrapes. If he was the same Mark, she knew she could do so now. She bit her lip. "He does not know I am here," she said softly.

Mark laughed. "Inwardly, still the same mischievous Tamara, I see. Now I recognize that expression. 'Tis the one when you are in trouble."

He looked amused. She glanced at him warily with her large violet eyes. "I have run away from my uncle's house, Mark."

"But why? Does he mistreat you?"

Tamara heaved a sigh. "Not exactly, but it was he who arranged my engagement to Lord Darrington, even though I protested. 'Tis the second time he has arranged a marriage for me."

"Ah, I see. You do not wish to marry this man."

"No."

"He seemed very attentive at the theater. I could tell he was enraptured by you."

"I did not encourage him," she replied spunkily. "I enjoyed his company, but I told him time and time again that I did not welcome his . . . his attentions."

Mark, genuinely amused, threw back his head and laughed. "Tamara, Tamara. You underestimate your charms."

"Please, Mark, I do not wish to go into the details, but I would rather die . . . than let him . . . than marry him. Will you arrange passage for me on one of your ships? Are any of them preparing to leave for the West Indies?"

She looked at him closely. Noticeably, he was physically more manly than when last she saw him, but the years had added sophistication, a cosmopolitan air to his personality. Experiencing life, its challenges, its joys, its adventures, gave him an appealing confidence that enthralled Tamara. The sense of ease and happiness she had felt in his presence when she was a girl had not altered. She wanted to put her life and soul into his keeping.

25

Mark struck a match and lit his pipe. "Dammit, Tamara, that is out of the question. To begin with, Schofield ships are freighters, merchant ships, which are not very comfortable. We take very few passengers, and certainly no unescorted young women. The *Mark Schofield*, for example, has a crew of forty. I would not want to risk a woman on board." He looked at her and chuckled. "No, that would be courting trouble. You are too young, too beautiful to make the trip unescorted. It would make the men nervous. Celibacy at sea is difficult enough without temptation thrown in their faces."

Tamara paled at his frankness. "If I promise to stay in my cabin and not cause trouble?"

"Why, Tamara," he chided. "You . . . not cause trouble? I have not forgotten some of your escapades. I am certain you have not changed that much," he said laughingly.

"You were willing to help me then, why not now? Please, Mark, this is very important to me."

He hemmed, nurturing his doubts. Silence filled the room as he considered her plight.

"Please," she pleaded.

"As it happens," he said thoughtfully, "I am preparing to leave day after tomorrow for Charleston, South Carolina, with a shipment of tools. I plan to be in port only a day or two, just long enough to unload and load the cargo of cotton, then get out of there as fast as possible and head for Barbados to pick up a consignment of molasses to bring back to England. War threatens, and I do not want to be there should it start."

"Then take me with you," she said resolutely. "Please, Mark. From Barbados I will be able to find passage to Jamaica. I cannot go back to my uncle's house. Ever! This is the second and last time I will run away."

"And what about your Lord Darrington?"

"I have written him a note expressing my regrets and begging his understanding."

"Tamara, I did not think cruelty was part of your nature."

"He will soon forget me. He has many opportunities to

116

find a woman who will truly love him and make him happy. 'Twould be more cruel to marry him."

Mark shook his head. "I think you should speak to him."

"No!" she said firmly. "Will you take me with you? If you do not, I shall kill myself!" she said emphatically, with conviction expressed in her narrowed eyes.

Mark tried to hide a grin; a twinkle flashed in his eyes. "Well, I would not want your demise on my conscience," he teased lightly.

She did not find his words amusing. Her lips tightened, causing him to turn serious.

"If you do not wish to return to your uncle, I have a town house in Kensington. You are welcome to stay there until you solve your problem. I can supply you with funds if you need them."

" 'Twould be cruel to leave me," she said fetchingly.

Mark rubbed his chin and stared at his pipe. "You do not understand. Should war break out, I might find it necessary to run a blockade. 'Twill be dangerous."

"The United States . . . at war? With what country? I have studied the ancient history of countries, but I am afraid my knowledge of present events is very lacking."

"No other country is involved, Tamara. It would be a civil war, a war between sections, North and South. They've been drifting farther apart economically and philosophically, arguing, bickering, threatening, compromising for the last thirty years. They are like two mad dogs, snarling, showing their teeth to each other."

Mark shook his head. "I doubt whether it will turn into a fight to the death, but the situation in Charleston is explosive. It is the focal point of dissension, a hotbed of anti-Northern sentiment. Back in December, after the Southern candidate lost the presidency to a man named Lincoln, delegates met in Charleston and passed an Ordinance of Secession, taking the state of South Carolina out of the Union. I am surprised they went that far. Thought they were bluffing. It set off a chain reaction. Other Southern states followed."

Tamara wrinkled her brow. "But why? Why would these states no longer want to be a part of the United States?"

Mark looked at her and smiled. "Do not concern your pretty little head with such matters."

Tamara frowned. "Mark, do not treat me like a child . . . or a frivolous woman. I want to know," she insisted.

"Honestly, Tamara, only those who are Southern-bred understand. I can give you reasons,—the simplest would be slavery. The South needs slaves for its economy. Northerers want to confine or abolish it. The real issue is more complex—the doctrine of nullification. Southern states declare the right to nullify federal laws that they oppose."

"Which is right, the North or South?"

Mark chuckled. "My dear, that is a matter of opinion, dependent upon whether you are a Northerner or a Southerner."

"Do you honestly think they will take the drastic step of war?"

Mark hesitated. "I honestly do not know, Tamara. I doubt it, but on the other hand, it is difficult to predict what will happen. A great deal depends on the new president. If he—"

"If, if, if! If there is so much uncertainty, then you cannot use the war as an excuse not to take me with you."

Mark breathed deep. "Even when you were little, you were obstinate."

Just when she thought he would agree to take her, he dashed her hopes. Tugging at his mustache, he said, "Sorry. The answer must be no, absolutely, positively no."

Tamara's shoulders slumped visibly.

"Before you go to my town house, if you are interested, I would like to show you my ship."

"Yes, of course I would like to see it. When are you leaving?"

"At dawn, with the tide, day after tomorrow."

26

Many ships with towering bare masts and hulking funnels were moored in narrow slips along the docks. Snugly cradled in its berth, the *Mark Schofield* was impressive-looking. Its sleek oak hull, painted black to the bulwarks, sank low in the Thames with a heavy cargo and large quantity of coal needed for power. Only a hairline of the red boot topping showed along the waterline.

The ship was equipped with both screw and paddle wheels, the paddle boxes located midship. Two hulky funnels, void of belching smoke, were being given a fresh coat of admiralty-gray paint. Although a steamship, it was rigged with four

118

masts pointing skyward—fore, near the stem; main, at the stern; mizzen; and jigger—their furled canvas sails used only in emergencies.

The *Mark Schofield*, though a merchant ship, was armed with a row of black twenty-four-pound cannons, starboard and portside. When Tamara queried about the gunnery, Mark explained it was necessary not only for defense against privateers and pirates, but that the British government encouraged privately owned craft to be constructed and outfitted in a way suitable for naval use in time of war.

Mark and Tamara walked up the slanted gangway of the sturdy ship. Tamara's first impression was that it was immaculate. As if he could read her thoughts, Mark said, "The decks must be swabbed constantly because of the black dirt in the coal smoke."

Three brawny barefoot yeomen, pants legs and shirt sleeves rolled up, joked and laughed as they swilled the main deck, warmed by the rays of the midmorning sun. A brisk March breeze rippled across the ship, brushing the smell of fresh paint from stem to stern, converting the deck's warm moisture into hot vapors that steamed upward.

Anticipation of the journey was evident on the faces of the brown weather-complexioned men and in their vigorous movements. Ships, like people, developed reputations. The *Mark Schofield* was a fine, honorable vessel, its captain engaged in honest trade. Honest men were attracted to it. Pay was about average, but the men knew by reputation and experience that working conditions on Schofield ships were the best on any afloat. They knew, too, what was expected of them when hired—their best, all-out service. Captain Schofield was demanding of his crew, ran a taut ship. In turn the men admired his expert seamanship, respected his fairness, offered him their loyalty.

Saluting Mark, the men lifted their hands to their caps. Mark touched his fingers to his. Curiosity entered the men's eyes upon seeing he was accompanied by a woman.

Adulation Tamara had felt toward him when she was a child surfaced and multiplied. Too young in Jamaica to consciously take into account his character, she only knew she enjoyed being with him, admired him in the way of a fascinated child. Now she could feel her admiration for him mounting. She saw him as a man of scruples, shrewd in business, skillful in dealing with men, respected, liked. She could tell he was a man who faced with vigor the problems and joys of his life. She got the impression that for him life was not to be observed from a secure vantage point, but lived to its fullest. Ostensibly, Mark was a man with the courage of his own convictions.

Tamara had observed wealthy men who had their riches and titles handed to them without lifting a finger. They did not possess that indefinable quality evident in self-made men. Mark and his father had it, that extra quality which made them more attractive as human beings and more masculine as men. Solid muscles and tanned faces were only a part of what made them virile-looking. There were intangible qualities, self-reliance, drive, sharp instincts.

As Tamara and Mark walked along the portside of the main deck, the pride of the ship's owner shone on his face. He slowed his pace, taking Tamara's arm as they stepped over coiled hawsers. The touch of his fingers was casual, but she felt it linger long after his hand returned to its resting place behind his back.

"She was designed by Isambard Brune, the same man who built the *Great Eastern*," Mark said proudly. "The hull is divided by iron bulkheads into eight separate watertight compartments. The paddle engine was made by John Scott Russell."

Tamara had never heard of these men, but from the tone of his voice, she concluded they were experts in their field.

"I have a crew of forty," he boasted.

"Forty! Upon my word! Where do they all sleep?"

Mark laughed easily. "In hammocks in the forecastle, which, to you, is off limits."

They walked to larboard before they went below to his quarters. Stepping over the coaming, they entered his rooms. He bowed stiffly and said, "Welcome to my home. I might add, you have the distinction of being the first woman to see it." He waited for her reaction, laughing when he saw her eyes widen at its luxuriousness.

"You are surprised. This is not only my office but also my home. Why should I not have it as comfortable as possible? I am not much of a Spartan. I enjoy comfort."

"There is plenty of room here for me!"

"You could not stay in my private quarters, Tamara. You know that."

"It is fantastic!"

"I admit I am extremely fond of worldly possessions. They make life enjoyable. Philosophers tell us the world has become too materialistic. I say 'poppycock.' Although riches alone do not guarantee happiness, they sure as hell help."

"Yes, I agree," said Tamara seriously. "And wealth is not fully appreciated until it is lost."

Mark smiled. "Oh, I assure you I appreciate mine. One of my faults is that I am a greedy man. I want more. This ship is mine. Someday I will own all fifty of my father's."

Mark stepped farther into the room, signaling Tamara to join him.

"How can a man be happy if he is poor?" he went on. "I would find that impossible and would spend all my energies to change it."

Tamara was glancing around the room.

"Is a man happy who sits in his shack not knowing when or where his next meal is coming from? How can he be happy living under such conditions? He is no man if he does not wish for a better house and food. He is no man if he is satisfied or allows others to supply him with necessities. There is something emotionally unstable about such a person."

Tamara looked into his eyes, thinking of all the misery she had seen in London. "It could be acceptance of his fate. He might have tried, failed, found it impossible to improve himself."

Mark shook his head in disagreement. "It is the man who goes out and tries, even if he fails at first, who eventually succeeds, not the man who gives up. The man who continues to work to improve his lot is the one following his natural instincts. When a man has one carriage, he should not be satisfied until he has two. Those who preach against materialism and those who say people are never satisfied preach against progress. Supposing Columbus had sat back and had not been interested in wealth. Supposing he had said he didn't give a damn whether the earth was flat, round, or shaped like a string bean."

Deep in thought, Tamara ran her finger along the edge of his desk. "I understand. It is unnatural for a woman to be happy in rags. The woman who wants satin gowns is normal."

"Exactly. The man who works in the pits would have to be crazy if he did not want shorter working hours and more pay."

Tamara nodded. "I comprehend. If the miner works only six hours a day, it would be natural for him to wish for five."

"Right." He flexed his hand through the air. "A man who owns fifty ships should not be content until he owns a hundred, and when he has a hundred . . . who knows? That is my philosophy. Call me avaricious, if you must."

Tamara viewed him closely. "And you do not believe in sharing your wealth, do you?"

"Absolutely not. Why should I work my guts out, then give what I have earned to those who have not?"

Tamara hesitated. "Then, if you saw a man starving and you had two apples, you would not give one to him?"

Mark smiled. "Sure I would, but only because I had two. If I was starving and had only one apple, would I give it to the man? That would be the greater test, would it not? Since I have never been in that position, I cannot tell you honestly what I would do."

He looked at Tamara. An amused expression entered his eyes. "When it comes to the woman in my life, I am rapacious," he said teasingly.

She gave him a look of mock annoyance. "Does that mean you like to accumulate beautiful women the way you do wealth?"

"No. It means when I am with a woman I am extremely demanding of her time and . . . her attention, to put it delicately."

"And do you love her in turn?"

Mark laughed. "Never. I have never been in love. Infatuated, yes . . . in love, never. But if I ever do fall in love, greedily I will insist she give me her undivided affections. If she fails to do so, I will shave off all her hair," he said, his laughter rising heartily.

"There is a bit of cruelty in you, Mark Schofield."

He chuckled. "I admit it."

Tamara took a deep breath. "You have disillusioned me. I thought you were the perfect man who could do no wrong."

He laughed. "Me! What have I done wrong?"

"You are forgetting the role your father has played in your success. I admire him."

The space between Mark's eyebrows wrinkled. "Father? Aye, he is to be admired, but at the same time, I hate him. I hate my father. What do you think of that, little angel?"

"Mark! I am certain you do not mean it."

"I assure you I do, but . . . that is another story. Let us proceed. Allow me to show you the rest of my quarters."

Mark's announcement that he hated his father had a sobering effect on Tamara. She had been close to her father, had loved him and lost him. She had assumed all children felt the same about their fathers.

Mark's living quarters were masculine, leaving no question of its being the home of a man. The walls of the stateroom were oak-paneled, the floor covered with rich crimson Persian carpets. A large brass lantern hung from the ceiling over a magnificent mahogany desk laden with sheaves of papers, charts, scrolls, ledgers, maps, a brass spyglass, a sextant, and a decanter of spirits.

An enormous globe stood in the corner. On the wall behind the desk hung three brass clocks, each the same size, showing the time in London, Sydney, and New York. Hanging on another wall, a huge map of the Caribbean. Two polished rapiers hung crisscrossed on the opposite wall as if their purpose was decorative rather than defensive. Tamara wondered whether he had ever used them in a fight.

They walked into the next room, which was a paneled dining area furnished with heavy mahogany chairs and a table fastened to the floor. A large portrait of his father hung on the inner wall.

A salon adjoined the dining room. The walls were lined with shelves filled with leather-bound books and objects he had collected around the world. The shelves were enclosed in wooden railings to protect the books from scattering in time of rough seas. A long cranberry-colored leather divan extended along the fourth wall, surrounded by deep leather armchairs.

"The carpets are beautiful," Tamara commented.

"I seem to have a weakness for Oriental carpets. Bought all of these in Constantinople."

A large casement window afforded a view of the sea. Rays of the sun slashed across the spacious room, falling on an immense mounted swordfish on the opposite wall. Mark pointed to it. "One of my hobbies."

Tamara peeped into his bedroom with its wide bunk and heavy mahogany closets and chests with polished brass hardware. The gallery was next to it, with bathtub and head and a washstand with personal shaving items.

"This is really amazing," she said with awe in her voice.

Mark bowed to thank her. When he straightened, Tamara noticed his head was only a few inches from the ceiling, making him look quite tall. "Glad you like it."

A serious expression came to Tamara's face. "You have been master of your life as well as your ship," she mused. "You have enjoyed life, Mark?" she asked.

"Aye," he replied lightly. "I enjoy the sea, its peace and quiet, its challenges in raging storms, its ports of call, the opportunity to see different cultures, meet many people." He shrugged. "Everyone has an escape or two. This is mine," he admitted. He turned serious. "But I've worked hard . . . at first, to please my father. I learned that that is an impossibility . . . a never-ending task. My father is a dour man, not bent on praising others, although he craves compliments himself. No matter how advantageous a contract, no matter how successful a deal, I can be assured he will find fault."

Mark insisted Tamara join him in the meal he was about to eat. The food was on the table. He must have just sat down to eat when he was called to his office to meet her. There were enough pancakes, eggs, and sausages for half a dozen people. His cabin boy, Jimmy, a gangly blond youth no more than fifteen, filled their coffeecups.

When the meal was over, Mark stood. "Now, young lady, come with me."

He hailed a hackney, gave the driver money with instructions to deliver Tamara to his town house in Kensington.

"I thought you were my friend," she said as he helped her into the creaky carriage, placing her valise on the opposite seat. "You are getting rid of me as if I had the plague."

"It is because I am your friend that I must refuse you. What I should do is send you back to your uncle. Come to your senses and return to his protection. Someday you will realize my good advice and thank me."

"Never! Can't you get it through your thick skull I want to go home—to Jamaica."

Gallantly, he took her hand and kissed it. "Not by yourself, you're not. Here is the key to my house. In this envelope are money and a draft for more funds, should you need them. Also, here is the name of my solicitor," he said firmly.

His parental attitude infuriated Tamara. "Mark Schofield, you wasted my entire morning!" she proclaimed, instead.

Mark guffawed. "*I* wasted *your* time!"

Tamara glared at him. "Mark Schofield, I hate you! I hope I never see you again!"

Knowing she did not mean it, Mark smiled. Her last action before he closed the carriage door was to hurl the envelope of money and his key in his face. "I don't need your help. I can take care of myself."

For one brief moment their eyes met through the windowpane. Thoughtfully he tapped the envelope against his thigh while clutching the key in his other hand, then slipped it into his pocket. Tamara squeezed her hands tightly in her lap and looked straight ahead.

What could she do? Tamara sulked. She would not go to his house, nor would she return to Park Lane. The first time the carriage stopped, she would jump out and run. Clasping her valise in her hand, she watched for the right moment. The carriage stopped at a cross street. Tamara flung open the door, leaped out, closing the door behind her. She stepped to the curb and watched as the hackney moved on without her. As if she could not help herself, she laughed, thinking how surprised the driver would be when he stopped in Kensington to find the carriage empty.

She glanced around, contemplating what she would do. Spotting a narrow walk-through park with trees and benches, she sat down, placing the valise at her ankles.

After Tamara had been sitting on the bench more than an hour, a plan came to her. She knew what she would do.

27

In the dark, without warning, a strong hand clamped over Tamara's mouth. She dropped her valise with a bang. From behind, an arm feeling like an iron bar tightened around her waist. Her frantic struggles to pull away from her attacker were in vain. She was roughly turned around. Before she could react, his mouth crushed down on hers. She squirmed, tried to get away, but her efforts were useless. A kind of fear she had not experienced before gripped her. It was accompanied by strange excitement. Was it because she recognized him? Her assailant's arm tightened. One hand came up to still her head. Helplessly imprisoned in his strong arms, she was too weak to fight. His lips pressed hard against hers. Tamara was startled by the effect the kiss had on her. It was not completely unpleasant. Her trembling was not entirely out of fear. His mouth tasted fresh and clean; his face smelled of a recent shave and felt smooth. She did not respond outwardly; but inwardly, teasing thrills ran through her veins, her mind and body pulling in opposite directions.

He released her so abruptly that she staggered backward, grabbed the railing to regain her balance.

"Hello, beautiful," said a rakish voice. The familiar words were spoken by the man Tamara would have recognized anywhere, even in the dark.

"Mark! Of all the unmitigated nerve! You scared me half to death!"

"That was my intent. Dammit, do you not realize what could befall you? That was but a hint of what could happen to you wandering about alone on the docks at night."

Tamara smiled coyly. " 'Twas not that bad."

"You say that because you knew who it was. Supposing a stranger, a ruffian . . ." He did not finish what he was thinking. "Have you come on board my ship to gain command, or was it your intent to become a stowaway with the mice?" he asked teasingly.

Tamara grinned mischievously. "I had not thought of piracy."

Mark chuckled. "I thought you said you never wanted to see me again."

She had waited in the park until nearly midnight before she made her way to the *Mark Schofield*. The gangplank was down for members of the crew who had leave for the night. Tamara watched the seaman on night watch as he paraded back and forth. From a distance she observed his movements carefully. When he was walking starboard with his back turned, she slipped on board, remaining in the shadows, groping her way to the companionway, thinking there must be a storage closet or cabin of sorts somewhere. It was at that moment that Mark came up behind her.

"How did you know I came aboard?" Tamara asked disbelievingly.

"I was standing up on the poop deck and saw you approaching. Nobody boards my ship without my knowledge."

He picked up her valise. "You are as willful as ever. I suppose if I do not take you, someone else will. At least I can keep an eye on you. I shall probably live to regret it, but . . . come along."

Mark led her to a small paneled cabin on the quarterdeck. It was sparsely furnished with a stationary bunk, chair, wardrobe, and washstand. Covering the floor, however, was a beautiful garnet-colored Oriental carpet.

"I feel guilty putting you in this small compartment, but I warned you accommodations would not be grand."

"It looks very comfortable, Mark."

"My own quarters are a short distance down the passageway. They are quiet and spacious, and when you feel cramped, you are welcome to them. I am sure you will enjoy relaxing in my salon."

"How long will it take to reach Charleston?" Tamara asked with a motive.

"Sailing west . . . seventeen or eighteen days. I expect to arrive April third. That is cut down from thirty-four on a sailing ship," he answered proudly. "Coming back to England, it takes somewhat longer. We will be traveling at a speed of thirteen knots most of the time."

"Mark, I left my uncle's home in a hurry, with only the few belongings I was able to stuff in my valise. Do you suppose I will have time to obtain a few clothes and books tomorrow morning?"

"Yes, but I will accompany you," he answered matter-of-factly. "As for books . . . you saw my well-stocked library. You are welcome to use it."

"I have very little money. I cannot go to my father's solicitor, for he would surely notify Uncle Arthur, so I must go to a pawnbroker with these." She pulled her mother's jewels from her reticule.

"I say, Tamara, don't do that. Keep your mother's jewelry," he said firmly. "I am certain it is very precious to you for sentimental reasons. Use the money and the draft I gave you today. I have funds for what you need."

Tamara shook her head stubbornly. "I could not ask you for more than what you have already agreed to do for me."

Mark smiled. "We will make it an official loan."

"That is very kind of you. You can be sure I will repay you for all my expenses," she answered earnestly. "As soon as I reach Jamaica, I will write to the solicitor."

"Do not worry your pretty head about it."

Tamara looked around her cabin. She walked to the porthole. "Is this the back of the boat?" she asked.

Mark joined her at the porthole, grinning and looking at her with mock dismay.

"Dammit, young lady, if you sail with me you will be required to learn the correct terminology. This is not a *boat*. 'Tis a ship, a steamship." He pinched her cheek teasingly. "And, yes, this is the back of the ship, but it is called the stern. The front is the prow, stem, or bow."

Tamara stood at attention and saluted him sassily. "Aye, aye, sir. Is this the stem or the stern of the ship, sir?"

He replied, chuckling, " 'Tis the stern."

"Very good, sir," Tamara countered, pumping a reproving finger into the air in his direction. "But if you say 'dammit' to me one more time, I am going to call it a tug! You curse like a common sailor."

Suddenly they were rollicking with laughter. Their eyes met, and they stared at each other. It was almost like times long ago, but not quite.

28

"Is that dress madam's size?" Mark asked the proprietress.

"I am sorry, sir. That gown is not for sale."

"Why not?"

"It has been made for one of my best customers, sir."

"Would it fit this lady?"

"It would have to be taken in at the waist and let out at the bosom."

"Mark, please. I do not—"

He waved his hand in protest. "I will pay you double the price for it. You can make your customer another."

First thing that morning Mark had taken Tamara to the fashionable couturiere who greeted him by name and excitedly promised to put her seamstresses to work immediately. Five outfits would be ready and delivered to the ship by nightfall.

While Tamara was being measured and fitted, Mark sat cross-legged on a comfortable red-velvet sofa. Unnerved by his unwavering eyes, Tamara squirmed and shifted from one foot to the other.

"Madam must stand still," the seamstress said patiently.

Mark looked away, his attention caught by the dress hanging on a door hook. It was soft tulle, white, the bodice embroidered with hundreds of crystal beads atop billowy layers and layers of skirts.

Now the proprietress hesitated nervously at Mark's insistence on buying the gown, in the end consenting reluctantly. Mark paid the entire bill, and they left the shop. Outside on the pavement, Tamara put her hands up to her face, red with anger.

"How could you!" she snapped sharply, stamping a foot. "That was most embarrassing!"

"Why, for heavens sake?"

"What must that woman think?" Tamara pointed to the

door of the shop. "Why, I am sure she believes I am your
... your mistress!"

Mark chuckled loudly. "Would that be so terrible?" He
shrugged his shoulders nonchalantly. "The dress suits you.
You will look superb in it. The hell with what she thinks."

"My head aches," she retorted crisply.

He grabbed her arm and pulled her along like an errant
child.

"Dammit, Tamara, stop fussing. I have got to get back to
the ship. We sail tomorrow at dawn with the tide."

The *Mark Schofield* came alive at the first hint of light, in
a gauzy, leaden-colored mist, which rose from the Thames,
floating up the sides of the hull and across the deck like a
harem girl's veil. It curled around the stacks, completely hiding the tips of the tall masts. The morose groan of a foghorn
was the only sign of life on the still-sleeping river.

The ship began its voyage down the gray waters of the
Thames. As it reached the open sea, the sun rose higher and
higher, magically causing the fog to disappear. From her
cabin Tamara heard the firm command "Full steam ahead!"

She looked out the porthole, seeing the sulfurous, feathery
trace of black coal smoke across the clear blue sky, and the
endless, wavy ocean. An hour after setting sail, having
reached the offing, heading for the sea lane to South Carolina, Mark knocked on her door and invited her to join him
for breakfast. Afterward she returned to her cabin with a
book.

Tamara complied with his wishes, spending most of the
day there, reading until he came for her at dinnertime. Mark
led her to his dining room, where he ate all his meals.

As Jimmy served them, Mark commented, "Enjoy the
good food while you can, Tamara. 'Tis not too bad the first
week. 'Twill get worse the second."

As they dined, they sentimentally reminisced about their
carefree days growing up in Jamaica.

"I am most anxious to see your mother," Tamara remarked. "She was very kind to me at a bad time in my life.
You know she took care of me until my uncle came for me?
I wanted to stay with her, but Uncle Arthur would not permit it."

A faraway look entered her eyes. "I needed affection and
understanding. She was the one person who could help me."

"Yes, she told me that." A tone of sadness entered Mark's
voice. "She was upset by it, wanted you to stay. I am sorry to

tell you she was bedfast for two years and died three months ago."

"Oh, I am truly sorry, Mark. I did not know. She was one of the reasons I wished to return to Jamaica. And what about your father?"

"He is fine. I am sure he will be happy to see you. He is away now, but should be home by the time you arrive. He is traveling to try to get over my mother's demise, so he says."

Tamara's eyes flickered over him. He was quite handsome wearing a black naval jacket with gold buttons.

"Is the beautiful woman you were with at the ballet in London your fiancée or . . . your wife?" she blurted.

Mark grinned. "Elaine? Of course not. I have known Elaine several years. She is an enchanting companion for an amusing evening whenever I am in London. She is a . . . she is the kind of woman who has many male friends among the nobility and wealthy."

Tamara's exquisite skin showed pink even in the dim light of the flickering candles. They had finished dinner. Mark casually poured two glasses of wine. He asked her approval to smoke. She nodded. He bit the tip off a cigar, then lit it by holding a candle to it and puffing.

"No, Tamara, marriage has never tempted me. I have no wish to be drawn into intrigues and problems created by a wife. Besides, 'twould not be fair to her, not with the life I live. I saw what it did to my mother," he admitted quietly.

Fleetingly, in her mind, Tamara questioned his words and the tone in which they were spoken, like a hidden annoyance that surfaced in his voice. She interpreted it as dissension existing between father and son. After a moment the idea was forgotten.

Mark dealt lightly with the many women he had known in countries around the world, enjoying their company and ardor, always escaping an affair of the heart. Emotional entanglements were not for him.

Frankly honest, he let them know from the beginning it was to be no more than an entertaining interlude. He felt no need for permanent attachments. He had a penchant for casualness. He never led them on with flowery promises or false declarations of undying love. It was never necessary to resort to such tactics. Women found him irresistible. His cool indifference was seductive, increasing their interest. He had a way with them which was appealing. His open, easy laughter, his continental manners, charmed them. They were thrilled to accept his attentions under any terms, hoping he would fall into a trap, each woman wishing she would be the one he would choose as his wife.

When a paramour became demanding, clinging, he stayed clear, backing away as he would withdraw from flames that threatened his safety. After the excitement of the newness of a charming woman wore off, after getting to know her intimately beneath the bedcovers, when he had learned all her charms and delights, he ended it before she became a habit difficult to break. Afterward, he hardly recalled what she looked like, if he remembered at all.

Escaping London and her relations added a new radiance to Tamara. In a euphoric mood, she became more talkative, aided by several glasses of wine, which she was not accustomed to drinking. At sea she felt free. With the effects of the wine and the feeling of security in Mark's company, she relaxed.

Mark remembered her as an effervescent, high-spirited little girl riding along the Jamaican shore. His memory of a child and the reality of the delicately boned beauty sitting before him mulled together. His mind confused, he could not accept them as one and the same. He knew not how to behave toward Tamara, child, girl, woman. This voluptuous sylph whose voice matched her soft features, her loveliness shining mystically in the flickering shadows of the oil lamp, could not be Tamara. Evanescently he wished she were a stranger so he would have no qualms about seducing her, inviting her to his bed.

Overwhelmingly aware of her presence, he could not prevent his eyes from lingering on the swell of her breasts showing bare above her bodice. He could not help observing the well-endowed roundness pressing firmly against the soft folds of her gown. He gazed at the deep-shadowed crevice indicative of their fullness. His eyes searched in the tufts and folds for a protruding nipple.

Mark refilled their glasses. While he lifted his and drank, his eyes fluttered upward to Tamara's mouth. A myriad of queries seeped through his brain. He wanted to know the feel of her lips, wondered whether they had felt a man's demanding kisses, the first clue to his passion. Girl, woman, girl-woman. Had she surrendered her body to desire? Had she known the feel of a man inside her, experienced complete fulfillment? Was she indeed a woman?

His eyes moved up to her eyes for the key. There was an aura of sweet sadness surrounding her, which intrigued him.

Was it the color of her gown or her expression that made her look innocent? The gown was of the palest pink satin over soft white tulle. A cluster of pink velvet roses bloomed at her bosom.

An indefinable expression of sorrow appeared, making her mysteriously appealing. Then, quite suddenly, her expression changed to enticing devilment, a glimpse of the Tamara he once knew. She would flash a beguiling smile or burst into merry laughter. One moment her eyes were filled with melancholy; the next, mischief. It piqued his curiosity.

When he had seen her at the theater, before he knew who she was, he was captivated by her ravishing beauty, finding himself staring helplessly at her profile and more vulgarly at her lovely throat, soft white shoulders, and the smooth pale flesh of her partially exposed high breasts above the immodestly low-cut basque. Envy of her escort had gripped him. He was not surprised when he saw the gentleman had persuaded her to leave the theater before the performance ended.

The smoke from Mark's cigar spiraled ceilingward. His senses enflamed, he felt guilty about the desire creeping into his loins and the thoughts that cropped unwelcomingly into his head. Christ, she is a child. No, she is not a child, he thought bemusedly. His mind was playing tricks. She is not a child. She is a woman. A damned desirable woman. His pulse raced, his manhood aroused unwillingly. Silently he rebuked himself. Dammit, what ails me? 'Twould be close to incest!

Tamara chatted on until he drained his glass, setting it down with a bang. Not trusting himself, he rose abruptly, threw back his shoulders to dismiss his thoughts and feelings. Walking to the porthole, he clasped his hands behind him, stared at the endless sea, contemplated the roll of the waves, the starlit sky. Tamara gazed at his broad shoulders as he glanced out to sea. A sweet thrill swept through her as her eyes lingered on his fingers. Finally he turned to face her. "It has been a long day, Tamara. Perhaps you wish to retire. Get all the rest you can while the sea is still calm," He suggested as dispassionately as he could. "In a few days it will turn rough."

"But you have not told me what you have been doing these past eight years," she protested. "I would be most interested to hear about your travels. Remember, Mark, when you left on your first sea voyage, you promised you would tell me about your adventures next time we met." More softly, almost to herself, she added, "No . . . of course you could not possibly remember that."

He turned briskly. "I *do* remember, but we have seventeen days. There will be plenty of time. I must report to the helm now," he remarked, sounding a little impatient.

"Yes, of course. 'Twas thoughtless of me to demand more of your time when you have so many responsibilities." She rose to leave. "Thank you for not turning me away. Thank you for bringing me with you," she said softly, smiling as she reached the door and put her hand on the knob.

Tamara's sweetness gripped him in the pit of his stomach. He hurried to her. "Wait. I will escort you to your cabin."

They walked slowly the short distance down the passageway. At her cabin he said good night, then headed for the companion ladder, climbing two rungs at a time to reach the main deck.

29

Tamara was confined to her cabin most of the time. The only member of the crew permitted to enter was the steward, who changed the bedding and kept the cabin clean. She read and sewed, finding herself waiting anxiously for Mark's tap on the door and his invitation to go up on the main deck. The more she saw him, the more she admired and respected him. He had worked hard, and since his father's retirement had become the head of the family's mighty shipping empire. He was a man of progress, having the best and latest navigational equipment available on board. He possessed the distinct quality to command and to gain the trust and respect of his men. He knew and called each one by his first name, which added to their eagerness to serve.

His knuckles rapped lightly at her door. "Tamara, I think you should come up with me now and get a bit of sunshine," he would say. "We must keep that lovely color on those cheeks of yours."

They would walk the deck together, Mark remaining at her side. Tamara suspected he did not quite trust some of the crew. Most were able seamen with years of navigation behind them, old hands who had sailed with his father. But he had taken on a number of younger men to perform the more demanding physical tasks. If the men resented her presence on board, it was not evident to her. Tamara was the only woman. She found their stares of admiration discomposing. When Mark returned her to her cabin, she locked the door until he came for her again.

With each day they sailed, the weather turned warmer. Tamara packed away the dark, heavy clothing she had worn when they left London and began to wear her new dresses. The third evening at sea, she chose a pale pink, deciding it would be a perfect color to wear with her pink silk shawl, hoping it would never be necessary to wear woolens or furs again. They dined alone. In his manly voice Mark told her of his trips to the Pacific and India. He described faraway places, exotic ports where he had stopped, sun-drenched islands of the South Pacific with lush green mountains and warm sandy shores, islands where tropical flowers grew in abundance and where natives were gracefully beautiful.

"The islands of the Pacific are exotic. You would enjoy them. They are very scenic, like Jamaica." He was a prolific storyteller, relating humorous experiences of his travels. Tamara laughed. Cheered by his tales, she found herself smiling more often. Displaying flashes of wit, she burst into untrammeled laughter, realizing she had almost forgotten how good it felt.

When the meal ended, he stood, a signal for Tamara's dismissal.

"I have a bit of work to do, but you are welcome to remain in the salon." He pulled several books from one of the shelves pertaining to the South Pacific, and another on the history of the United States. Handing them to her, he said, "You might be interested in taking a look at these."

Leaving her, he went into the other room and sat down at his desk with its mound of charts and maps. Tamara tried to concentrate on the pages in front of her, but her eyes consistently lifted, strayed to watch the man leaning forward over his desk studying the ledgers. The brass ashtray clicked as he banged his pipe against it to empty the ashes and refill the bowl. Surreptitiously Tamara watched as he lit the pipe. She felt his gaze upon her and turned the page of her book, although she had not as much as glanced at one word of it.

She sighed, absently turning the pages of the book on the United States, stopping at the chapter on the founding of the original thirteen English Colonies. She skimmed over the next few pages, looking for South Carolina. Her interest perked when she read the second paragraph.

"Oh, my gosh!" she said aloud. Mark looked up from his desk.

"What is it?"

"I cannot believe what I am reading. The colony of South Carolina was founded by eight noblemen who had been given a land grant by Charles II as a reward for helping restore him to the throne."

"So?"

"One of the noblemen who helped plan the city of Charleston was the first Earl of Shaftesbury!"

Sitting at his desk, Mark looked puzzled. "And?"

"About two years ago I met the seventh Earl of Shaftesbury. Have you not heard of his work of improving working conditions among the laboring class in mines and cotton mills and the slum children?" she rambled excitedly.

Vaguely Mark recalled the name.

"It did not mean anything to me at the time, but I believe he mentioned something about Charleston."

Mark unrolled a map and spread it out on his desk, studying it, puffing on his pipe.

"Tamara, would you like to have a look at Charleston harbor on the map?" he called.

Tamara put down her book and joined him at his desk. He rose and slid his finger across the map. "Here is the Ashley River . . . and this is the Cooper River."

"Ashley . . . Cooper. Why, that is the family name of the Earl of Shaftesbury! Anthony Ashley Cooper!" As she leaned closer to study the map, she became aware of Mark's nearness. Instead of looking at the map, she found herself gazing at his suntanned hand and the dark hair at his wrist. Tamara's breath caught in her throat. His hand grazed hers as he pointed to the islands in the harbor. The movement sent a wave of excitement coursing through her body, which overpowered her elation at discovering Charleston's founder. Sensing rather than feeling his strength, his strong-muscled thighs, Tamara felt her emotions somersault. While the thrill of his nearness distracted her, she tried to concentrate on the map and what he was saying in a voice that was not entirely steady.

Tamara was always delighted when Mark invited her to accompany him on his evening rounds. At first they stood along the railing marveling at the dusk sky streaked deep pink by the red-colored sun.

He showed her his ship with obvious pride. His father had started the company, had become a shipping magnate. When Mark took over, he did it to please his father, but he became caught up in the challenges thrust upon him and had played a large role in expanding their empire. But this was his. The *Mark Schofield* belonged solely and completely to him. It was his castle, which he showed to Tamara as proudly as Lord Sheldon had shown his ancestral estate.

Tamara welled with excitement when he allowed her to take hold of the helm. He explained the usefulness of the sextant, how it was used to observe altitudes so as to ascertain latitude and longtitude. She looked through his spyglass, observing a close-up view of the horizon, pointing it skyward to look at the multitudinous planets. He taught her the names of the prominent constellations used as navigational guideposts—the North Star, Jupiter, the Big Dipper—instructing her in his rich voice.

Six members of the crew who were off duty sat at the base of the mizzen, playing cards. Tamara and Mark stopped to watch. All sturdy, able seamen, their skins bronzed by the nature of their work in the tropical sun and sea air, they bet heavily on wages not yet received. The dealer shuffled and dealt the cards expertly as Tamara and Mark continued on their walk.

As they strolled along the quiet main deck, they fell silent, a serene, contented reticence with no need for constant talk. Idly they observed the whitecaps crest and break. Dusk had turned to night, taking with it the colors of the sunset. A black filmy cloud obscured the topaz moon hanging low in front of them.

Standing beside the capstan, Mark puffed on his pipe. In the moon's partial light, his eyes lingered on Tamara as gusts of wind tousled her hair. He had often wondered what it would be like to have a woman on board with him. He had been told it was romantic. At sea one relaxed, the senses sharpened. Qualms about getting romantically involved with Tamara cautioned him. Had it been a mistake to bring her on board? It was only the beginning of the voyage, and already he was spending more time with her than he had planned, and he found that when she was not with him, she occupied much of his thoughts. No matter how romantic the setting, he knew she was not a woman to trifle with in a mere dalliance while at sea. Unknown to Tamara, she had aroused all his senses to the point where he gripped the polished railing to prevent himself from sweeping her into his arms. No matter how tempting she was, he resolved to treat her as a friend, and not to woo her into his bed.

30

The weather was changeable. There were bright, sunny days with white clouds reflected on the rolling waters. Then the sky became overcast and dreary. For several days the sun did not appear; then it came out in full force with a beautiful sunset. The brilliant red ball dropped slowly until only half of it could be seen, then sank completely beneath the surface of the water on the horizon.

The next evening Mark invited the first officer, Roderick Moran, to join them for dinner, and occasionally after that, another officer or two. For the remainder of the voyage they never dined alone. Mark pondered which was worse, being alone, tempted, unable to touch her, or watching Moran's eyes upon her, noting the growing friendship between them. He identified his feelings as protective. He was responsible for her well-being as long as she was aboard his ship. He knew Moran's reputation with women, which was no better than his own.

Physically, Roderick and Mark could have been taken for brothers, although Mark was more handsome, Roderick younger. Their coloring was similar, but Roderick was not quite as tall and was slightly heavier in build. He did not wear a mustache, but was clean-shaven.

Most of the time Tamara was not included in the conversation. She listened to Mark and his first mate spinning yarns of past experience. From their conversation she gathered they had had many adventures together and shared a close camaraderie. Their personalities, however, were different. Where Mark was outgoing, quick to grin, laugh, take command, Moran was quiet, with a serious expression in his eyes most of the time. Where Mark was a leader of men, Moran was a follower. Mark knew he was fortunate, for Moran had been his dependable, efficient first officer for six years. In that time Mark found he could depend on him as a friend as well as an officer.

As Mark had warned, meals did not improve. The menu dwindled to salt pork, biscuits, and freshly caught fish that Tamara had watched being gutted and scaled. For breakfast there were freshly laid eggs. Chickens were kept on board until the end of the journey, when they would be killed and eaten. After the first week, the casks of water began to turn slimy, and Mark warned her not to drink water unless necessary, except boiled for tea, encouraging her to drink wine instead.

Tamara had no idea why she and Mark no longer dined alone. She knew he was avoiding her and wondered what she had done to displease him. His insouciant behavior confused her. She had remained in her cabin as she had promised. What had she done to warrant his censorship? Since she could think of nothing, she concluded it was simply because of her presence on his ship. He was anxious to reach his destination so that he would be rid of her and she would no longer be his responsibility. She sighed, believing she had been relegated to the position of a boring, tiresome obligation, or even worse, a nuisance.

The feeling that her presence annoyed him and that she was nothing but an irritation upset her to the point that she was unable to sleep. The sound of the ship's bell drifted through the porthole of her cabin. It was only nine o'clock. With dismay she glanced at the book she had finished reading. Why had she not returned it for another? Certain that Mark was making his rounds and that no one was in his quarters, she put on her slippers and pink silk robe and walked the few steps to his door. She would return the book and get another before he came back, one about the United States, which she was about to visit for the first time.

Tamara walked through the empty stateroom, dining room, and into the salon, putting the book she had read back in its place on the shelf. Scanning the books, she spotted two volumes, but they were on the top shelf. She looked around for a stool on which to stand, but there wasn't any. Her arms stretched upward, but she could not reach the books she wanted. At that moment the door opened and Roderick Moran entered.

"At your service, ma'am," he said politely. He circled her waist with his fingers and lifted her up so that she could reach the volumes. Tamara laughed gaily as she attempted to remove the books from the partially enclosed shelves. They were large, and she had difficulty. Moran chuckled as a slipper fell from her foot.

Mark walked in while she was in midair. He looked at one, then the other. An angry violence swept through him at the sight of another man's hands touching Tamara, at the joyous moment they were sharing. He felt like an intruder in his own salon. He was enraged.

"Mr. Moran!" he commanded in a deadly tone.

Roderick put Tamara down, turning to his captain. "Aye, sir?"

"Touch Lady Warde one more time and you are fired!"

His words stunned them. Tamara and Roderick looked at each other, then at Mark, in disbelief. For a long moment silence strained the room.

"Please leave my quarters at once, Mr. Moran," Mark ordered irrationally.

Tamara waited and was disappointed when the young first officer, his face inscrutable, did not attempt to explain, but answered simply, "Aye, aye, sir."

When Roderick was gone, Tamara exhaled a gush of air she had been holding inside. She glanced at Mark quizzically, still not fully aware of his wrath.

"Mark! For heaven's sake, what has gotten into you?"

"I might ask you the same," he scoffed. "What the devil are you doing in here alone with him . . . and in your bedclothes? Where's your modesty? A more blatant display of wantonness I have never witnessed." This, he knew, was not true. Why had he said it? he wondered.

Flushing deeply, Tamara dropped her head to look down at her appearance. The garment with long sleeves and high neckline covered more than her gowns. The flesh of her body was completely hidden. What she did not realize was that her classical contour was not. The soft silk hugged voluptuous curves, slim waist, outlining her shapely hips and legs, sharpening Mark's imagination more than if she were exposed.

"You promised me you would behave. Do you call flaunting your body in that provocative thing, flirting like a common trollop, behaving?"

Tamara's eyes flew open wide and her mouth dropped. "Mark! How can you accuse me of such a thing? Please. Let me explain what happened."

"I am not interested in your goddamned explanation," he thundered "I saw for myself. In the future save your passion for when you are no longer my responsibility. I trust it will not be too much of a hardship."

He glared at her and she glared back. Turning a deep shade of red, she swallowed hard. Her breathing was heavy as her eyes narrowed, showing a suspicion of tears. Her lips tightened in anger.

"I am sorry if I am an annoyance to you. I want you to know I am grateful you brought me with you, so forgive me for what I am about to say," she said calmly, trying to hide the raging turmoil inside. Much louder she yelled, "You are detestable!" Abruptly she swung around with the books on her arm. Minus one slipper she hobbled toward the exit, then turned back to face him again. "In case you do not realize it, you made a blundering ass of yourself."

For a moment Mark stood dumbfounded, then recovering, bent and retrieved that which was causing her limp. He followed her down the passageway, carrying the lost slipper like Cinderella's handsome prince. "Tamara! Wait!" Tamara limped forward with grim determination. "Tamara," he called, louder and sharper.

Tamara's door was ajar. When she reached it she pushed it open further with her elbow and entered. Mark stood at the door, intent on apologizing. "Tamara, I . . ." Tamara turned, jerked the slipper from his hand, and banged the door in his face.

She held her breath and listened. After what seemed a long time she heard his retreating footsteps.

Too upset to concentrate on reading, Tamara slammed the book closed and sighing heavily stared up at the flickering patterns of light from the oil lamp on the ceiling. Sleep eluded her for a long time.

Suddenly the phantoms returned, storming her peace of mind. Three bearded men violently pushed open her door and ruthlessly ripped off her clothes, tearing the pink silk robe and nightgown beneath into shreds. In her dreams, instead of being a spectator to a rape, she was the victim. A shiny-headed man with a thick black beard, tall, muscular, naked to the waist, stood looking down at her on the bunk. He did not speak. His hands reached down. Mechanically he pulled a rope from his trouser pocket. He tied her wrists behind her. Her ankles were tied to the bedpost. When this was accomplished, he bent to kiss her. The dream was so real she smelled the rum on his breath, the stench of his dirty, sweaty body. Morosely she cried out in her sleep. He punched her, knocking out several front teeth. He hit her again across her face. Blood trickled from her nose and mouth. He pulled a knife from his belt and held it between her legs, poking her private parts with the tip of the blade, then suddenly plunging it inside her.

Tamara heard a bloodcurdling scream, awakening to realize it came from her own throat. Disoriented, her arms flailing, tears rolling down her cheeks, she bolted upright, feeling sick. Her body trembled uncontrollably, the nightmare having shaken her mercilessly. Her hand flew up to her mouth to check her teeth. They were all intact.

Mark pounded on her door. "Tamara, it is Mark. Open up. What is wrong?"

"Go away."

"Tamara, unlock this door immediately."

"I am all right. Go away," she insisted.

"I am not going away until I am sure. Open up." He rattled the knob, then pounded on the door. "Must I take off the hinges?"

Tamara swung her feet to the carpeted floor, walked to the door, unlatched it. Instinctively she plunged toward him, wrapping her arms around his waist, clinging to him, frantically seeking his protection.

He held her comfortingly, feeling her soft, curvaceous body, clad only in her nightgown, pressing against him. He cursed the callowness of his feelings, picking her up and carrying her to the bunk, where he set her down gently. As he viewed her closely, a crease showed in the flesh between his eyes. He saw the tears, her pale face, the frightened look. Her soft hair fell in disarray around her shoulders.

"Do not move. I'll get brandy." When he returned she was as he had left her. He looked down. Accidentally, from his vantage, he saw a pair of mellow breasts, the most perfectly molded he had ever seen. Had he taken clay and formed them himself with his own hands, he could not have made them more to his liking. He ground his teeth. A muscle twitched in his cheek. He leaned over, holding the glass of brandy to her lips. She pushed it away half-empty.

"All of it," he demanded.

Obediently she drank again until all the brandy disappeared.

"Lie back. Cover yourself."

Tamara obeyed, slipping beneath the covers, looking up at him warily. "I am sorry I disturbed you. I had a bad dream, that is all."

"Are you sure you are all right?" he asked concernedly, noting the perspiration on her brow and her damp hair.

"Yes," she whispered softly.

He tucked the covers under her chin, stared at her for a long moment. "I want to apologize for what I said earlier."

141

She did not reply, but he saw renewed defiance in her eyes, and reached down to brush his fingers beneath her chin. "Jesus, you have a temper."

Tamara's face turned expressionless. "Speak for yourself." Mark's brow creased in a frown. "I am trying to apologize."

Unmoved, Tamara studied the nail on her index finger.

"Tamara?"

Tamara glared up at him. "I despise being accused of something of which I am not guilty!"

Mark sat down on the bed beside her and took her hand. "I am sorry. I made a mistake. I am a bungler." He saw a slight smile on her lips and could not refrain from smiling to himself. He put her hand down and left, clicking the latch behind him. She was alone.

Tamara heard his footsteps retreating down the passageway toward his quarters. There, he lit a cigar and poured a glass of brandy, drinking it empty. Pacing restlessly, firmly imprinted images of Tamara's expressive eyes, sometimes frightened, other times defiant, and then, mischievous, appeared before him. Clearly she was a woman with passionate responses. Visions of her satiny, pink-tipped breasts kindled a fire within him. There was no mistaking, evading, or denying the impact her loveliness combined with her vulnerability had on him. It was plain and simple. He wanted her. He wanted to put his lips all over her sweet, luscious body. Mark stopped pacing to make his self-confession. Dammit, he wanted to make love to her.

Mark cursed himself for agreeing to bring Tamara on the voyage. Not only were women aboard ship bad luck, but they had a way of beckoning, worming their way into a man's heart, drawing him into a snare . . . then whang! Before he knew it, he was wed. Mark liked his life the way it was; he did not want his situation to change. Confronting his predicament head-on, he was determined to be cautious and not find himself in the trap of matrimony.

Gravely he looked at the tip of his cigar glowing red in the darkness. He smashed it in the ashtry, convincing himself avoiding Tamara would put an end to the problem.

31

Tamara's nightmares were devastating. It took several days to shake off their effects. At breakfast she was glad Mark did not mention what had happened the previous night, but she noticed he watched her closely, his green eyes serious.

That evening at dinner the first few moments were strained, all three wishing to avoid any mention of what had happened in the salon. Tamara did not know Mark was cursing himself for his conduct, and she had no idea whether he had discussed it with Roderick, but no mention was made of it. Instead, they talked about Charleston and the impending war.

"Sir, do you really think there will be a war?" Roderick asked Mark reservedly.

"I doubt it. Each is making threats. 'Tis but a bluff."

"If war does come, will it hinder your trade agreements?"

"No. The South is not industrially equipped. It will need supplies for her army. Profits in war are tremendous, but so are the risks. I plan to look into the entire matter when we reach Charleston. If there is war, I intend to make the most of it. The possibilities are gigantic. Profits are worth the risks. No contraband, mind you, but cloth, shoes, tea, medical supplies, will bring high returns. Our textile mills in England will demand the raw cotton we will take back." Mark looked at Roderick cautiously. "Are you with me?"

"Aye, all the way," replied Roderick, nodding. "Why not trade with the North as well?"

Mark chuckled, breaking the strain between them. "Precisely. Why not indeed? It could be extremely dangerous, should the North decide to blockade Southern ports, which I am certain it will do."

Again the fair weather broke. Obscure signs of rough waters appeared, at first noticed only by the experienced seamen. The barometer readings, then more obvious telltale signs, all indicated an approaching storm. The wind slapped and howled with increased ferociousness. Gathering clouds piled in layers on top of each other.

By evening, the ocean was choppy. The vessel pitched and heeled forcefully. In her cabin Tamara was jolted back and forth. It grew so stuffy she had difficulty breathing. Opening the porthole for fresh air, she heard the frightening sounds of waves thundering and slamming against the hull.

On deck, Mark thought about Tamara in her cabin. He knew she would be afraid. She was his responsibility until they reached Barbados. Telling himself he would be shirking his duty as the ship's captain if he did not check on the safety and welfare of his passenger, he went below and knocked on Tamara's door.

She staggered toward it, opening it and gesturing for him to enter. He was relieved to see she was all right. "Tamara, do not be frightened; this will pass. The area we are sailing through is normally rough."

Struggling to maintain his balance, he viewed her more closely and noticed her pallid appearance.

"You look a bit pale. You have been cooped in here most of the day. Come up on deck with me." As she grabbed her shawl, he walked across the cabin and closed the porthole. "Sorry, Tamara. You must keep this closed for the time being."

The ship rocked. He took her arm to steady her. Up on deck the wind whipped a strand of her copper hair across her face. Momentarily forgetting his vow of the night before, he reached out and brushed it back. The wind caught her skirts, billowing them like sails. Forceful spindrift touched their faces. They walked astern.

"That shawl is not enough. Here. Put my jacket around you," he said protectively. They laughed because it was much too large, hanging loosely over her shoulders. She stood in front of him as he wrapped it around her, pinning her hair beneath it. He was very tall. His thick dark hair fell across his forehead. She looked up and smiled uncertainly as he brushed a tendril of damp hair away from her eye. They swayed unsteadily. Mark guided her along starboard. It was difficult to walk. Tamara stopped to catch her breath.

"Perhaps this was not such a good idea after all, but I felt you needed the fresh air and exercise," he yelled above the sound of the crashing waves. "We will walk around the deck once and then I will take you below."

He accompanied her to her cabin, checked to be certain the porthole was secured.

"Sorry, I will have to turn off the lamp for the time being. You understand . . . on account of fire."

144

The room was plunged into darkness. He opened the door to leave, admitting a shaft of dim light from the passageway.

"Oh, Mark. Here is your jacket. Thank you."

The ship pitched rhythmically with the heavy roll of the sea. Suddenly, as she handed him the coat, the vessel lurched forward in the surging waters. Instinctively Mark reached out in the dark to grab her, sweeping her into his arms to prevent her from falling. He was struck immediately by the desirability of her exquisite figure, hinting of pleasurable delights, malleably fitting his body. Possessively he pulled her closer, feeling the pressing softness of the breasts he had seen and could not chase from his thoughts. As it brushed his cheeks, he smelled the fresh fragrance of her recently shampooed hair. His heart pounded. His senses reeled. His strong arms clasped her tightly, exciting a storm of passion. His swollen loins throbbed. His lips planted a soft kiss on her forehead, then her cheek, then sought her sensuous mouth. Their bodies rocked together with the sway of the ship.

Then Tamara went rigid. Unknown to Mark, in the inky blackness a bearded man appeared out of the past and flashed before her eyes. Seeing herself on the floor being raped, she panicked. Breaking into a cold sweat, she twisted in his arms, jerking her head viciously from one side to the other, trying to avoid his searching lips.

At first Mark thought she was teasing, being playful. He chuckled huskily and pulled her closer. Her hands pushed ineffectively against his muscular chest. Her frantic struggles to free herself became more desperate. With all the force she could muster, she slapped him across the face. Shrieking, she clawed at his face like a trapped animal. The stinging blow thrust him back to reality. Astounded by her violent rejection, he released her.

"Tamara!" She was on the verge of hysteria. He grabbed her arms and shook her. "Tamara!" He attempted to subdue her by grasping both her hands. She sank her teeth into his arm just above the wrist. His right leg wrapped around hers, pinioning her to him so that it was impossible for her to move. She struggled until she was weak, sensing he was waiting for her to stop. She went limp. He released her. She groped in the dark and flung herself down on the bunk, panting nervously. Her hand pressed against her chest. For a moment she feared she was going to retch.

Mark stood very still. Staring at her through the darkness, he clenched his fists, his mind searching for a plausible explanation of her rejection until it found one.

"Aye," he said quietly at last. "The barriers of class, that is it. I crossed the line, did I not? You are of noble birth. I am a commoner. The difference has become important to you," he accused. "Your years in England have taught you well. Your aristocratic friends have done a thorough job. My apologies, Lady Tamara Warde," he said stiffly, rubbing his arm where she had bitten him.

Tamara sobbed as he continued.

"I failed to tell you my friend and competitor Samuel Cunard and I were made baronets in recognition of service during the Crimean War. Our vessels were used as hospital ships and mail carriers. Would that I had known it was a requirement for your kisses!" he said mockingly. "I would have informed you."

Tamara put her hands over her face. " 'Tis not that!" she sobbed imploringly. "Whatever else you may think of me, that is not the reason," she choked hysterically, tears streaming down her cheeks.

"Do not fret. You cannot help you were born and bred a lady," he said sarcastically.

"Mark Schofield! You speak of it as if I was born with some kind of disease."

She stood up.

"I thought you were different . . . but you are like all the rest. The only emotion you possess is lust. Men!" She fluttered her hand through the air. "They are all like wild animals, stalking their prey, pouncing, devouring! I hate men," she screamed above the noise of the storm. "I hate you! All you think of is ravishing women," she sobbed, as hot tears poured down her face.

Stung and perplexed by her hysterical outcry, Mark turned to light the lamp. This was no simple rejection. This was a matter that needed reckoning, and at once.

"I see we have more than one storm to outride tonight," he said in soft, patient tones. "Confound it, Tamara, I have never ravished a woman in my life! Rape is an act of violence. I have no taste for it . . . nor have I ever found it necessary to use force. Is that what you thought I was about to do?" he asked, a note of disbelief in his voice. Tamara continued to weep uncontrollably.

"You categorize all men as being beasts. Are you not being unfair? I am none of those things of which you accuse me."

Good God, he thought, he was needed at the helm, and here he was attempting to placate this young woman . . . or was he seeking forgiveness?

146

"I am sorry to have frightened you. I seem to make a habit of upsetting you. I assure you my intention was not to rape you."

The ship heeled. Instinctively he reached out to steady her, but withdrew his arms, not daring to touch her again.

"Tamara, please sit down before you fall and injure yourself," he said firmly.

Her eyes downcast, Tamara did as he asked. She hid her face in her hands and sobbed. Mark sat down beside her, realizing her reaction was more than the rejection of his kisses. Something was tormenting her, and he would get to the bottom of it.

"Pl-please, Mark," she stuttered. "Just leave me alone. It is my problem. Please . . . gooooo awaaaaay!"

Mark drew a handkerchief from his pocket, lifted her chin, and dabbed her eyes and wet cheeks.

"Such beautiful eyes. You must not hide them with tears," he said soothingly. "Your face has turned the color of whey, except your perky nose, which is as pink as a rosebud."

She blinked and smiled weakly. He half-rose to leave, then sat down again.

"Will you be all right? Can I get you anything?" he asked solicitously, stroking her hair. "Shall I send to the galley for something to eat? How about a cup of tea?"

Tamara shook her head, not looking up, but staring at her fingers. Mark raised her chin with his hand until their eyes met.

"You do not really hate me?" he asked quietly.

Tamara shook her head from side to side, aware that her feelings for him were quite to the contrary. His overpowering presence, the heat of his body so close, the touch of his thigh against her, wrought havoc with her emotions.

"I must leave you now," he announced, rising reluctantly. She did not look up. He hesitated.

"You do forgive me, Tamara?"

Her eyes, still moist, found his. "Yes," she whispered softly. "I am sorry. And I am sincerely happy about your title. I am very proud of you. Congratulations, Sir Mark Schofield." A sweet smile spread her lips.

Mark had always found women flattered by his overtures. They were more than willing to receive his kisses, returned them eagerly. As he walked the deck alone, deep in thought, he shook his head. The wiles of women! Had it not been the natural thing for him to do? To kiss her when she was in his arms? Her reaction slapped at his pride. He was both intrigued and puzzled by her behavior. If it was not because he was a commoner who had overstepped his bounds, then why had she responded with so much vengeance? Without conceit he was certain it was not because he repulsed her. A thought nurtured in his brain that some man must have hurt her. It must have been that nobleman, Darrington. What other reason would she have for running away? He should have known.

In the recesses of his mind he groped for ways to win her confidence. Having had only a detached interest in women, he had never delved into their inhibitions and idiosyncrasies, but dismissed them lightly as the artifices of their gender. With Tamara it was different. She evoked in him emotions he had never experienced in the countless women he had known. His feelings defied description. At first he credited them to knowing her in the days of his youth. She was a friend who had come to him for help. He refused to acknowledge he was drawn to her physically, that he wanted her as he had never wanted a woman before—until honesty forced him to admit the truth.

If he was to learn what her problem was, he would have to move swiftly. There was very little time left. In two days they would reach Charleston, South Carolina.

32

Tamara sighed onerously. Mark had sent for her. What had she done now to displease him? Since the night he tried to kiss her, their behavior toward each other had turned to strained formality. Since that moment, his mood had changed. More often than not he was ill-tempered, as if something was eating at him. From her cabin she could hear him snapping crossly at his men. At mealtime he had very little to say.

Expecting to remain in his salon only a few moments, until he told her what he wanted, then dismissed her, she sat on the edge of her chair, demurely clasping her hands in her lap, pretending to take an intense interest in the stitching on her gown. She wondered what arrangements he had made for her, suspecting that what he had in mind was to book passage on another ship in Charleston, one that would sail directly to Jamaica. Her heart sickened. For eight years she had longed to return to the home of her childhood. Suddenly, it no longer mattered. What mattered was that she wanted to be near Mark, wherever he was, wherever he went. If he sent her out of his life, he would also send her desire to go on living, but she was determined he must never know how she felt. Loneliness gripped her, striking at her heart mercilessly.

On what was to be the last evening at sea they dined on roast chicken basted in a wine sauce. The last of the plump hens that had supplied them with fresh eggs had been slaughtered that morning in preparation for the final meal. Determined to win her confidence, after Roderick had left Mark's quarters, Mark asked Tamara to join him in the salon. He was determined to win her confidence. He would talk first about what it would be like once they reached Charleston. He would look for an opening to probe subtly without her becoming suspicious.

Now, as she waited for him to speak, she stole a wary glance, not knowing it made Mark fight back a chuckle. Her expressive eyes attracted him strongly. She looked quite adorable, innocent, with a haunting winsomeness, but appearing at the same time, to carry all the world's problems on her shoulders. Staying his distance the past week had not been easy.

Contemplatively, he rubbed the tip of his nose with his finger, trying to decide how to begin. He began matter-of-factly. "Tomorrow we land. Although I do not expect to be in port long, you will meet some of my friends. I believe it essential under present conditions in Charleston for you to understand what has been happening there so that you will be on guard about what you say."

The ship rocked cradlelike in the calm sea. Mark settled back in his red leather chair, resting his elbows on its arms. Tamara waited attentively.

"The state in which Charleston is located is South Carolina. As it happens, South Carolina is no longer a state in the United States. For the past four months it has been part of the Confederate States of America, a newly formed nation."

Tamara's expression was one of puzzlement.

"Why would it no longer be in the United States?"

Mark shifted in his leather chair. "Tamara, the reasons are complex. There are geographical and sectional differences.

149

Only born-and-bred Southerners can truly understand the reasons for secession. Southerners are like the people of Ireland. Only the Irish can fully understand their feelings and reasons for fighting the crown, for wanting to break away from Great Britain. Southerners have a fervent love for the South."

Tamara sighed deeply and nodded. "One always has strong feelings for the land where one was born. That is how I feel about Jamaica."

"Me, too." He paused before he went on with his explanation. "For one reason or another, Southerners feel the central government has failed them, that it is bent upon ruining them and that they would be better off not being a part of it. To them the central government has encroached upon powers belonging to the states. They believe their choice is submission or secession. They chose secession."

Tamara nodded understandingly.

"What I want to emphasize, Tamara, is that South Carolinians are very serious about this. Charleston is a spawning place for secession. They consider their cause sacred. Although you will find them friendly, soft-spoken, with impeccable manners, they are high-strung, especially now. At first glance, slavery would be the easy answer to give to your question on why they want to leave the United States. Slavery is an important part of the Southern economy. Their slaves are a form of wealth, their property, a way of life. The abolitionist movement in the North has increased their fear of slave insurrection. Many slaves are content, accept their lot. Others, who have waited a long time hoping to be free, have reached the point where they believe Northern promises of a better life are possible only by insurrection. They are through with hopes and dreams and talking."

Mark looked into Tamara's eyes, keen with interest. "Can you imagine living on an isolated plantation with your husband, outnumbered by, let's say, fifty slaves? There have been uprisings where the master and his entire family were wiped out, brutally slaughtered, and homes set afire."

"Just the thought of it is horrible. Does the United States government want to abolish slavery?"

"Confine it. Stop it from spreading. The United States is expanding westward. Each time a territory applies for statehood, the question of slavery arises. Southerners want the right to take their slaves with them to the new west."

"Thank you for explaining all this to me. I would have been unprepared."

Mark crossed his legs casually. "But there is a more complex principle behind the secession movement, the doctrine of nullification. Southern states demand the right to declare laws made by the central government unconstitutional if deemed harmful to their states. You see, Tamara, the South is an agricultural section, which must import most manufactured goods. The central government over the years has continually increased tariffs on their imports. I have seen it myself. Revenue agents are at the docks when my shipments are unloaded. It galls the South that the money they are forced to pay in the form of import duties goes to build roads to the west, where they want to keep slavery out. I have a great sympathy for the Southern cause. In this I believe they have reason to gripe."

Mark looked at Tamara, pausing in his explanation, half-suspecting she would ask questions. She had an inquisitive mind, and he feared it would get her into trouble in Charleston if she did not understand the political situation. Any other woman of his acquaintance would have yawned with boredom and insisted he drop the entire subject, asking instead what was in Charleston to amuse her. It was because of her innate curiosity that he feared she might unknowingly, unintentionally say or do something regrettable. He noted how easily she absorbed what he was telling her. Finding masculine satisfaction in explaining what she did not understand, he was flattered by her alert attentiveness, her innocent-looking eyes watching him intently, piercing his as he spoke.

He found that to be disconcerting, making it difficult to concentrate on what he was saying. While his words were about secession, shipping, and slavery, he imagined her violet eyes looking at him longingly as he held her in his arms. The fantasy interfered with his flow of thoughts and words. Dammit, why did he find it difficult to steer the conversation to a more personal level? He had failed to get her to talk about herself. When he tried, he was as awkward as a tongue-tied schoolboy in the throes of his first love.

"Now I understand," she said, breaking through his thoughts. "If they form a nation of their own, there will be no tariffs on imports."

"Precisely." Mark nodded emphatically. "They believe themselves wronged and resistance to be the only action left."

Now that she knew their discussion was not about her, Tamara relaxed. She wanted to kick off her slippers and tuck her feet under her, but she remained sedate. She slipped back in her chair. Tugging her skirt, she pulled it up slightly, unknowingly displaying her pretty ankles and slippers as she crossed her legs. Mark's eyes lingered on the slim ankles before they moved upward, following the contour of her shapely legs outlined against the soft fabric of her gown. He blinked before he looked away, a faraway expression entering his eyes.

"I recall Uncle Arthur discussing the role Great Britain should play if war comes. If I remember correctly, he sympathized with the South, too."

"Not surprising. Most of the ruling class does, and the cotton merchants, who would lose financially. The working class in England supports the policies of the North, since it is opposed to slavery."

Mark drew on his pipe, to discover it was no longer burning. He looked at it contemplatively, gripping the bowl in his hand, debating whether to light it again. He decided to put it on the pipe rack standing on the table beside him.

"South Carolina is part of what is known as the Deep South," he continued. The people you will meet are aristocrats who control the oligarchic government. It's an aristocracy minus the fancy titles. After leaving England, many of their ancestors settled in the West Indies first, just as yours and mine did—Barbados, Jamaica—before coming to Charleston. That is why in the marketplaces and throughout Charleston you will see and hear things which will remind you of Jamaica. My friends are also important customers. Some are merchants, others plantation owners where cotton is grown. They ship it to England."

This information caused Tamara to think about the time she had worked in the Tufnel Texile Mill. Most assuredly the cotton she had handled was brought to England by Mark.

Mark's words drifted through her thoughts. "I am hoping some of my friends will be at their town houses. Most of the year they live on their plantations, worked by hundreds of slaves. If I get a chance before we leave, I will take you to one of the town houses. If I do, remember, all the servants are slaves."

Tamara smiled. "I would like that very much," she said readily. "You have made me curious."

Mark smiled. "I don't know what has occurred recently. Two months have passed since I left. Tension was mounting because of the abolition movement in the North and the election of President Lincoln."

Mark half-rose, reached for the box on the table, flipping

open the lid, digging deep inside to take out a cigar and light it.

"Whatever your views on the subject, I suggest you keep them to yourself, Tamara. Do not become embroiled in their arguments."

Puffing on his cigar, he walked to the table and poured a glass of brandy. "Will you join me?" he asked before putting the stopper back on the bottle.

She shook her head. "No, thank you."

Mark returned to his chair. He tilted his cigar to study the burning tip. "I was in Charleston last December. Spent Christmas with friends. When news arrived of Abraham Lincoln's election, crowds gathered in the streets, stores closed, not to celebrate his victory, but to celebrate the Southern Confederacy. The people of Charleston were certain their state could no longer remain in the United States with Lincoln as president. Most Southerners were confused. Didn't know what to do and simply followed whatever direction their officials took. In South Carolina the leaders did not hesitate. They had supported a Southerner by the name of John Breckinridge, who was a states-rights' man, a secessionist."

"Sounds like an English name," interposed Tamara. "I suppose this Lincoln is an abolitionist."

Mark shook his head. "No. He did not propose interfering with slavery where it already exists, but he insisted it be confined to the states where it is practiced, and not be allowed to spread into the new territories in the west." Mark lifted his arm, flexed his wrist. "Hypothetically, suppose a Southern slaveowner wished to sell his plantation and move beyond the Mississippi River. According to Lincoln, he would not be permitted to take his slaves with him."

"If this Mr. Lincoln had not come along, would the United States have remained intact? Would the South have stayed a part of the nation?"

Mark shook the glass in his hand, swirling the brandy. He held it up and looked at it steadily, as if expecting to find the answer to her question in the amber liquid. "Historical processes are like the elements of a tornado. They combine, fuse, increase in velocity, until no human can control them."

Tamara shifted in her chair. "It all sounds so . . . complicated. Since the South practices slavery, why do you support it? I would think you would not be in favor of slavery."

Mark tilted his head back. A smoke ring from his cigar escaped his mouth and floated ceilingward. "Two reasons," he answered. "It is more than a question of slavery. The South

153

wants independence. You know the second reason. Business. At any rate, South Carolina has seceded. It would have been like trying to control a tornado. Robert Rhett demanded secession. His Charleston newspaper, the *Mercury*, printed big headlines, 'The Revolution of 1860 Has Been Initiated.' Soon after that, I left for England. Of course, my primary concern is the effect it will have on my shipping. Whether other . . . What the hell!"

Mark stood up abruptly and walked to the center of the room, balancing himself with his feet firmly planted on the floor. Puzzled, Tamara watched as he studied the motion of the ship. She had not noticed anything unusual, but apparently he had. He walked to the port window, looked out, then turned brusquely. "Excuse me, Tamara. I'll be right back."

"What is it?"

"I hope I am wrong, but there are indications we are sailing into a squall."

He returned a few minutes later. "It is a squall. They come up suddenly. Usually last no more than fifteen minutes."

Schofield's words were interrupted as the ship pitched forcefully. Tamara grabbed both arms of her chair to prevent herself from being tossed to the floor. Mark flung himself in front of her to protect her.

"We are going down," she cried.

He pulled her to the floor and held her in his arms. "No! We are not going down. I know my ship. It has been tested many times in squalls such as this. All precautions are being taken. It is as seaworthy as any ship afloat."

As raging waves swirled around the *Mark Schofield,* battering the hull from all directions, Mark helped Tamara back to her cabin, ordering her to lie on the bunk and remain there. "At the moment, that is the safest place. Stay there," he ordered before he disappeared.

Gusts of wind roared in fury like a mad giant. The ship plowed through rolling, mountainous swells, dipping down into deep valleys. Rain came in a solid sheet. Huge waves lifted the helpless vessel, hurling it forward, then backward, taking it far off course. Submerging, it heeled deep into the roily sea, then popped up like a cork.

As the *Mark Schofield* was borne aloft by mighty waves and forceful winds, Tamara was tossed back and forth on her bunk, slammed against the wall. She could hear Mark calmly shouting orders. It was frightening to be alone, not knowing what would happen next, but she was determined to remain where she was, trying to force from her mind the inconceivable thought that Mark might drown. "I know he will come for me if it is necessary to abandon ship," she reflected aloud. She remembered seeing lifeboats, in her mind tried to locate them, concentrating on what she would take with her—her mother's jewelry, nothing else. She looked around. The cabin had never seemed so small, pressing her in.

Tamara heard shouting above the baleful moaning of the wind. "Reef off starboard bow!" She squeezed her eyelids tightly closed, waiting for the crash. Millions of thoughts and scenes flashed through her mind. She wanted Mark. If only he were with her. Her thoughts reverted to another time. She was lying on the floor in her home in Jamaica, and the same prayer was in her mind during that crisis. If only Mark would come to her. If they were going down, why could they not be together? If, if, if. Life without him would be no life at all. He had been the one person important to her, always there, in the back of her mind.

A stool slid back and forth across the tilted floor, first this way, then that. The lamp hanging from the middle of the ceiling swayed like a pendulum. There was a thunderous crash as the rolling waves tossed the laden ship against a reef. It listed starboard. On her lopsided bunk Tamara rolled against the wall; then the ship was washed free of the reef and returned to an even keel. Tamara noticed that the obstreperous wind had died down. The storm subsided, having lasted less than fifteen minutes but seeming like a lifetime.

Mark banged on her cabin door and entered, soaked to the skin. Cautiously he sat down on the bed, then lay down beside her, taking her into his arms.

"You are all right?" he asked quietly.

She managed a weak smile and nodded, mollified by the protection of his strong arms.

"I was worried about you, but I could not come to you. It was necessary for me to keep command of the men. We relied on the navigational safeguards the ship provides."

Mark saw Tamara's lower lip tremble. "I was worried about you, too," she said softly. "I was afraid you would be washed overboard."

He made no move other than to comfort her, ease her fears, assure her they were safe, but she became conscious of a change in the tone of his voice as he spoke. She felt his fingers shake. It came as a shock that he desired her. He wanted her sexually, a man desiring a woman. She looked up and saw it in his eyes. Her heart fluttered. The discovery thrilled her like nothing had ever done before.

By habit she had thought of him as a friend, someone to respect, look up to, a pleasant part of her childhood. She was aware of his handsomeness, his masculinity, proud of it as she would be of an older brother. She refused to try to explain his attempt to kiss her the night of the other storm. Storms seemed to arouse him. Insidiously, the awareness crept into her subconsciousness of thrilling sensations when he was near, and a lost feeling when he was not, until that moment when it struck her conscience full force. Hopelessly she knew that her emotions had taken a turn from that of a friend to something more personal and much deeper. She was lying in his arms. Her body stirred in response to his masculinity, something which had never happened before. She wanted him to kiss her passionately on the lips. He did not.

"Will . . . will the ship stay afloat?" she asked falteringly. He planted a reassuring kiss on her brow. "Of course. Do not worry your pretty head. The paddle wheel has been crushed, the propeller and bowsprit lost, but we will be able to reach Charleston without abandoning ship," he went on. "It is equipped with sails for just such an emergency as this. It will take a little longer than I planned, but we will arrive safely."

He held her a moment longer, reluctantly releasing her to return to the main deck, giving orders to unfurl the canvas sails, which ballooned, billowed, and cracked as the breeze found them, plunging the vessel forward.

Tamara remained on the bunk, momentarily bemused, until doubt became her conqueror. The longer she thought about it, the more fervently she was convinced she had been mistaken about Mark desiring her. How absurd of her to think it! It was not her he wanted, but someone else whom he loved and missed.

33

By morning the sea was calm. Tamara did not see Mark or Roderick Moran. She ate her breakfast and lunch alone, assuming they were kept busy with the damaged ship. It was not until late in the day that they appeared in Mark's quarters for the evening meal. Exhaustion showed on their faces.

They greeted Tamara politely, then resumed their conversation.

"Looks as if we will be spending more time in Charleston than I thought," Mark said, looking at Moran.

Moran smiled. "That is fine with me, sir."

Tamara gathered he had a lady friend in Charleston and wondered whether Mark did, too. Shyly she looked at Mark. As if he knew what she was thinking, he turned toward her and smiled. She could feel her face turn pink.

The men spoke briefly of repairs to the ship that would be necessary and of the problem of sudden storms that arose without warning. Tamara picked at her food contemplatively, listening quietly as their conversation reverted to the difficulties in the country they were about to approach, whether a war would be the end result.

As they spoke, Tamara mused that while she was growing up at Lady Bedford's school in England, struggling to overcome her own inner fears, the South struggled with fears of its own, the fear that slavery would be abolished and ruin them completely, that abolitionists would incite the slaves to insurrection, that the South was falling behind the North in wealth and population and was therefore too weak to influence the government to do anything about it.

When her thoughts came back to the present, she heard Mark say that it was during the period following the United States–Mexican War, when the United States gained vast western territories, that the question of slavery was brought out into the open. The South demanded these new lands be open to slavery, the North insisted it be prohibited and confined to the Old South. Southern fear became acute when, a few days before the treaty ending the war was signed, rich deposits of gold were discovered in that part acquired from Mexico known as California. The result was a sudden mass influx of people, mostly Northerners opposed to slavery. The increased population qualified the territory for statehood.

Mark commented that in the Northern states a growing number of people were convinced the institution of slavery was morally wrong and should be limited or abolished. At the same time, Southerners believed more fervently than ever that slavery was vital to their very existence.

"The last time we were here, slavery had become the dominant political issue. Every public question was scrutinized from the point of view of its effects on slavery," added Roderick, "extending railroads, building roads into the west, supporting a national bank, western migration, immigration from other countries. The debates grew more bitter, compromise increasingly difficult, violence more frequent."

Mark turned to catch the cabin boy's attention. "Jimmy, bring us a bottle of red wine," he ordered.

Tamara glanced at the gangly youth, lean and pale of face because his duties kept him from the decks. He had confided in Tamara about his hopes for the future. One day when he was old enough, he would be out there with the rest of the crew. As Jimmy poured the wine, Moran continued: "The American people and sections of the country were divided not only on whether slavery should be abolished, confined, or expanded, but what branch of the government had the power to act upon it. The theory of popular sovereignty was the view that people living in the territory should decide whether they wanted to legalize slavery. Others thought the Supreme Court should decide. And there were those, like Abraham Lincoln, who argued that only the United States Congress, through legislation, had the power to act upon slavery."

Tamara sipped her wine slowly as the men continued their discussion. Back in December, while Mark was enjoying the hospitality of his friend Stephen Walker and his wife, Rosabelle, in Charleston, word reached the city that Lincoln had been elected to the presidency. It triggered the secessionists to action. A convention that had been meeting in Columbia, the capital of South Carolina, fearing an outbreak of smallpox, adjourned and came to Charleston. When the delegates arrived they were greeted by salvos of artillery, bands playing "Dixie," and boisterous, cheering Charlestonians. Mark recalled the headlines in the Charleston newspaper, which called for secession, emphasizing the right of a state to leave the Union. Editorials declared the right of Southern independence, declaring that South Carolina wanted to leave the Union in peace and did not believe withdrawal would lead to war.

Mark looked at Tamara directly. "We were in Charleston when the delegates, lawyers, planters, scholars, doctors, reconvened in St. Andrews Hall on Broad Street. They deliberated in secrecy for two days. Then, on the morning of December 20, word spread throughout Charleston that an ordinance was likely to pass. By noon the streets were packed. People gathered around St. Andrews waiting for an announcement. Of course, I was curious and joined the crowd."

Mark had been a spectator when the ordinance was announced: "The union now subsisting between South Carolina and the other states under the name of the United States of America is hereby dissolved."

"I watched the rejoicing that followed. I found myself caught up in the excitement. People flooded the streets waving Confederate flags and promenading through the streets of Charleston. Boys selling newspapers shouted the headlines."

Mark was a shrewd businessman, and a shrewd businessman finds out all he can about his customers and the political situation in the country in which he is dealing. In this case, it was Southern merchants and planters. It was vital to his interests to understand the political events sweeping the country in which he dealt, indeed, made his fortune. He felt personally involved and pondered each succeeding event in an attempt to determine how it would affect his company. If it meant a curtailment of shipments of cotton, a drop in the importation of British goods, it could mean financial disaster. It was important for him to decipher what complications would result or what advantages he could derive from Southern secession.

Tamara drank a second glass of wine. She forced herself to concentrate on what Mark was saying, but found herself drifting, paying more attention to his masculine voice than to what he was saying. Her heart palpitated as she studied his facial expressions and watched his gestures. Her eyes fell on his lips. She was shaken by the feelings that swept through her. Even her eyelids were affected, growing very heavy.

Mark continued to describe what he saw in Charleston the night of secession. "That same evening, I accompanied Stephen Walker through the streets of Charleston. Bonfires were started throughout the city. There was cheering and dancing in the streets. Rockets burst in the night sky. Cannons boomed, church bells rang. But not everyone was happy. Many were somber. I saw weeping. There were many who disapproved of secession and grieved because their state had left the Union."

"What did the government do . . . the president . . . in Washington?" Tamara asked.

"Conditions were tantamount to perplexed disorder, according to reports reaching Charleston," Mark answered. "Desperate efforts were made for more sectional compromises. Southern congressmen resigned and left the capital. In his last message to Congress before leaving office, President Buchanan denied the right of states to secede, stating that secession is neither more nor less than revolution.

My friend Stephen Walker was madder than hell when he heard that."

Mark did not know that following his departure from Charleston in January 1861, Mississippi, Florida, Alabama, Louisiana, Georgia, and Texas had followed suit and severed connections with the United States. In February delegates from these states had gathered in Montgomery, Alabama, to organize the Confederacy. On February 16, Jefferson Davis of Mississippi, a graduate of the military academy at West Point, an officer in the United States Army, took the oath as the first president of the Confederate States of America. He had done more than any other Southern leader to delay secession, but finally went along with it.

After that, events happened rapidly. On February 28, in a desperate attempt to save the Union, Congress passed by a two-thirds majority a proposed constitutional amendment to legalize slavery forever in the states where it already existed. It was too late. The Confederate States of America had been established. No coaxing would bring them back into the Union.

In March, when Abraham Lincoln took his oath as sixteenth president of the United States in Washington, D.C., seven Southern states had seceded from the Union. Few men, including his own supporters, had confidence in the new president's ability to deal with the most serious crisis since the founding of the nation. He showed kindness toward the seceded states, appealed to patriotism, begged that the Union not be destroyed. The world held its breath, waiting, watching.

Thus it was when Lady Tamara Warde arrived in Charleston on April 4, 1861.

34

"Land ho!" shouted the lookout two days after the squall had crippled the ship. On the morning of April 4, 1861, as the brisk sea air filled the sails and scudded a cobweb of soft white clouds across the livid sky, the *Mark Schofield* nosed its way past the red buoys of the channel toward Charleston harbor.

Mark joined Tamara standing at the railing of the main deck. Gingerly, as the saline breeze fluttered her skirts, she pressed the palm of her hand on top of her bonnet to keep it in place. She turned and smiled. They stared toward land.

"Originally it was named Charles Towne, in honor of Charles II," Mark proffered, puffing leisurely on his pipe. "'Tis a splendid harbor," he remarked proudly. Tamara made no comment as she watched sunbeams ricocheting from the gold ball on the towering spire of Saint Michael's Church. Her excitement at arriving in the United States was building. There was a long, easy lull, moments best enjoyed in silence. Then Mark said "You understand, I shall be required to put the ship in dry dock for the repairs. Might take several weeks, depending on the parts needed." Another lull. "As long as it is in dry dock, I will put my men to scraping the barnacles from the bottom of the hull and giving it a good coat of paint." Another lull. He ignored the wind-tousled hair across his suntanned brow. He pulled his gold watch from his pocket and checked the time. "When I left Charleston, the country was on the verge of civil war. I am anxious to learn the current situation," he mused almost to himself. Nonchalantly his left leg came up as he planted his booted foot on the lower railing. The movement brought him closer to Tamara. His right thigh touched her lightly. She thought he was going to put his arm around her, but instead he leaned his left arm across the top railing and turned to face her. She could feel his gaze upon her.

"We will stay at the Charleston Hotel on Meeting Street. It is the city's most fashionable. I am truly sorry for the delay in getting you to Jamaica. I will find a maid for you."

Tamara broke her silence. "Oh, that will not be necessary. I can manage just fine. The delay is not your fault."

"I am sure you can manage. The point is, I will be at the docks a good deal of the time, and I do not want to worry about you being alone." When she made no further comment, he added, "We'll see."

Looking inland, he commented, "The British held Charleston for two years during the war for American independence."

"I read a little about the city's history on the way over, but I do not recall reading that."

Mark chuckled, looking at her with affection. "I have a sneaking suspicion that once again Charleston is about to be taken by storm by a British subject."

161

Tamara laughed delightedly. "At the moment, all I crave is a fresh drink of cool water and a good hot bath."

"You will have them soon."

The vessel entered the main ship channel, passing Morris Island and Cummings Point on the left, Fort Moultrie on Sullivan's Island to the right. It skirted Fort Sumter, rising from a shoal almost in the middle of the harbor. Straight ahead, over the ship's bow, the church spires of Charleston served as a guide.

"Won't be long now, Tamara. We are three miles from port. I notice the flag of the United States still flies over Fort Sumter," he said.

Charleston was located on a narrow peninsula formed by the Cooper and Ashley rivers, which unite and widen into a capacious harbor. The *Mark Schofield* made a slight turn to the left and entered the harbor. The sun was still in the eastern sky, slanting its rays on the buildings along the wharves when the ship quietly slipped into port.

At the waterfront Mark sent Moran to the customs office and hired an open carriage to take Tamara to the hotel. He wanted to get her settled before making arrangements for the repairs on his ship. They left the Battery as the bells in Saint Michael's Church sonorously chimed twelve o'clock noon.

Tamara felt heady as she looked with awe from one side of the carriage to the other. Charleston basked in tranquillity in the noonday sun, which had turned the sky bright. The tangy odor of blooming chestnut trees hung heavy in the air.

"Oh, how lovely! Oh, how charming!" Tamara kept repeating. "This is the most beautiful city I have ever seen."

Agog, she leaned back against the black leather tufting of the carriage seat. "I like it already," she concluded. "It reminds me of Jamaica."

Mark smiled, the tanned flesh at the corners of his eyes crinkling. "I knew you would think so. Perhaps it is because of the many blacks, but also years ago many settlers came here from the West Indies, particularly from Barbados. Notice that house we are passing, for example, the one with the long balconies running its length. That is for cross-ventilation. It is distinctly West Indian architecture. There are many single houses one room deep and two wide, built perpendicular to the street. The balconies here usually face the south to catch the warm winter sunshine. Probably you were too young when you left Jamaica to remember, but many of the houses there are built that way."

162

"No, I do not remember, but that is very interesting to know."

Mark looked at her closely. "This is the most beautiful time of the year to be here. Maybe the ship's damage was a blessing in disguise.

When he saw how much she was enjoying herself, he instructed the driver not to go directly to the hotel, but to drive around first to give her a glimpse of the city. Charleston was a serene, drowsy place. Tamara noticed the pace was slower than in London. People walked and spoke unhurriedly. For a city on the brink of war, it was deceptively serene. The only visible evidence was the group of uniformed militiamen who drilled and paraded through the streets.

Tamara and Mark passed handsome three- and four-story Georgian mansions, many displaying intricate wrought-iron gates and fences. Tamara noticed blacks working on the well-groomed lawns, pulling weeds and raking the dried petals of magnolia blossoms that blanketed the ground.

The streets were lined with palmettos and oaks draped with long moss. Azaleas, pink, red, white, glowed profusely. The horse obeyed the driver's command, clip-clopping along East Bay Street to Broad, passing the Exchange, turning right on Meeting, coming back on King Street. Tamara viewed the houses gleaming in the sunlight. She marveled at the pale brick walls with fancy gates enclosing sprawling lawns and partially hidden houses with wide piazzas.

"Where do your friends live?" she asked Mark.

"The Walkers? On Legare Street. I'll show you later, when we have more time. You will meet them."

Tamara and Mark ate with gusto in the hotel's spacious dining room, doing ravenous justice to the warm cornbread with creamy fresh butter and honey, the fresh meat and vegetables. For dessert Tamara popped huge plump strawberries into her mouth and ended by devouring a large wedge of freshly baked rhubarb tart.

"You keep that up and you'll be as fat as a pig by the time we leave," Mark chided.

"Staying here is going to add to your expenses, Mark. Please keep a record of mine so that I will know how much I am indebted to you."

Mark's green eyes sparkled. "We could save a great deal by sharing a room," he jested.

Tamara blushed hotly, which caused him to chuckle. She looked around to see whether guests sitting at nearby tables had overheard.

"I should not tease you," he said apologetically.

Tamara grinned fetchingly. "And I should not have taken you seriously, Mark Schofield."

"I promise we shall be most circumspect. Your reputation will not suffer."

Their luggage had arrived, brought to the sitting room that separated their spacious bedrooms. There, Mark told Tamara he was returning to the ship.

"Do not venture to the waterfront. Stay here. That is an order, which I expect you to obey. Rest until I return later this afternoon. I have ordered your bath. It should be here shortly."

35

Mark paced up and down in the sitting room. It was late afternoon. Where the devil was Tamara? He had specifically, emphatically requested she remain in her quarters, and he had expected her to obey. At times she could be a most exasperating woman, and at other times . . . He left the sitting room and walked down the hall, intending to check with the clerk at the lobby desk. Standing at the top of the stairs, he gave a sigh of both relief and exasperation as he watched her climbing toward him. Her vision of gracefulness softened him a bit. How lovely she looked, carrying her bonnet and closed parasol in one hand, daintily lifting her skirt to her ankles with the other. Her yellow gown trailed like a large petal touching the edge of the steps in back of her. She was humming prettily until she looked up and met Mark's eyes, followed by his tirade.

"Where in damnation were you?" was his greeting.

Tamara smiled. "I could not possibly stay penned in a moment longer. I walked to Saint Michael's. I saw the steeple from the harbor and—"

"You could have waited until I returned and could accompany you," he interposed, a note of irritation in his voice. "We are leaving," he added, entering the sitting room.

Tamara followed on his heels. "Where are we going?"

"To the Walkers'. Stephen insisted we stay with them . . . wouldn't hear of our remaining at the hotel."

Tamara glanced at him warily. "I am sure the invitation did not include me. They do not know me. You go, and I will stay here."

Mark looked at her directly. "Don't be an ass. I told Steve about you, and the invitation does include you."

Tamara stamped her foot obstinately. "I am not going to encroach upon those strangers."

Mark narrowed his eyes and glared. "Are you going to make matters difficult? I cannot leave you here at the hotel alone. True, you do not know them. If you did, you would realize they will feel insulted if you insist on staying here."

"Pooh! Insulted, indeed."

"Yes, dammit, insulted," he said firmly. "You will find Mrs. Walker gracious, and Lila will be a good companion for you while I am at the docks."

"Who is Lila?"

"Their daughter. Now, come on."

"How old is she?"

Mark was ostensibly agitated. He was in a hurry and his patience had grown short. "How the devil should I know? Nineteen . . . twenty."

Tamara narrowed her eyes accusingly. "Oh, now I understand. One of your numerous paramours. 'Twill be more convenient for you under her roof."

Mark blinked. "Dammit, no! Now, hurry along, Tamara. They are waiting for us."

When Mark had left to return to the ship, Tamara shampooed her hair and after a bath felt clean and refreshed. She tried to sleep, but found it impossible. The bells in Saint Michael's chimed four o'clock. Mark had not returned. She could not remain in her room one moment longer when there was so much to see. She donned a dainty lemon-yellow afternoon frock with its matching bonnet and ribbons. Carrying her closed lacy parasol like a cane, she stepped onto the second-floor balcony and faced fourteen huge Corinthian columns. Walking to the wrought-iron railing, she looked down on Meeting Street. Suddenly a stiff draft caught beneath the brim of her hat and ripped it from her head. Tamara leaned over the railing to watch it twirl through the air and land on the pavement below.

A well-dressed gentleman about to enter the hotel saw what happened, turned, and ran down the pavement after the bonnet. Succeeding in retrieving it, he brought it back and looked up at Tamara, who was smiling. "I will be right down, sir," she called. She ran down the flight of stairs, through the lobby, and out on to the wide portico, smelling and looking as fresh as the blossoms of Charleston.

With a breathless broad smile the man nodded as he handed Tamara her bonnet. "At your service, ma'am."

"You are very kind, sir. Thank you," she said as she clutched the bonnet in her fingers.

The young man bowed. His lips widened into a smooth smile that spread to his eyes. "Allow me to introduce myself. Oliver Bickley, ma'am. Dr. Oliver Bickley."

"Tamara Warde, sir. Lady Tamara Warde," she countered, smiling. She had not meant it to come out that way. It made them laugh. "You do not look old enough to be a physician," she said lightly.

"Twenty-six, ma'am." There were tones of laughter in his voice, a very pleasant gentleman, Tamara thought.

He was tall and manly, with thick soft brown hair, clear blue eyes, and heavy eyebrows. He was an attractive man, not ruggedly handsome like Mark, but nevertheless good-looking in Tamara's eyes. He wore doe-colored breeches that disappeared into shiny black boots. His waistcoat was the same color as the trousers and nearly reached his knees.

Slyly he took account of Tamara's attributes, his eyes revealing that he liked what he saw. "Do I detect a British accent?" he asked cheerfully, intent on keeping the conversation going.

Tamara grinned. "Yes, sir. I arrived from London this morning."

Tamara knew she should not be talking to a stranger. If Mark knew, he would be furious. She dipped a curtsy by habit and turned to leave.

Oliver Bickley followed alongside. "Are you a guest at the Charleston Hotel?"

"Yes, sir. Our ship, the *Mark Schofield*, was damaged at sea and must go into dry dock for repairs. Its owner is a friend of mine. Do you by chance know him?" Tamara would have felt more at ease if he did.

"No, ma'am. Sorry to say I have not met him. I've only been in Charleston four months. Came down from Baltimore."

Tamara started to walk away again.

Oliver attempted to detain her. "Ah . . . how long will you be here, ma'am?"

"Mark . . . Mr. Schofield estimates several weeks."

Dr. Bickley smiled. "How fortunate for Charleston. Lady

Tamara, I hope I will have the pleasure of seeing you again, but not on a professional basis, of course." He pushed his broad-brimmed panama hat back into place on his head and bowed. "Please excuse me, ma'am. I am here to treat a patient, and as much as I regret leaving you, I must hurry."

Tamara opened her parasol and strolled down the sidewalk on Meeting Street, using the church spires she had seen from the ship as a guide to Saint Michael's Episcopal Church on the southeast corner of Broad and Meeting streets. She gazed in wonderment at its Doric portico, and tilted her head back, raising her eyes to the storied steeple rising skyward. Then she turned left on Meeting Street, coming to Church, stopping to marvel at the fruits and vegetables displayed along what was known as Cabbage Row.

Everywhere she looked the sun-soaked flowers bloomed in colorful profusion. The southern end of the city was a popular area for residences. She paused at a sprawling white three-story house whose black shutters were closed to ward off the afternoon heat. Verandas arched across the front of each level. She craned her neck, glimpsing the house set back, barely visible through the oaks and pines that graced the lawn, sheltering the lower, flowering shrubs, azaleas and rhododendron, brilliant in spills of sunbeams. She admired the aureole of yellow flowers encircling the porch. Never had she seen a more beautiful home or setting. A high wrought-iron fence ran along the public pavement. Shadows of its gate of wrought-iron scrolls and lilies cast deep patterns on the pale-colored gravel lane leading to the house. Tamara thought the scene so beautiful as not to be real.

Saint Michael's bells told her it was five o'clock, and she feared Mark would be annoyed if he returned to the inn to find her gone. Turning to continue on Meeting Street, she spotted a shingle swaying from its hinges on a post: "Dr. Oliver Bickley."

At that moment a man hurried from the house, down the driveway, and through the gate. Dr. Bickley, standing on his porch, saw Tamara and waved. He walked toward her.

"How nice to see you again," he called as he approached her.

Tamara's eyes lit up. "Dr. Bickley. I was just admiring your home."

The doctor smiled. "Thank you, but I regret it does not belong to me. I am leasing it."

"Do you know the name of those lovely yellow flowers in your yard? I see them everywhere."

"I believe they are called Carolina jessamine . . . but your loveliness outshines them by far."

Tamara twirled her parasol. Palm fronds swished in the strong breeze blowing in off the harbor. She had given up on the bonnet and carried it hanging from its ribbons over her arm. Raptly, Dr. Bickley stared at her alabaster complexion, flushed from the sun. Her hair whisked about her shoulders, gold and russet strands competing for brilliance in the sunlight. Her eyes flashed deep violet.

"You are most generous, Dr. Bickley."

"Truthful, Lady Tamara," he corrected, open admiration in his eyes. "My last patient for the day has left. Will you come in and join me in a glass of lemonade?"

"No, thank you. I am afraid Mr. Schofield would not approve. I must return to the inn."

The physician hesitated. "Is your relationship with Mr. Schofield a personal one?"

Tamara looked puzzled.

"Are you affianced to Mr. Schofield?" he clarified.

"No, of course not, but he feels responsible for my welfare, since I am a passenger on his ship."

His eyes filled with pleasant laughter. "Perhaps another time, then. I'd be beholden to you if you would accompany me to the horse races tomorrow."

"I would like to check with Mr. Schofield first. Perhaps he has other plans."

"I will call for you at two."

Before she had a chance to protest, he turned and went back to the house. Tamara went on her way, walking back to the hotel, thinking how much she would enjoy the races. She felt lighthearted, and hummed, until she saw Mark scowling at the top of the stairs.

36

Lila welcomed Tamara as if they had been friends all their lives, which, at first, made Tamara feel guilty, because she had not wished to come to the Walkers'. As soon as Mark introduced Tamara, Lila clasped her by the hand and whisked her inside the spacious home and up the graceful, winding staircase to show her which guest room she would occupy. Lila bounced on the white-ruffled bed, pulling up her skirts, displaying a pair of shapely legs. Her blue eyes twinkled with devilment. A pretty young woman with a delicate frame, she had auburn hair in waves to the middle of her back. Her complexion was creamy and flawless, except for a tint of pink on her cheeks. She was slender-waisted, with a tiny bust. She spoke with a delightful Southern drawl, and her blithe personality was contagious. Tamara, liking Lila immediately, found herself laughing and talking effusively.

Upon her return to the Charleston Hotel after meeting Dr. Bickley, Mark and Tamara had left immediately for the Walker town house, which was located on Legare Street between Tadd and Lamboll. When their carriage drew into the circular gravel driveway, Tamara gaped at the grandeur of the Carolina red-brick Greek Revival mansion, which exemplified Southern opulence. Mr. and Mrs. Walker and their daughter, Lila, came forward, eager to welcome them. They stood in the shade on the Italian marble portico, amid Ionic columns, smiled warmly, kissed and hugged Tamara, displaying open affection, calling her "deah" and "dahlin'." Their sincerity was obvious, and Tamara understood what Mark had tried to tell her. They would have felt insulted had she remained at the hotel.

Rosabelle Walker, a gentle-faced, doe-eyed lady, was completely at ease. Her soft auburn hair framed a relaxed, pleasant face. She spoke softly, unhurriedly. "It is a pleasure to welcome you to Charleston and our home, Lady Tamara. I am Rosabelle, named after one of Sir Walter Scott's heroines. He is the favorite English author among Southerners, you know."

A self-confident man, Stephen Walker was short and round and chuckled jovially. His eyes were a bluish-gray, his silver hair thick and wavy. He held a long smoldering cigar between the fingers of his left hand. With his right he held Tamara's hand and kissed it gallantly.

Now, as Lila sat on the bed, she rattled on. Tamara was fascinated by her slow drawl and expressions she had never heard before.

"You must tell me all about London," Lila insisted. "Are you and Mark lovers?" she asked forthrightly without batting an eye.

"No, of course not. I knew him when I lived in Jamaica. I have lived in London the past eight years. Now he is taking me home."

"Good! Then you and I can be friends, because I intend to seduce him," she said bluntly. "I do declare, I have had my eye on that good-looking rascal for a long, long time, ever since Christmas. He spent the holiday with us, and I spent my time trying to lure him into my bed, but I never succeeded." She sighed heavily and fell back on the bed. "I can imagine what it would be like if that strong, virile man took me in his arms, looked into my eyes with desire, and kissed me passionately." She sighed again and sat up. "I would simply die . . . I just know I would. And in addition to all his charms, Daddy tells me he is very rich. He is absolutely the most handsome man I ever did see!"

Tamara made no comment. She sat on a blue boudoir chair, listening to Lila bubbling with plans.

"Daddy's friend General Pierre Beauregard is coming for dinner tonight—the most dashing man in the entire Southern Confederacy," she said exuberantly. "When he is not brooding," she added. "His hair is so black it is rumored he dyes it. He can charm the pantalets off any lady in Charleston." Lila rambled on. "Daddy will get us tickets for George Christy's minstrel at the Dock Street Theater. And Friday night, we are having our annual ball right here in our own ballroom," she gushed. "You will meet Governor Pickens and his wife." Lila paused to look at Tamara. "Gosh, you are beautiful. Sure you and Mark . . . ?" Before Lila could complete the question, Tamara moved her head slowly from side to side. Lila continued. "You will have every man in Charleston on his knee."

Tamara giggled childishly. "That would certainly be a silly sight."

"Wait until my brother, Steve, sees you. He is at the Citadel, the military academy here in Charleston. He is coming home in time for the ball. Oh, dear, I just had a great idea. Maybe we can coax him into taking us to the races."

Tamara's hand flew up to her mouth. "Races! Good heavens, Lila, I completely forgot!"

"What, dahlin', did you forget?"

"Dr. Bickley is calling for me at two o'clock tomorrow at the Charleston Hotel. He plans to take me to the races."

Lila's eyes lit up. "Dr. Oliver Bickley?" she asked with surprise in her voice.

"Yes. Do you know him?"

"Of course. Why, he is the most divine man in Charleston," she drawled. "Women have suddenly developed all sorts of maladies just to pay a visit to his office. So far, he has paid absolutely no attention to any of them."

Tamara laughed. "What shall I do, Lila?"

"Why, play hard to get, of course. It works every time."

"You mean . . . ignore the appointment? It was not definite that I would go with him."

Lila thought for a moment. "Noooo," she said meditatively. "That would be rude. Write him a note expressing your deepest regrets. Tell him where you are staying. If I know men, he will make every effort to get in touch with you here. I will send the note with a servant."

Tamara hesitated. "I really do not know whether I should. I do not want to appear bold."

"Stuff and nonsense! If you are not interested, I am."

A note was sent to Dr. Oliver Bickley. When the servant returned, he had a reply that the doctor would contact Tamara in the near future.

Shyly, a colored girl wearing a black maid's dress and a little white apron stood at Tamara's bedroom door. " 'Scuse me, missy."

"You may come in," Lila said.

"Yas, missy."

She was petite, with almond-shaped eyes, a pretty girl. She began to unpack Tamara's clothes.

"Tamara, this is Pansy. She will be your maid. Pansy, see that you obey Lady Tamara. You hear me?"

"Yas'm, Miss Lila. Sho will," she drawled.

Lila turned to Tamara. "If you want anything, tell Pansy. Would you like lemonade?"

"No, thank you."

"Mama has a few peculiar ways. She insists on naming all the household slaves after flowers. It gets to be rather confusing. Besides Pansy there are Petunia, Primrose, Iris, Tulip, Magnolia, Daisy, and Violet. The cook is Geranium, and my old mammy is Verbena."

The two young women laughed heartily. Even Pansy failed to keep a straight face.

"And I am named after a tree," Tamara said lightheartedly.

Pansy was a slave. From the stories Tamara had heard, she had visualized all slaves in shackles, with whip marks. Pansy appeared happy. She was free to come and go in the household, looked well-fed.

Lila glanced at the fancy little porcelain clock on the bureau. "Good heavens, we should be dressing for dinner." Lila scooted to the door. "When I am ready, I will stop for you."

Tamara found herself caught up in the excitement. The idea of spending the next few weeks in Charleston filled her with delight. Pansy helped her change into one of her new gowns, an off-shoulder mint-green chiffon evening dress. The shade was becoming. With the assistance of the stays of her French corset, her breasts pushed proudly against its yoke.

Pansy became less shy. "Lawdy, mistress, dat gown sho' pitty."

"Thank you, Pansy. You are very pretty, too."

The compliment confused the slave girl for a moment, then encouraged her to do her best to please the lady. She parted Tamara's hair in the middle and pulled it back softly to form a wave above each brow and a halo of coiled curls on the back of her head. When it was completed, Pansy stood back to admire her work.

"Theah! Ah sweah, yer de mos' go'jus lady ah evah done seen."

When Lila stepped into Tamara's room, she gushed flattering words. "General Beauregard will eat you alive, Tamara."

As the two young women proceeded toward the dining room, Tamara noticed all the high-ceilinged rooms were painted pale blue, giving the home a cool, airy feeling. Before entering the elegant dining room, they gathered in the drawing room. Tamara saw the large harp in one corner and learned that both Mrs. Walker and Lila played. She looked forward to hearing them after dinner.

There was one other guest besides Mark and Tamara, a family friend, the forty-three-year-old Brigadier General P. G. T. Beauregard, resplendent in a new Confederate gray uniform with two rows of shiny brass buttons down his chest and a brass belt with an elaborate wide brass buckle at his waist. His broad shoulders were straight, his masculine, military bearing easy, natural. When Tamara was introduced to him, he bowed politely, gallantly taking her hand and kissing it. He reminded her of a romantic medieval knight.

Lila had seen to it that she was seated next to Mark at the table, which meant that General Beauregard was beside Tamara. It was a delightful evening. As Mark's friend and guest, she was accorded every courtesy. General Beauregard was especially attentive, holding her green damask chair back until she was seated, paying her lovely compliments and asking questions about her life in London.

Mrs. Walker was a gracious hostess. Ostensibly the Walkers

entertained for the sheer enjoyment of it, taking pride in their friendly hospitality. Their pleasure was a contagion to their guests, so there was no lag in the conversation or laughter. Given command of all military operations in Charleston, General Beauregard had received a hero's welcome upon his arrival. The Walkers considered it a great honor to have him as a friend and as a guest in their home.

Tamara savored the perfect dinner, a meal that might have been enjoyed in the noblest castle of England, served by well-trained liveried slave-servants. Tamara particularly enjoyed the she-crab soup, which she had never tasted before. There were also shad roe; oyster pie; paella, a dish of rice with seafood; black-eyed peas; fresh asparagus; baked ham; and spiced pears.

"Steve still at the Citadel?" General Beauregard asked Mr. Walker.

"Yes, sir. He wanted to be here this evening to thank you personally for using your influence in getting him enrolled, but he will not be free to come until tomorrow night."

"I am certain he is getting excellent training. Cadets from the Citadel proved invaluable in helping to train South Carolina troops who fought in the war against Mexico."

"I am thankful for the experience he is getting," interjected Stephen Walker. "He was one of the Citadel cadets on Cummings Point when they opened fire on the *Star of the West*. They prevented the merchant ship from getting supplies to Anderson."

"Yes, yes. So he was with that group?" countered Beauregard. "Very good."

Tamara found the general quite dashing, with dark eyes and complexion, and a thick brown mustache that turned down at the edges of his lips. He turned his attention to her. "How do you like Charleston, Lady Tamara?" he asked in his clear, masculine voice, looking directly into her eyes.

"I adore it," she answered charmingly. "This is my first visit to the United States."

"My dear, this is *not* the United States. That nation is farther north. This is the Southern Confederacy . . . the Confederate States of America."

Embarrassed, remembering Mark's warning, Tamara flushed. The evening had just begun, and already her tongue had gotten her into trouble. She glanced across the table to Mark. Fortunately, he was talking to Lila.

"I . . . I beg . . . beg your pardon," she stammered.

The general's eyes dropped to feast on the rounded flesh

above her immodest neckline. His lips curled upward before his eyes returned to hers. "Perfectly all right, ma'am, a natural mistake. It is something we must all get accustomed to, ma'am." His gaze did not waver.

"Your accent is different from that of the people of Charleston, sir."

He smiled and nodded. "My home, my plantation, Contreras, is in southern Louisiana. I was born in St. Bernard Parish, below New Orleans. The accent is French-Creole. Lost some of it when I went to school in New York, then West Point."

General Beauregard's parents were aristocratic Creoles. They had sent their son to a school in New York operated by two Frenchmen who had served under Napoleon. Beauregard found a hero in Napoleon, after whom he modeled himself. He built a brilliant record at West Point, graduating second in his class in 1838. From there he entered the Engineer Corps, considered the elite branch of the United States Army.

"I suppose everyone asks you, so forgive me. What do your initials represent?"

He smiled brightly. "My name is French, from beginning to end. Pierre Gustave Toutant Beauregard," he said, glowing with pride. "Officially I am known as Peter, but I do not like that. Please, ma'am, call me Pierre."

"I have never met a general before," Tamara said fetchingly.

"Brigadier general," he corrected. "Fought in the war with Mexico."

At the mention of the Mexican War, his eyes turned a darker shade of black. An angry expression crossed his face.

"My superior officers took all the credit for my accomplishments," he said dourly. "General Scott saw to that."

During the Mexican War, Beauregard was a young man with driving ambition, expecting a call to greatness, thinking of himself as a man of destiny. When the war ended, he was an embittered man, believing he had been treated unjustly by his superior officers. He brooded, threatened to leave the army. Disgusted with the low pay and slow rate of promotion, he considered improving his fortunes in the service of William Walker, an adventurer who became dictator of Nicaragua. Stephen Walker, the silver-haired man sitting at the head of the table, was a distant cousin.

Beauregard decided to remain in the United States Army. Perhaps the chance of greatness was yet to come. Briefly, he had served as superintendent of West Point. When his state of Louisiana seceded from the Union, he resigned his commission in the United States Army. He refused a commission as colonel of engineers in the Army of Louisiana, thinking the Louisiana command belonged to him, not to Braxton Bragg. Enlisting as a private in the Orleans Guards, he received a commission and was sent to Charleston to command the Confederate forces.

Mark was aware of the attention the general was paying to Tamara. "General Beauregard," he said from across the table, "our shipping interests would be helped by an independent South. Do you anticipate the North will use force to try to bring the seceded states back into the Union?"

"I doubt whether that Illinois ape named Lincoln has the guts," interposed Walker.

"If he does, the South will never be defeated," Beauregard said confidently, looking at Mark more closely. "We fought for our freedom from you English in seventy-six. We will do it again if necessary. As a political minority we have been continually overlooked."

"But, sir," said Mark, "I have read there are just as many slave states as free. Does that not mean you are equally represented in your Senate? And over the years there have been more Southern presidents than Northern, four out of the first five."

"Not in the House, where tax legislation originates, not in the economic wealth of the country."

Beauregard took a sip of tea. "My spies in Washington inform me that Lincoln is about to make a decision. I am prepared to counter and block any move he makes on the chessboard of war."

Walker looked at the general. "We are now an independent nation. United States forts in our midst are intolerable. The United States flag flying over Fort Sumter in our harbor is an offense to South Carolina and the Confederacy.

"What are you going to do about it?"

The general's face remained expressionless. "Of course, you understand I am not at liberty to disclose my military plans, but we should never have allowed Major Anderson to transfer his men from Fort Moultrie to Fort Sumter back in December. It was an act of aggression. I have sent two demands to him to surrender the fort to the Confederacy. He stubbornly rejected both. Therefore, I have two alternatives in dealing with this enemy. Wait until he runs out of food or order an attack."

"An attack would surely mean war," commented Mark. "Perhaps Lincoln will order an evacuation."

"Never," expounded Beauregard. "He knows it would destroy Northern morale, and secondly, he realizes that would be regarded as giving recognition to the Confederacy, which he has no intention of doing."

"I do not understand why Governor Pickens gave authorization for Anderson to purchase fresh meat in Charleston," said Walker.

"Up until recently, wives and children were at the fort," proffered Rosabelle Walker.

"I assure you selling meat to Anderson is going to be stopped," replied Beauregard firmly. "I think his mail should be cut off, too."

"If war comes, the South will surely suffer from lack of supplies, sir," said Mark, moving his body to one side to make room for the servant to refill his wineglass.

Walker answered his question. "It is true we do not have industries, no gun or ammunition factories. We plan to send all available cotton to England to build up our credit before Lincoln can declare a blockade of our ports. Cotton is the king of the world's economy. Our cotton will finance a war, should it come to that, which I personally doubt."

He noticed the skeptical expression on the general's face.

"Mark, back in February the citizens of Charleston met to consider the proposal of A. M. Weir. I am sure you know him."

Mark nodded. "Yes, I know him. He represents the shipbuilding firm of Laird and Company."

"Correct. The plan is to establish a Charleston–Liverpool Steamship Company."

Beauregard smiled, and referring to the English, said, "When they need each other, old enemies become friends."

"I can guarantee the Schofield Shipping Company will put at least twenty ships at your disposal," Mark said.

Stephen Walker smiled. "Good! We will need your ships, Mark. Your country and mine need each other. Your cotton mills are starving for our raw cotton."

Tamara had a fleeting glimpse of the bales of raw cotton brought to the carding room at Tufnel Mill. Her mind flashed back to the time she had worked at the mill, helping to open those bales, mixing various grades, cleaning the dirt and seed from the fibers. The recollection plunged Tamara deep into thought. Here she was, sitting at Stephen Walker's table, enjoying his hospitality, a man who lived opulently because he raised cotton and sold it at a high profit in England, three thousand miles away where cotton could not be grown. It was needed to run the textile mills, giving work to many people, however dire the working conditions. In turn, those mills wove cloth needed by the Southerners. Mark needed the business of transporting the raw cotton to England and returning with the textiles in order to keep his shipping company going. Up until now Tamara had thought only about the little circle in which she lived. It was like thinking only of the earth and ignoring the existence of the rest of the constellations in the universe. That the whole world was made up of interdependent communities was a new concept to her.

Lila's voice cut into Tamara's musings. "You see, dahlin', how important you are to us," she said with sugary tones in her voice. She had been fluttering her long lashes at Mark all through dinner, her manner an open invitation. The kindled look in her eyes was inescapable.

Mark ignored her, looking at her father instead. "Perhaps I should clarify my stand, sir. Mind you, I will not ship contraband, rifles, or ammunition if a blockade comes. I will take the risks with cotton, medical supplies, necessities. We will sail in convoys."

The dinner concluded, the men drifted toward the drawing room to continue their discussion. Tamara and Lila went outdoors, leisurely walking to the garden. Before they parted, General Beauregard had taken Tamara's hand, kissing each fingertip. "I look forward to holding you in my arms in a waltz at the ball, Lady Tamara," he said in a low voice so that the others could not hear.

The warm night air was fragrant with the scent of flowers in the Walker garden. The two young women sat on a marble bench. Tamara inhaled deeply, enjoying the scent of the blooming pomegranate tree overhead.

Softly Lila said, "If you hear General Beauregard leave, tell me. Mark promised to meet me by the fountains."

Tamara turned toward her friend. "How did you learn to flirt like you do?" she asked curiously.

"Oh, that's easy, dahlin'."

Lila stood up and strutted back and forth in front of Tamara, holding her head high, pushing her shoulders back and her breasts forward, wiggling her hips provocatively.

"When you know a man is watching you, walk like this. When he looks at you, look into his eyes as innocently as you can. Flutter your lashes like so, then lower them shyly." Lila fanned her lashes up and down to demonstrate.

"Like this?" Tamara asked, mimicking her new friend.

Lila giggled gaily. "Oh! Yours are really long! The men will not only be down on one knee, they'll be unbuttoning their breeches as well." She laughed impishly.

Tamara was aghast. "Lila! You must not say such things! I have no wish to be gawked at by men."

Lila sat down beside Tamara. "Hush, silly. You are joking, of course. Otherwise, why did you ask how to flirt?"

The question confused Tamara, and she did not know the answer. Was she beginning to enjoy the attention of men, which had once repelled her? Did she want to flirt?

Lila looked at her doubtfully. "Flirting is the most fun thing there is. With your looks you can get a man to do anything you want, enslave him, torment him, do your will, make a fool of him, if you like. A man turns to mush around a pretty girl. You should be enjoying your beauty."

"I was told beauty comes from within. My insides are full of fears, scars, and ugly fantasies," Tamara answered seriously.

"Why, you ninny!" Lila squirmed on the hard marble bench, waving her fan in front of her face. "Take two women. Both are sweet, kind, loving . . . beautiful inside, in other words. One is lovely to look at. The other has buck teeth and crossed eyes. Which will find greater happiness? Which will have more fun, pleasure, love in life? Which will snare the richest husband? Gracious me. It does not have to be one or the other. Silly you, you've got both, and you cannot tell me differently. You are beautiful inside and out."

Tamara smiled weakly.

"Wait and see," Lila continued confidently. "Watch me at the ball Friday night."

Tamara became intrigued with the idea of flirting. She had not considered her looks an asset, a power to get what she wanted. She had modestly treated them as a curse, insulted rather than complimented when a man desired her, paid attention to her. It never occurred to her that her femininity could be put to use as an instrument of gain. Commencing tomorrow, she would act differently.

The young ladies heard General Beauregard leave. Tamara said good night to Lila and went to her room. From her window, through boughs and leaves, she could see the figures of Mark and Lila close together in the moonlight. She heard a cat meow, the eerie sound of a feline calling its mate. She turned from the window feeling melancholy, longing for something—she knew not what. Why did her heart pain at the sight of the couple in the garden? Was it that she needed someone to look at her the way Mark looked at Lila? Was she longing for tenderness and affection, someone who would speak to her softly as Mark spoke to Lila? Tamara sighed deeply. I bet he never says "dammit" to *her*.

37

In the morning, Tamara was awakened by a mockingbird singing its matinal song in the magnolia tree outside her room. The mellifluous tune muddled in concert with the morning rays of the bright sun filtering through the open window to arouse her from a restless sleep. She went to the window and leaned out, bending her head, trying to get a glimpse of the cheerful bird.

Mark had left early for the waterfront. He spent most of his time at the docks supervising the repairs on his ship. After breakfast, Tamara accompanied Lila and her mother to their dressmaker for last fittings on the ball gowns they would wear Friday night. From the tone of their voices, Tamara concluded the ball was a highlight on Charleston's social calendar. They spoke of little else.

The women returned home in time for lunch and before the heat of the afternoon sun made it uncomfortable. A little after one o'clock, Dr. Oliver Bickley paid a call. After Tamara introduced him to Lila, the three headed for the races, Tamara and Lila sitting in Oliver's open carriage facing him. The weather was mild and humid. The sky was overcast, with a hint of showers. They commenced their ride across town, pulling into the stream of carriage traffic. Oliver asked Tamara whether she had been to the slave market, a site on the agenda of all tourists.

"No, sir. I do not think I would like—"

"Oh, let's stop," interrupted Lila. "We have time," she said enthusiastically. "It's the most fun thing to watch."

A cynical smile crossed the doctor's face. He commanded the driver to take them to the slave market on Chalmers Street, where a crowd had gathered at the arcade to gape at the slaves in leg and wrist irons. Not all the people were prospective buyers, but, like Tamara, Lila, and Oliver, spectators. The bidding on bucks and field hands was in full swing. A tall muscular black, approximately eighteen years old, Tamara's age, was being prepared for the auction block. Prospective buyers examined his teeth to estimate his age and physical condition, his ears for sores. He was forced to run around what looked like a small racetrack to test his wind, his strength, heart, and lungs. One planter, who was particularly interested, lifted the Negro's soiled loincloth and cupped his dark genitals in the palm of his hand. The planter moved his arm up and down as if guessing the weight of a melon. He poked and squeezed the testicles, then moved the skin back on the man's large, limp penis. The rotund slave trader watched, puffing nervously on his cigar, pushing his chest out, proud of his first-rate merchandise.

Lila stood on her tiptoes to watch. Tamara clutched Oliver Bickley's arm, pulling him aside. "You should not have brought us here," she reprimanded firmly.

A cryptic smile plied his lips. "They are not recognized or treated as humans. I wanted to show you what slavery is all about. And besides, your friend Miss Lila insisted. See what a good time she is having."

Tamara flinched. "I did not realize . . . You knew . . . You should have refused to bring us."

For reasons of his own, Tamara recognized the physician's wish for her to see what took place at a slave market. Buying and owning a human being repelled her, but it did not disturb the planters. They could just as well have been purchasing horses or cattle. She realized that, indeed, they were thought of as subhuman.

The planter who had appraised the buck so closely was the high bidder. This was the last male field worker to be sold. The coffled women were led to the bidding block. The first one put up for sale was about fifteen. The puny girl stood naked on the vendue table, her hands clasped tightly in front of her, her head bowed. It was clear she knew no English and had no idea what was going to happen to her. Tamara blinked back tears.

Lila nudged Tamara. "Oh, dahlin', look at that poor creature. Do you see how flat-chested she is!"

Inwardly Tamara cringed. It was the first time she had seen people sold, and it shocked her. She tried to hide the emotions sweeping through her, but they showed on her face. Confusing thoughts flooded her mind. How must that poor girl feel inside? It must have been like this in Jamaica before slavery was outlawed, she thought. Tamara felt relief that the scene she was witnessing would never again take place there. In a sense, the Negros in Jamaica were still slaves. Those who could find work earned very low wages. Many were not nearly so well off as some of the slaves Tamara had seen, but at least they were their own masters.

Tamara was bewildered. She tried not to let her warm sentiments toward her new friends change. She liked Lila and her parents. That they owned slaves, that slavery was an important, accepted part of their way of living, had not bothered her until now, when she saw how they were sold. She had fallen in love with Charleston, but buying and selling human beings was wrong. Mark had warned her that since she was not a Southerner she would not understand. She glanced at Lila. If I had been born here, if I were Lila's sister, I would be the same. Tamara looked around. I would accept all this without question, she thought.

The girl was sold to the same planter who had purchased the young field hand. As she was led away, she looked back longingly at an older woman who could have been her mother.

Tamara twirled her parasol nervously and looked beseechingly at Oliver. "Do you not think we should start for the racetrack?"

The Washington Race Course was outside of town, giving Tamara her first glimpse of the countryside—rolling acres, not as fertile as they had once been. Continuous planting had depleted them of energy. Sprawling plantations immured behind white clapboard fences were barely visible, hidden amid the long gray moss draping the giant oaks, elms, pecan, and sycamore trees. The earthen road on which they traveled curved through graceful green hills speckled with buttercups and daisies. Dust clouds hovered over the road, whipped up by carriages traveling ahead of them, their destination the same, the racetrack.

A dilapidated barn, gray, unpainted, its roof collapsed, gave evidence the land had been occupied a long time. Tamara noticed a mule to which a plow had been attached standing in the middle of the field. The mule swished its tail back and forth, patiently chasing away pesty insects. Close to the plow, kneeling on the ground, a slave struggled to roll a large boulder from the furrow. Eight or ten slaves knelt close to the ground planting tobacco.

Tamara stared at the sweep of the terrain. The land matches the personalities of its people, she thought—gracious,

181

gentle, friendly, lively, exciting . . . beautiful. She made no comment when they passed slaves bent in the cotton fields. The slave market had made her melancholy. Chimerically she imagined herself naked on the vendue table before the eyes of the crowd. Was it any wonder they rebelled? She would think less of them if they did not. The slaves she had seen at the Walkers' and in the cotton fields were better off than some of the people she had seen in her own country, in the cotton mill in London, or the half-starved children in the slums of Whitechapel. The negroes looked strong and healthy in comparison, but their plight was more tragic.

Tamara pushed the dismal thoughts from her mind. This was a beautiful day, to be enjoyed. She must not dwell on conditions over which she had no control.

The racetrack was crowded. She was amused to see so many people strutting in their finery, ignoring the races. It reminded her of the promenades through Hyde Park with Lord Darrington.

Dr. Bickley excused himself briefly, leaving the two young women to enjoy their lemonade while he spoke to a man. Tamara saw the man hand the doctor a paper, which he folded and tucked into the inside pocket of his frock coat.

Tamara enjoyed looking at the beautiful thoroughbreds more than watching the races. One of the frisky mares reminded her of Little Lady, her horse when she was a child. She knew nothing about betting on races, but before each one she and Lila chose a horse, and each tried to cheer it on to victory. Oliver placed bets on several races, but lost.

It was late afternoon when they headed back to Charleston. Dr. Bickley was invited to stay for dinner at the Walkers'. Seated next to Tamara, he was most engaging. She found herself following Lila's instructions, looking directly into Oliver's eyes when he spoke to her, then lowering her long lashes coquettishly. Oliver interpreted the look in her eyes as an invitation and smiled boldly. But it was not Oliver with whom she longed to flirt. It was Mark Schofield. She would not dare put the test to him. His presence filled the room with potent masculinity. More aware of him than of any other person, when she looked at Mark she could hardly breathe.

Unobtrusively, a change was taking place in Tamara. At first the symptoms were too subtle to notice. Inside, the healing power of time was slowly beginning to take effect.

She assimilated easily into life in Charleston. The gaiety of the city was a poultice to her spirit. Unknowingly, Lila served as a cure, a potion, becoming a strong influence, helping to give her confidence in herself. She was Tamara's first woman friend and confidante.

An important part of the change in Tamara was a new determination to rid herself once and for all of the visions that had plagued her. Elusive images of her mother and father appeared less often. She tried to convince herself they were only bad dreams. Sleeping dreamlessly now, the disturbing nightmares became less and less frequent.

There was still another miracle ingredient taking effect, a balm which she was unprepared to identify or acknowledge. The strongest force of all. Love.

"You have not lived in Charleston very long, have you, Dr. Bickley?" Rosabelle Walker asked.

"No, ma'am."

"We will need all the doctors we can get if war comes."

"Yes, ma'am. That is true."

While Mark's attention was occupied by conversation with his host and coy daughter, Lila, beside him, he had not failed to notice what was taking place on the other side of the table. Where in hell had she met Bickley? he wondered silently.

Tamara had been fascinated by the white balustrade on the rooftop of the Walker mansion, called a widow's walk, supposedly the place where a wife could look out to sea, watching for her husband's ship to return after a long voyage. She asked Mrs. Walker for permission to show it to Oliver. While tactfully trying to pretend he did not care, Mark glared angrily. He attempted to keep his rage under control and hidden, but his eyes turned steely. His hands were white-fisted when he saw them leave, Oliver's hand cupping Tamara's elbow familiarly.

Brilliant moonlight touched Tamara and Oliver when they stepped out onto the rooftop encircled by the fancy wooden balustrade Tamara had seen from the street. They stared at the view of Charleston harbor, clearly able to identify streets, docks, and the lay of the land.

"That is Fort Sumter in the middle of the harbor," Oliver said. "The Confederates have practically ringed it in."

"What is that island to the left?" Tamara asked.

"Fort Moultrie."

Alone with Oliver Bickley, Tamara grew a little edgy. The bravery she had enjoyed earlier evaporated, especially when he stepped closer to her.

"I must admit Schofield is a real man. How many ships does he own?" he asked.

"The *Mark Schofield* is his. His father owns in the neighborhood of fifty merchant ships."

"Is he planning to use them to bring goods to the South?"

"He told General Beauregard last night he had twenty available."

"Oh, was Beauregard here last evening?"

"Yes, for dinner."

"Tell me, what does Schofield plan to ship?"

"Mostly cotton to England, bringing back cloth and medical supplies."

They sat down on a marble bench, still able to look at the view between the posts. Oliver took her hand and held it in his. "Is he planning to ship contraband if war breaks out?" he asked cagily.

"No. He was emphatic about that last evening."

"Did Beauregard say what he plans to do about the Union occupation of Fort Sumter? . . . I suppose not."

"He said he was waiting for orders. He has sent the surrender terms, but they have been rejected. He said there was an alternative—wait out the time for hunger to force surrender."

Dismissing the subject of war, sliding a bit closer, Oliver Bickley turned to Tamara. The smoldering look in his eyes belied his nonchalant behavior. He smiled broadly, then his hand came up and grazed the creamy flesh of her shoulder. His eyes strayed to her lips.

"You're beautiful. Your skin feels like magnolia petals," he said quietly. "The Walkers have invited me to the ball Friday night. Will you dance with me?"

"Yes, of course."

"I must confess," he said deeply, "you have been on my mind." He rose, taking her hands, gently pulling her to her feet.

Tamara did not know what to do. She was certain he intended to kiss her. Her flirting had encouraged it. Now she regretted the way she had acted. He placed his hands on her waist and planted a soft kiss on her cheek first. Tamara tried to step back, but his hands tightened.

"It is a perfect night for love," he whispered huskily, his hands wandering upward from her waist. "Could we—?"

"Dr. Bickley," came a familiar deep voice. Mark stood before them, a whimsical expression on his face. "Please oblige me. Release the lady," he demanded coolly.

38

Oliver Bickley took his arms from Tamara. His eyes turned the color of cold steel. He stepped back, awkwardly bumping into the sundial. "Of course. No problem." The two men stood motionless, measuring each other, before Oliver bowed to Tamara, then headed for the stairs.

"A pox on you," snapped Tamara.

"You could have at least invited Lila to accompany you," Mark said acidly.

"I am sure she has seen the widow's walk many times. And besides, I did not want to tear her away from you." Tamara countered sarcastically. He scowled in response.

The silence was unbearable. In the moonlight, Mark's eyes became intense, dropping insolently to her low, square-cut neckline, stripping the ice-blue heavy French satin gown from her body. His eyes traveled up and down before they settled on her mouth. She blushed clear up to the roots of her hair, including the tips of her ears, beside herself with anger. Smiling roguishly, without uttering a word, he put one arm around her. He pulled her closer with a jerk.

"You know nothing about that man," he admonished huskily. "He could be a blackguard. I forbid you to see him again." Mark's other arm went around her, locking her to him. "If it is kissing you crave, let me accommodate you."

Tamara tried to pull away from his grip, but his arms were like ropes of iron binding her to him.

"Let . . . me . . . go!"

"Dammit, hold still! You should be swooning in my arms, not squirming," he bantered playfully, meaning only to teach her a lesson, finding it difficult to admit that the purpose of teasing her was to hide his own deep feelings. Considering jealousy an objectionable trait in any man's character, he refused to acknowledge it in identifying his emotions; but in truth, it was jealousy that had driven him hastily to the rooftop, steaming inside with the knowledge that Tamara was alone with the doctor.

It struck him warningly that Tamara was unlike any woman he had ever known. A serious kiss, a gesture of passion, would mean a commitment he had no intention of giving. He had meant only to kiss her briefly. Finding her lips, he covered them with his, touching them lightly as the mere jest he planned, but once his lips met hers, he was powerless to remove them. He used pressure to open her mouth. Her parted lips had a tumultuous effect. His reserve shattered. His plan backfired. He was totally disarmed. The kiss lingered on and on, turning from lightness to tenderness to deep intensity. As his arms tightened around her in a forceful embrace, he felt the swell of her tantalizing breasts, the softness of her body pressing against his.

Neither Tamara nor Mark anticipated the response that swept through them, striking both of them unexpectedly. No man had ever aroused Tamara before. It was like nothing she had ever felt, a new sensation she did not recognize. A teasing warmth spread through her body. Instead of being frightened, repulsed, she responded, wanted more. Warmth turned into raging heat. She was conscious of the power of the man who held her in his arms, and did not feel threatened; although aware of it, no force on earth could have stopped her. The pressure and heat of his body made her pulse race. A thrill from her lips surged through the rest of her body, generating a throbbing between her legs, bringing a moisture that was never there before. With her soft mouth she clung to his hypnotic lips, pushing against the firmness of his thighs with hers. Tamara swayed, feeling as if she would truly swoon.

Mark's intended ruse scattered like pollen in the spring breezes. In a spurt of passion he went on kissing her, holding her in his arms, until it was necessary to stop to catch his breath, regain his equilibrium. But his burning lips reluctantly left hers only to press possessively against the rapid pulse at her slender throat, before they returned to her honey-sweet mouth. Thrown off guard, he became dizzyingly aware of her curvaceous body crushing against him. His hands slid up to the middle of her back, clasping her tightly, pressing her closer. About to be swept over a thundering waterfall of desire, he saved himself in the nick of time. He released her abruptly. Standing very still, Mark stared in amazement. Before Tamara noticed, he covered the befuddled expression on his face with an invisible mask. He stiffened, threw back his shoulders to conceal the effect the kiss had on him.

Tamara put her hand to her chest to slow her palpitating heart, calm her breathing. Awkwardly she looked at the view of Charleston, turning to face him only after he spoke, noting

186

disappointingly that he had not been moved by the kiss. His eyes flashed icy green. There was a look on his face that she did not understand, an expression that did not match the words that were forthcoming.

"And if you are curious about what it is like to lie in a man's arms and be made love to, I will oblige you with that, too," he said mockingly, but failing to hide the passionate hoarseness in his voice.

His sarcastic words infuriated her, wounded her pride, struck at her dignity. Defiantly she raised her chin into the air, daintily flapping her mother-of-pearl fan back and forth in front of her face. His hand came up to caress her cheek. She ducked, thrusting it away with all her strength.

Her fan moved faster. She glared. "Hush your mouth, silly. I am sure you are quite the expert when it comes to seducing innocent women."

Mark narrowed his eyes. " 'Hush my mouth,' " he mimicked with a drawl. "Christ, Tamara, you sound just like Lila. Stop imitating her, dammit."

Tamara's eyes turned glassy in a hint of tears. "I do not," was her testy riposte.

"Hoodwinker. You do," he accused firmly. "You even wiggle your pretty ass like she does," he chided, reaching back and playfully pinching her derriere.

Tamara's eyes enlarged to the size of saucers. "How dare you!" she gasped. "Of all the gall! You are certainly no gentleman."

With all the strength she could muster, she threw her fan at him. It bounced off his chest and fluttered through the air, over the balustrade. Tamara walked to the railing to watch the beautiful fan drop into the Walkers' yard, but a gust of wind caught it, zooming it through the night skies of Charleston.

"Do not worry. I will find it for you."

"Do not bother," she answered tartly.

Mark shrugged. "Very well."

Tamara looked at him cautiously. "I am sorry. 'Tis a beautiful fan. Would you please?"

"If I cannot find it, I will buy you another." Flashing a discomposing grin, he reached out to cup her face with unexpected tenderness. She slapped his hand away. He frowned. "Tamara, be yourself," he said more quietly. "Your theatrical behavior is phony. Acting the flirt does not become you. I liked you much better the way you were when we arrived in Charleston."

His words surprised her, and it showed on her face. He had noticed.

"You never told me," she answered softly.

"There are some things that should not be necessary for a man to say."

"But . . . but . . . nevertheless, a woman likes . . . to hear them."

The damned vixen was disarming him again, he thought to himself. Aloud he said, "I did not think my views mattered to you. To you I am an instrument for what you want, a return to Jamaica. Last night you had eyes only for the smooth-tongued Beauregard. I should warn you, he has the reputation of being a ladies' man. Tonight, it was that damned Bickley. Do you enjoy having men lust after you?" Tamara cringed, but he continued to lash out at her. "I am sick to death of watching you enjoy men drool over you. You are like a butterfly flittering from one attraction to another," he accused. His words sickened her inside and weakened her spirit.

"Not so. Your opinion of me . . . has always . . . been important. When I was little, I thought of you as a handsome prince who would one day rescue me. You were my hero," she said wistfully.

"Dammit, now don't get sentimental on me. Rescue you from what?"

Tamara frowned. "Why must you always treat me like a child?" she complained crossly.

"That was hardly a kiss I would give to a child." He paused. "And it was not the kiss of a child that was returned," he mused.

Her face burned. Her body and mind were in turmoil. "What kind of friend are you? You toy with me," she accused. Unthinkingly, Tamara fluttered her lashes at him. Roughly he grabbed her by the arm. She felt his fingers digging into her flesh.

"Ouch! You are hurting me."

"Tamara, I warn you! Do not flaunt your charms at me! You play a dangerous game, young lady," he said bitterly. "Did Lila explain the consequences?"

With an iron grip he held on to her arm, jouncing her until her teeth clicked.

"Now! If you think you can behave like a lady, we will return to our host and hostess."

Tamara glared. "What if I do not feel like it?"

He shook her again. "Do not act huffy when we get there,

or I will send you back to the hotel. And no long face, either."

Tamara wrenched herself from his grip. "I am not your sister. Must I remind you again you are speaking to a woman, not a child?"

"Then act like one."

Strains of the harp in the drawing room became louder as he whisked her across the roof to the stairs. By the time they reached the first floor they had calmed down. Tamara walked sedately toward her hostess.

39

Not sleepy, Tamara sat in her room gazing out the window at the stars. A tremor ran through her as she thought of the potency of Mark's lips and the incredible effect of his kiss. Unknowingly she sighed audibly. He had kissed her in jest. It had meant nothing to him. What would it be like if he took her in his arms and kissed her with meaningful passion? She closed her eyes to search for the answer. Her thoughts drifted into a world of romantic fantasy in which Mark was embracing and kissing her. So vivid was it that the sensations returned, crazily churning within her. She was shocked by the feverish longing between her thighs. Bemused, she rested her head on her arm on the windowsill, thinking that daydreams were so much nicer than her terrible nightmares while asleep.

Tamara rose early the following morning, too early, for the house was still quiet at eight o'clock when she left her room. As she stood outside her door, closing it softly behind her, she stared at Pansy, tip-toeing from Mark's room, his clothing draped over her arm, his boots in her hand. "Mornin', ma'am," Pansy whispered.

Tamara thought the maid looked suspicious about something. "Pansy," she greeted in a low voice. "What are you doing with Mr. Schofield's boots?"

"Aw's goin' to shine 'um."

"Is Mr. Schofield still in bed?"

"Yes'm."

They began to descend the stairs. "What are you doing in his room when he is still asleep?" Tamara persisted. "You will waken him." She hesitated on the steps. The girl was guilty about something, she was sure. "I demand to know what is going on."

Pansy looked at Tamara skeptically. "Massa send me to Mistah Schofield las' night . . . to pleasure'm. Aw pleasured'm all night. Mus' obeys mah massah," Pansy said sheepishly. Then she could not help herself and grinned.

They reached the bottom of the stairs. Tamara paused, whispering "What do you mean pleas . . ." She stopped the susurrant question abruptly when realization struck her, gawking at the girl in disbelief. Dumbfounded by Pansy's confession, Tamara opened her mouth in a wide gape. Flabbergasted, first she turned white, then red. The thought was abhorrent. Pansy could be no more than fifteen. Surely Tamara must have misunderstood.

At that moment Mark bounced down the steps whistling "De Camptown Races." He stopped in the middle of the song when he saw Tamara talking to Pansy. As he bid her good morning, she pushed her chin into the air and walked past him, careful not to sway her hips. Mark's right eyebrow shot up into a high arch. He spun around and tried to grab her, but she eluded him.

"Now, what in damnation ails *you* this morning?"

She tried, but it was impossible to hide the shock mixed with hurt. "Nothing," she answered waspishly. "Just keep your filthy hands off me!"

Mark's hands dropped. He shrugged, grinned, then with deliberation reached out to grab her hand. She put it in back of her and took a step away from him. He persisted, taking her arm and pulling her to the stairs.

"What are you doing?" she snapped indignantly.

He bowed stiffly. "Your ladyship, may I presume to suggest you go back to bed and get out on the right side?"

She glared, jerking herself free of his grip.

" 'Tis you who appears to lack sleep," she countered brusquely. "You look awful. You have black circles under your eyes."

A tense moment followed. The luster in his eyes dimmed momentarily, then recovered to flash brightly. He chuckled devilishly, looking at Pansy, who stood fearfully frozen in the spot.

"Pansy, have you been blabbering?"

"No, sah. Et jes' slip out, sah. 'Cos Lady Tamah t'ink aw be stealin' yuah boots," the girl drawled nervously. Fright entered her eyes before she bowed her head, shamefaced.

"Shall I tell your master, Mr. Walker?"

"No, sah," Pansy replied firmly. Having no notion of how he would punish her, the girl feared the worst, a beating with a whip.

Tamara continued to glare, remained silent, turning a deeper red.

"Well, then, don't do it again," he warned, speaking to Pansy as if she were a naughty child. He turned to Tamara and bowed. "Excuse me, Lady Tamara. I am late in getting to the docks."

Stephen Walker III was not what Tamara expected. Surprising to her, he looked very young, like a boy come home from military school for the first time to show off his uniform. His hair was the same dark shade as Lila's, and like her, he favored his mother, full-lipped, high cheekbones, deep-set blue eyes, the same straight nose. Unfortunately, though, he had inherited his father's short stature.

The resemblance to his parents and Lila ended with looks, their personalities being disparate. Lila and her parents were friendly and unassuming, but Steve was stiff and pompous. Tamara took an instant dislike to him. He displayed a highly inflated opinion of himself and walked rigidly with his chest pushed forward. At the dinner table he boasted of his achievements, stating he was better than anyone else in his unit. He snobbishly criticized his superior officers, their treatment of him, and the way they conducted the training of new cadets. In between his bragging, in an attempt to impress Tamara he lorded it over the servants.

Steve's position as the son of the master gave him confidence, as did his ability to command and control a horse, an animal far beyond his own strength. The shortest man at the academy, he had put forth strenuous effort to excel, and had succeeded. His drive to prove himself to his taller peers had triumphed. Not only was he their equal in most things, but their superior in his mastery of horsemanship and sharpshooting. The uniform gave him additional courage. His countenance was an unconscious attempt to hide his feeling of inferiority because he was not as tall as the other men and because he was not as successful with women.

As he dominated the conversation with his boasting, his mother listened proudly, his father swelling with pride, Tamara's mind drifted. She relived the sensations of Mark's kiss. The feel of his strong arms pressing her close persisted in her memory. The thrill of his fingers touching her flesh

191

caressingly stayed with her. A glance at him across the table, and her breath quickened. As hard as she tried she could not veil her feelings. As far as Tamara was concerned Mark was the only person in the room. When their eyes met, she found herself returning his gaze. When he grinned at her with a twinkle in his eyes, hers lit up, and she showed her ill-concealed delight by smiling sweetly.

Disquietingly aware of his presence, covertly she eyed him, thinking he was the most exciting man she had ever known. She felt a sense of loss whenever he left her side. Earlier in the evening there had been moments when she did not see him, but sensing his presence, knew he was watching her. When he was not in the same room, it seemed empty, devoid of life, and thoughts of him tumbled through her mind. She refused to define or analyze these strange new emotions. As if mesmerized, she gave little thought to where they would lead. She wished with all her heart he would find her attractive, but she told herself, dispirited, that he was not interested in innocent women. Deep inside Tamara knew she wanted him to seduce her.

40

Friday, April 12, was greeted with excitement in the Walker household. Preparations and last-minute decorations for the ball began early. Lila and Tamara tried to relax most of the day. In the late afternoon, after Tamara's nap, Pansy shampooed her hair, pinning it up in a pompadour until her bath was completed. The young slave closed the shutters at the bedroom windows and drew the draperies to keep out the heat of the afternoon sun. When Pansy left to press her gown, Tamara stepped into the white porcelain claw-legged tub patterned with purple violets and green leaves.

Tamara leaned back, dipping and splashing her hands in the cologne-scented water. She looked down, inspecting her body as she would a new gown, noting her breasts were larger than Lila's. They were the size and shape that excited the male of the species, brought a glint to their eyes. Idly she wondered why men found breasts so fascinating. What was magical about a woman's bosom that caused their eyes to linger there? Why not a knee or an ear?

Her nipples hardened. She smiled naughtily, sliding her hands down to her belly, and farther, down there. A delightfully wild feeling spread through her. Was that what a man felt? she wondered.

Lying back, she slipped farther down into the cool water. Her legs unfolded. Like deep-sea divers her fingers explored the hidden mysteries of crevices, discovered and probed the cavern beneath the surface of the water. Tiny pearls of perspiration gleamed above her parted lips. Her eyelids grew lustfully heavy, and her breathing quickened. Closing her eyes, she transposed herself into Mark's arms, pretending he was caressing her. Involuntarily, her fingers beneath the sudsy scented water moved faster.

Tamara's eyes shot open when Pansy reentered the room holding the filmy gown with wispy layers of tulle, the creamy color of jasmine. Briskly Tamara sat up in the tub, overcome by a guilty conscience at her unwholesome wantonness. She reviled herself for the immoral act she had committed. Although not a religious person, she prayed silently for salvation and God's forgiveness, begging him for atonement, pleading she would never again allow her fingers to drift.

She stepped from the tub and when dry gargled with strong mint tea to sweeten her breath. She donned her lace-trimmed silk pantalets. Pansy helped her with her strapless corselet before she sat on the white brocade-upholstered bench in front of the dresser mirror to await the arrival of the leading coiffeur of Charleston.

Lila bounded into the room to show Tamara the black velvet dog collar she was going to wear.

"Are you wearing a choker?" she asked Tamara. "It is the latest fashion."

"No. It looks lovely on you. I tried one on, and I looked horrible. Besides, it does not go very well with my gown." She shrugged her shoulders. "Why wear something simply because it is fashionable if it is not becoming?"

The gala affair was an elegant assemblage of Charleston's leading citizens. Outside, there were so many carriages, both sides of the street were lined for blocks. The liveried carriage drivers huddled in groups along the pavement, gossiping about their masters, laughing, joking. One slave, familiar with the long waits for his master, brought his banjo with him.

Inside, the mansion was ablaze with hundreds of candles

193

flickering brightly in the cut-glass tiered chandeliers. A festive spirit permeated the ballroom, which dominated the left wing of the mansion. The motif for the ball was patriotic, with Confederate flags, the Stars and Bars, displayed on the walls. After the Walkers greeted each guest, servants scurried to serve them punch.

Tamara and Mark moved slowly through the short receiving line. They were introduced to Governor Francis Pickens and his wife, Lucy. Lawyer, wealthy slaveholder, advocate of nullification, he was a stout man with a large head and flabby features. His pretty young titian-haired wife smiled politely when introduced to Tamara, a smile that turned coy when she met Mark.

"The governor and I have been looking forward to this evening. We left our plantation, Edgefield, to attend." She complimented Tamara. "Your gown is magnificent. Was it made in Paris?"

Tamara curtsied. "Thank you, ma'am. It was made in London," she answered politely.

"How nice. Mine was made in Russia," she said, dismissing her to greet Mark. He bowed. "A pleasure to meet you, Mrs. Pickens."

Lucy Pickens extended her hand. "Have you ever been to Russia, Mr. Schofield?" she asked effusively.

"No, ma'am."

"Well, then, you remind me of someone I met in St. Petersburg. My husband was minister to Russia under President Buchanan three years ago. I liked Russia, but my husband tired of it."

Tamara and Mark moved away from the line to meet William Simms, considered the most prolific historical novelist of the age. Next to him was Thomas Rhett, captain in the United States Army during the Mexican War, who resigned his commission to be appointed a major general by the governor.

After all the elegantly dressed guests had gone through the receiving line, the band played a medley of tunes including "Dear Land of the South," "Yellow Rose of Texas," and a mixture of popular Irish, English, and American ballads—"Kathleen Mavourneen," "Annie Laurie," and "Home, Sweet Home"—ending with "Dixie." Everyone cheered and clapped.

Soldiers of the local regiment marched into the large ballroom wearing gray uniforms, frock coats, crimson sashes, hats with plumes, virgin sabers flashing at their sides. They performed a routine of precision marching.

Governor Pickens welcomed the richly attired guests, spoke briefly, and encouraged everyone to have a good time. Living up to his reputation of being a brilliant orator, he spoke eloquently, leaving no doubt that he was greatly disappointed in not having been appointed president of the Confederacy, but he went on to state that President Davis had his full support and asked everyone to back the new president. Whistles and cheers went up whenever he used the word "Confederacy," and boos when he mentioned "Yankees" or "Federals."

Mark knew several guests and introduced Tamara to them. She met so many distinguished people she feared she would never remember all of them. They came upon a small circle of people. A man of about sixty was the center of attention. He was tall but slightly built. Tamara was attracted by his distinguished, intellectual air. Behind gold spectacles were friendly blue-gray eyes. When she was introduced to Robert Barnwell Rhett, he bowed politely.

"I have enjoyed my visit and have fallen in love with Charleston, sir. I could easily make my home here," Tamara said.

Pleasure showed on Mr. Rhett's face. "Lady Tamara, buy a copy of my newspaper, the *Mercury*, tomorrow," he suggested charmingly. "There will be an item about your visit to our beautiful city."

Governor and Mrs. Pickens started the dancing. Others soon joined them on the floor. The women's gowns of satin, taffeta, and tulle provided an array of vivid colors, skirts spreading round with the help of stiff crinoline underneath, decorated with satin and French velvet ribbons, sprays of flowers, ruches at the sleeves and hem. Many of the gowns were off-shoulder. Black velvet collars similar to Lila's were worn around the throat, with gold pendants decorating the neckline.

The gentlemen, too, looked distinguished in their finery. In prominence were men in gray uniforms, a small army of officers, the gray of their outfits a subtle background for the brilliant colors worn by the ladies.

Tamara was claimed by one partner after another. She danced with Colonel Benjamin Huger, one of Charleston's most distinguished citizens. She was flattered when the flamboyant General Beauregard, who charmed all the ladies, asked her to dance several quadrilles. He seemed the most honored guest at the ball. Upon his arrival many gathered around eager to shake his hand. Now he held Tamara at a proper distance, looking directly at her with dreamy, sensuous eyes. Smiling bewitchingly, he flashed sparkling white teeth beneath his attractive mustache.

"Lady Tamara, you make a steadfast soldier's heart flutter madly. What a magnificent woman you are, ma'am! I would like very much to . . . get to know you better." Tamara blushed. Before she had a chance to reply, he twirled her across the ballroom floor, laughing good-humoredly at her flushed response, his dark face expressing amusement. At the end of the dance he kissed her hand. "Soon I must return to my headquarters at the Charleston Hotel. In the morning I shall say a prayer for you at Mass."

She danced a Virginia reel with Mr. Walker, a cotillion and several waltzes with Oliver. While she was in his arms he apologized for causing her trouble a few nights earlier.

"'Twas nothing," she murmured as he swung her around.

Oliver looked at her closely. "Schofield is very protective. He is in love with you and insanely jealous of every man who comes near you." He chuckled. "I feel as if I have put my life in danger by asking you to dance."

Tamara smiled constrainedly, shaking her head slowly. "No, you are mistaken," she said softly. "He knew me when I was a little girl and thinks I have not grown up. He feels responsible for me because he agreed to take me back to Jamaica. Love . . . jealousy . . . have nothing to do with it."

"Aaaahh, my dear. No offense, but I doubt the accuracy of what you are saying," he said. "It is jealousy. You should be flattered. Jealousy is a compliment. The way he looks at you . . . take my word for it, the man is in love with you. I had planned to court you myself, but then I saw the expression in his eyes when he looks at you. And you . . . it is in your eyes, too, Lady Tamara. Why is it that neither one of you wants to admit it?"

Tamara's lips curled upward. She shook her head spunkily, swishing the russet-gold coils at the back of her head, tears on the verge of breaking through. "You are imagining it. He has not claimed one dance all evening. Look at him now."

They both glanced in the direction of Mark waltzing with Lila, holding her much too close. He was a striking man; there could be no denying his superb looks. Mark was devilishly handsome, wearing tight-fitting striped trousers, a soft white shirt and neckcloth, and a long black jacket ending just above his knees. His countenance was of natural confidence devoid of conceit.

"Well, then, come to lunch," Oliver said. "I will be out of the city next week, but the following Monday . . . please. You would like to see my house . . . let's see, that would be April 21."

Mindless of Mark's warning, Tamara was flattered by his attention. She agreed to have lunch with him at his home.

41

Joviality filled the atmosphere, but constant reminders of the impending war were in evidence. The air was rife with rumors. When not dancing or eating, guests huddled in small groups and spoke of war, not morosely or in terms of its horrors, but as inevitable to gain Southern independence. Lincoln would not stand by and allow the Union to break up. He would insist their contract on entering it was irrevocable. The president had announced he would hold all federal property, mentioning Fort Sumter in Charleston harbor in particular. Would he adhere to his policy? They were not sure, but felt the time for action was upon them.

It was known that supplies in the fort were almost exhausted. Reports of the president's most recent actions circulated at the ball. Governor Pickens had been notified officially by President Lincoln that he was sending provisions to Major Anderson, the Union officer in charge of the fort. Emphasis had been made that food would be sent, but no additional federal troops or ammunition. Cleverly, the president did this to avoid the charges that he was taking warlike steps against the South. In spite of warnings from members of his cabinet about difficulties in aiding the fort, the president had dispatched food supplies by ship to relieve the Union soldiers. Forewarned of their arrival, the Confederates demanded surrender of the fort. Major Anderson refused.

As rumors drifted from one guest to another that four of Beauregard's officers were presently at Fort Sumter giving Anderson another ultimatum, Oliver Bickley twirled Tamara across the ballroom floor.

"I saw you dancing with General Beauregard. Is he planning to be in Charleston long?"

197

"I have no idea."

"I thought he might have mentioned it in casual conversation. Did he say anything about an attack?"

"What attack?" Tamara asked, trying to avoid his eyes, becoming suspicious of his questions.

"On Fort Sumter."

"No. He said nothing about Fort Sumter."

"Haven't you noticed the increased military personnel in Charleston? The harbor is seething with activity. Take a look around you right now. Look at all the Confederate officers here."

"I have been here in Charleston only a short time, and as a foreigner I have paid no attention to political or military matters. Mr. Schofield warned me to stay out of it," she commented firmly.

"Three of Beauregard's aides visited the fort yesterday afternoon," he persisted. "It is common knowledge that they went back again tonight. Possibly negotiating the terms of surrender," Oliver mused. "But rumors are often inaccurate," he stated wisely.

The truth of the matter was that Beauregard had been waiting for a supply of ammunition from Atlanta. When it arrived, he sent three aides with written demands for surrender. Another ultimatum was on its way to Anderson. It demanded that if the fort was not evacuated in an hour, he would open fire.

Toward the end of the evening a tenor sang a number of Stephen Foster songs. Tamara's eyes searched for Mark and met his eyes across the room. Her heart surged. She did not know how long he had been watching her.

Mark held her eyes compellingly before he looked away. The dancing started again, the orchestra playing "The Blue Danube." Tamara watched him, her heart beating wildly, knowing he was coming to claim her, walking slowly, purposefully, weaving through the dancers until he reached her. He bowed. Without a word he took her hand in his possessively. Feeling her fingers tremble, he tightened his grip. He slipped his other arm around her waist, holding her a correct distance from him. They circled the dance floor. He was an excellent dancer, graceful, confident. He tightened his hold on her fingers and drew her closer than was appropriate, until their bodies touched. His unwavering gaze discomposed Tamara. She missed a step. His arms tightened, lifting her up to him. Before he spoke the words, his eyes told her he thought her beautiful. He wanted her. Her awareness of it filled her with joy. That her looks delighted him, brought that expression to his face, entranced her.

"You are dazzling," he said, looking into her eyes.

Tamara felt suddenly shy. "Thank you, Mark. Thank you for buying this dress for me."

He grinned handsomely, the suntanned skin at his eyes crinkling. "I was not speaking of the gown."

Tamara's blush deepened. Bringing her closer, he twirled her around, their bodies pressed together.

"In certain species of birds the wooing is done by a love dance before they mate." There was a devilish glint in his eyes. "Our rhythms are perfectly matched, are they not?" he whispered.

The boldness of his words, their innuendo, affected her strangely. She knew she should have been outraged, but she wasn't. Said by someone else, they would have sounded crude, but his did not. They were spoken caressingly, thrilling her. She gave a wisp of a smile. Nodding, she brushed her cheek up and down against his.

In the middle of the waltz, he led her to the piazza, down marble steps toward the stately gardens enclosed by a wall of pink brick and flowering shrubs. The night was sultry. Fronds of palmettos moved sluggishly. Fireflies flew and blinked their lights in harmony with the music wafting from the ballroom.

Dreamlike, Mark and Tamara strolled across the shadowed lawn, followed a serpentine brick path through pruned boxwoods to the misty fountains. The air was heavy with the fragrance of boxwood. The night's stillness was broken by a softly strumming banjo in the distance.

What has come over me? she asked herself. Her heart beat erratically. Bathed in patches of moonlight, the crystal beads on her bodice and skirt glistened like the stars in the night sky. Mark stood in back of her with his hand resting lightly on the curve of her waist as they gazed into the glistening spray of the fountains, silent, spellbound, absorbing the beauty of the moment.

"Tamara."

Mesmerized, caught up in the enchantment of the night, she did not move, but stared into the fountains without blinking her eyes, concentrating on the spray, finer than spindrift.

"Tamara," he whispered again. "Turn around. I want you in my arms." At first she thought she had not heard him correctly. He reached up and touched her hair. "You must know I love you." Still she did not move, except her eyelids, which closed. She felt the soft touch of his fingers on her bare upper arms as he spun her around slowly to face him. Turning gracefully, she looked like a doll atop a music box. Her violet eyes opened wonderingly, seeing the inescapable expression on his face. His eyes burning into hers grew lustrous with passion. Consumed by the caress of his gaze, she shuddered. He wanted her. Instantly she was in his arms in a famished embrace. Limply, dizzily, in a haze of desire, she clung to him. Her legs felt weak. The ground spun beneath her. She knew her behavior was unladylike, that she should protest, put her hands against his chest and push him away. If her life had depended on it, she could not have done so.

Time lost meaning. Transfixed, she wished it would stop completely so she could remain in his arms forever. She did not know how long he held her close before he lifted her chin with tremulous fingers. The pounding in her ears blurred the distant sounds of the solitary banjo. Vaguely she was aware of the fireflies which blinked around them, seemingly encouraging her. "Step closer, closer. Kiss. Fall in love," they seemed to say.

Mark held her as if he would never let her go, as if he was afraid she would disappear. "Tamara, what are your feelings for me? Tell me. I demand to know. May I hope that they have developed into more than friendship as mine have for you?"

"I . . . love you," she whispered shyly.

As his grip tightened, she could hardly breathe, but she wanted to be even closer to him. "Mark . . . oh!" His lips rubbed across her cheek and down to her neck. Spontaneously their mouths moved toward each other, her sounds of breathtaking pleasure silenced by his lips. He tasted the sweet nectar of her trembling mouth and was lost. The twinkling stars and fireflies were the only witness to their magical moment of rapture.

Tamara gave herself to the moment, losing herself in the wonders of his embrace. After the long, demanding kiss, she listened as he said, "My love for you is so compelling, I do not know what I would have done if you had said otherwise. My dear love," he whispered softly, his voice trembling. "I find it impossible to delay one moment longer telling you and showing you how I feel about you. I want you! How much I want you!"

Tamara was afraid she was dreaming. All this time she had feared love and happiness were unattainable, and now it was happening. Her eyes leveled to his sensuous mouth, then closed as his lips came down on hers.

His lips left hers to touch the smoothness of her cheek. Consumed by scorching desire, he moaned softly, crushing her so tightly she could barely breathe. Safe in his arms, she forgot her fears. He loved her. She knew this was what she wanted to hear, but never expected she would. All that mattered was that their futures would be together.

"Put your arms around me," he whispered caressingly.

She complied, wrapping her arms around his waist, embracing him with all her strength. A low groan escaped his throat. Their lips came together again. With each kiss her heart beat faster. The fountains began to spin. The music blurred. His lips left hers. She lifted her face to them again, raising herself on the balls of her feet, stretching, searching for his mouth.

"Tamara, I think of you all the time. You occupy my mind constantly. What have you done to me?" he asked quietly, not waiting for an answer, but pressing his lips demandingly against hers. She could feel her heart thumping against his, his insistent lips, strong arms caressing her. She felt warm and secure. Shoving the world into oblivion, they drifted weightlessly, swept with feelings for which there were no words.

"Hold me. Mark, please hold me," she begged. "It feels so good to be in your arms."

His arms tightened. He drew in his breath sharply. "And you feel marvelous in mine. You are sweet . . . soft . . . so unbelievably lovely. I love you, you know that."

A physical magnetism drew them to each other. In a tender moment their lips touched again.

"Most beautiful of goddesses, I humbly worship you as one, but thank God you are flesh, warmth, emotions, feelings." Between each word he kissed her, sending pulsating vibrations through her body.

He went on kissing her as if he could not stop, sweeping her into a world of longing for more than his lips. She pulled her mouth away from his. He followed, capturing it again. She leaned her head back. Their eyes locked.

"Do you really . . . love me?" she asked, a tone of wonder in her voice.

"My love for you is immeasurable," he murmured intimately. "I fought it, but you have succeeded in capturing my heart. My soul is yours. You have become a necessary part of me which I cannot live without." He brushed his lips across her cheek. "I know, now, it happened the night of the ballet in London. Although I did not recognize you, I knew if I never saw you again the vision of you would haunt me the rest of my days. Tell me you love me," he demanded, his voice unsteady. "Please."

"I love you. I love you. I love you," she whispered emotionally.

"I am positive it was meant to be. Long before we realized it ourselves, the gods ordained we fall in love and spend our lives together. I want to make love to you, possess you, claim you for my own for always."

Conscious of his powerful body, his masculinity, Tamara was moved by the passion in his voice.

"Yes," she purred, "I know now I have always loved you."

He brushed a stray curl from her temple, then gently clasped her face between his hands and looked deep into her eyes. When his mouth came down on hers, she felt the hunger in his lips, the sweet wanting.

The tranquillity of the garden was contrary to the passion engulfing them. The bright stars appeared close, matching the sparkle in Tamara's eyes.

Mark released her, taking her hand in his, kissing her palm, then each finger. "We will be leaving Charleston in a few days. The ship is nearly ready. We must make plans."

"But—"

"No buts."

Tears blurred her vision. "I love you with all my heart, but—"

"I said no buts. You don't think once I get you back on the ship alone I'll be able to stay away from you?"

42

Back in her room Tamara thought about Mark, dreamily reminiscing about the events of the evening in detail, hardly believing he loved her. How glorious it was to be in love and to be loved . . . and by Mark. Colors appeared more brilliant, the fragrances of the night air filtering through the window sweeter, the moon brighter.

Tamara prepared for bed, undressing, washing her face and hands. Groggily, while brushing her hair, she envisioned intimate moments of married life with Mark. Vagaries of her imagination flashed before her. Supposing her fears returned? Supposing she froze when he came to her bed demanding his marital rights? Supposing she was frigid? Being kissed in the garden was one thing, but when the moment came for consummation, would she shrink from physical contact until he would be forced to rape her? She loved him too much to condemn him to a frigid wife. Mark was a virile man. If she refused him, he would turn to others. Their marriage would be a mockery, and it would be her fault. There would be disillusionment, a drifting apart, love turned to hate. Even his friendship, which she cherished, would be lost. The marriage could turn into a hell on earth for both of them.

Tamara stopped brushing to confront herself in the mirror. She would not deceive him. When she looked at her situation objectively, there was only one recourse. No, she would not run away this time. She was determined to face the problem head-on. For her own peace of mind, she must confront it.

As she resumed brushing her hair, an idea came to her. She brushed more vigorously. She would go to him now and prove herself a woman, prove to herself she could do what she wanted to do with all her heart, give herself to him. Nothing could ever be of any significance except to belong to him, to have his love as she loved him. If she succeeded, she would marry him. If she failed, if she could not submit willingly, she would not bind him to a marriage contract. A mystical smile crossed her face. Out of gallantry she was certain he would insist they go through with it, but she would simply refuse.

Tamara stood in front of her mirror, nervously checking her appearance, putting a dab of perfume behind each ear. Her apricot-colored nightgown of soft silk clung provocatively. She pulled on the matching robe, a precaution in case someone saw her in the hall. Poking her nose out the door, she looked up and down the dim hallway. Arranging her loose hair around her shoulders, she shoved aside apprehension—for a moment. She heard the clock in Saint Michael's strike three o'clock. She took a deep breath. The house was quiet. The hall was deserted. She walked a few steps toward Mark's door, veering now between continuing or returning to her room. Shrouded by hundreds of established conventions, she was well aware that what she was doing was contrary to a lady's proper behavior and the inescapable rules of morality. Motivated by the growing importance of the only man who could ever make her happy, a desperate need of his love, she placed her hand on the doorknob of his room. Self-justification and sophistries encouraged her. Gingerly she turned the knob.

Tamara was thankful the room was pitch-dark inside. With a do-or-die, totally unromantic attitude, she walked to the bed, where she dropped her robe and nightgown unceremoniously and slipped into bed beside half-asleep Mark, who moved over to make room for her, groggily unsuspecting who the intruder was. He had undressed and lay naked between the sheets. He took her in his arms and held her. He yawned sleepily.

"Pansy, I hope you took a good hot bath before you came here."

Tamara did not reply, but slipped her arms around his waist. She felt his soft breath on her cheek. Bare stomach touched bare stomach. His turgid manhood poked at the junction of her thighs. She closed her eyes, trembling, not from fright, but desire. Never had she experienced the thrilling sensations spiraling through her naked body pressing against his. Relieved, she believed she could give herself to him without the reappearance of bearded phantoms to stop her. Her love for him had replaced fear.

Tamara's hips moved in thrilling surrender. His hand came up and grazed her hair flowing down her back. Instinctively he stiffened. The slave girl's hair was short and woolly. He flung his arms from her and pulled on the sheet.

"Lila, what the hell are you doing here?" he demanded. "Get dressed and on your way. Your father and I are friends. Suppose he catches you!"

Shaking her head, Tamara rolled over and clung to him tightly. Mark hedged, asking himself why he should not enjoy the opportunity presented to him. A man would be a hell of a fool to refuse. He told himself it would be downright unmanly of him.

"You are not a virgin, are you, Lila?" he asked in a low-pitched voice.

Tamara shook her head.

Lila was Lila, but at least she was not chattering incessantly, he thought. Caution abandoned, he drew her closer, kissing her lingeringly.

"Mmmmm, you smell good," Tamara whispered impulsively.

"So do you," he replied huskily. His breathing grew shallow. He kissed her again. "Christ, that was sweet. Are you sure you know what you are doing?" he asked in a fleeting attempt to cajole his conscience.

Tamara nestled in closer and nodded invitingly. Her fingers brushed across his chest. She was amazed how the feel of his downy hair excited her. His hands slipped to her breasts and began to fondle them. His fingers froze, knowing immediately whose body they adorned.

"Jesus!"

He rolled away from her, leaping from the bed, groping for his robe in the dark, tying it with a jerk of the belt.

"For Christ's sake, Tamara, get out of here before I take you over my knee and spank you! What a foolhardy thing to do!"

"No!" Tamara answered curtly, clutching the pillow as if it were strong enough to sustain her. His response when he had thought she was Lila piqued her. Only a short time ago he had said he loved her, and now he was ready to make love to the first woman who crawled into his bed. How could he!

Tamara's incredible behavior in coming to him was so totally unlike what Mark expected of her that he stood motionless, dumbfounded. Bemused into silence by the inconsistency of a woman's behavior, he bent down and picked up her nightgown and robe, shoving them into her hand. "Get going," he ordered, turning his back, waiting to hear her rise from the bed.

Tamara flung the clothes on the floor again. "No," she said defiantly.

"The devil! That does it! You are acting like a cat in heat!"

"If that is true, where else would I go except to a tomcat?" she asked mischievously, putting her finger on her lips to stifle a burst of laughter.

"I did not intend my words to be amusing," he snapped.

Turning, he grabbed her, pulled her from the bed, twisting the robe around her shoulders, awkwardly forcing one arm into one sleeve, then doing the same with the other in an attempt to cover her, very much aware of her tantalizing naked body before him. With her robe secure, he lifted her up in his arms, flung her across his shoulder like a sack of wheat, and headed for the door.

"Mark! Are you crazy! Put me down," she said firmly in a low voice. Tamara's head was upside down, her long hair dangling toward the floor. Her gown slipped, exposing thighs and well-rounded buttocks.

She resorted to name-calling as her fists drummed on the muscles of his back. "Damn you, Mark, put me down."

"Jesus, be still. Someone will hear you!"

"Ninnyhammer, renegade, dolt, cad!"

Mark snickered, amused. "My, my, your vocabulary amazes me. Any more endearments before I open the door?"

Pommeling his back relentlessly did not faze him, but her arms began to ache.

"Clod, rapscallion, cur, brute!" Never had he been called names so charmingly, tough invectives intended to sound like insults, but which came out as caresses.

"Wow!" he chided. "Those were dandies. Where did you learn such language?"

"Lout!" He chuckled heartily. "Nincompoop."

Tamara continued to punch ineffectively up and down his back with her fists. "From you, you pigheaded sailor. They serve the purpose of getting rid of my hostilities against you. Vermin, vile snake, lecher, brute!" She stopped the tirade.

"And?" He shook her up and down, as if by doing so, more words would drop from her mouth.

"I could think of a few more, but I do not wish to shock you." She kicked, her legs flying in all directions. "Damn you, Mark. You treat me like a child," she accused, not for the first time. "Put me down this instant. The blood is rushing to my head."

"Maybe it will wash some sense into you."

Mark chuckled at her predicament. "You hardly resemble the sedate Lady Tamara I saw dancing in the arms of General Beauregard earlier tonight."

She struggled and kicked. He slapped her firm posterior, the cracking sound of his palm on her bare flesh echoing through the room.

"You were perfectly willing when you thought I was Pansy or Lila," she said sulkily. "Brazen lecher. Womanizer. Libertine. How could you kiss Lila when you told me you loved me?" she gasped upside down.

"That is absurd! My need of you cannot be appeased by another woman's kisses."

She hung like a koala bear. "Mark Schofield, you are despicable. How can I talk upside down?"

"You are doing fine."

A wicked urge attacked Tamara. The temptation was too great. Impulsively she slid her hand between his legs and pinched him. It was so unexpected that Mark laughed outright. "You little vixen. I've a good mind to show you what that is really for." He chuckled lightly.

Relenting, he deposited her in a boudoir chair. She looked

up at him warily, hardly able to see him in the dark, not bothering to put her hair back into place.

"You told me you would show me what it is like to . . . to make love," she said tartly.

"You little idiot. You came here out of curiosity?" he asked disbelievingly. "I am to be the victim of a clinical test? That is hardly flattering. And you know perfectly well I did not mean it. Please return to your room. It is late. We will discuss this in the morning."

"No," she snapped loudly.

His voice dropped. "For God's sake, Tamara, keep your voice down. Soon the entire household will know you are here in my room."

He knew it was vital to send her back to her room before his carnal appetite got the better of him. He grasped her wrists, pulling her from her chair, and practically dragged her to the door. He opened it and tried to push her out into the hall, but she stiffened, stubbornly hanging back. She dipped down out of his reach and fell backward into the room.

Mark cursed soundlessly and closed the door again, looking down at Tamara sprawled on the floor at his feet. Suddenly she was crying. "You do not want me." Her outburst bemused him.

This required different tactics. Sitting down on the floor beside her, he leaned over and kissed her on the cheek, chuckling to himself. It was the first time he had ever kissed a woman to persuade her not to let him have his way with her. Turning serious, he positioned himself alongside of her on the floor and took her in his arms. Seconds of silence stretched into minutes before he spoke.

"Darling, I love you. What we have is something quite special . . . almost sacred. More than anything in the world I want our marriage to be a happy one for both of us. As much as I want you, I cannot treat you as I would Pansy or even Lila. The bond between us goes deeper than desires of the flesh."

Tamara sniffled. "You did not even ask me to marry you."

"Lying on the floor is hardly the place I expected to propose to you," he said huskily. "Once upon a time a wide-eyed little girl looked up at me and begged me to take her with me as cabin boy to sail around the world. Do you remember?"

Tamara smiled sweetly. "Yes, I remember. How tiresome it was of me."

"How would you like to come with me as my wife, on our honeymoon?"

Tamara lowered her lashes so that it was necessary for him to lift her chin until their eyes met in the dim light.

"Will you do me the honor of becoming my wife?"

"I would go anywhere with you," she said softly. A pained look crossed her face, mirrored in her eyes. "But—"

"No buts," he interposed, briefly silencing her with his lips on hers.

When he lifted his head, she continued. "You made it clear you had no wish to marry."

He grinned devilishly. "I am no longer averse to the idea. Suddenly the thought of permanence appeals to me. I would like a home on land, a family, and most of all, I want you as my wife to have and to hold forever." He kissed her lightly. "I warn you, though, I will be very demanding. I need you to be all things to me, my passionate love partner, my friend in whom I can confide and trust, mother of my children. I need your affection, your concern for my well-being, as I will be for yours. I need you to talk to and hold in my arms in the night." His lips pressed against her cheek. "Oh, there are bound to be choppy waters, but we will weather them together."

Mark worshiped her. In his eyes Tamara was the embodiment of all that was good and beautiful. His determination not to take her as he had taken numerous others without thought or hesitation was proof of his love, his respect, his protective attitude toward her, which he felt for no other woman. Tamara nuzzled closer, resting her head on his shoulder.

"I want everything to be right with us, Tamara, always. Nothing must supersede our long-range happiness together, and that means wait," he continued. "In my dreams I have made love to you a thousand times. Knowing you are in the adjacent room, I have longed to come to you in the night, hold you in my arms like this, and make you mine, but I have vowed to wait until you are my wife. By coming here you are tempting me beyond reason. Do you know what your kisses do to me?"

She nodded knowingly, stretching to kiss him.

"You are deliberately ignoring my pleas," he said lightly. "I wonder how courageous you will be when the time comes." He waited for her to reply in words, but clutching him, she said nothing. Unaware, furtively, her lovely femininity was ensnaring him. Without realizing what he was doing, he kissed the velvety lobe of her ear. His face nuzzled in the heavy mass of her sweet-scented hair. His fingers searched, charting thrilling routes, pausing to caress her thighs. His lips found the spot in her neck where her pulse thumped wildly. What sweet madness!

His lips returned to hers in a long, fiercely demanding kiss, touching off another wave of emotion over which he had no control. She responded with equal fire, feeling the prelude of womanhood, her first yearning to give herself completely to the man she loved. His desire stampeding, carrying him beyond his control, he slipped the robe from her shoulders, exposing her weighty breasts. Noble intentions evaporated. Somewhere in the back of his mind he meekly condemned himself for what he was about to do.

43

"Not here on the floor, you lecherous ass," said the voice of Mark's conscience, gnawing cruelly, berating him. He argued back and forth with himself. She was bred and strictly reared as a lady of quality. True, she had disregarded, indeed defied convention by coming to him, thrusting upon him the responsibility of treating her as was expected of a gentleman. "She is going to be your wife. You cannot use her as a common harlot. You will regret your conduct in the morning," it said. But a stronger, more influential voice intervened. "How could any man withstand the temptation thrown in front of him? Not he," it said at the same time his hands traveled over her nude curvaceous body, feeling the voluptuous breasts he had longed to caress and kiss. He slid his head down until his tongue found her nipple, encouraged by the groans of pleasure that escaped her lips. His deft fingers and lips sought signposts of approval to continue their journey to paradise. The course was unquestionable, the directions explicit.

It flashed through his mind that she might have known other men. His Tamara, impure! Vagaries flooded his brain. Who had despoiled her? Was it that damned aristocrat in London to whom she had been engaged? Tamara would not surrender willingly. The son of a bitch had raped her, and that was why she had run away. The thought cooled his passion. Battling to constrain himself, gaining control with an effort, he sat up.

Tamara pulled on his arm. "Show me how Pansy pleasures you."

"Whaaat!" he blurted incredulously, arching his brows. "So . . . you came here for a lesson in fornicating, did you?" he asked in a tone of utter disbelief.

She sat up, leaning close.

Calming down a bit, instinctively he put his arm around her, his lips brushing her cheek.

"What is the difference between fornicating and making love?" she asked with incredible frankness.

He pressed her close to his side. "For one, it is not proper for ladies to utter that word."

"Fornicating?" In pronouncing the word her voice went up a pitch. "Poppycock! Come now. Do not pretend to be a prude with me, Sir Mark Schofield. Tell me. What exactly is fornicating?"

Mark's body shook from an internal chuckle. As if he could not help himself, it burst forth into throaty laughter, which he tried to muffle. This had to be the strangest conversation, the most unique experience of his life. "Fornicating is something I am determined not to do with you, my sweet." His voice turned impersonal. "Technically, it is the sex act between an unmarried couple."

They sat close together on the floor, his arm around her intimately. She rested her head on his shoulder. Not a sound came from the rest of the house. Hopefully, all were asleep and no one knew of her presence in his room.

The night breeze pushed its way through the two windows facing the Battery, cooling the room, bringing with it the mixed fragrance of the blossoms nearby. No noises came from the outside. The carriage traffic on Legare Street had stopped for the night. The birds were still asleep, but not for long.

Mark pulled his robe across the front of him to conceal his manhood. His fingers strayed once again to her nipple, pressing it gently between his fingers until it was hard and erect. "I think of it as satisfying one's lust," he continued. "Lovemaking is quite different. It is something much more between two people who love each other. It is a communion of their souls as well as their bodies." He kissed her forehead. "What we have found is so perfect I am afraid of ruining it. Tomorrow we would regret it." He grinned in the dark. "At least, I am sure *you* would."

His fingers traced a circle around her face. "You are pure, untouched, the way a man wants his wife on his wedding night. If you do not go to your room now, you will not be a virgin for your husband on the bridal bed." He cradled her. "In the world of art, the painter strives to achieve his goal as an individual artist. So do the pianist and the poet. Lovemaking is an art in which two people in love cultivate a skill by learning what thrills and pleases the other," he said knowledgeably.

He looked down and frowned as he saw Tamara smile naughtily. "How many women have you fornicated?"

"What!" His frown deepened. "A lady in your position does not ask a question like that."

"In my position? I am on the floor in the arms of the man I love. Tell me. How much do they charge?"

He scratched his head in an effort to untangle his perplexing thoughts, then ran his fingers through his hair. He had credited himself with understanding women.

"For the life of me, I do not understand you. When I tried to kiss you on the ship, you clawed me and accused me of rape, and now . . . now you are greedy." He leaned over and kissed her, pushing her down until she was flat on the floor, pinioning her with his arm and leg, running his fingers through her thick mass of hair. Her hands went up to the nape of his neck, fingers entwining in his thick dark hair, arousing strong sensations of desire, chasing away all his resolutions to wait.

"Hold me tight. Tighter," she whispered.

There was nothing between them except their robes. He wanted to remove that barrier, and told her so. "I want to hold you naked in my arms without these damned robes between us. I want . . . I want . . ." He mumbled incoherent words of passion, lost in the sweetness of her lips, the softness of her yielding body, her enticing fingers.

Mark cursed the rules of propriety as a contradiction to the laws of human nature. A gentleman was expected to put valor first, to refrain from showing his true feelings for the woman he loved and expected to marry. He was not a prude, but dammit, he wanted to do what was right, what was expected of him as a gentleman. He should be allowed a free rein to demonstrate his love, but on the contrary, propriety inhibited him. It was so damned ridiculous pretending to be a gentleman, masking his true desires. He was a man with needs. His prolonged unfulfilled desire increased in intensity. His swollen loins throbbed. Dammit, he wanted to take her, but at the same time he received pleasure in the wanting, which would be spoiled if he made her his at that moment.

He wanted to be the first with her, but it was so much more than that, for which he could find no explanation. How could he take advantage of her innocence? Formulated reason, a sense of morality that mystified him, commanded him in one direction; the pulsating needs of his body, compelling, tempting, pulled him in another. As its victim, he cursed propriety, the established customs of his time and country, the standards by which a man is tested and judged.

Tamara's hand slid to the front of his robe and attempted to open it. She lifted her head from his shoulder and glanced down. "I want to look at it."

"Tamara!" He recovered. "I think not tonight."

"Why?"

"First things first. I want you to enjoy the feel of it before you see it." Mark grinned a little. "The sight of it might scare you."

She sat up. "Is it that big and ugly?" she asked in astonishment.

His attempt to stifle a chuckle dissolved into husky laughter. "Big, but surely not ugly," he said teasingly, grinning at his own intimate private humor. He pulled her down into his arms. "When shall we be married?" he inquired. "Before we leave Charleston, I hope, or would you prefer waiting until we reach Jamaica?"

Tamara put her hands up to his face, which was very close. As much as she loved him, felt secure in his arms, doubts drifted through her mind. She shook her head. "You must make love to me first. Otherwise . . . otherwise, I cannot marry you."

"That has to be the most idiotic statement I have ever heard!"

"You do not understand," she said in a small voice.

"Exactly. I do not understand," he said gruffly. He waited for an explanation, which was forthcoming.

"Before we make a commitment, there is something I must explain," she said quietly.

He pulled her head against his chest. "We need no confessions from our past. Our lives begin tonight," he interposed.

"But you must understand the problem which has plagued me, because it is likely to affect our marriage," she protested.

"What is the problem? Whatever it is, we will work it out together."

Slowly Tamara proceeded to explain her deep-rooted fears, leaving nothing out. Before this, there had been no one in whom she wished to confide. For the first time, she described the scene of her parents' death and how it had haunted her ever since that fateful day. She gushed a confession of her nightmares in detail, expressing her deepest fears of being brutalized, of her vow never to let a man near her, of her determination that she would never submit willingly to the horrors of any man's lust.

Mark held her close, stroked her hair affectionately. "You poor darling. You are not afraid of me, thank God."

"At . . . first I was," she confessed.

His fingers caressed her throat, rubbed her neck. He was the only person to show her sympathy since his mother had embraced her. "And that is what you were dreaming the night you cried out in your sleep on my ship?"

"Yes."

"Why didn't you tell me then? Have you had any since we arrived in Charleston?" he asked with concern in his voice.

"No."

"Now I understand many things, including your motive in coming to me tonight. You fear you cannot consummate our marriage. I am gratified you trusted me, loved me enough to come to me in an effort to break those vows you had once made to yourself. I did not realize you still suffered so deeply. He caressed her gently. "There is no need for you to worry, and you must promise me you will not be concerned. Nothing will interfere with our happiness. I will teach you to forget. I will show you the rapture in our love. There is no fear that our love cannot overcome."

Tamara ran her fingers across his mustache. "It is much better since I am with you."

"The men you described. I think I know them. When I left Jamaica, they were members of the crew. They caused so much trouble, by the time we reached Curaçao the captain paid their wages and ordered them off the ship. They have been looting and attacking cargo ships ever since, particularly Schofield ships. I myself have encountered them."

"I know I must put it all behind me, but it is difficult to do."

"Try to remember the joyous times with your parents. It seems to me you have dwelt on their murders to the point of obsession."

He kissed her cheek. "You kept it all locked inside, didn't you, love?"

Tamara nodded. "I had no one I wished to talk with about it . . . you were not there," she whispered.

Mark was moved by her words and the tone of voice in which they were spoken. "It will be different from now on."

His hold on her was gentle, protective, making her feel deliciously warm and secure. She tilted her face, her mouth reaching for his in a sweetness indescribable, in a kiss that left them both shaken.

"You see how different it is when there is love," he asked softly, tenderly. "Do you not feel it in our kisses?"

"Yes . . . yes I do," she whispered feelingly.

Mark smiled. "I assure you, it is only the beginning, my darling. If you were really frigid, you would not respond to my touch and my kisses the way you do. There is fire in you, Tamara, not ice."

Mark stood up, pulling Tamara to her feet, holding her in his arms. Their bodies trembled with desire. His lips pressed hers, stirring excitement in her loins. Her arms slipped up around his neck, her body tight against his, sending him to a height of desire approaching agony. With an effort, he took his lips from hers.

"If you do not return to your room within the moment, I will not be responsible for what happens," he said hoarsely. "Go before I change my mind."

Obsequiously she left his arms. Before he opened the door for her to leave, he gave her a last kiss, one that was more tender than passionate, a wordless gesture of commitment.

"It is almost four o'clock. Sleep late, my love. We will make our plans tomorrow," he whispered.

44

Tamara felt the strain of the late hour and the excitement the evening had brought. Back in her room, in her lovelorn state, she glanced at objects dazedly. Everything had developed a dreamlike quality, the elegant furnishings, the papered walls, the richly carpeted floor, porcelain figurines and knickknacks. She had not intended that going to Mark's room would be a test of his love, but it had turned out that way. A knot formed in her throat when she thought of his indomitable restraint. It broadened her respect, added new faith, and deepened her love to an intense glow. She resolved that their love was meant to be from the beginning of time.

As much as they wanted each other, that they had not been united in passionate fulfillment made her feel good inside. Their denial brought them closer together. In a strange way, she felt she belonged to him more than if their desires had been satiated. Attempts to bridle the demands of their love, anticipation of what it would be like when released, intensified their need and want of each other.

Once in bed she stretched sensuously, aware of the longings of her body, which had not subsided. The touch of his lips, his words and laughter, persisted long after she left him. Wanting to be close to Mark, she curled her arms around the downy-soft pillow. She could still feel his love, his kisses. A trace of his cologne lingered on her flesh where he had touched her.

At last she would belong to someone who loved her. Their expressions of undying love and her confession had drawn them closer. By telling him her burden, she had made it his.

For eight years her mind had wanted to remember the murder scene and the faces of the murderers, clinging to their images revengefully. Speaking about it openly to Mark resulted in a feeling of relief.

Tamara sighed deeply, staring into the darkness, her luminous eyes wide with wonder. Then she closed them, fashioning dreams of their future, wishing to escape with Mark to Jamaica, where she could lie in the sand in his arms in total abandonment. She trembled thinking of it. Afterward, they would frolic in the waves and race their horses along the shore.

Drifting off to contented sleep, she felt loved and cherished. Her last thoughts were whether she wanted the wedding to take place in Charleston or Jamaica. Romantically, nostalgically, she preferred Jamaica. It was where she had first met Mark. It was there that their friendship had begun. In retrospect, she realized now that a strange bond had existed and been nurtured between them, in spite of the difference in their ages, which had been of greater significance then.

Boom! . . . Boom! . . . Boom! At first, thinking she was dreaming, Tamara sat up with a jerk. Wondering what in the world was going on, she glanced at the banjo-shaped gilded clock on the mantel, noting it was four-thirty. She had been in her first sleep and it took several minutes before she was wide-awake.

Shortly, Lila pounded on her door, bounding into the room before Tamara had a chance to respond.

"Hurry, Tamara. Get dressed. General Beauregard is attacking Sumter. Daddy and Mama have gone up to the widow's walk to watch. Steve has hurried back to the Citadel. Hurry! We do not want to miss the excitement!" Lila prodded as Tamara slipped on her pantalets and dress, brushed back her hair and tied it in a ribbon.

Appearing half-asleep, Mark was waiting for them in the hall. He looked at Tamara. Their eyes held for a moment as excitedly Lila said, above the sound of exploding shells, "Let's go to the Battery."

Lila, Tamara, and Mark followed the curious crowd headed in the direction of the Battery, hurrying along Legare Street. Soon the streets were packed. Lila was separated from Tamara and Mark by the surging throngs. Mark, holding Tamara's arm, propelled her through the streets, steering her across Lamboll to South Battery, then onto East Battery.

"Yoo hoo!" women yelled, vigorously waving Confederate flags from second-story windows, balconies, and rooftops.

"Hip, hip, hurrah!" shouted a young stentorian.

The smell of salt water, fish, and the bay hung heavy in the air. A predawn mist rose from the harbor, lifting like a flimsy net curtain for the spectators to look upon the stage of action, the squat five-sided brick fort under siege in the mouth of the harbor. The audience, the people of Charleston, looked on excitedly, the entire nation an interested, invisible observer. The men with the leading roles were General P. G. T. Beauregard and Major Robert Anderson, the remainder of the cast consisting of nine commissioned officers, sixty-eight noncommissioned officers and privates, eight musicians, and forty-three construction workers.

Orange-red flames glowed, lighting the dark, thick clouds of smoke buffeting into the early-morning sky. A projectile from a ten-inch mortar burst inside the fort. Fire broke out in the magazine. One by one Southern batteries on shore fired, the thunderous noise bouncing across the surface of the water. Heavy cannon fire erupted from Fort Johnson and pounded Fort Sumter with shrapnel-filled shells. Showers of cannonballs rained into the fort like a downpour. Shells arched across the sky in bright orange patterns. The smell of gunpowder floated through the heavy sea air. Booming sounds volleyed across the water toward the shore, vibrations striking the cheering spectators lined along the Battery.

The entire operation was an artillery engagement. Ironically, the officer who led the attack against Major Anderson in the beleaguered fort was General Beauregard, who had studied the uses of artillery under Anderson at West Point. Anderson had taught his pupil well. Beauregard had graduated second in his class.

Mark learned from conversation with a bystander that across the harbor at Fort Johnson, a man by the name of Edmund Ruffin, a secessionist from Virginia, had pulled the lanyard firing the first shot in a symbolic gesture. The shell had arched across the black sky, bursting directly over Fort Sumter. Confederates waiting in the batteries at Cummings Point and Fort Moultrie opened fire.

On the South, Morris Island was the seaward limit of Charleston harbor. The limit on the north was Sullivan's Island near Fort Moultrie. Twenty-seven hundred yards apart, these two points determined the entrance to the capacious harbor. Within minutes a barrage of gunfire and mortars had encircled Sumter, property of the United States government, built on a shoal in the narrows of the harbor. It was designed for two tiers of guns in casements and one in barbette with five-foot-thick walls, thirty-eight feet high, pierced for heavy cannons, many unmounted.

When the attack started, the unfinished installation, constructed to accommodate six hundred fifty men, was being prepared to withstand a siege. Thirty-eight guns were mounted in the first tier of casements and along the parapet. A number of thirty-two- and forty-two-pounders and three howitzers were assembled about the sally port on the gorge, a total of sixty guns mounted in the open terreplein. Since not enough men were available, guns had not been erected in the second tier of casements.

People silently stared toward the little garrison in the harbor, watching the flashes of light from cannon fire, knowing that the attack was a symbol of the beginning of war. The tension of waiting was over.

Mark put his arm around Tamara as she craned her neck above the milling throng. "This means it will be necessary for us to leave Charleston at once," he said.

"Are we in danger?" she asked.

"The war between the North and South has begun," he informed her. "The South is now a nation at war."

"War? Then why are people cheering? In my confusion, I thought this meant an end to the problem."

"Fort Sumter is the death knell of peace and unity in this

217

country." He hesitated a moment before he went on. "Certainly a Northern blockade will be formed around Charleston, making it dangerous for ships to leave."

Promising his ships to bring supplies to the South if war developed had been mere speculation. The events taking place in the harbor made Mark's commitments a reality, but he did not tell Tamara, for fear she would begin to worry.

"My goodness! I cannot believe that only a few hours ago I was waltzing with General Beauregard," Tamara exclaimed.

"Beauregard is provisional commander of Southern forces. His brief appearance at the ball must have been an intentional cover-up, a tactical distraction. There are Northern spies in the area."

"How could he possibly remain calm when he knew what was about to happen?" Tamara marveled. "He gave no hint at all of the impending crisis."

" 'Twas his duty as an officer. He is a professional soldier with a high sense of duty. Highly regarded, and rightly so."

Mark looked around. "I wonder what happened to Lila. I hope she is all right."

"I am sure she is. She probably met some friends."

"You look exhausted, darling. I think I should take you back to the house," he said possessively. "Neither of us has had any sleep, and it is after seven o'clock in the morning. The siege could go on for hours."

"There has been no firing from Fort Sumter," Tamara commented. Barely had she spoken the words when the cannons on Fort Sumter began firing at Cummings Point. The Union cannons opened fire, aiming at three targets—nearby Sullivan's Island, Morris Island batteries, and those on James Island. Failing in their objective, the Yankees turned their fire on Fort Moultrie, but sandbags and cotton bales gave protection.

Tamara and Mark watched a little while longer before they headed back toward the house, pushing in a direction opposite the crowd. Tamara clasped Mark's fingers tightly to hold on as he led her through straggling roisterers.

"Oh, there is Roderick . . . Mr. Moran," Tamara exclaimed, trying to catch his attention. Clinging to his arm was a raven-haired Southern beauty, a buxom woman with too much rouge on her cheeks.

Tamara had not seen the first officer since their arrival in Charleston. He nodded, smiling coolly, and proceeded on his way. Tamara looked askance at Mark, who guffawed.

"Poor fellow. Lost his heart to you on the crossing. He has

orders to stay clear. It didn't take him long to find it again, though. It never does," he mused lightly.

"Who is the woman?"

"Someone he . . . stays with when in Charleston."

45

The city of Charleston was in an uproar. Business was at a standstill. The bombardment continued throughout Saturday, April 12, and into the night. That evening there were no guests for dinner at the Walkers' except Mark and Tamara. Sitting around the oval dining-room table, they heard the windowpanes rattle from concussions caused by the booming of cannons. It had begun to rain. A strong wind whipped in from the harbor across the city.

"Can't see how Anderson can hold out much longer," commented Stephen somberly.

"Dear, have you heard anything about casualties?" Mrs. Walter asked.

"No, ma'am. As far as I know, there haven't been any on our side. Don't know 'bout inside the fort. I was told that about one-thirty this afternoon the Union flag was shot down, but it was raised again. Last I heard, Colonel Wigfall went over in a small boat to ascertain whether Major Anderson would surrender."

Unknown to Stephen Walker, at that moment, seven-thirty, General Beauregard's chief-of-staff returned from talking to Anderson with a report that he agreed to the Confederate officer's terms of surrender: evacuation, taking all arms plus private and company property, safe transportation to a Northern port, and permission to salute the flag as it was lowered.

Tamara and Mark did not mention their plans to wed. Uppermost in Mark's mind was leaving Charleston safely and as quickly as possible. He was concerned about a Union blockade and spoke at length about it to Walker.

"All Schofield ships are British-registered. According to international law, a belligerent is required to give notice to neutral powers before it establishes a blockade. Thereafter, any neutral vessel attempting to enter or leave can be treated as an enemy and may be destroyed or captured and condemned as an ordinary prize of war," Mark said, hesitating before he continued. "With a valuable cargo, I would be willing to risk it, but not with Lady Tamara aboard."

Stephen nodded. "That's understandable," he replied.

"I am anxious to see whether my government will recognize the Southern Confederacy. That will make it easier for me," commented Mark.

"I have heard through the grapevine that Lord Russell and Gladstone are in favor of recognition," said Stephen, motioning to a servant for the silver tray of sliced baked ham.

"It is a little early to be sure. England's government moves slowly," Mark added.

"I think you will be safe if you leave within the next few days. Lincoln will be required to announce the blockade and then establish it effectively," said Walker.

"You are right, Stephen," Mark continued. "A mere declaration that a port is closed is not enough. It will require an adequate naval force to carry it out. Until then, it will be a blockade on paper. My vessel will be slipped from drydock Monday morning. We'll take her for a test run. If she proves herself capable, we'll leave within the week. Your cotton will be loaded. I'll take it as far as Nassau. Have it transferred to one of our other ships for England." Mark hesitated, trying to think of a possible alternative.

"Either that or I could turn command of the ship over to my first officer, Roderick Moran. In Nassau, Lady Tamara and I could lease a small craft to get us to Jamaica," he mused. "I won't make a decision until we reach Nassau."

Tamara had been very quiet listening to the men. She looked at Rosabelle Walker. "I have certainly enjoyed our stay with you," she said sincerely. "I wish there was some way of showing you my gratitude. It has been simply marvelous, and I shall always have a warm place in my heart for you and Charleston."

Rosabelle Walker smiled. "Delighted to have you, my dear. You are always welcome."

"Yes," added Lila. It has been wonderful having you with us. Let's correspond."

"Oh, yes, let's," Tamara replied enthusiastically. "I will hate to leave you, Lila. Maybe you could visit us in Jamaica."

"Us?" repeated Lila mockingly.

Tamara blushed. Mark laughed good-humoredly and came

to her rescue. "I have asked Lady Tamara to be my wife," he announced.

Instantly the somberness of the evening turned to celebration, congratulations, hugging and kissing and toasting.

"So you see, Charleston will always be very special," Tamara managed to say between the well-wishing.

Feeling the toll of not enough sleep the night before, the household retired early. At her bedroom door, in eloquent silence, Mark took Tamara in his arms, burning with love, ravenous for her kisses, finding it difficult to say good night and part.

"How dearly I love you," he whispered, raining kisses on her face and hair.

"I love you," she answered between caresses.

"I love you so much," he murmured, awakened to the realization that their love was not a sudden gust of passion. He had loved her as a brother would love a little sister, feeling wise and protective, a feeling that became stronger, developing into the love of a man for a woman he liked and admired, respected and thought very beautiful. Possessing charm and intellect, she was the woman whose company he sought and enjoyed above all others.

"Soon we will not part at your door," he said huskily. "You shall be in my arms throughout the nights."

"It is what I wish for with all my heart."

"If you do not object, under present circumstances I believe we should wait until we reach Jamaica to marry. Many matters occupy my mind. I will be glad when we are out of here. I want to be completely free of concerns when I make you mine."

"It sounds marvelous, darling. We will be wed in Jamaica."

He held her at arm's length. "In the meantime, keep your door locked," he teased. "I might weaken." He kissed her long, averse to leaving her. "Get a good night's sleep, my darling love. Tomorrow the shops are closed, and Monday I will be busy, but Tuesday, would you like to go shopping to buy the Walkers and Lila a present?"

"That would be wonderful."

Mark smiled impishly. "And how about an engagement ring?"

She slipped her arms around his neck and kissed him.

"See you in the morning," he whispered.

Sunday, after lunch, Mark and Tamara strolled to the Battery. The thunderous noises of the battle had stopped. People

221

crowded the streets. Searching for vantage points, they climbed out on roofs and stood on balconies. Tamara and Mark watched wherrymen steering their brightly decorated boats back and forth, carrying curious sightseers out to the island.

"Would you like to go out on the boat?" Mark asked Tamara.

She shook her head. "Not really, unless you do."

At two-thirty Tamara and Mark watched in solemn silence as Major Anderson started a one-hundred-gun salute in honor of his flag before it was lowered to formalize the surrender of the fort, which had been named in honor of the Revolutionary War hero General Thomas Sumter. Although Tamara was not an American, she was very moved. A lump formed in her throat and she found it difficult to swallow. Silently she counted the shots: one . . . two . . . three . . . At fifty they stopped abruptly. A charge of powder exploded, killing the gunner, Private Daniel Hough—ironically, the only life lost in the long bombardment.

Hence the flag salute stopped at fifty and the exodus from the fort began. The crowd was silent. People had arrived by train, horseback, and carriage from across the South. Tamara shivered. Chills ran up and down her back and arms.

Anderson did not glance back, but stared straight ahead. A South Carolina vessel, the *Isabel*, transported him and his men to the United States ship *Baltic*, waiting outside the harbor to take the passengers north to New York. General Beauregard was not present for the departure. He did not wish to see his friend Major Robert Anderson in defeat and wanted to spare him as much humiliation as possible.

The control of Charleston harbor was in the hands of the Confederacy. Church bells pealed throughout the city. Brass bands played "Dixie." Volunteers rushed to join their companies. Soon flanks of men wearing Confederate grays paraded through the streets.

"Gray columns of war," Mark mused.

The marchers were a mixture of boys, experienced veterans of the Mexican War, scholarly men of good breeding, raw recruits with little or no training. As Tamara watched the pathetically ill-trained troops, she recalled the snap precision of the crack guards at Buckingham Palace and the Parade of Troops.

"Atten-shun! Fo'wahd mahch! One-two-three. *De*tail . . . halt!" Mass confusion followed. There was a shuffling of sabers. Soldiers bumped into each other. Finally the men stood at attention in a crooked column. Mark shook his head. "They've a long way to go," he remarked.

Tamara felt disheartened. She knew nothing of the North. Her sympathies lay with the South, whose people had become very dear to her.

News of the events at Fort Sumter spread out across the continent, moving northward and westward with great rapidity. Monday, April 15, President Lincoln called on the states for seventy-five thousand militia. Southern officers in the Union Army hurried to their home states.

Mark came home early from the docks that Monday, going to Tamara in the garden. When she saw him approaching, she ran to him, looking fresh and lovely in a light blue voile gown. Mark took her hand. "You are incredibly lovely. I want to gobble you up." They sat down on a marble bench in the shade.

"I am beginning to look forward to getting back on the ship. We are never alone," he complained. "Will you come with me now for a carriage ride?"

"Have you not noticed the way the men treat their ladies here in Charleston . . . with utmost courtesy and gentility. Tsk! Tsk! A southern gentleman would never suggest being alone with a lady," she retorted teasingly.

"The devil he wouldn't!" he said, smiling brightly. "That is, if the lady looked like you. I can vouch for it. He would get her alone by hook or by crook."

They laughed together, before Mark's expression turned serious. "Then you do not find the suggestion attractive?"

"Marvelously so," she answered quickly, "but it would be impolite not to invite Lila."

"The devil with Lila. I want to be alone with you."

"Mrs. Walker will think it unladylike of me."

"Rosabelle will understand. Come along."

They left for a drive in the Walkers' small, one-seated, elegant carriage, which seemed to have been built for courting. Sitting close, Mark squeezed her hand. As soon as they were out of the city, he put his arm around her. Dreamlike, she snuggled up close to him, resting her head on his shoulder, paying no attention to the scenery. In the country they came to a picturesque stone-arched bridge, where Mark tethered the horse. Arm-in-arm, the lovers stood on the bridge gazing at the rippling water. They turned toward each other at the same moment, reaching, embracing, kissing, passionately murmuring words of love.

"I have something for you. I hope it fits," he said quietly, placing a dainty ring on the third finger of her left hand, a pear-shaped diamond sparkling in the center of a plain gold band.

Tamara's eyes welled with tears. " 'Tis too beautiful for words," she said softly, slipping her arms around his neck to thank him. He pulled her hard to his lips.

Back in Charleston they went to an art gallery, where they purchased a painting by Adrian Persac that Lila had admired when she and Tamara visited the gallery. Mark and Tamara presented it to the Walkers before dinner that night.

The women admired Tamara's ring, and there were toasts with champagne. At the table the men reverted to talk of war. "The aim of the Confederacy will be to fight for its independence," said Stephen.

"And I suppose the North will try to keep the Union together," added Mark.

"I have received word that my cousin Leroy Walker of Alabama has been named first Secretary of War for the Confederacy. Knowing him, I am afraid the job is over his head."

"Both sides have a great deal to learn," Mark commented.

Wednesday, April 17, Virginia seceded from the Union. Robert E. Lee, who rejected Lincoln's offer of field command of the Union armies, went home to become commander-in-chief of the Confederate forces of Virginia, stating, "I cannot raise my hand against my birthplace, my home, my children."

Throughout the South, volunteers flocked to answer President Davis' call for an army of one hundred thousand. April 19, the Confederates took the federal arsenal at Harpers Ferry and the United States Navy Yard at Norfolk, and on this day, President Lincoln announced a blockade of Southern harbors, making Mark more anxious about leaving.

He was spending most of his time at the dock, preparing his ship for sailing. Problems had to be ironed out before he could put the vessel to sea. The crew had taken it out twice and had run into difficulties, reporting it was unseaworthy.

Monday, April 22, Rosabelle Walker and Lila went to the Citadel Baptist Church facing Marion Square on Calhoun Street to attend a meeting of the concerned women of Charleston. The purpose of the gathering was to determine what role the women would play in the war effort and to organize committees.

Tamara, alone at the house on Legare Street, walked through the garden. The sun was bright, making the sky a brilliant blue. The air was clear, but there was increased humidity. Tamara knew in a short time it would turn uncomfortably hot. She meandered to the front yard, went up the steps, and stood on the portico gazing out on the busy street, thinking she would hate to leave. If the test run of the *Mark Schofield* proved satisfactory, Mark told her they would depart Tuesday morning with the tide. She watched unconcernedly as a carriage pulled to the curb. A liveried Negro walked toward her.

"Docta Olivah Bickley's carriage, mu'um."

"Good heavens! With all that is going on, I completely forgot I was to have lunch with him today."

Tamara was about to write a note sending her regrets, but felt impelled to keep the appointment. She remembered she would be leaving, and wanted to say good-bye to him. Twisting the engagement ring on her finger, she smiled. She wanted to tell Dr. Bickley his diagnosis had been correct after all. She and Mark were in love.

"I will be ready in a few minutes," she told the servant.

Having no time to think, she raced to her room, changed dresses, grabbed a bonnet, and off she went to Dr. Bickley's residence.

46

The wrought-iron gates swung wide and the carriage entered the private driveway of Dr. Oliver Bickley, coming to a stop beneath the large oak at the side of the house, a cool, shady spot. Oliver was there to help Tamara down. He did not take her inside, but led her around the back to a small piazza overlooking the garden, where a table had been set for two. White-blooming clematis covered both ends, making the piazza quite private.

Oliver kissed her hand, then seated her at the table, telling her that he would show her the house after they dined. He sat opposite her, waiting while a servant fluffed a white linen napkin and placed it across Tamara's lap.

"Charleston has turned into one immense lunatic asylum, has it not?" he said.

"Yes. A great deal has happened since I saw you at the ball."

He smiled warmly across the table. Their eyes met. "That's for sure." He seemed to be groping, finding words difficult.

Tamara made an effort to ease the tension. "You were right, Oliver. Mark and I love each other," she blurted, holding up her hand to display the ring. "We are engaged and will be married when we reach Jamaica."

The silence was so great Tamara could hear the droning of bees gathering nectar in the clematis. She saw the muscles in his cheeks twitch. For a moment he said nothing; then: "Under different circumstances I . . ." He stopped, straightened his shoulders, and cleared his throat. "I envy him and wish you every happiness," he said forcefully.

"Thank you, Oliver," she answered softly. "We are leaving tomorrow."

"Then Schofield's ship is ready to sail?"

"Yes. In a way, I hate to leave."

"Is he sailing empty?"

"No. He is taking a shipment of Mr. Walker's cotton, which will be transferred to another ship in Nassau."

Oliver lifted his wineglass. "Then my intuition was correct. It told me this would be a farewell." He cleared his throat. "So . . . a toast is certainly in order." He raised the small crystal glass of white wine toward Tamara. "To the most beautiful woman I have ever known. Under different circumstances, I would have tried to capture your heart."

Tamara blushed and turned the ring back and forth on her finger beneath the tablecloth. "I have enjoyed meeting you. If you ever come to Jamaica, I hope you will call on us."

He smiled ruefully. "I doubt whether your husband would approve of that. He is most certainly aware of my feelings for you. What did he say when you told him you were coming here today?"

She could not tell Oliver she had forgotten the luncheon date and said simply, "I forgot to tell him."

"Then he has no idea of your whereabouts?"

"No. I will tell him when I return to the Walkers'."

Oliver looked at Tamara with a serious expression in his eyes. "If I were he, I would be furiously jealous. I do not wish to cause trouble for you. Perhaps we should begin to eat. I will return you to the Walkers' as quickly as possible."

He signaled to the liveried servant standing at the door. "Reuben, you may serve."

The meal was delicious, a cup of vichyssoise, shrimp and rice made with a wine sauce, and a cold artichoke salad. Tamara was halfway through a slice of fresh coconut cake when there was a disturbance in the front yard. Before Oliver had time to rise from his chair, six Confederate soldiers surrounded them.

"Dr. Oliver Bickley?" snapped the officer in charge.

"Yes, sir," he answered resolutely.

"You're under arrest," he proclaimed. Looking at Tamara, the officer asked, "Lady Tamara Warde?"

"Yes, sir," she said, surprised that he would know her name.

"You're under arrest."

"Oh, no!" she moaned. "What will Mark think!"

Oliver sprang up from his chair. "Now, just a minute. Leave the lady out of this. She is completely innocent."

The officer did not waver. Tamara was manacled, as was the doctor. She looked totally confused. "Why are we being arrested?"

"I told you Charleston has become a lunatic asylum. This is war. Anything can happen."

They were put on the back of a military wagon, sitting facing each other on backless benches. Jouncing in pensive silence, Oliver never took his eyes from Tamara. "Sorry to drag you into my affairs, Tamara. I had no intention of doing so."

Tamara tried to move her arms, which had begun to cramp. Leather thongs fastened them to hooks screwed into the wooden sides of the wagon. People stared as the cart rumbled and bumped along the tree-lined thoroughfare to the Provost Dungeon under the Exchange Building on East Bay Street, close to the wharf. The small Charleston jail at the corner of Magazine and Franklin streets was overcrowded; therefore, military authorities resorted to the use of the Provost Dungeon, which had served as a British prison for American patriots during the War for Independence.

Upon arrival Tamara was placed in a tiny windowless cell with two other women. The iron-barred door clanged shut.

"Why are you here?" she asked after the door banged closed and the soldier disappeared. The woman whose name was Jean laughed. "Ah'm a regulah visatah heah," she said lightly. "Fo' solicitin'," she added. "Propositionin' a soldiah." She shrugged. "Jes' doin' mah duty." In her twenties, she had cheeks rouged the color of her red wrapper. Her raven-colored hair was tangled. White powder lay thick beneath her eyes in an attempt to cover the purple circles. She wore gaudy jewelry on her wrist and around her neck.

Tamara looked at the other woman huddled in the corner,

noticing her dress was threadbare. Her brown eyes were dull, her hair mousy-colored. Her yellowish complexion was spotted with pimples on her forehead and cheeks. Tamara guessed her to be middle-aged, although it was difficult to tell.

"And why have you been arrested?" Tamara asked her with the purpose of trying to find out why she herself was in such a predicament.

"Says ah'm a lush," the woman called Grace answered. "Why yo'all heah?"

"I have no idea," Tamara answered emotionally, her eyes welling with tears, finding it impossible to heed her own advice and remain calm. In the back of her mind she knew the answer. It had occurred to her before her arrest, when Oliver asked her questions. Oliver was a spy. She was believed to be an accomplice. She had not seen him since their arrival at the prison.

The two women laughed unsympathetically. An intense wave of indignation gripped Tamara. She grabbed hold of the bars and tried to shake them.

"Let me out of here. There must be some mistake," she cried. "Won't anyone listen to me?"

No one heard; or if they did, they paid no attention. Finally Tamara gave up and sat on the floor. It was hot and clammy. Perspiration seeped from her pores, trickled between her breasts. She mopped her forehead with the back of her hand. Wet circles under her arms and down her back stained her expensive gown. Sleep overtook her at last, but not for long. She awakened with a start when she felt a hand on her breast, fingers rubbing her nipple. Her eyes flew open. It was Jean, sitting close to her. The other hand of the prostitute had slipped up under Tamara's skirt, searching amidst her underclothes for the center of her thighs.

Tamara squeezed her legs together tightly. She grabbed Jean's hand and removed it. "Get away from me," she ordered forcefully.

An orderly arrived at the cell, bringing a tray with three bowls and three tin cups of water. He unlocked the cell door and slid the tray on the floor.

Tamara walked up to him. "May I please send a note to Mr. Stephen Walker? He lives on Legare Street," she pleaded to the burly orderly.

"No, ma'am." Tamara looked at him warily. "General Beauregard is a friend of mine. May I send him a message?"

The soldier laughed outright. "Yeah, ma'am . . . an' Pres'dent Davis is mah daddy."

228

"Will you not tell me why I am here?" she asked with desperation in her voice.

"Ah'm not supposed to talk to the prisonahs. Orders, ma'am." He banged the door closed and left.

"Goddammit, mush again," complained Jean.

"Yeah," said Grace in agreement, sitting on the floor with her back braced against the stone wall, her legs spread wide. The bare, dirty balls of her feet pushed through the circular holes worn through the soles of her shoes. She played with the mush in her bowl, stirring it round and round with the spoon, then lifting the spoon heaped with mush high above the bowl. Slowly she turned the spoon downward. The mush plopped back into the bowl, some of it splashing on the front of her dress.

Tamara could not eat. Her one concern was that Mark did not know her whereabouts. She wondered whether he would be furious when he learned she had been with Oliver Bickley. He would think the worst, she was certain. Sitting on the damp cell floor, berating herself for not leaving a note when she left the Walker residence, she waited anxiously, expecting to be released momentarily.

Darkness crept over the city. Time passed agonizingly slowly in the dungeon. Overhead, on East Bay Street, the interval between the noises of horses and carriages lengthened until there was complete silence. Weak, flickering light leaked between the metal bars from a lantern hanging on a wall outside the cell, far from the reach of the prisoners, casting diagonal shadow lines across dreary walls.

Tamara felt bereft. In the dark, Jean's hand slipped inside Tamara's bodice, cupping her breast. Tamara slapped her hard across the face. Jean only snickered.

"If you come near me one more time, I am going to scream as loudly as I can," Tamara warned. "What kind of woman are you?" she shrieked.

Jean laughed. "Let me show you. C'mon. If you'd let me show you, you'd want mo'ah," she predicted.

"No, I would not," Tamara snapped. "Stay away from me."

The three women settled down, each taking a wall to lie against. Grace curled up, her knees touching her chest, moaning for a drink.

Tamara was afraid to go to sleep. She looked around the vile cell and cringed at her bizarre companions and surroundings. A chamber pot, its handles and the knob on the lid broken, stood in the corner reeking the foul odor of their excrements. Tamara moved as far away from it as she could, but the nauseating stench was as much a prisoner in the cell as she.

47

Tamara paced back and forth in her cell. Taking her metal water cup, she scraped it over the iron bars. "Help me! Someone. Let me out," she yelled, then waited. There was no reply. Tamara listened to the precision of the sentries' booted footsteps in the distance. There were no windows. She estimated the time by the arrival of food. An orderly approached bringing dishes of hominy grits, which announced that it was morning as plainly as if he had spoken the words. She grabbed the cell bars with both hands.

"Let me out," she pleaded. "There has been a grave mistake. I demand to see General Beauregard." The orderly was not the same one as the night before. This one was shorter, thinner, with blond hair. About eighteen.

"The general left fo' Vaginny, ma'am."

"I tell you, this is all a mistake! You cannot keep me in prison without explaining why," she gasped, on the verge of hysterics.

"In time o' woah, a writ of habeas corpus can be suspended, ma'am. This is woah!" he declared, setting down the tray.

Mark had planned to leave at dawn. Tamara, knowing he was anxious to depart, wondered whether he had sailed without her. The grim prospect that he would break their engagement preyed on her mind. She would never see him again, never have the opportunity to explain her innocence. Never again would she know the thrilling touch of his lips on hers. She whimpered, breaking the silence. Bracing her back against the cell wall, slowly she slid to the floor. Not hungry herself, she watched as Jean and Grace slurped their breakfast.

Hearing someone approaching, she looked up and saw a sergeant standing at the cell.

"Name?"

"Me?" Tamara asked, pointing to herself.

"Ah ain't cross-eyed, ma'am. Yo'ah the one ah'm lookin' at."

"Lady Tamara Warde," she said anxiously.

"Lady? Humph! Done 'way with that nonsense when we fought ol' King George III, ma'am."

"I demand to see the British consul. He will rectify this gross error you have committed against a subject of Great Britain."

"Well, now. Is that a fact, ma'am?"

She heard footsteps. Mark stood at the cell, staring in disbelief. Instinctively she stretched her arms toward him through the bars.

"Thank God you have come for me," she sobbed, a flood of silent tears gushing down her cheeks. It was then she noticed the dour expression on his face and clasped her hands together behind her. He looked terrible. He was grimy. His eyes were bloodshot. She stared at his unshaven jaw, amazed at the length of his one-day growth. In a week's time he could grow a full beard, she thought.

"What a ridiculous situation!" he barked. "After all I explained to you, how could you get yourself in such a mess! Goddammit, they could put a rope around your neck."

Disheartened that he was not more sympathetic, she bit her lip. "Of . . . of what am I accused?" she asked, knowing the answer. She wanted to hear the incredible charges spoken.

He scowled, looking at her as if she had committed murder. "Explain yourself," he demanded gruffly.

He waited for a reply, looking dismayed when none was forthcoming. The lump in her throat prevented her from answering.

"Well?" he asked laconically.

It flashed through Tamara's mind that if he loved her, truly loved her, he could not show such a lack of understanding. Bravely she pushed her chin into the air. "I do not recall asking for your help," she said with asperity, attempting to hide her disappointment and distraught emotions. "Oh, please, sir, spare me the concerned look."

One of Mark's eyebrows arched. The slight indentation in his chin deepened. His nostrils widened.

The previous afternoon, when it was realized she had disappeared without a word, he had been scared out of his mind that she was involved in a tryst, that he had lost her to the arms of another man. After a night of searching, when he learned what happened, anger replaced fear. As he looked at her now, knowing that she was safe and still belonged to him, her hair in disarray, her lilac silk dress wrinkled and stained, her face smudged, he was flooded by a mixture of sympathy and at the same time amusement.

The picture of innocence, she looked ridiculously pathetic behind bars with the drunk and the prostitute. Although Mark regretted she had been put through the unpleasant experience, felt sorry for her, at the same time he could not help but be amused. Meticulous about her appearance, she had never been so untidy, but the smudges on her face and her ruined dress did little to mar her beauty and natural grace. She always wore her long hair neatly arranged in a nest of coiled curls at the nape of her neck. Now it hung loose down her back. He thought it was the most beautiful hair he had ever seen, and falling as it did, made her look provocative. Her shoulders were straight, her head held high. Admiring her spunk, he believed her to have more mettle than any woman he knew.

"What an ungrateful, cantankerous woman!" he fumed tersely. "I have been out all night looking for you, and this is the thanks I get. Very well. Rot in your dungeon if you are so hell-bent on it. I do not care one iota." He turned, feigning departure, expecting her to cry out for him to rescue her.

"Precisely," she yelled in a high, nervous pitch. "Why did you come here in the first place?" She answered her own question. "To gloat. You lied to me. You said you loved me. Do not pretend to care when *you do not*. You did not mean any of the things you said, those deceitful words of love." She twisted the ring from her finger and threw it at him through the bars. "If I committed a crime, I said *if*, it should not alter your love—if it was there . . . if it had been true love."

Picking up the ring, Mark put it in his pocket, realizing she was putting on an act of bravery. He stood with his back to her, listening to her rant, believing it best for her to release the pent-up nervous tension. He could tell now she was distraught. He knew she did not mean the hastily spoken words.

"You are not even concerned that I might hang . . . and innocently." she accused sullenly. "And the food is terrible. I hate hominy grits and mush!" Mark was forced to refrain from smiling as she continued to rave.

"You will be glad if they hang me. You are angry because I was with Oliver. I thought you were a brave man. You are a coward, Mark Schofield. Do you hear? A coward. You misled me. What a sneaky way to get out of our engagement."

He chuckled inside, not believing his ears. She was blaming him for her arrest. It had gone far enough. He swung around. "Where the devil did you get that foolish notion?"

As she detected a softening in his voice, her behavior turned vapid. Her shoulders slumped. Her brave words belied the trembling of her lower lip. When Mark saw the expression of anguish on her face, he cursed himself for the way he had acted. "Oh, please, Mark. Do not leave me here." She cupped her hands at her mouth to whisper to him so that the others would not hear. "That . . . that woman, the one in the red dress, has been trying to get . . . familiar with me," she whispered.

"Whaaat!" he barked in a loud voice, rage entering his eyes. "What has she done?" he demanded to know, not as loudly.

"She has tried to . . ." Tamara covered her face with her hands, unable to explain. "Oh, Mark, I cannot tell you."

Mark muttered an oath. "Guard!" he yelled, wondering where the devil Stephen and General Beauregard were. They were supposed to have met him here by this time. Mark looked at Tamara anxiously. "Are you ready to explain what happened?"

Tamara looked around. "Could we speak somewhere in private?"

Mark went to the guard, who refused his request.

"This will have to do, Tamara. Now, tell me how you got yourself into this predicament."

Tamara hedged.

He looked at her. "I am waiting."

"On the night of the ball, Dr. Bickley asked me to have lunch with him. I admired his house."

She paused as she saw Mark frown.

"Proceed," he snapped.

"While I was there, we were arrested."

She stopped again.

"Go on. I'm listening."

"You did not sail without me," she said quietly.

"Do not digress."

The soldier on guard duty snapped to attention when he spotted General Beauregard. So did the orderly, who stood gawking while dangling the large ring of keys.

"Imbecile, unlock this cell immediately," commanded Beauregard.

Tamara, not wanting to cry in front of the general, blinked rapidly to keep the tears hidden.

"Are you all right, my dear?" he asked comfortingly.

"Yes, sir."

"My deepest apologies for this gross error. I hope you will not think badly of the Confederacy, ma'am."

"Oh, I could never do that, sir."

"I gave orders for Bickley's arrest and any suspicous persons seen in his company the last month. I certainly did not mean you, ma'am. What can I do to rectify this mistake?"

"Just get me out of here."

Stephen Walker hurried toward them, accompanied by a man Tamara assumed was his lawyer. "Sometimes mistakes happen," he was saying as they approached.

"Here I am, Schofield," Stephen greeted, out of breath. "It is all straightened out." He nodded to General Beauregard and smiled at Tamara.

"About time," Mark said impatiently.

The instant Tamara was released, she was in Mark's arms. He stroked her back consolingly. Kissed away the tears that slid down her cheeks. His day-old beard scraped her face, reddened her cheek and chin. Jean and Grace gaped silently.

"I am still not certain why I was arrested," Tamara said, clinging to Mark, relishing the security of his arms.

"The bloody ass is a spy," proffered Stephen Walker's lawyer, a short, chubby man with a paunch and a bald head.

"Oliver Bickley is intensely loyal to the North," said Beauregard. "He came to Charleston as an intelligence agent. A dossier has been found which includes Southern strength in arms, names and classes of ships, ship movements, location of magazines."

"His medical practice was a front," added Walker. "He has contempt for all slaveowners. Has assisted runaways."

"Then why did he accept your hospitality?" Tamara asked.

"He hoped to gain information. He knew we were making a shipment deal with Mark."

Mark's fingers slipped beneath Tamara's hair, rubbing away the tension that gripped her neck muscles. She bit her lip nervously.

"His house was watched for months," said the little lawyer.

"He exploited your naiveté, ma'am," said Beauregard, trying to ease her mortification. "You were seen with him on several occasions. My intelligence officers suspected you were supplying him with information."

Mark felt Tamara stiffen. Her face turned red. She slapped the heel of her hand against her brow. "I was a fool!" she blurted. "I did answer questions he asked, but at first I thought he was just being curious. I never dreamed he was a

234

spy." Tamara paused. Her hand went up to her cheek. "I just remembered. I took him up to the widow's walk to show him the panorama from the Walkers' rooftop. He had an excellent view of Charleston harbor with all its installations."

"I am sure he had all that information before he went up there," opined Beauregard.

"What will happen to him?" Tamara asked, shuddering.

"Strong, healthy young fella like him, would be a shame to hang him. There will be a serious shortage of doctors. We will put him to good use until the war is over," Beauregard answered.

"Then he is a doctor and not masquerading as one?" Mark asked.

"Yes. He is a medical doctor," answered Beauregard, "but Oliver Bickley is not his real name."

They left the prison. Tamara squinted, momentarily blinded by the sudden brightness of the sun. Figures around her were blurry until her eyes adjusted to the light. Mark was shaking hands with Stephen, the attorney, and Beauregard. Tamara thanked them.

"C'mon," Mark said to Tamara, appearing anxious to leave. He took her arm and led her to a carriage. Flicking the reins, he informed her they were going to the ship. They had only a short distance to travel.

"I need a bath."

"Later. I will take you back to the Walkers', but first there is something I wish to show you."

48

Mark watched the expression of incredulity on Tamara's face as she gaped at the freshly painted ship. Her eyes widened before tears pushed to the surface. Her hands flew up to her flushed cheeks in disbelief.

"I cannot believe it!" she gasped. "It is a great honor."

Mark bowed. "A small token of my love."

Tamara stared at the ship's bow, reading the red printing carefully. It was no longer the *Mark Schofield*, but, the *Lady Tamara*.

Tamara hugged and kissed Mark enthusiastically, thanking

him for naming his ship in her honor. They went on board. In his salon he seated her and poured each a glass of brandy. He raised his glass. "To Tamara . . . both of them. They are all the world to me." She placed her glass to her lips and drank.

Mark sat down opposite her, stretching his legs. He looked exhausted.

Tamara glanced at him warily. "May I please have my ring back?"

"Only if you promise never to remove it again."

She made a face, wrinkling her nose. Her fingers pressed against her brow. "God, I was hairbrained!"

"At least you admit it," he said with a gleam in his eye while digging into his pocket. He went to her and placed the ring back on her finger.

"Stephen and I searched all night for you," he said after returning to the comfort of his leather chair. "Now I know what hell is. At first I feared . . . an accident; then I was afraid you had been kidnapped. There were moments when I believed you . . . had run away from me. And when Lila suggested Bickley, I died a thousand deaths. I thought you were meeting him clandestinely." He looked at her straightforwardly. "I did not think it conceivable that you would be in prison. Indeed, I did not consider that possibility at all.

"But you considered it possible for me to be deceitful, disloyal."

"I apologize for that."

Tamara sipped the brandy, feeling it burn going down her throat. She began to relax. "I am sorry," she said softly.

He waved his hand through the air. "I apologize for not trusting you. I should have had more faith in your love." He put his empty glass down and crossed his arms in front of him. "We searched everywhere. By process of elimination we reached Bickley's house. Lila suggested him. His servants told us of his arrest."

He looked into her eyes.

"I cannot believe you went to his house alone . . . and without telling me. Is this the sort of behavior I can expect in the future?" he asked with a note of reproof in his voice.

Tamara hesitatingly explained how she had forgotten about the luncheon until Oliver's carriage arrived for her. "I was going to refuse," she insisted, "but I wanted to tell him of our engagement. He informed me at the ball you and I were in love, and I insisted he was wrong."

Feeling guilty for all the trouble she had caused, she low-

236

ered her lashes. Looking at her fingers resting on her lap, she said, "He did not take me into the house," which was her way of assuring him that nothing indiscreet had happened between them. "When he learned we were to be wed, he was anxious for me to return to the Walkers'."

"At least he was that much of a gentleman." Mark took a deep breath of air and exhaled it slowly. "I know you are exhausted and want a bath, so I am going to take you back to the Walkers'. I insist you rest the remainder of the day." He paused before he continued. "We are getting married at eight o'clock tonight."

"Tonight! What will I wear?"

"Yes, tonight. You do not have to worry about a thing. Lila and Rosabelle have selected your gown. They are getting everything ready. Steve's lawyer handled the legal end of it. You have nothing to do except rest. We sail at midnight."

Lila and her mother performed a miracle. They succeeded in turning the garden into a fairy-tale-like chapel. A small altar had been erected, banked with palms, white flowers, and candelabra. Mrs. Walker played her harp, which had been brought from the drawing room.

Tamara wore a white organza dress with a pink satin sash at the waist and insets of pink satin ribbon in the puffed sleeves and along the full hemline, matching her pink satin slippers. Rosabelle Walker's Belgian-lace veil, hanging magnificently from Tamara's crown, rippled gently in the slight breeze blowing in from the harbor. When they met at the altar, Mark looked deeply into her eyes. "Hello beautiful," he whispered, a familiar greeting from the past, which reached back into her memory, flashing a view of Mark, her heraldic prince, riding toward her on the beach in Jamaica.

As she stood beside him, facing the altar, her fingers trembled, clutching the bouquet of white rosebuds. Her heart pounded erratically. Promptly at eight o'clock, Sir Mark Schofield and Lady Tamara Warde were united for eternity by the Walkers' pastor, the Reverend Mr. Charles Michael. Millions of stars twinkled in the night sky. The quarter-moon appeared to be smiling down on them. Stephen, Rosabelle, and General Beauregard watched. Lila, who was maid of honor, wore a pink gown and carried red roses. Roderick Moran was Mark's best man. The ceremony was solemn, more moving than if it had been witnessed by many guests. Mark looked deep into Tamara's eyes, penetrating her soul, and repeated his vows with confidence. Tamara said hers softly, feelingly.

After the ceremony, champagne was served in the garden. Toasts were given, followed by an elegant dinner in the dining room. Tamara smiled as she watched Lila flirting with Roderick, ready to claim another conquest.

The tiered wedding cake was cut with Mark's polished rapier and served with coffee. Taking Tamara's hand in his, looking at Stephen, Mark said lightly, "When I was here at Christmastime, if you had told me I would be a married man, I would have said you were crazy."

The guests laughed, and Tamara blushed, looking at Mark with starry eyes. General Beauregard came to her, took her hand gallantly. "It is my distinct pleasure, ma'am, to wish you happiness." He raised her hand to his lips.

Close to midnight the guests went to the dock, waving happily and throwing rice at the newlyweds standing at the railing on the main deck of the *Lady Tamara*. As the breeze pushed piles of clouds across the night sky, the command was given. "Weigh anchor!" Rolling up thick cable, the steam-operated winch lifted the heavy iron anchor dripping with salt water and draped with slimy seaweed. The ship tooted her farewell and slowly steamed out of port, leaving a sooty streamer blacker than the midnight sky.

General Beauregard had ordered two armed Confederate ships to accompany the *Lady Tamara*. When she cleared the harbor, as Mark scanned the horizon with his glass, looking for Union gunboats threatening the area, he told Tamara to go below and wait for him in his quarters. He wanted to remain in command until he was assured they were safe. So far, the Union blockade was ineffective. No Union gunboats, which would attempt to capture any ship trying to get out, were sighted. The *Lady Tamara* sliced smoothly through the calm water of the harbor into the open sea, then turned south-southeast into the choppy, whitecapped Atlantic.

However hard he tried, Mark had been unsuccessful in getting a full supply of coal to power his ship to Nassau. In order to save the slender reserve of fuel, once they were out of dangerous waters the engines were shut down and the main, mizzen, and fore sails were slowly unfurled. The ship would travel at a slower speed, but there was actually no hurry.

When the sails caught the wind and the *Lady Tamara* was on her tack, Mark ordered a keg of wine to be opened for his crew to celebrate his wedding. He left his men with a smile on his face, giving orders not to be disturbed unless a dire emergency arose.

49

Several members of the crew had purchased banjos in Charleston and had learned to play some of the popular tunes. The music drifted to the salon, where Tamara waited for Mark. Thinking of what would take place when he arrived made her feel hot all over. Filled with heady excitement, she went to him the second he came through the door, offering him her warm lips, seeking, yielding.

"Your body feels wonderful in my arms," he whispered, cradling her. She trembled as he reached behind her to unbutton the pearl buttons down to her waist, as he kissed her. With ease, he slipped off her petticoats and pantalets until she stood before him completely nude. Tamara thrilled as his eyes and hands swept over her body. She delighted in the way he murmured her name over and over in passionately husky tones. She wanted to run her fingers through his thick hair and rumple it. An inexpressible yearning quivered at the apex of her thighs.

Mark swept her into his arms, mumbling incoherently in her ear as he carried her to the bedroom and put her down on his bed. He took off his clothes. The mattress depressed when he joined her, rolling her close. She snuggled in the sanctuary of his arms, marveling at the pleasure the feel of his naked body pressing against hers brought. It began subtly, with tender touches of his lips on hers again and again. She returned each kiss more eagerly than the one before, until sublimely they lingered longer and longer, becoming more and more demanding, until their lips were welded together.

Unhurriedly his deft fingers trailed up and down her spinal column, sending thrills through her body. Gently his hands glided over her full breasts, fondling them, expertly fingering her nipples, triggering them to turn hard. His hand moved down her belly, to the reddish triangle where her legs met, between her legs, touching, kissing, licking sensuous spots, arousing smoldering embers in her loins until they burst into

239

flame. Murmuring private words of endearment, while turning her over on her belly, he kissed the curve of her waist as she rolled. His lips lingered on the middle of her back, then moved down. She felt the touch of his tongue on her buttocks, the light brush of his mustache as he kissed her there, before his lips moved upward. He pushed her hair away from her neck and kissed her. Rolling her over on her back again, he turned her face up to his and saw the wild desire in her eyes.

"We need each other, love. You are my wife. I want you. I need you desperately." As he snuggled his nose between her breasts, sounds and movements of the ship became diffused. Tangible objects turned obscure. The room seemed to vanish.

Tamara's hair formed a cape around her bare creamy shoulders as she tossed her head on the pillow from one side to the other. Her fingers brushed across the soft silkiness of hair covering his chest. He took her hand and guided it.

"Touch me."

Shyly, her arm stiffened.

"Please," he said pulling her hand toward the place. "See how much I want you." Hesitantly she felt his turgid manhood, at first prodding it cautiously with one finger, then with several, until she held his rigid erection in her hand, sending swift currents of desire through his body. A guttural groan escaped his throat. He rolled toward her, spreading her legs. An overwhelming ebullience of passion coursed through his veins as his body covered hers.

Perceptive of her feelings, sensitive to her responses, the second he was on top of her he felt her stiffen and knew what had happened, recognized her reaction as more than apprehension. Her passion, so quickly aroused, plummeted when his body was over her. A feeling of being stifled attacked her. Panic struck, and she went rigid.

"No, no," she moaned, flinging her head back and forth on the pillow. She tried to twist away from him.

"Darling, it's Mark. Mark. Tamara!" He shook her. "Tamara!" His voice grew louder in an effort to get through to her.

She squeezed her eyes tightly shut, vividly seeing the scarred face and beard of her mother's murderer.

"Open your eyes and look at me, darling. It's Mark."

"Get away from me."

Mark did not know what to do. Was his insistence the only way she would begin their married life? How long would he have to wait until she came to him of her own free will? He

240

feared that forcing her would bring disastrous effects. He could lose her forever if he chose the wrong direction for his actions. He hesitated before he moved from her placatingly, coming to rest by her side. He took her in his arms and held her. He was breathing rapidly.

"It is all right, darling. All virgin brides are apprehensive on their wedding night. Relax. I am not going to do anything you do not want me to do. I promise," he said, kissing her cheek, pulling her closer, feeling her body go limp.

Tamara struggled to be free of his arms, wrenching herself from his embrace. She left the bed, thrusting her feet into her slippers. When she looked around dazedly for her robe, Mark jumped from the bed, went to her, grabbed her shoulders. "Where the devil do you think you are going?"

She bowed her head so he could not see the pain in her eyes. She sobbed silently. "To my cabin," she said, choked. "Don't you see, Mark, I cannot go through with it. It is what I feared. My heart is drawn to you. My body responds, but my mind rebels and tears me apart. My mother's rapists— not you—were on top of me!" A sob escaped her lips. "I should not have agreed to the marriage." She covered her confused, hurt eyes. "You can get an annulment in Nassau or when we reach Jamaica," she sobbed resignedly. " 'Twill be better now than later."

His fingers pressed her more firmly. "Never! How can you imagine for one moment I could ever let you go, now that I have found you? I love you, Tamara. I did not realize how lonely my life was until you came back into it. I can no longer contemplate a life without you. You have become a necessary part of me . . . of my future."

He wrapped his arms around her so that she spoke with her head against his chest. "You understand . . . don't you? I cannot . . . help it. It is not that I do not love you," she said almost inaudibly. "It is because I love you that I wish to release you from your vows." A stream of tears spilled from her eyes, dropping on his downy chest. "I shall always remember you loved me enough to marry me."

A heart-rending sound rose from her throat. "It must end now. It should have ended before. If you sought the arms of another woman, which you would have the right to do, I would . . . die."

He kissed her cheek. "Get that out of your head." He paused before he continued. "I never thought of you as a quitter when matters become difficult." She did not reply.

Mark held her at arm's length. "You cannot leave my

quarters. There are few secrets on board a ship. Moran . . . my men would know immediately. This is our problem, yours and mine, husband and wife. It is a problem we will solve together."

He took his arms from her, brushed the tears from her cheeks with his fingers. "Now, get back into that bed," he said with gentle persuasiveness, whacking her bare behind playfully.

She obeyed, and when she was settled, he slipped in beside her, holding her close, stilling her trembling lips with his. His words and actions instilled renewed confidence. Instinctively her hands went around his bare shoulders, fingers entwining the dark hair at the nape of his neck. Tamara felt a tremor go through him.

"Darling, I will show you the way of it," he whispered hoarsely, kissing her temple, lips, neck, rubbing the smoothness of her belly and thighs. Her nipples puckered at his touch.

"Tamara, love, let me take you with me to paradise," he pleaded. His lips followed the trace of his fingers, touching her thighs, kissing away the invisible barrier of fear from her mind and body, replacing it with desire. He was no amateur. He spread her legs. Demonstrating his prolific skills, his questing finger probing until it found her most delicate spot, he awakened her slumbering innocence, raptly transporting her into untraveled depths of passion.

Tamara responded in mind and body. She was inflamed. Stars flashed before her eyes. Writhing with passion, she pressed the back of her hand over her mouth to imprison the cry of ecstasy. So intense was her desire, she wondered whether she would not die.

Mark's finger moved skillfully, until her body shuddered in pulsating waves of pleasure, bringing her to the threshold of . . . something she wanted desperately, but knew not what. Just when she was on the brink of whatever it was—madness, perhaps, not quite reaching the pinnacle of what must be assuaged or she would surely die—Mark felt the need to slow down, to prolong the rapture, to prepare her for his entry.

As Tamara's hand left her mouth to run her fingers through his hair, she shrieked ecstatically. He stopped. Leaving a searing trail, his lips slid upward, along her side, pausing at her waist. Then he cradled her in his arms.

"Hush, love. My men will think I am torturing my bride."

"You are . . . Sweet, sweet torture," she gasped.

His arms encircled her. He held her tighter and tighter in a crushing embrace. She could feel his strong manhood pressing between her legs.

"I did not know anything could be so thrilling," she whispered.

"It will be more so when you feel me inside you . . . if you will let me."

Mark sensed she smiled beguilingly. "If it is any more sensational, I shall die of it."

He kissed her, feeling the heat surface to her lips. His fingers found hard, erect nipples. He put her hand on his demanding erection.

It was on a week-long stop in Constantinople that he had sought to learn the technique known as *imsak,* in which he could withhold from orgasm. His aching desire put him to the test. He knew he would be unable to contain his passion much longer. He had wanted her from the moment he set eyes on her at the ballet in London, a want that had increased in Charleston and turned to a desperate need. There could be no more waiting. Impatience brushed tenderness aside. He kissed her violently, bruising her lips. His controlled voice hid the frustration slowly creeping up on him.

Tamara knew. Clinging to him, she begged emotionally, "Be patient with me, Mark. Love me. I beg of you, love me."

"You need not beg for my love. 'Tis yours forever," he replied thickly.

"Love me. Be my lover. Make me yours *now,*" Tamara implored.

50

Thump! Thump! A most inopportune fist banged with desperation on the thick oak door of Captain Schofield's quarters.

"Captain, sir. Moran here."

"Son of a bitch!" Mark cursed but did not move. Another banging on the door, this time three thumps.

"Goddammit, I left orders not to be disturbed," Mark uttered, still not moving, holding Tamara close.

Again Moran's fist banged on the door. "Sorry, sir," he shouted, then paused. "Sail ho! Unidentifiable ship on the horizon, sir."

Mark lifted his head and took his arms from his bride grudgingly, "Be right there," he yelled.

Tamara watched as he slipped into trousers and a long-sleeved white shirt. Reaching the bedroom door, he looked back at Tamara. Her hair spilled out across the pillow. Her naked body stretched sensuously on top of the sheet, her legs apart as he had left them. Her lips were slightly swollen from his kisses. Her cheeks were pink from the brush of his mustache. He grinned at the picture of sensuality. Returning to the bed, he bent over and kissed two pink suck marks on her belly.

"Stay put. I'll be right back," he said, then disappeared.

The ship's whistle screamed the alarm, a call for all hands to report for duty. Tamara heard the shuffling of booted feet. Shouting. She slipped on her robe and slippers and looked out the porthole, using one of Mark's spyglasses. A square-rigged vessel came into view, its skull-and-crossbone flag clearly visible. She rode high in the water with the speed of a shark, gaining steadily on the slower-moving *Lady Tamara*, weighed down by her heavy cargo of cotton bales.

Dumping the cargo overboard would do little to increase her speed to escape her pursuers. There was no time to start coal fire to build up steam and pressure in the boilers. Mark's only chance was yawing, maneuvering, attempting to foil the pirate ship. His shouting commands were audible in his quarters.

"Hard to starboard! Heave to!"

The gap between the two ships narrowed. Even with full sail it was obvious escape was impossible.

"Man the cannons, Moran!"

Tamara turned as Mark rushed into the salon. "I expect you to obey me, Tamara. Do as I command. These are well-known pirates preying on merchant ships sailing the Caribbean. I do not want them to know a woman is on board. Your femininity will be difficult to disguise, but try. Wear these. They belong to Jimmy." He handed her a pair of the boy's trousers, a shirt and cap. He spoke rapidly. "The captain's quarters will be the first place they will search for gold if they are successful in boarding. Go to your cabin down the passageway and lock the door. Stay there. Do not open the door under any circumstances." He was gone in a flash.

Tamara followed his instructions, donning the cabin boy's trousers and shirt, which were too large, rolling up the sleeves, which extended from her hands. She tucked her long hair up under the cap, pinning it to prevent it from falling loose. When she had done all she could, she returned to her former cabin and lifted the spyglass to watch the pirate ship coming into range off portside.

"Stand fast! Ready the cannons, Moran!"

There was a pause; then: "Ooooopen fiiiiire!"

Tamara could not see the cannons from the porthole of her cabin, but watched the streak of orange-red fire and smoke that shot low across the water. She felt the recoil, heard the roaring boom. The cannonballs fell short of target, sending up sprays of sea water.

Cannons thundered from the pirate ship. Tamara held her breath. A cannonball ripped through the stack of the *Lady Tamara*, jolting the vessel, knocking Tamara to the floor. She pulled herself up and retrieved the spyglass, which she had dropped.

"Ooooopen fiiiiire!" Silence before the roar of the cannons. Boom! Boom! Boom! Tamara stared through the glass. The enemy ship was struck. Its mizzenmast was shattered and crashed to the deck. Gunfire boomed from the pirate ship, hitting the *Lady Tamara* broadside, leaving a gap in her hull above the waterline.

The two ships were side by side. A sharp thud shook the *Lady Tamara* as the hulls bumped. Chaos broke out immediately. Tamara heard shouting, a scurrying of boots, a clash of metal as the pirates boarded. Hand-to-hand combat broke out on the main deck. Pistol shots cracked. Cutlasses swished through the air. Men wrestled, wielding knives in their hands, ready to plunge into their victims. They shoved and pushed, punched, kicked, skidded on pools of blood.

Dawn arrived bright and clear. The shouts of the men, the slashing of metal hand weapons, echoed across the calm sea. Tamara heard descending steps on the companionway as the pirates rampaged through the ship. The hurried footsteps came closer, along the passageway. She held her breath, looking around the cabin for a hiding place. There was no room to crawl under the bunk, no closet in which to hide. Feeling helpless, she slid to the floor on her knees, burying her face in her hands. She began to pray for Mark, his crew, and herself.

Tamara stopped to listen. Men ran past her door. Mark had been correct. They had entered his quarters, were ripping them apart in search of gold. Tamara squeezed her eyes shut tightly and resumed her prayers.

The doorknob rattled. A pistol shot rang out. The door was thrust open. Tamara, sitting on the floor, raised her eyes slowly, hoping it was Mark. She stared in horrified disbelief. The menacing pirate was tall and muscular. His beard was dark and bushy, sprinkled with gray. His badly soiled shirt was torn into threads. He was out of breath and panted noisily. Tamara's eyes were frozen on the jagged red scar extending from his left ear to his lip. It was Jack. She let out a bloodcurdling scream. Jack tucked the pistol back into his belt, checking to be sure his dagger was in its scabbard at his hip. He stood with legs apart and crossed his arms in front of him. "Well, well. Whut 'as we 'ere?"

Tamara moved backward, sliding on her buttocks away from him. He took a confident step closer and laughed gruffly. "Yer no lad," he accused.

Evil leered from his eyes. Tamara crouched in the corner. He reached down and grabbed her, his fingers digging painfully into the flesh of her upper arms. The color drained from her face. He pulled her to her feet. His hands probed for hidden breasts. It was as if her nightmares had turned to reality. Her eyes enlarged with fear. She shuddered with revulsion.

"Get away from me! You vile creature, how dare you touch me!" She kicked his shins as hard as she could. He sneered. She struggled to escape his grip, but she was no match for his strength. She bit his arm. The pirate flung back his head and laughed. Pleading with the maniac was useless. Resistance was futile. She knew it would do no good to scream. Every man was fighting to defend his life.

"Oi got no time now fer what oi 'as in mind fer you. Oi'm takin' you with me."

She dared not close her eyes. They widened as she saw Mark sneak up behind him. Savagely his arm came around Jack's neck. The pirate hissed. With amazing speed he turned and threw Mark off balance, punching him on the chin, sending him reeling across the cabin.

"That be fer firin' me an' chasin' me off yer ship, Schofield. Oi swore to git even someday," he growled.

Mark recovered and rushed Jack. His left fist connected with the pirate's eye. Mark ducked a pounding blow to his face, which knocked Jack off balance. Mark punched his right fist into the pirate's gut. He staggered. Strong-muscled arms and legs tangled. Jack reached for his knife, brandishing it precariously. Mark parried, grabbing Jack's wrist, twisting his arm until he dropped the weapon. Mark kicked it toward Tamara, keeping his eye on his enemy.

They circled. The pirate leaped. Mark deflected. The pirate reached to his belt for his pistol. Mark kicked it from his hand with his booted foot, then somersaulted backward, away from him. Bodies came together in a clutch.

Tamara retrieved the weapon, cocked it. Aimed. Her hand trembled. She had never fired a pistol before. Her eyes froze on the man who had denied her the love of her parents, the man who had haunted her dreams and was now attempting to kill her husband. She was afraid to pull the trigger, not from any qualms about killing the murderer, but from fear of missing her target and hitting Mark.

Mark grabbed Jack's arm and twisted it back relentlessly at the same time he tripped him with his right foot. Jack was forced to his knees, then onto his back on the floor. The pirate growled. Mark pulled a shiny rapier from the wall, pressing the point dangerously against Jack's throat. Mark's boot came up to rest on the pirate's stomach.

"Scum. Order your men off my ship before I run you through."

"Wha guarantee oi got yo won't anyways?"

"Absolutely none." Mark pressed the point harder until the pirate winced. "Murderer of this woman's mother and father in Jamaica eight years ago. What chance did you give them?"

The pirate's face turned red. "Desist!" he shouted to his men.

The noise on deck drowned his order. Mark seized him by the throat, lifted him to his feet, and pushed him to the door. "Again," he commanded.

"Desist!" the pirates' captain shouted.

This time he was heard. The men stopped fighting and scrambled for the railing, climbing over onto their own ship. With the swiftness of a leopard, Jack threw himself down against Mark, grasping his legs to throw him off balance. Mark struggled, rallied, and pinned the pirate to the floor with the slender sword. With one forceful thrust Mark rammed the weapon through both cheeks, skewering Jack's grizzled face to the wooden floor. Mark turned to assist Tamara.

A second pirate entered the cabin. "Cap'n Jack? Bes' we scat. That British frigate stalkin' us be on the 'orizon."

The pirate looked down and gasped. Seeing what had happened to his captain, he grabbed the rapier and attempted to pull it with all his might. The rapier was pulled free from the floor, slipped from the force, cutting Jack's face wide open, assuring sudden death. When the pirate saw what he had done accidentally, he dropped the bloodied weapon and fled up the companionway.

A third pirate entered the cabin to rescue his captain, not knowing he was dead. He came up behind Mark, wielding a metal bar. Tamara let out a demonic scream. Mark swung around, but too late. He was felled by a hard blow on his head. Moaning, he dropped unconscious to the floor.

Tamara crawled to him. Blood gushed from the wound on the top of his head. He did not move. Unsure whether he was dead or alive, her trembling fingers hesitantly touched his cheek. Feeling its warmth and seeing the rise and fall of his chest, a flood of relief swept through her. She took her petticoat, which she had hidden in the bottom drawer of the chest, and held it to the wound. She trembled and felt an ache deep in the pit of her stomach.

Tamara ran up the companionway to look for Roderick Moran. The blood-drenched deck was a glimpse into hell. She stepped over mutilated bodies, corpses, several decapitated. She paused but briefly to look at the pirate skewered to the deck with a rapier, one of Mark's. The dead man's arms and legs were spread wide and he was lying in a carmine pool of thick, sticky blood. He was bald. She knew his name was Wally. Two of the men who had murdered her parents, Jack and Wally, were dead at last. She had no time to ponder the matter. That would come later. The important thing at the moment was to save Mark. She must find Roderick.

The surviving pirates, spattered with blood, escaped to their ship which was drifting away from the *Lady Tamara*. The crew from the *Lady Tamara* hurled torches onto its main and quarter decks, which caught fire. Men could be seen tossing barrels of water on the flames, which leaped higher and higher. The *Lady Tamara*'s cannons fired, giving the pirate ship a shattering blow. She began taking in water through the enormous gap in her hull. Men jumped into the sea to escape the bursting flames.

At that moment Tamara recognized the third pirate who had helped to murder her parents. He was at the railing of the other ship. She had known she would never forget his face and there it was, not in a dream or fantasy, but in the flesh. She gasped as she saw his clothing ignite, the flames spreading from his trousers upward to his shirt, then his hair. His entire body was engulfed in orange tongues of fire. In horror Tamara watched as Pete jumped over the railing, dropping like a shrieking torch. The sea drew him under.

The battered vessel wallowed. Her bow sank deeper into the water. She listed helplessly as her men lowered the longboat and rowed away from their sinking ship, stopping to rescue those who had survived the jump into the sea. Pete was not among them.

Cheers went up from the crew of the *Lady Tamara* as the pirate ship went down. Tamara called for Roderick Moran above the shouting. She groped her way, stepping over the dead and wounded. Fearing he was lying dead among them, despair swept over her.

"Over there, ma'am," A yeoman pointed.

Roderick, cut and bruised, was giving orders to have the bodies tossed overboard and the deck swabbed.

"Mr. Moran, come quickly. Mark is injured badly."

The first officer returned with Tamara to the cabin. Mark, unconscious, had not moved. There was a deep gash in his skull. Roderick checked his breathing, then set about to cleanse the wound and stanch the blood. He was relieved to see signs of clotting; otherwise, cauterizing would have been necessary.

Mark mumbled deliriously as Roderick worked skillfully, expertly. He shaved the hair from around the wound, being careful none got into it. Tamara, following Roderick's instructions, made pads out of clean white linen, which would absorb the drainage. She cut strips to wrap around his head in order to keep the pads in place. Surprising herself, she remained quietly calm throughout the entire procedure.

Healing salve was applied and his head bandaged. He was carried to his cabin and placed on the bed.

Roderick looked at Tamara. "Nothing more can be done for the moment."

"Is . . . is he in danger?"

"It is difficult to tell with a head injury. I must be honest with you. Right now it doesn't look good. Come with me before you collapse."

Tamara protested. Moran insisted, leading her to the salon. She sat down heavily, raising her hand indifferently for the glass of brandy he offered her. Tamara put her head back and gulped the brandy, nearly choking.

"Here, now. Take it easy. Sip it slowly," Moran advised comfortingly.

Tamara's voice caught in her throat. "We have just found each other. If he dies, I would not wish to live."

"Now, now. He will be all right. He is strong and healthy . . . and . . . has good reason to live," Roderick said, looking at Tamara with smoldering eyes. "We will bring a doctor on board as soon as we reach Nassau."

"When will that be?"

Moran thought for a moment. "The ship's damages are not so severe that we cannot proceed. Our sails are intact, so I should estimate we will reach Nassau by tomorrow morning."

He set his empty glass on the tray and excused himself, saying he would return as soon as matters were under control. When he was gone, Tamara went to Mark's bed and looked down at him. The flesh around his left eye was badly bruised and had turned black and blue. Abrasions marred his chin. Her eyes fell on the red spot oozing through the bandages on his head. His white long-sleeved shirt was torn and smeared with blood. The shirt was open, exposing his broad chest covered with dark ringlets. Her eyes outlined his lips, soft but masculine. She noticed the brown of his mustache was a deeper shade than his thick side whiskers. His lashes were darker, almost black. God, she loved him! He had been so gentle with her, so patient and understanding.

Carefully Tamara removed the shirt, then his boots. Sitting on the edge of the bed, she bathed his face with a cool wet cloth, then pulled a blanket over him, up to his shoulders. Bending over him, she touched his lips with hers before she dropped to her knees beside the bed. Clasping his limp hand in hers, she kissed it, then rubbed it up and down against her cheek. Scalding tears burned her eyes. "Please do not die. God, do not let him die."

51

Gripped with trepidation, Tamara's lips moved in silent prayer, begging the Lord to spare Mark's life and bring him to complete physical and mental recovery. If he died, so would she. How could she go on living without him? He was her life, her happiness, her future. Without him there would be nothing. A sob rose straight up from her heart as she envisioned his death and burial at sea. She had heard or read that a blow on the head could cause forgetfulness, even idiocy. Tamara prayed he would be saved from that fate. Knowing Mark, if that happened he would be better off dead. That he should die or be mentally incapacitated was incomprehensible. He must live and he must have no ill effects from the injury.

At Tamara's request, a comfortable armchair was carried from the salon and placed in the bedroom close to Mark's bed. She refused to leave his side. All through the day she watched him intently for signs of regaining consciousness, feeling his forehead with the palm of her hand, checking for fever, thankful it was cool. She saw his eyes flicker and bent over him, waiting for them to open, but they did not move again. He rolled his head back and forth on the pillow, mumbling incoherently.

The ship was silent in its sea-rocking cradle as it sailed toward Nassau. When night seeped over the horizon, spreading darkness across the wavy waters, the Caribbean moon flashed its silvery bright beacon through the porthole of Mark's room, making it unnecessary to light candles or lamps. The troubled night went on and on. During her vigil Tamara found time to mull over the events of the predawn hours. Mark, her love, her husband, her prince, had saved her from ravishment, the most dreaded of her fears. He had slain the stealthy killers, rapers of innocent women, roughnecks who had condemned her to a life of fear and suspicion, barbarians who had altered her life so dramatically.

There was no hate in Tamara's heart. It was not revenge she felt, for her loss could never be measured in their destruction. It was a sense of awe and gratitude toward the man lying before her, the man who had done the merciful deed. It was not gloating vindictiveness she enjoyed, but relief, as if a great weight had slipped from her shoulders, a feeling of being free for the first time since she had walked into the drawing room of her home and come face to face with tragedy.

Jack, Wally, and Pete were no longer hidden, surreptitious phantoms whom she must search for and find. They were dead men at the bottom of the sea being devoured by hungry sharks. The search was over. The nightmares ended. Mark, her Aesculapius, god of healing, was taking her home at last.

Humbly Tamara went down on her knees beside his bed. She kissed his limp, motionless hand, rested her tear-covered cheek on it. She closed her eyes.

Roderick came to the door. "How is he?"

"The same. He sleeps fitfully."

"If you need anything, send for me." He left.

Thinking she had fallen asleep, she believed she was dreaming when she felt Mark's hand slip from under her face and stroke her hair. Slowly she lifted her head. His eyes were open, watching her mistily, his mind disoriented.

He moistened his lips with his tongue. "Brandy," he demanded in his manly voice.

Tamara held the glass to his lips. As he became more alert, his incapacity embarrassed him. "I can hold the glass myself."

When he had emptied it, he asked questions. After Tamara told him all that had happened, he went to sleep again. He awoke an hour later and consented to eating hot broth with rice, then drifted in and out of consciousness.

During the night the *Lady Tamara* docked at Nassau, chief port in the British Bahama Islands, in a harbor glutted with ships, several of them Schofield-owned. The physician Moran brought on board checked Mark's wound and general condition. There were no signs of infection, thankfully no evidence of mental disability.

Mark grumbled when the physician ordered him to remain in his quarters for several days of rest. He was allowed to get up and walk around, with periods of sleep in between, but no strain or tension.

The first day, Mark paced back and forth like a caged lion. Although Tamara offered, he insisted on shaving himself. He looked at his black eye in the shaving mirror. "I fought deadly pirates in the Indian Ocean and came away unscathed. Now this!" he complained as he scraped the dark bristles from his chin with his razor. "I feel perfectly fine. Why must I remain here? Where is Moran?" he barked.

As the day wore on, he grew noticeably exhausted. Tamara watched as he rubbed his forehead. She was certain he was in pain, but too stubborn to admit it. Finally she was able to give him a sedative and persuade him to lie down.

From then on, Roderick Moran, having taken command, reported to Mark regularly. He took charge of the temporary repairs on the hull and stack that would enable the *Lady Tamara* to continue to Jamaica. Mark sent him to the British Customs office, always a hassle Mark dreaded. The duty officers who checked his records of shipment and bickered about import duties had time and time again tried his patience. Mark was happy to send Moran this time.

The cotton was unloaded and reloaded on the *Drake*, another Schofield merchant ship in port, which would take the cargo to Portsmouth, England. Food and water supplies were replenished on the *Lady Tamara* in preparation for her journey to Jamaica.

Not getting enough sleep, having but napped on and off in the armchair, Tamara was exhausted. She applied clean dressings to Mark's wound, saw that he was settled for the night, and waited until she thought he was asleep. Now that he was out of danger, she would undress and go to bed. Since the pirate attack she had remained in Jimmy's clothes, and she was glad to be rid of them.

Mark feigned sleep. He watched her covertly as she stood naked, almost within reach. She turned her back to pour water from the ewer into a washbowl and began to wash herself. Fascinated with her shapely body, his eyes followed the fine curves, stopped to caress the indenture at the small of her back, kiss the superb roundness of her buttocks.

He closed his eyes and gulped hard. Would that it were his hands going over her exquisite skin. He found himself shaking. His blood coursed hot through his veins.

Passion opened his eyes to slits. Tamara was covering her creamy flesh with a sheer lavender nightgown. She ran a brush through her hair before she crawled slowly into bed beside him, careful to stay close to the edge so as not to disturb him. Weariness overcame her. She fell asleep the moment her head touched the pillow.

Mark, with his eyes open wide, turned his head to gaze upon his young wife. He smelled the sweet fresh scent of her soap upon her flesh. Her lovely face was relaxed. He stared, unable to breathe. She did not look old enough to be his wife. His stomach took a somersault. Tenderness gripped him. Protectiveness and possessiveness joined in. Love planted itself firmly in his heart. His hand slid across the sheet and touched her silken tresses.

Mark was smitten. He could feel the perspiration gathering on his brow beneath the bandages. His maleness was churning up a storm beneath the bedcovers. His loins throbbed. His hard erection pushed assertively against the sheet. He glowered. What the hell could he do about it? She was fatigued, and he . . . he was flat on his damn back with a gash in his head and ordered to rest as if he were an invalid.

Mark reproached himself for behaving like a driveling callow lad eager to hump his first woman. Tamara had worn herself out waiting on him. She was fatigued from worry. He would be worse than a cad if he wakened her, but being tired and sleepy, she was less likely to resist him. Although he had no doubts whatsoever about his virility, if Moran and his men knew she was still a virgin they would think him less of a man.

He watched the slow rise and fall of her breasts, listened as she breathed in and out, deep in slumber, never realizing before what a beautiful sound it was. His arms ached to reach out and pull her close. He could see her round breasts and nipples clearly through the diaphanous lavender gown. He gaped and was lost. He had to touch her. He had to have her. He rolled to his side and stretched to slip his arm across her waist and draw her to the middle of the bed. She stirred in her sleep, snuggled closer, and sighed. Her lips parted, her arms extended in his direction. He swallowed with difficulty, pleased and encouraged by what his mere touch could evoke in her even when she slept. He could wait no longer. He turned sharply to take her in his arms, lifting his head to lean over and capture her sweet lips. A cutting pain sliced through his skull. His movements had been too abrupt. He groaned loudly and fell back on the pillow, wincing in pain. His hands flew up to his head.

Tamara sat up with a jolt. In doing so, the strap of her gown slipped from her shoulder. Tantalizing breasts tumbled out before his eyes. Mark gritted his teeth and turned his head away from the enchanting vision. A slow moaning sound escaped his throat as he pulled the covers up to his neck.

"I will send Jimmy for the doctor."

"No!" he resounded. " 'Tis just a headache." He turned to watch her comely figure leave his bed, gazed at her graceful movements as she prepared a sedative for him, which the doctor had prescribed, should he complain of pain.

He cursed to himself as the temptress stood before him and gave him the drug.

"You need rest, darling. Tomorrow you will feel better," she said in her soft, tender voice.

Mark shut his eyes. "What I need is you, Tams," he mumbled groggily as the laudanum took effect.

52

Moran was very considerate of Tamara's needs and comfort. While Mark rested, he accompanied her to the shops and straw market, where she made several purchases. He rented a carriage and took her for a ride around the town. He anticipated her every wish, including a hot bath when they returned to ship. Unknown to Tamara, before they went ashore he had ordered a barrel of fresh water set on the deck to be heated by the sun for her bath.

With the knowledge that Mark was going to be all right, Tamara relaxed in the tub. She moistened the lavender-scented soap Lila had given her, luxuriously spreading its globules of fragrant suds all over. She closed her eyes and sighed deeply, slipping down into the sun-warmed bath, savoring the clean, refreshing effect the water had on her tired body.

Tamara's eyes sprang open when a noise intruded upon her sweet reverie. Mark had entered the gallery. His lingering gaze turned her cheeks rosy. She smiled shyly, feeling a warm pleasure in the way he looked at her. Modestly she slipped farther into the water.

"A breathtaking sight to behold, my lovely wife."

"Pain gone?"

"All gone."

His fingers went to the buttons of his shirt, which he removed while walking toward her. Naked to the waist, he grabbed a stool and straddled it beside the tub and took the soap and sponge from her hands. The sight of his splendid physique caused her breath to quicken.

"Bend forward, love," he ordered softly. Tamara leaned over, her breasts dipping into the water. He massaged her neck and shoulders with the scented lather, sending tingling sensations through her body.

"You were gone two hours. Where did Moran take you?" he asked as he scrubbed.

Tamara glanced up warily. "Roddie took me to the straw market and then on a tour of Nassau. The governor general's mansion is lovely."

Mark scowled. " 'Roddie,' is it? I am your husband. You should have waited until I was able to take you."

"I am sorry, darling. The doctor told you to rest and remain in your quarters. I did not wish to bother you."

A sound of displeasure escaped his throat. "From now on, be it understood that I will be your escort."

His fingers spread suds up and down her back. He rinsed them away with the sponge, then bent over and kissed her smooth nape and shoulders. His lips lingered. His hand came around the front beneath the sudsy water and fondled her breasts.

"Now, lean back, love."

She rested her head against the back of the tub, tilting her face to meet his lips, which swooped down on hers, pressing heavily, parting hers hungrily.

He rubbed suds around her neck, across her collarbone, and up and down each arm. At the slightest touch of his finger, a nipple sprang erect. He grinned with pleasure at the noticeable response. His fingers made circles of bubbles around each distended nipple. Before he kissed each one, he dipped the sponge into the soapy water, and holding it high over her breasts, squeezed it. The water streamed down upon her shimmery flesh.

He brushed the sponge back and forth across her belly, fanning the longing deep inside. He grabbed a slim ankle and lifted one shapely leg from the water, meticulously covering it with lather, then the other. He sponged her toes and the soles of her feet, which made her laugh. He kissed the arch of her dainty foot. His fingers, an instrument of joy, moved upward beneath the water, touching, teasing the intimacy between her thighs. He brought to this wooing of his wife all his experience, all his knowledge of arousing a woman.

His need of her had gone unfulfilled for a long time. Never had he wanted a woman as much as he wanted Tamara. Rampant desire pounded at his loins. The throbbing became so intense it hurt. His mind rejected all possibility of her refusal.

Tamara, whose emotional wounds had healed, possessed deep, burning hungers. She trembled not from fear but passion. Mark smiled, encouraged when her lips parted and she whimpered. Her eyelids grew heavy, her eyes became smoldering embers of desire. She closed them while savoring the feel of his finger touching sensuous nerve endings in the warm, moist recess of her body. Feeling as if he had cast a potent spell upon her, she mumbled, "Mark . . . love me."

He gave her a quick kiss. "I do, darling. Stand up," he said huskily, taking her hands and helping her. As if in a dream she stood up, looking down at herself, watching the water slide from her body, feeling wickedly excited by Mark's eyes upon her. When the dripping stopped, he wrapped a large towel around her and dabbed her dry. She stepped from the tub, her trembling fingers reaching out, brushing the soft down on his chest. Arms slid up around his brown, muscular shoulders. Her lips sought his and found them as he rubbed the towel up and down her back, across her buttocks, between her legs. She clung to him, kissing him with wild abandon, sucking the tender flesh on his neck. He dropped the towel in a wet heap. One by one he pulled the pins from her

256

hair, which had been piled on top of her head to prevent getting wet, tossing them carelessly on the towel. Golden-red tresses fell like soft panels around her shoulders. He gathered her into his arms. His flesh burned to the touch. He carried her to his bed, where he placed her in the middle, and completed his undressing. When he went to her on the bed, she noticed the bandage wrapped around his head.

"Your head!" she protested. "I have forgotten to change the bandage."

Mark chuckled lightly. " 'Tis not me head that requires immediate attention."

The room whirled as their bodies pressed together, afire, searing flames rising toward a pinnacle.

"Mark . . . make me yours," she gasped in a pleading voice.

"Yes, love . . . now. Keep your eyes on my face. I want you to know it is me."

In Tamara, love released nature's instincts held in check until now. Passion, mired once in an undercurrent of fear, rose to the surface. Inhibitions, apprehensions, uncertainties, phantoms slid from her body like the water of her bath. No disruptive words were spoken. Beyond thought, she looked with unseeing eyes. She did not hear the splashing waves, the creaking of the ship, or the familiar noises of the quay, but heard only the silence of his lips on her body, his caressing hands. Sight, hearing, all senses merged into one violent force, fusing together in the insistent craving of her body for his. The need to be touched, the feverish longing, the urge to be possessed, the thrill of yielding. The pressure of his strong, demanding manhood against her, piercing the bridal veil. In a delirium of desperate passion they became one, unified in body and soul, man and woman, lovers, husband and wife.

For a long time afterward, they stretched, entwined in each other's arms, cuddly, affectionate, basking contentedly in the afterglow of their first love ritual. They whispered promises to love each other forever.

"There is blood on the sheet," Tamara said, lifting her hips and looking down. "Oh, dear God, your wound has opened!" she exclaimed frantically.

Mark laughed. " 'Tis not from me, my virgin bride." He groped for his white linen handkerchief and dabbed it between her legs, wiping away traces of red along with his own essence. "It will not happen again," he assured her.

Their honeymoon had begun in the coziness of Mark's

quarters on board the *Lady Tamara*, where they dined heartily on a feast of lovemaking, quenching their salacious thirsts with kisses, satisfying demanding hungers by partaking of each other.

With the last flicker of daylight, when night prevailed over dusk, the lovers were famished for nourishment. Mark ordered a meal sent to his quarters, which they devoured with relish. While they drink wine leisurely, Moran set the ship asail for Jamaica.

Mark and Tamara watched from the window of his salon, Mark confident that Moran could handle matters without him. As Nassau disappeared, he pulled her onto his lap on the divan, raining eager kisses on her face and neck. Lightly his fingernails traced zigzag lines up and down the silk robe covering her back, spreading gooseflesh, sending chills of desire through her body, arousing the love and passion trapped inside for such a long time.

He laid her down, resting her head on the crimson pillows. Standing motionless, wearing only his dark blue night robe, he looked at her closely in the flickering candlelight. Dropping to his knees before her, he opened her silk robe, touching the exquisite flesh that awakened his desire, flashed fire in his devouring eyes.

She was different. What had changed her? He found it difficult to comprehend that sedate, shy Lady Tamara Warde, his wife, was one and the same with this temptress, conqueror of his heart, enslaver of his emotions, lying before him naked with her lips and legs parted, smiling beguilingly, beckoning him with her seductive eyes and hard-tipped breasts.

That she was his overwhelmed him. Without warning she had. crept into his ordered life, disarming him completely, making herself his life, his reason to live. On his knees, he admitted all to himself, made a silent confession. He was hopelessly in love. He adored everything about her, her beauty, poise, mind, purity of heart, her passion . . . ah her passion, which he had unleashed . . . her body . . . ah, her body, thrilling him totally like a bewitching illicit lover.

For years his love affair with the sea and his ship was all he had wanted. There was no place in his life for a wife. Now, looking back, he recognized many lonely days at sea. A captain's life was different from that of a yeoman or captain's mate, especially if he was also the owner. He could not mingle with his men or while away the nights playing cards. He spent most of his late hours alone in his quarters mulling over ledgers and charts. He had sailed the seven seas like a vagabond. Had he used the family business as an excuse for his wanderings? Being a solitary man had not been all that glamorous. He had used women to satisfy his basic animal needs, but by his own choice had never permitted one to enter his heart. What about companionship and love, the need to belong to someone special? Were these not also basic to a man's true happiness? Looking back, he was surprised that he had not realized it before. He was stunned at the knowledge that until now his content had been a semblance of happiness and not the real thing.

As he knelt before Tamara a new thought crept into his head. Had falling in love with her been his destiny? He wondered whether subconsciously he had been waiting for her. He had thought about her often, hoping she had found happiness. Uncertain of what their future would be, he vowed to use all his power to make her happy. She had suffered enough. Content with the present, they had not discussed their future. He made an oath to himself he would not treat her or their children as his father had treated his mother and him. He swore he would not, could not leave her to go to sea again.

Mark was recovering miraculously from the ill effects of his bout with the murderous pirates. The deep gash was mending beneath the white linen bandages that Tamara changed twice daily. Wrapped around his head to protect the wound from dust and dirt until a scab formed, they gave him a heroic appearance.

"Tamara . . . you are outrageously lovely. I did not know how lovely until this moment." She raised her arms to welcome him. For a moment her eyes clung to his with the power of magnets that drew him to her. He threw himself beside her on the divan, sweeping her into his strong arms, passion barely held in check.

"Unknowingly, I have searched for you, the woman of my dreams, in faraway places, Calcutta, Sydney, Paris, Rome. Now I know it was you. You were born to be mine."

He pulled her on top of him. He showered her face with kisses. His questing hands touched her everywhere. Her fingers brushed across his mustache, then traced the curves of his lips. He smiled sensuously, then snapped, mimicking a dog, pretending to take a bite out of her fingers. His arms clamped around her. Desire surged through his veins. Her hand guided him to entry. Their bodies and hearts locked together.

His lovemaking became fervent, all-consuming. Bodies still

259

joined together, they rolled from the low divan to the floor. He reached up and rolled one of the pillows down, placing it beneath her buttocks. Over her arched body, he thrust deeper, accelerating his movements, on and on, sending electrifying sensations through them. Wrapping her legs around his hips, she moved with him in an unbroken sonata, vibrating in a convulsion of ecstasy. He placed his hands beneath her buttocks, pressing her body upward, closer to his, bringing her nearer to the moment of true bliss. Her body shuddered as he introduced her to fulfilled womanhood, presenting her with its ultimate experience. At the same time, feeling, knowing what he had done, excited him beyond control, brought him to his peak, and his seed burst forth within her.

"That was . . . incredible," he said, placing himself beside her and gathering her into his arms. "There are no words in the English language or any other to describe how wonderful that was," he whispered movingly.

53

In the calm of dawn, when the day's light emerged pale along the distant horizon, Mark moved his shoulder where Tamara rested her head in peaceful sleep. He maneuvered to reach her lips with his. When she felt their gentle touch, she blinked her eyes drowsily, stretched her long slender limbs, arching her bare leg across his. She closed her eyes again and nestled her head on his chest.

"Is it time to get up?" she asked sleepily.

"No, sweet. 'Tis time to make love."

"Oh, is it still night?"

"No. 'Tis morning."

Tamara smiled and knit her brow. She slipped her arms up around his neck. Tilting her head back, she searched his face, reveling in the adoration and tenderness she found.

"Love . . . so early in the morning?" she quipped lightly.

He flashed a broad, devilish grin and pressed her body tightly against his, imprisoning her with his arms and leg.

"Morning, midmorning, noon, teatime, nighttime, anytime is love time when you are near me. I've a desperate need for you this very moment."

Tamara smiled fetchingly, the corners of her lips curving sweetly upward. "Show me," she challenged coquettishly.

Completely awake now, she looked down and blushed seeing she was naked and the covers had been kicked from bed to floor in careless disarray. She blushed deeply when she looked at Mark's naked body and saw indeed that he needed her. She bent over the side of the bed in an attempt to retrieve the covers, but Mark, chuckling, pulled her back.

"You are not cold, my warm sweet love?" His arms encircled her, brought her close to the heat of his body. "The temperature will rise soon," he whispered, covering her body with his, kindling her flesh with kisses until she was breathless and the simmering fire raced through her blood like a burning inferno.

He murmured, "I love you, Tamara."

"I love you, too." She enjoyed hearing his reaffirmation over and over.

He wanted to hear hers, too. He tightened his hold on her. "How could I have surmised we would find perfect love?"

She had no answers in words, but in kisses.

He murmured more endearments. "I love your lips on mine, your arms and legs around me. It thrills me when I kiss your breasts, drives me wild when I pulsate inside you." The rest of his words were incoherent as his lips began an intimate tour of her body, stopping when he reached her thigh.

"I must have you now," he said, overcome with violent desire that demanded satisfaction.

It was midmorning when Mark signaled to Jimmy to serve their breakfast. Afterward he insisted on going on deck and resuming command of his ship. Tamara went with him. Now that she was his wife and under his full protection, he gave her more freedom to come and go as she pleased. At first she faced Roderick and the crew self-consciously, blushing, wondering whether they noticed any difference in her appearance or countenance as the result of her first night of love. Could they tell by looking at her what had taken place?

With his finger Mark had traced their route for Tamara on his large chart of the Caribbean. Their destination would take them southward through the azure waters of the Caribbean Sea between the Great Inagua Island and the eastern tip of Cuba, past Port-de-Paix, Haiti, on the east, to Kingston on the southern coastline of Jamaica.

The *Lady Tamara*, relieved of her cargo, rode high in the

water and was carried smoothly by wind-filled sails. Mark estimated they would reach Jamaica within five days.

Tamara was never happier. During the day when she chanced to see Mark, if only for a moment, she flirted with him, distracted him, possessed the urge to devour him. In the late afternoon when she returned to their quarters to take a nap, Mark followed her, telling his men he was not fully recovered and needed to rest. In the privacy of their rooms, they undressed and eagerly fell into each other's arms. "I have been thinking about this all morning and afternoon. The night's love does not last me through the day, Tams."

Each time they made love brought new delights. Tamara learned soon that he enjoyed intimacy in a variety of ways and places. He invited, excited, coaxed, led, commanded, demanded her passion, which responded, arose, and followed dreamily.

Tamara relished the knowledge of his need of her, of the effect she had on him and he on her. Love's fulfillment cast a new radiance on her face. Her eyes, clear violet, sparkled like sapphires. She walked and talked with new confidence in herself as a woman. Even her appetite, which was never wanting, improved enormously.

Each night before retiring they took several turns around the ship's deck, walking arm in arm. Then in their bedroom he swept her into his arms. They came together in a maelstrom of passion, rediscovering rapture all over again. Sometimes the loving was slow, gentle, unhurried. They allowed passion to creep over them slowly until the last phase which erupted tumultuously. Other times he picked her up and carried her to bed taking her without preliminaries, urgently, fiercely, not able to get enough of her, apologizing needlessly afterward.

"Will you not give me time to change into my nightgown?" she asked, playfully, pushing him away. He grabbed her, picked her up, and carried her to bed, laughing hoarsely.

"Not tonight, Tams. I want to look at you, feel your body against mine, touch you, kiss you all over," he said in possessive tones, kissing her breasts, her mouth, then reversing himself to kiss her other lips.

Tamara appeared so proper and sedate when in the presence of others that at times her abandonment when in Mark's arms shocked him. They did not hold back. Kisses and touches fanned tenacious fire, and when the climax came, tremor upon tremor, he smothered her cries of delight with his lips. When the flames dwindled to embers and extinction, they remained in each other's arms, enjoying the lazy contentment and idle chatter of love's sleepy aftermath.

One night, just when he thought her asleep, Tamara laughed outright.

"What is so amusing, love?"

"I was wondering . . . my eyes are violet and yours are green. What color will our babies have?"

Mark smiled, drew her closer, tightened his hold around her waist.

"Either will do, just as long as it is not one of each."

Tamara laughed.

Mark was silent for a moment. "Do you want babies, Tams?"

"Yes, don't you?"

"Oh, I suppose two or three will do."

When she was alone in the salon she went over every intimate detail, reliving again and again his expert lovemaking, going over every word and gesture. She groomed to make herself as attractive as possible for him. Ever since she had begun to choose her own clothes, she wore only the most stylish outfits. She changed dresses several times, glancing in the mirror before deciding which she thought Mark would like best. Her efforts did not go unnoticed or unrewarded.

54

"Tell me," Tamara coaxed playfully, tickling Mark's ribs. Her eyes danced with laughter.

Between chuckles he admonished her. "A lady does not ask that question," he said, cuffing her backside.

Tamara leaned her naked body over his and tickled him again, jabbing his bare rib cage with her fingers. His hands flew up to protect himself. Inner laughter exploded openly.

They were in bed in his quarters. It was their last night at sea. The next day toward noon the *Lady Tamara* would dock in Kingston. Tamara would be home. After dinner Mark had opened a bottle of champagne, which now stood empty on the floor. Bits of their clothes were strewn in a path from salon to bed. They both felt heady. His captain's quarters had provided their honeymoon at sea, a love nest that had sheltered them like a cocoon from the rest of the world. Taking pleasure only in each other, they did not need or want the company of others. In five days, love had brought them more happiness than either had thought possible. They had come to know both gentle and wildly passionate love, fulfillment, contentment, affection, companionship. They enjoyed a familiarity, an intimacy that was new to them, such as at this moment.

"Tell me," Tamara repeated insistently. "Are you circumcised?"

Mark's body shook from his guffaw. "No," he answered, laughing. His lips grabbed the lobe of her ear.

"No, you will not discuss it, or no, you are not circumcised? Which is it?" She continued poking him.

"Tams, you truly shock me." He feigned surprise.

"Well, are you?"

"Why is it so important to you?"

"Important? I do not understand. I am curious, that is all."

"Some women prefer . . . Never mind."

Incredibly, he, Mark Schofield, was suddenly shy with a woman, with his wife. He felt his face turn scarlet.

Tamara's hand roved down to his chest, then his taut belly, and below, approaching the point of discussion.

Mark's voice turned husky. He nuzzled her head against his shoulder. "Hush, now! 'Tis time to go to sleep."

"I am not sleepy, and why won't you tell me?" she persisted.

"You know what is happening, don't you?" he warned. His questing hands found her breasts. "Your chatter has aroused me. I am getting wicked ideas. In another moment I will be making love to you."

"Greedy, you just did for the last hour," she quipped.

"You are tempting me to start all over again." He rolled on top of her, pinning her to the bed. "Spread your legs."

His need had grown acute, but once he entered her, he remained quite still, completely in command of the moment. She pretended indifference. His virility and the scent of his cologne struck the first blow at her defenses. She felt her pulse increasing, the heat rising. She faked a yawn in pretext of being bored. He advanced his siege with an onslaught of gentle touches with his masculine hands on her sensuous zones, further weakening her pretense. She closed her eyes, acted as if she had fallen asleep, secretly, so she thought, savoring the slow spread of pleasure through her body. His errant lips attacked the smooth flesh where her neck and shoulder met, causing her arms to go up around him, her fingers to entwine in the thick locks at the nape of his neck. His mouth encountered no resistance when it met hers, long, demandingly, undermining her bluff. Her lips parted to return his kisses, an outward clue of surrender. She felt his hardness increasing within her, his coup, his master stroke. Her blood turned molten. Her body could no longer remain outwardly passive. Beleaguered by unrelenting internal and external forces, she succumbed, wrapping her legs around him, clutching her hands to his back. She moved her hips up and down, slowly at first, then fiercely increasing her pace.

Mark reveled in his *tour de force*. His lips left hers and he looked into the dark purple pools of her eyes, shimmering with passion. "Now who is being greedy?" he teased, but after a moment found himself surrendering to her sensuous delights, reversing his position from captor to captive, groaning as her hips moved wildly to meet his rhythm. She arched her back, feeling the force of his love flow into her body.

After their journey of passion, which took them beyond understanding, his hair damp, his body moist, he lay beside her breathless. He hugged her, kissed her cheek, rubbed his hand up and down her arm. Relaxed, he closed his eyes until he felt her move as she lifted her head.

"Now are you ready to tell me?" she whispered.

His naked abdomen waved in spasms of chuckles.

"Do I amuse you?" she asked crisply.

"I am sorry, darling, but . . . dammit, yes! I was hoping you would forget."

"Then you refuse to tell me?"

"No, I am not circumcised. Now are you satisfied?"

"Not exactly. I do not understand what is done to a man when he is circumcised. Will you explain it to me?"

"I can see it is necessary if I am to get any sleep tonight."

With candor he proceeded to explain the procedure of circumcision and then showed himself to her, pointing out the loose foreskin, explaining how it would be snipped in the operation, how his phallus was different from a man's who was circumcised. She touched him and pushed the skin back, felt how thick and stiff he had grown again. He took in his breath sharply.

"Someday your curiosity is going to get you into trouble," he moaned, grabbing her hands and holding them. He pushed her head against his shoulder. "Now, let's get some sleep."

She lifted her head again. "Just one more question that has bothered me."

He waited, not knowing what to expect.

"What is castration?"

Mark's eyes flew open. He did not answer immediately. "It is when a man is emasculated."

"How is it done?"

"There are various methods. Sometimes a sharp knife is used to sever the genitals."

"Ugh! I am sure it is very painful. Is it not dangerous as well?"

"Of course, if infection sets in. Then there is the problem of urination."

"Oh, God, the thought of it is horrid. I am sorry I asked," she said, reflecting revulsion in her words.

"I met several such men when I was in Morocco. They are then eunuchs, unable to perform sexually. When this is done to a male horse, it becomes a gelding," he said matter-of-factly.

"Have you ever been unable to perform sexually?" she asked with curiosity in her voice.

He guffawed. "Yes. I am in that condition at this very moment."

Satisfied with his explanations, Tamara nestled in his arm and went to sleep.

In the morning Tamara was occupied getting her belongings in order when Mark rushed into the bedroom. "Hurry, Tamara. I have something to show you."

She went with him to the main deck, where he pointed to the horizon straight ahead, handing her his spyglass. Seeing a speck of green, she gasped with delight. "It is Jamaica! We are home at last!"

"She is farther away than you think, though. 'Twill take another hour."

That hour passed slowly for Tamara. As they approached Jamaica, a haze hung like a curtain in front of the looming Blue Mountains. A backdrop of dark, fast-moving rain clouds, like a foreshadowing, brought showers, then disappeared. As they sailed into the harbor, which was just as she remembered, the clouds broke apart. Sunbeams danced across the deck. Tamara sniffed the tropical air, drawing it in deep, enjoying its sweetness, feeling its warm gentleness against her face. Seagulls greeted them, flying low over the hull and alighting on the masts. The crew of an outgoing vessel waved. Tamara and Mark smiled and waved back.

"I forgot how truly beautiful the island is," Tamara mused.

Mark was delighted to see her eyes sparkle and her cheeks flush with excitement. "Since I know how much Jamaica means to you, I am glad to be the one to bring you home."

"Thank you for bringing me, darling."

Tears filled her eyes then as the crystal-clear memory of her departure flashed before her. She slipped her hand into Mark's, remembering where his parents had stood on the quay and waved.

"It makes me sad to know your mother will not be here to welcome us."

Mark squeezed her hand and smiled ruefully. "I am sure she would have approved my choice of a bride."

Mark understood Tamara's preference to remember her home as it was when she left. His intention was not to destroy her childhood memories, but feeling protective, he saw a need to prepare her for a change. "I believe your home has been boarded closed all these years, love. Do not expect it to look as it did when you lived there," he warned.

"Of course not. I understand that."

"I think it best we stay at Schofield Manor, at least for the time being, unless you would prefer to live on the ship."

Tamara hesitated. "Let's see what we find, before we decide."

55

Tamara gaped at the tranquil Caribbean Sea mottled brilliant azure, crystal-clear turquoise, deep blue, purple, and pale green. She inhaled deeply, taking in the sweet smells of the tropics and the sounds of the harbor. Her hungry eyes feasted on the towering Blue Mountains.

As soon as they disembarked, Mark whisked her away before she had a chance to get her fill of the scene. He leased a horse and calash with the top folded back, stating that he would send a wagon from Schofield Manor for their luggage.

"Mark, could we stop at Montjoy first . . . just for a few minutes? Please."

At first reluctant, not knowing what they might find, Mark hesitated, but when he saw the pleading look in her eyes, he could not refuse. The small carriage left Old Hope Road, turning right onto Montjoy Lane, which would take them to the Warde estate. The road was deep-rutted and rocky, washed out by heavy downpours. They had not driven far when it grew narrower and narrower, until it was impossible to go any farther and the horse stopped without Mark pulling on the reins. Lofty grass and thicket ruled the road ahead, too overgrown for the carriage to get through. They went the rest of the way on foot.

Briers clung to Tamara's long skirt, pulling on it like groping fingers attempting to stop her. Mark took her arm as they stepped over fallen trees and broken limbs. He waved away silky spiderwebs woven from branch to branch like Christmas-tree ornaments.

They bypassed jungle-thick trees hanging full of large brown termite nests. When they came to a clearing, Tamara stopped and stared for a long silent moment. Symbolic of what happened a long time ago, the house seemed to tell her it was useless to try to recapture what had once been. It looked dead, rotting in its grave. Vines twisted up over crumbling walls, their tendrils crawling across the partially caved-in roof. Windowpanes were smashed. Loose, weatherbeaten shutters, barely fastened by rusted hinges, swayed precariously. Steps leading to the verandas were broken and unsafe to tread upon. Eight years of neglect had worked their toll.

Tamara remembered it the way it used to be. A melancholy expression entered her eyes. She had expected the home to be abandoned, boarded closed, but the crumbling view before her was a heartbreaking disappointment.

"I should have known it was impossible to go back. Nothing remains the same," she said softly, continuing to stare in disbelief.

"We will look to the future together," Mark replied, trying to comfort her. He put his arm around her shoulders as they proceeded toward the front entrance. "Are you certain you are up to going inside today?" he asked warily, mindful of her feelings, afraid of how she might react. She had not been in the house since that fateful day she ran to his home seeking help, and he was certain a flood of memories would sweep over her.

"I must. I want to walk into that drawing room and face it head-on. Otherwise I shall never be completely free of it."

"That's my brave darling. I will go with you."

They discovered all doors nailed and boarded shut. Mark walked to one of the broken windows. Cautious not to cut himself on the sharp, jagged edges, he reached inside and unlocked the latch. He pushed the window open and helped Tamara crawl into what had been the parlor.

It felt damp inside. A musty odor hung heavy in the air. The room smelled of dust, mold, and mouse droppings. Walls were damaged from leakage. Silk papering that had been bright and beautiful was crisp and brown, water-spotted. Broad strips of it had peeled from the walls and hung to the floor. The bare walls were covered with green mold. Mice and large black bugs scurried across the dirty tile floor. Spiders dropped from their webs.

Mark looked at Tamara hesitantly. "Tamara, I am afraid termites have done a great deal of damage," he commented, sweeping away a large spiderweb. "It is not safe to walk across the floor. Should we fall through, we could be trapped, and no one knows we are here."

The door to the drawing room was ajar. Tamara froze. She had been brave up to that moment. Now her courage failed her. She looked at Mark for guidance.

He squeezed her hand comfortingly. "Maybe it would be better to wait until another day, Tams."

"Yes, I think I will do that, if you promise to bring me here tomorrow."

"Of course I will. Let's go back to the carriage."

Tamara was pensive as they drove toward Schofield Manor. Finally she spoke, but so softly Mark could barely hear her. "It cannot be repaired, can it?" she asked gloomily, a woebegone look crossing her face.

A lull followed her question. Mark considered carefully before he answered. "It would not be feasible. Termites have taken over. If that is where you wish to live, it would be advisable to tear the structure down to the ground and build a new house."

"I have the funds to do that. The money from my father's estate was put in trust for me until I was of age or married."

"Tamara, you still do not know what kind of man I am. Do you think I would tolerate that? Your money will not be touched. We will use mine. I will build you the home of your dreams."

The Schofields' sprawling stone mansion was cool inside. Richly decorated, every room was exquisite with furniture, draperies, and works of art that Mark's father had collected around the world, chairs and crystal chandeliers from France, divans from India, marble statuary from Italy, tables and cabinets with inlaid mother-of-pearl from the Orient. Areas of the marble-tile floors were covered with Aubusson and Bessarabian carpets. What Tamara liked best was something that could not be purchased or imported, the breathtaking view from every window and balcony that circled the house.

Two faithful Schofield servants, a Negro couple, Dodie and Arona Brown, occupied the rooms on the third floor. Born into slavery in Jamaica, freed by British emancipation, now middle-aged, they had worked for the Schofields for over thirty years. Both displayed genuine happiness when they saw Mark. They had received no notice and were surprised when he showed up and introduced Tamara as his wife. Tamara remembered them vaguely.

Arona had helped to bring Mark into the world, assisted in caring for him when he was little, doted on him like a mother hen. Throughout Mrs. Schofield's long illness she had been a dependable housekeeper and companion to the sick woman.

Matronly, Arona was a tall, buxom woman with a flawless dusty-rose complexion and short silver-gray hair. She ruled her husband, Dodie, with a firm hand. Easygoing Dodie needed ruling and prodding. His nature was such that he refused to allow his wife's bossiness to rile him. He loved her and accepted his waspish ways, ignored them most of the time. As domineering as she was, she turned soft, passionate, and submissive in his bed.

Dodie was thin, not quite as tall as Arona, and slightly stooped. His ebony-colored complexion was darker than Arona's, and where her face was smooth, his had begun to wrinkle. His kinky hair, black, gray, and white, was as multistriate as the feathers of a guinea hen. Dodie smiled a great deal of the time, proudly displaying a gold eyetooth. The smile broke into a hearty laugh whenever something struck him as amusing. He never hurried, never got excited, but he was terrified of spirits and ghosts. A firm believer in obeah, the native religion brought from Africa by his ancestors, he was afraid of the obeah priests and what they might do to him.

Dodie never walked. He either ambled or shuffled. He didn't talk much. He left that to Arona, but he whistled all the time.

With her hands on her hips, Arona examined Mark from his head to his boots. "Aw t'ink you turn into good-lookin' mun. 'Bout time you marry." She looked at Tamara with a

270

warm, welcoming expression in her eyes. "Aw 'member you, po' chile. Do Mark treat you right? Bettah o'aw box his ears if do'an. Not too ol' fer dat."

Tamara laughed. "I will remember that."

Arona looked at Mark. "You catch turtle, aw makes snappa soup you likes." She shook her head, and her eyes returned to Tamara. "When he little, always git hisself dirty catchin' turtles." She punched him playfully on his arm. "Break his mama's heart he go 'way. Nebba sass his mama. Bettuh do same wis you."

Dodie laughed. "Mistah Schofield, Arona try boss you jes' like she do me. Do'an mind her. Arona got sharp tongue, but soft heart."

Mark and Tamara laughed. Mark looked at Arona with affection in his eyes. "Arona, it is good to be home. Do you know when to expect my father?"

"Do'no zackly. Maybe two, three week."

Dodie led the horse and wagon from the stable, sitting slouched on the wagon seat with his banjo beside him, which Mark had given him several years earlier. Holding the reins in his hand, he waited for instructions, restless to be on his way to Kingston, since he planned to use the opportunity to stick a chew of tobacco in his mouth.

Arona forbade tobacco chewing. She could not stomach the constant spitting of brown tobacco juice mixed with spittle. Dodie hid his tobacco pouch in a rafter in the stable. He looked forward to errands in Kingston or going fishing, for as soon as he was away from Arona's sight, out came the tobacco pouch. He would stuff a big wad in his mouth, packing it into his cheek firmly with his finger. Feeling like a king, he would sit back on the wagon seat, spitting tobacco juice in an arched, spurting stream that splattered the bushes along the road to Kingston and back.

Arona knew of his transgression, but pretended otherwise. It was a game they played. She actually delighted in her secret indulgence, believing he enjoyed it better chewing behind her back. She saw the telltale stains on his mouth and chin even when he was cautious to gargle with water at the horse trough, wiping his face dry on the sleeve of his shirt. Regardless of whether he managed to remove the golden-brown visible evidence, Arona's nose, as sharp as a bloodhound's, picked up the tobacco scent.

Dodie's attempts at discretion amused Arona. The only time she fumed about it was when he spattered the juice on his shirt. She realized he knew she would see the brown spots and felt compelled to make a raspy fuss about it, taking pleasure in bawling him out, acting as if she did not know what he was doing all along. When this happened, he argued unconvincingly that he chewed tobacco because he thought he had worms.

Dodie was content with his life. Never ventured beyond the circle from Schofield Manor to Kingston and back. Dodie was a man happy on a road to nowhere. When in Kingston, he became a sinner, buying chewing tobacco and a bottle of rum if he possessed enough funds for both, taking delight in smuggling them into the stable on his return.

"Pay 'tention, Dodie," Arona snapped, telling him what supplies to buy at the Kingston market after he picked up the luggage on board the *Lady Tamara*. Since neither Dodie nor Arona could read or write, she could not give him a list of what to bring back. Reluctant to rely on his memory, she asked him to repeat the items—grouper, lobster, yams.

"Do'an you dally," she warned. Aw needs dat flour and sugar."

"Uh-huh." Dodie had his mind on the tobacco pouch hidden beneath the floorboard of the wagon.

"Be mir'cle if you 'members ever'thing," commented Arona.

"Would you like me to write a list?" Tamara asked.

"Yas'm. Dat best ideer. Aw t'ank you, ma'am. 'Preciates it."

"Stop fer Thelma on de way back," Arona called as Dodie flicked the reins and was off to Kingston. Thelma was their married daughter who helped with the cooking and cleaning when Mr. Schofield was in residence. Most of the servants had been dismissed after Mrs. Schofield died and Mr. Schofield departed on his travels to forget.

Arona prepared the bed in Mark's suite of rooms on the second floor. She gathered bunches of jasmine and filled a large vase for the bedroom and another for the center of the dining-room table. She began to prepare food for the evening meal, remembering some of Mark's favorite dishes—banana biscuits, rice with a white wine sauce, pork tenderloin preserved in glass jars when they last butchered a pig. She peeled a coconut, grapefruit and bananas to make a salad.

That night a lingering malaise caused Tamara to be restless. Mark rubbed her back soothingly. He held her close in his arms as she drifted in and out of sleep, afraid she might have a recurrence of the nightmares.

Next morning, after a breakfast prepared by Arona, the stablehand saddled two horses for their ride to Montjoy. This time they entered the drawing room unfalteringly. Noticing the tears welling up in his wife's eyes, feeling her tremble, Mark put a comforting arm around her. Through blurred vision, Tamara looked at the floor where her parents had lain. Her eyes rested on the bare space where her childhood rocker had stood. Speechless, she turned in her husband's arms, which closed around her.

Draperies torn and faded, water-marked, hung in threads. The room was bare except for one dusty painting that hung crookedly on the wall.

"I wonder what happened to all the furniture and rugs. I suspect Uncle Arthur sold them."

Mark did not answer. She waited several minutes. "Are you ready to leave now?" he asked softly, anxious to get her away from the unpleasantness. Tamara nodded her head up and down, ready to put the traumatic experience behind her once and for all.

"I would like to visit the graves of my parents before we return to Schofield Manor."

It was difficult to get through. Dense undergrowth, weeds, and bushes had taken over the path to the little graveyard. Mark tried to make it easier for her by trampling them with his boots.

Barely visible amid the grass waving in the tradewind, two crooked headstones covered with bird droppings marked the graves of Lord and Lady Readington, showing that both had died June 3, 1853.

"The graves have been sadly neglected," Tamara remarked sorrowfully, placing small bunches of pink hibiscus at the tombstones.

"I will see to it that the graveyard is cleared," Mark promised.

Subdued by nostalgia and remembered love—a fleeting glimpse of how it had been—she rested her head on his shoulder; then he led her back to their horses.

"When I was a child, I took for granted that my mother and father would always be at hand. Then, abruptly, they . . . were gone," she mused. " 'Tis the same with my home. I thought it would be almost the way it was when I last saw it. I did not expect this."

Mark's hand came up and stroked her hair. "I understand perfectly, darling. When I left Kingston to begin my career, I took my folks for granted. Most of us are guilty of that. I thought my gentle mother would always be here. I never thought of her aging. Then one day I came home to find she had grown old. And yesterday I returned to find her gone. 'Tis life's way, Tamara. We must accept it. We have a great deal to be thankful for, eh . . . you and I? We have fond memories and . . . we have each other, do we not?"

"Whatever differences you have with your father, I wish you would settle them before it is too late."

"I will try. Everyone has an Achilles' heel. Mine is my father."

56

Mark placed his hands on Tamara's waist and lifted her, easing her into the saddle. As they left the little graveyard behind them, he spoke once again of his father. "I never really knew him. I seldom saw him when I was a boy. He was away most of the time. Consequently I built a marvelous image of him. I worshiped him—looked up to him as the perfect man, with all virtues and no faults."

Mark gave a bitter laugh. His eyes hardened. Tamara remained silent, hoping he would continue to talk about his father.

"It was not until I reached my teens that I realized I was wrong. My mother was a lonely, neglected woman. I cannot prove it, but I suspect he was unfaithful to her. I swore it would be a cold day in hell before I would marry and treat my family the way we were treated. I could not ask a woman I loved to put up with that."

He shook his head. "All those years wasted when we could have been together."

Mark regarded his lovely wife sitting erect on her mount. He held the reins with one hand, made a gesture with the other.

"At any rate, I cannot remember a time when my father showed genuine affection for either of us. He castigated us at every turn. He was always irritable. Desperately searching for approval, no matter how hard I tried to please him, I received nothing but criticism. He struck at my self-confidence time and time again. I grew up believing the only one who could do anything right was my father. I thought I was the one who was wrong, that I had done things that displeased him. Dammit, Tams, we could not even please him with the Christmas gifts we chose for him, and he let us know it."

Tamara looked at him warily. "You are not lacking in self-confidence now."

"It was something I was determined to overcome."

They came to a part of the path too narrow for the horses to walk side by side. Mark pulled in his reins to allow Tamara to go ahead.

She looked back at him. "Some men simply do not know how to show love. They think demonstrating affection is a sign of weakness. I am positive your father loves you."

Mark scowled. "He has a hell of a way of showing it," he said sourly. "The time came when I realized I had to shrug off this notion that I was too stupid to do anything right. The fault was not in me, but in my father, a flaw in his character. At first I felt guilty about my change in attitude toward him, but the older I grew, the more I understood our home was no more than a place for him to hang his hat when he was not in some port on the other side of the world."

The trail widened. Mark drew up his mount alongside Tamara's."

"He came home whenever he was ill. He suffered periodic bouts of malaria. My mother nursed him devotedly, waited on him, catered to his every whim, but she could never please him or do anything right."

Mark shook his head.

"She tolerated so much and never complained. She kept it all hidden inside, until it burst forth in her fatal illness."

He looked across to his wife. "I blame my father for what she became, the shell of a woman who prayed to die."

Tamara looked at him questioningly. "Does your father know how you feel?"

Mark smirked. "Heavens no. At times guilt-ridden, I have gone out of my way to mask my feelings—filial respect and all that. I was the obedient son, the only child to carry on my father's wishes. Christian doctrine demands: Honor and respect thy father. Whenever he snaps his fingers, I jump to attention. When he commands, I obey. There was only one time when I defied him. During the Crimean War my father balked at using his ships. I went over his head in committing them and myself to the cause."

On the surface, Mark had shown respect, but deep within, known only to himself until now, he possessed a festering loathing for his father. Part of his drive stemmed from that hatred, an obsession to do better than he. Mark blamed it on his father and gave little credit to his own ambitions and self-willed urge to excel.

He took a deep breath and exhaled forcibly. "Father wields power, but he is not the man most people think he is. He's vain, lacks understanding and compassion. He is a man who craves compliments but is unable to give them."

Tamara cleared her throat as her eyes considered him with anguish. "I always thought of him as a kindly man. He was good to me."

Mark nodded emphatically. "Oh, he has his good points. I don't deny it. He might not be generous with praises for his son and wife, but he has helped many people, if only to nourish his own ego." Mark shrugged. "My mother didn't want a large mansion. It was vital to my father to amass a fortune and own the most luxurious home on the island—his way of compensating for not being born with a title. Ironically, I was the one to receive those honors without seeking them."

Mark pushed back the limb of a tree extending over the trail so that Tamara could pass.

"When he grew tired of roaming, he turned the company over to me. I am surprised he had enough confidence in me."

"Mark, he must have a great deal of confidence in you or he would not have done that."

Mark frowned. "Sometimes I wish I had refused to go to sea and had gone out on my own."

He held the reins in one hand, flicked the other through the air. "Done something on my own, something entirely different just to prove I do not need his influence. I might still do that, if only to prove it to myself. No one likes to feel indebted, not even to one's father."

Tamara gave him a sweet wifely smile. For a moment it distracted him. He liked to look at the perfection of her teeth.

"You would be successful no matter what you did."

Mark laughed. "My sons, which you are going to give me, my beautiful wife, shall feel differently about their father."

Tamara noticed his spirits had lifted. He was not as sullen as when he first began to talk about his father. The confessions to Tamara seemed to have brought some kind of inner relief.

"At any rate, I was determined to make the most of it, not only learning the ins and outs of a gigantic business, but negotiating agreements, improving and increasing shipments—doubling profits—which, I am proud to say, I did." He flipped his hand through the air. "I did it honestly—no

276

cheating on shipments, no underhanded deals. I could not live with myself if I were guilty of deception. I want to be able to sleep nights. I prefer everything open and aboveboard. But however successful I was, Father was always critical. The stipulations were not clear, the rate of exchange not to his satisfaction, not enough profit."

Mark shrugged as if he did not know what to do about it.

"Be kind to him, Mark. He is your father. If only mine were still here. I loved him so."

They reached the stable and dismounted. Linking hands, they walked toward the house, passing a tamarind tree. Mark picked one of the yellow blossoms and tucked it in her hair. He looked at her fondly. "I did not realize how well your name suits you." He took her hand affectionately, and they entered the house to change for dinner.

Tamara had learned a great deal about her husband that afternoon. She vowed to try to bring him and his father closer together, certain that much of the difficulty was due to a clash of two strong personalities.

In spite of the dilapidated condition of Montjoy, the days and weeks that followed were blissful. Mark and Tamara settled comfortably in Mark's suite of rooms on the second floor at Schofield Manor until they could move into their own home. Tamara wrote to the Warde solicitor in London, informing him of her marriage and return to Jamaica, certain that he would notify her uncle. This knowledge gave her satisfaction, for she did not want to be the cause of worry for her uncle.

Mark gave his crew leave, maintaining only a skeleton force on board the *Lady Tamara* while the damages made by the pirate ship were fully repaired. Roderick Moran returned to England.

Together, Mark and Tamara planned their home.

"I would like a courtyard with splashing fountains, lots of flowers, and terraces. Our bedrooms shall have a balcony facing the sea."

Mark laughed. "I want a boathouse down at the beach for the new sailboat I intend to buy."

Mark took their ideas to an architect in Kingston. Preparations were begun immediately to tear down the old house and clear the land. He hired several men to clean up the graveyard and landscape it with flowering shrubs.

Mark found it difficult to break his habit of rising at the first signs of dawn. Tamara discovered she adored it when he roused her with kisses and drowsily they made love in the pale light of morning.

Part of each week Mark went to the Schofield shipping office in Kingston, but he found time to spend with Tamara. They went riding along the beaches and up into the winding mountain passes. They swam in the surf and made love in a secluded cove. They went fishing, enjoying the way Arona prepared what they caught, using butter and special herbs.

"When you lived here before, did you swim in the pool on Rainbow Mountain?" Mark asked one night as she nestled in his arms.

"No, only in the surf. My parents forbade me to ride alone in the mountains."

"It is several miles northwest of Schofield Manor. It's quite secluded. I came upon it by chance. In those days I went there often." Mark pulled her closer, nuzzled his face in her hair. "In the morning, tell Arona to pack a food basket. We will ride there if you like."

Dense tropical greenery cloaked the narrow mountain trail that wove to avoid boulders and large tree trunks. Their sure-footed mounts trod slowly. Toward dawn a cool rain had fallen, bringing refreshing moisture to grass, flowers, and trees, making their ride more pleasant. When they arrived at the pond, Mark dismounted and helped Tamara. He made a valiant bow. "I welcome you to my secret paradise."

At first Tamara felt like an intruder in the awesome sanctum of the primal surroundings unchanged for centuries, but the pool seemed to beckon them. The glassy surface reflected trees and bright-blooming flowers basking in tropical splendor.

"I never knew this was here!" Tamara exclaimed excitedly.

Mark picked up a pebble and skidded it across the mirror-like water, animating the reflected scene.

They undressed. Tamara hung her clothes on a sun-dappled fern tree. She watched Mark as he dived in immediately, surfaced, and swam the length of the pool and back with strong, vigorous strokes. He made Tamara laugh as he mimicked a well-trained Labrador retriever, swimming doglike with a stick protruding from the corners of his mouth. He removed the twig and tossed it onto the bank. His sportiveness made Tamara exuberant, but she was not as brave. She stretched her long, exquisite leg and dipped her toe in first, then stepped into the cool mountain water up to her ankles. Mark waited for her in the shallow part, gazing with unblinking eyes. She stood as straight and graceful as the trees around her. She was not shy or in the least immodest before his devouring eyes. Her sensuality—her hair falling freely around her shoulders, her rose-tipped nipples, melon-like breasts, the curves of her waist, lean-tapered limbs—caused an unabashed grin to spread across Mark's face, set his temples pounding. He gave a long, low whistle.

Tamara treasured the look of approval in his eyes. A tingling sensation swept through her, and she smiled provocatively as she stepped deeper into the crystal-clear water, dipping down to her waist, catching her breath.

"It's just until you get wet, Tams," Mark called, his voice echoing across the water. He drifted closer. Laughing hoarsely, he splashed her ample breasts. She immersed, swam underwater, surfaced in back of him. She splashed him, then minnowed to escape. But he was too swift for her. His arms crushed her wet naked body to his. His lips came down on hers. He lifted her out of the water until his mouth found her breast. Before he put her down, sliding her body along his, his teasing tongue hardened her nipples. They stood close, facing each other in the water. He cupped her face with his wet hands. "Would you be averse to making love in broad daylight?" he asked, the timbre of his voice deep and compelling.

Taking a step closer, she answered by putting her arms around his neck, pressing her breasts firmly against his dark-haired chest, softly touching her lips against his.

"Feel my cheeks. They burn."

Jesting, Mark slipped his hands beneath the water to her buttocks. His eyes glistened. "They feel cool under the water."

"Not those, you guff. Here, on my face." Mark burst out laughing, then squeezed her tightly.

"My body aches for your love," she said softly.

Mark smiled. "And mine is on fire." His voice was low. He grabbed her hand and submerged it. "Touch me."

She clasped his member with her fingers. In spite of the cold water, it was hard and erect. She dived down into the transparent water, taking him into her mouth and kissing him until it was necessary to surface for air. He lifted her up in his arms and carried her to the edge of the bank, where he seated her, her feet dangling in the water. He stood waist-deep in the water between her legs and eased her back until her head and shoulders touched the cushiony green-covered earth. Her body tingled in anticipation. Her temples beat like the obeah drums of the Jamaicans she heard on dark nights.

His questing lips found her feminine mysteries, spawning thousands of rippling sensations. Tiny shock waves escaped from where his tongue touched her, sending scalding desire through her body. Abandoning herself to the passion he aroused, she moved her legs up around his neck. His tongue spurred her on to the brink of madness. Whimpering sounds of ecstasy escaped her throat. It was almost too much to bear, but her body screamed for more, until the final moment, when the bursting sensations began and went on and on.

After she stopped quivering, he grabbed her hands and pulled her into the water. She flung herself into his arms, the water splashing up around them. Passionately he returned her spontaneous kisses. She clung to him, her arms becoming ropes of flesh around the hard muscles of his back. Water dripped from her heavy mass of hair. She brushed the water from her wet lashes. He swung her around, playfully plunging her up and down in the water. Then, laughing mirthfully, he lifted her up in his arms and carried her to the shore.

Mark put her down on the verdant moss-covered ground, kissing her ardently, pinning his body against hers, uttering her name over and over in his thick emotional voice. Their breath mingled. He fondled her breasts. His hands caressed her rounded buttocks. Her flesh was keen to his every touch. He smiled to himself when he felt her quick response, marveled at her swift recuperative powers. Would that he could be reinvigorated and ready for more so quickly. How annoying it was for a man to wait for nature to perform its duty.

He bent over her, looked into her eyes, and whispered, "Keep your eyes open. Watch me enter you."

Tamara had always closed her eyes. She lifted her head and looked down. He entered her with unconstrained ease, feeling her warm, moist, clinging flesh, filling her with his passion. Giving and taking pleasure, they commingled rapturously in a harmony of bodies and souls. As they climbed the lofty slopes of passion together, he looked up to see her watching. Their eyes met. The magnetism was always there, but in that moment the exquisite flames of desire soared higher, shooting currents of rapture through their veins.

"Looking at your body and seeing the expression in your eyes thrills me beyond description," he murmured deeply, his huskily spoken words igniting more fires.

"You feel so wonderful inside me," she mumbled. They moved together, seeking and giving pleasure, not in a calculated way, but as instinctively naturally as breathing. When he knew she was on the verge of release, he withdrew, leaving her gasping and reaching out to pull him to her. Wetly he entered her again. They rocked in rhythm toward a single-minded goal. She had become so sensitive to his touch that she could feel he was on the brink of bursting. The thrilling sensation hurled her to join him in a mutual explosion. Tenderness vanished with the full force of his passion, sending them to the summit, where they were overwhelmed by its exultation, then descended with the contented knowledge that they had reached the pinnacle of bliss.

Shakily Mark eased himself to her side. His limbs were weak. He was unable to move. "That went beyond paradise, Tams," he murmured placidly.

"Mmmmn," Tamara hummed in agreement. Eyes half-shut, relishing the delicious aftermath, she sighed and glanced up at the emerald canopy of trees, a bell jar of lush green foliage, their temple of love. White clouds floated in filmy skeins across the blue sky. She took a deep breath as she felt the warmth of the sunbeams penetrating through the branches. Exhilarated, she stretched luxuriously, then nestled in the curve of her lover's arm, secure and content.

But not for long. Soon she reached for him again, finding him limp. He winced in exaggerated dismay. "For shame, my greedy little lover. A virtuous woman does not have the impulses you do. A wife is not supposed to enjoy this sort of play or behave as you do," he teased, expressing the common beliefs of the time.

Tamara thumped her fist on her forehead mockingly. "Then I beg you, sir, divorce me and make me your mistress," she chided wistfully. They laughed and rubbed noses. He clutched her possessively.

"I love you. Do you think I want a passive lump of ice for a wife, who would force me to seek a mistress? I have been fortunate in finding a wife who is also my mistress."

She looked into his eyes, her fingers reaching for him again.

He chuckled. "You must give me more time, love."

But in a few moments he was in her, remaining inside her until he was hard enough to maneuver. They moved together as softly as the gentle winds rippled the leaves, until he felt compelled to plunge fast and deep. When he felt her quaking contractions of ecstasy, he withdrew, still hard and erect, and moved to her side.

"I failed you," she blurted.

Mark laughed. "That you will never do. It is because for the moment I am replete. You have satisfied me completely."

The scent of tropical flowers and the clean earth surrounded them. He rolled on his side to face her, propping his elbow up to support his head. He wrapped his leg over hers. Idly the fingers of his other hand traced her mouth. His thumb touched her relaxed lips, rubbed back and forth.

"Have you ever stood before a table of tempting desserts? Not being able to make a choice, gluttonously you try a little of each, a dab of pudding, a slice of rich walnut torte, a helping of chocolate mousse, until your plate is covered. Halfway through the feast, you discover you cannot possibly eat another bite. Your eyes and desires were greater than your physical capacity." He made a face, swelling his cheeks as if they would burst. Tamara laughed.

"You put the plate aside, hoping that within the hour you will be able to finish what you have started."

He brushed his lips down along Tamara's throat and across her breasts, then pulled her into his arms.

"That is exactly what I intend to do with you, my creamy *pièce de resistance*. We will take a nap, and then . . . look out! You know how it is with me the second time around. I want it to be as long-lasting as possible."

He closed his eyes and cradled her in his arms. Dreamily she spoke of what she would do to him after their rest. "I shall do what you want . . . as you instructed me," she said softly. "I have learned when to hold back, when your gestures mean stop and when they mean continue." As she became more explicit, her fingers caressed him. She smiled wickedly in an unspoken invitation.

"Pretend you are that sheikh in Morocco you told me about. I am your favorite concubine. Lie back while I work my magic," she instructed soothingly. She knelt and made a deep obeisance, her head touching the ground at his feet; then she looked up into his eyes. "You summoned me, master?" she asked enticingly.

Lifting his gaze to meet hers, he played along. "Yes. Proceed immediately."

She stood at his feet, lowering her lashes and bowing humbly. She swayed and circled her hips, undulating provocatively, with undeniably seductive movements. Her fingers outlined her nipples, then her hands cupped her bare breasts suggestively, before they slid caressingly to her thighs.

Tamara saw his sharp intake of breath and smiled secretly. She picked two long fern leaves and used them as fans, waving them in front of her face like veils as slowly she knelt between his legs. She ran the soft green plumes over his body, up and down his erect manhood, causing gooseflesh. Gracefully she tossed the feathery fronds aside and began to kiss him, starting at his feet and moving upward.

Mark savored the hot spirals of pure passion swirling through his hard-muscled body and settling in his loins. He reached for her breasts to fondle them. Tamara stopped when she reached his thighs, removing her hands and lips. She sat back on her heels and waited for his response. He opened his eyes and stared at her.

"Would you like me to continue, master?"

"Yes, yes," he urged impatiently, it no longer being a game. His composure was beginning to desert him. She bent toward him and began again, moving her tongue, using her mouth, kissing him with her throat the way he liked, drawing him into an abyss until she knew he was on the brink of release. Then she stopped again, to prolong his pleasure. He imagined an earthquake shook the ground beneath him. He groped for her head to return it to the place between his thighs. She started again, then stopped again, tantalizing him until in a foray he pushed her down, almost roughly, and entered her, thrusting deep at first, then deliberately slowing his pace to a stop. She looked at him through eyes bleary with desire. His mouth came down on hers. He partially withdrew, remaining just inside her entrance, moving in a short, slow love rhythm that touched her most sensitive flesh, awakening every nerve in her body, coaxing her to unite with him in a vortex of passion whirling their desire to a peak simultaneously. She found it impossible to remain still. Her body matched his slow rhythm, then moved faster, and faster. He stopped completely, allowing her to move her hips at will. She arched her back.

"Oooohhhh!" floated from her throat. He felt her shudder and heard her climactic response. His heart beat wildly. Her husky sounds inflamed him until he could no longer control the release his manhood demanded.

When it ended for him, he remained on top of her, lingered inside her, reluctant to withdraw. He cupped her cheeks and looked deep into her eyes. "This physical thing between us . . . as wonderfully perfect as it is . . . it is only part of my love for you."

"Oh, I love you, too," she whispered.

57

Nine weeks after their arrival in Jamaica, Mark and Tamara came home from the beach one afternoon to find Thomas Schofield waiting on the veranda.

"Father!" Mark exclaimed, hurrying to him. The timbre of his voice led Tamara to believe he was happy to see his father, giving her hope that they would be drawn close to each other.

Thomas Schofield nodded coldly. "Mark," he greeted with a stern expression on his face and a note of irritability in his voice. He ignored Tamara completely. She was so happy to see him she wanted to reach out and kiss him, but she remained stoically quiet beside her husband.

Thomas Schofield was fifty-seven years old. He looked older. His hair had turned almost white. There were creases at the corners of his eyes and deep ridges across his sun-tanned brow.

"What is the meaning of these shenanigans?" he snapped. "You defile my home by cavorting with this . . . this unchaperoned woman you picked up somewhere."

Tamara felt Mark stiffen, saw hatred glaring from the narrowed slits of his eyes. His hands clenched into white-fisted balls. Outraged, he looked at Tamara. "Do you understand now what I have been trying to tell you?"

Tamara winced and looked pleadingly at Thomas Schofield. "Since Mark will not explain, I will—"

"Save your breath," Mark interposed, and started to walk away. Tamara grabbed his arm and held him back as she continued to explain. "Mr. Schofield, sir, you do not remember me. I am Tamara . . . Tamara Warde . . . that is . . . formerly Tamara Warde."

"Oh." Thomas Schofield looked at her now. "I didn't recognize you. How are you?" he asked curtly.

"I am fine, sir. Mark and I—"

"This is my wife you have grossly insulted, and I demand an apology," Mark interrupted.

Thomas Schofield did not apologize. "How the devil was I to know? Haven't heard from you in months," he snapped.

Admittedly, Tamara could tell Mr. Schofield was an irascible man. Her heart sank to see father and son get off to such a bad start. Partly blaming herself, she sought to make amends, when out of the corner of her eye she saw the outline of a woman approaching. At first, seeing only a blurry figure, she thought it was Arona. The slight rustle of satiny skirts told her it was someone else. She turned her head and saw an elegantly dressed young woman. Her gown, much too formal for the afternoon, was of ivory satin, cut low in front to expose the upper half of heavy, deep-creviced breasts. Her bright red hair was brought together in one large coil draped over the front of her shoulder and hung like a bell rope down her chest. Around her throat she wore an ornate necklace of diamonds and emeralds.

"Come here, my dear," Thomas Schofield commanded.

Mark turned. "Elaine!" he gasped. "What are you doing here?"

"Mark, darling, is that the way to greet an old friend?" she asked silkily.

"I didn't realize you two knew each other," barked Thomas Schofield.

"Ooooh, yeesss," Elaine replied too emphatically.

She looked familiar to Tamara. Slowly recognition set in. She was the woman with Mark on the night of the ballet in London. Tamara turned white. A foreboding, jealous, sick feeling gripped her.

Elaine looked at Thomas Schofield. "Well . . . aren't you going to tell your son?" she asked fetchingly.

"Yes, of course. Mark, Elaine is my wife. We were married in London. I expect you to welcome her and treat her kindly."

Tamara noticed the pallor of Mark's face, but he responded magnificently without faltering. "Congratulations, sir. I wish you happiness, which is more than you did me."

"You wouldn't understand, but I was a lonely man after your mother died. I saw Elaine and fell in love with her. I need her."

Tamara recovered from the surprise announcement. She looked at Elaine and smiled. "How wonderful for you. I wish you both happiness and a long life together."

Elaine smirked.

With the return of Thomas Schofield and his bride, an uneasiness filled the air around Schofield Manor. Mark had warned Tamara that Elaine was the kind of person who used people to her own advantage, but Tamara made a special effort to be kind to her. Nothing seemed to work. Elaine simply took advantage of her kindness and began ordering her around, demanding that she do errands for her as if she were a servant. It reached a peak one evening at the table. Elaine looked with disgust at her fork. "This silverware is so tarnished it is not fit to put in one's mouth. Tamara, see to it that it is polished."

Mark boiled inside and had difficulty keeping himself in check. He came to his wife's defense in as gentlemanly a way as he could.

"Elaine, you are the mistress of this house, not Tamara. You see to it."

Elaine looked indignant and glanced at her husband for support. He came to her rescue.

"I will ask Arona to hire Thelma full time. We need more servants around here."

Elaine looked at Tamara and smirked.

Tension mounted in the household. Arona turned sullen. Dodie stopped whistling. It was as if everyone waited for a catastrophe to happen. Tamara longed for the day when Montjoy would be completed so that she and Mark could move into their own home and away from Schofield Manor. This was Mark's father's home, and his stepmother's, and she no longer felt welcome. Mark suggested they stay on board the *Lady Tamara* until the house was ready, but Tamara refused, fearing it would only widen the gap between Mark and his father if they moved out.

Tamara and Mark went to the beach frequently, sometimes for only an hour, sometimes for an entire afternoon. As often as they could, they escaped to their mountain pool, where for a few hours nothing existed except their love. They swam, picnicked, and made passionate love, as if warding off threats to their happiness and the deep love they had for each other. Elaine scowled when they did not invite her to join them, not knowing that it was partly to escape her that they went. She spent most of her time in her room lounging on her bed, building up boredom until she thought she could stand it no longer.

"May I go with you?" she asked brazenly one day when Mark and Tamara were preparing to leave for the pond.

"Sorry, Elaine," Mark answered immediately, swinging the hamper of food on his arm. "We are meeting a Moroccan sheikh," he added, looking at his wife with a twinkle in his eyes.

Elaine's lips tightened. He was making a fool of her. Her curiosity aroused, she decided to follow, staying a discreet distance behind them on the winding mountain trail.

When she saw them stop and dismount, she led her horse to a spot where it could not be seen. Slinking like a prowler, darting stealthily from one tree to another, she made her way until she saw Mark and Tamara. They stood naked facing each other at the water's edge. Looking at each other, they did not touch, but Elaine felt the short space between them was charged with a magnetism, an invisible attraction which drew them together. Elaine could not see, but she was certain Tamara was trembling as she herself trembled.

Then they touched. Mark's hands petted Tamara's face, then moved down. He caressed one nipple with his fingers and the other with his tongue. Elaine could almost feel the thrills Tamara was experiencing, and was overcome by a pulsating sensation between her thighs.

Just when she thought she could watch no longer, the lovers dived into the water and swam, then floated, reveling in their secret, enchanted world. They splashed each other and cavorted like two bear cubs. Then they clung to each other and kissed.

Hidden among the tall ferns, Elaine stared with fascination as Mark carried Tamara out of the water and they stretched on the sun-warmed grass. Her eyes fell to his well-endowed manhood, swollen to bursting proportions. As she remembered the thrills that magnificent instrument had given her and the expert way he had used it, her breath came quickly and heat seared through her body. How long had it been? ... More than six months.

Mark kissed Tamara's breast. Taking a nipple between his lips, he pulled gently, elongating it, then doing the same with the other. Elaine watched, careful not to move. If a twig cracked, she would find herself in a compromising situation. She stared spellbound, shuddering with desire as Tamara straddled Mark's chest, facing his loins, lovingly cupping and caressing his turgid maleness with her fingers. A weakness pulled at Elaine and struck her legs as she watched Tamara lean down and kiss its inviting tip. She heard Mark groan while he reached to fondle Tamara's ample breasts.

Transfixed, Elaine observed the lovers closely through heavy-lidded eyes. Lust became her captor. Erotic sensations coursed through her body. She wanted to rip off her clothes and join them.

Elaine experienced the thrills herself when Tamara took

Mark deep into her mouth. Gripped by a surge of desire, she squeezed her eyes shut and leaned back against the trunk of the tree. Her thinking was paralyzed. Her body cried out for Mark's hard shaft. Her trembling hand slipped up under her riding skirt and silk undergarments until her fingers reached the hot, moist flesh of her womanhood. She jerked her fingers rapidly as she watched Mark put Tamara beneath him.

Elaine almost groaned aloud, the sounds sticking in her throat as Mark teased Tamara between her legs. He held his manhood in his fingers, rubbing her moist opening, stroking her with it as he had done with his fingers. Then he entered Tamara, plunging deep, until that marvelous tool disappeared inside her and their bellies were pressed tightly together. They began their love rhythm. Elaine worked her fingers faster. If she did not find release immediately, she would disintegrate. All her thoughts were on one objective, until she reached the apex and liberated her passion from its agonizing imprisonment. She pulled her long skirt down into place. Finding it impossible to watch anymore, she staggered noiselessly back to her horse.

When she arrived at Schofield Manor, the stable lad was rubbing down her husband's steed, and she knew he had returned from Kingston. Covertly she eyed the strong Negro lad who took the reins and led her horse to the stable. She took in his splendidly virile physique, his muscular arms, the large bulge straining against his tight trousers. Her fingers had relieved her temporarily, but here was something more adept for the purpose.

"How old are you?" she asked the groom.

"Sixteen, ma'am."

"What is your name?"

"Seth, ma'am."

"You sleep here?"

"Yes'm. In the loft."

Elaine reserved the information in the back of her mind and went to her room. She entered her husband's bedchamber, to find him stretched naked on his bed. He was snoring sonorously. Quickly she disposed of all her clothes and crawled into his arms. He awoke and kissed her lovingly. Her hand slid down to his drooped member. She slipped on top of Thomas, placing herself in the same position as she had seen Tamara on Mark.

"What the devil are you doing?" Thomas snapped. Elaine did not reply, but bent down and took the lifeless appendage into her mouth and sucked. She reached back for him to place his hands on her breasts, but he removed them immediately and remained motionless as she tried unsuccessfully to arouse him.

Cursing, she left his bed. Wringing her hands, she ranted, fretfully pacing back and forth before her husband. She hated Jamaica. She was beginning to detest him. Secretly knowing her efforts to ensnare Mark had been in vain, she wanted to return to England to the gaiety of city life. Craftily she used every argument she could think of, putting the blame entirely on her husband.

"I have tried everything I know, but you have not been able to make love to me more than once since we arrived." She flung her hands back and forth through the air as if warding off insects. "You have absolutely no imagination," she complained.

At his wife's outburst, Thomas Schofield looked down with frustrated dismay. He sat up and poured himself a drink. "You knew you were marrying an older man. You are never satisfied, Elaine. Your appetite for sex is insatiable. What can I do to make you happy? I have bought you jewels, expensive clothes, and furs."

"Furs! What good are they here?"

Thomas drained his glass.

Elaine stopped in front of him and looked at him with rebellious eyes. "You can take me back to London. Perhaps away from the tension of this house you will be more of a man."

What she really wanted was to return to London to her many lovers.

Thomas Schofield smiled indulgently. "If that is what you wish, my dear."

58

Early the next morning as the birds began to sing in the predawn darkness, Elaine made her way to the stables. Seth was asleep in the loft and awoke when he felt someone kick his legs. When his mind and eyes focused and he saw who it was, he jumped to a standing position.

"Mrs. Schofield, ma'am."

"Strip."

Seth looked at the woman disbelievingly. Instinctively his eyes enlarged, the whites showing clear around the black centers. He began to back away. He raked his memory, making a desperate search for what he might have done to displease her.

"You heard me. Strip."

The frightened groom thought he was going to be whipped. He studied her measuringly, trying to remember what he had done to deserve it as his trembling fingers went to the buttons of his shirt. He removed the shirt shyly. His trousers came off next. He was bare beneath. Shamefaced, he bowed his head, unable to look at the woman, embarrassed by his nakedness and his large erection. His arms hung in front of him in an effort to hide it. Elaine reached out greedily, and pushing his hands aside, grabbed it roughly. She was taken aback by its hardness and strength, and squeezed with all her might. The lad tried to take a step away from her, lost his balance, and fell backward into the straw. Elaine lifted her skirts. Seth saw she was not wearing undergarments. He got a glimpse of her bare thighs, smooth and white. A vein twitched in his neck. While his eyes bulged in excitement, the woman impaled herself on his hard swollen shaft. She gasped as it entered her. Crooning, she moved her body up and down, swirling her hips, seeking the pleasure his instrument could give her. She gave no thought to his pleasure, only what she could get from the use of his manhood as a tool to satisfy her lustful needs, which her husband was not equipped to do.

Seth decided to lie back and enjoy his good fortune. Without any effort on his part, she was thrilling him as he had never been thrilled before. Through lustful eyes he watched as she released her large breasts, hanging before his eyes. He noticed a mist of perspiration covering her flesh. She indicated he was to take her nipple into his mouth. For a moment he stared, never having seen a white woman's breasts before.

"Suck, you idiot." He complied eagerly, sucking one, then the other. Elaine's body moved faster and faster, until she collapsed in her climax of waves of convulsing contractions. She took a deep breath and stood up. Straightening her skirts, she brushed the straw away. Looking down at Seth, who had not moved, she was relieved to see he was still hard and erect. Good, she thought. His seed has not spilled into me.

"Not a word of this to anyone or your life won't be worth

the straw you're lying on," she warned, turning on her heels and leaving him. She climbed down the ladder, her soft-soled slippers arching over its rungs. About to step from the stable, she heard someone approaching. Her hands flew up to her hair, patting it into place. Cursing to herself, quickly she checked her habit to be sure there was no telltale straw.

She was elated to see it was Mark. This was the opportunity she had been hoping for. She remembered how they had made love in London and was certain her charms could arouse his manly appetite again. Perhaps she would not beg her husband to take her back to London after all. She walked toward Mark, swaying her hips. Impudently she draped her arms around his neck and beguilingly pressed her body against his.

Mark was madder than hell. He cursed beneath his breath. His arms came up with a jerk as he unclasped her hands and wrenched himself from her grip.

"Mark, darling. You are avoiding me. Do not be so cruel. I married your father because it was the only way I knew how to get close to you. Where can we meet? My body aches for you."

Mark glared disgustedly, but she paid no attention.

"Your father and I have separate bedrooms. He sleeps soundly. Come to me at midnight tonight." She beckoned flirtatiously.

"Are you out of your mind?" Mark snapped, barely able to contain his anger.

Elaine pouted. Her voice deepened. "Please, darling. Your father is so ungodly dull. And he cannot—"

Mark pushed her roughly from him. "Do not say another word, and stay out of my way!" He called for Seth to prepare his horse for the ride to Kingston. "Let me make one thing clear, Elaine. I love my wife. I have no wish to carry on a clandestine affair, and certainly not with my . . . stepmother."

The two couples ignored each other except at dinnertime, when it was impossible to do so. Each evening they gathered promptly at seven o'clock. Elaine, seething with jealousy at the love obviously existing between Mark and Tamara, displayed the expensive jewelry Thomas had bestowed upon his bride. Before Arona served them, Elaine, a vision of piety, offered a long prayer, her voice sweet, her hands folded, her eyes closed. At the conclusion of the prayer, Thomas

Schofield would lean back in his chair and proudly say, "That was lovely, my dear."

Even though Tamara was certain Mark had rejected Elaine's overtures, she was uneasy. She did not want to appear to be a jealous wife, so she thought it best not to say anything. She saw the coquettish way Elaine looked at her husband, and wondered whether Mr. Schofield did not notice. She knew Elaine used every opportunity she could to get Mark alone. She flaunted her bosom. Her gowns were cut low, and at night she walked through the upstairs halls in a diaphanous peignoir, hoping to entice Mark.

Mark was aware of his wife's uneasiness and wished to assure her he was not in the least interested in Elaine.

"She is a petty, selfish woman who thinks only of herself. She has driven a wedge between father and son by complaining she does not feel accepted here. She says she feels like an intruder."

"I cannot say I blame her entirely for the rift between you and your father. It was there before Elaine came on the scene."

Mark, cradling his wife in his arms, placed a kiss on her brow. "You are right. That was unfair of me. In looking for an excuse, I have blamed her entirely."

"She appears to be a very sweet person, almost devout. She attends church regularly, and she prays beautifully."

Mark rubbed his cheek against Tamara's. "Do not let that act fool you. 'Tis a thin veneer you see. Underneath she is a sly, ruthless, calculating woman."

"She seems to have made your father happy. You should be glad for that. He was a man who lost his wife of many years. I am sure he was lonely and very vulnerable."

"And I am certain Elaine knew his vulnerability and took advantage of it," he said with a tone of dismissing the conversation, but Tamara had the final word. "Your father is a strong-minded person. I am certain he cannot be coerced into doing anything he does not want to do."

"Enough talk." Possessively Mark held Tamara in his arms as they cuddled, petted, and stroked each other lingeringly. She felt cherished and loved, and generously reciprocated. Feeling guilty because he had not told her of his encounter with Elaine in the stable, he was especially attentive. He pulled her closer, holding her a long time, running his hand up and down her back, murmuring intimate love words, lavishing unhurried kisses on her, caressing her until the fire kindled. The heat began to build, and waves of passion swept through both of them, every nerve demanding satisfaction. His mouth moved against hers, more demandingly now. Her fingers rubbed the dark mat of his chest and then traveled down between his thighs. He kissed the satiny column of her throat, then drifted down to capture one rosy-tipped breast. As if his tantalizing lips and tongue were not enough, his mustache excited tender nerve endings, sending little jolts of pleasure through her body. Mark smiled as a lusty whimper escaped her throat.

Their tender passion climbed simultaneously. Mark moved on top, covering Tamara's naked body with his. She opened her thighs, her body arching to meet him, her soft, moist flesh locking his throbbing manhood inside her. He began to move with a gentleness she never dreamed possible in a man of Mark's physique and nature. With every tender movement their desire rose higher and higher, drawing them into a golden abyss. Each thrust made them greedy for more. Mark tried to hold himself back, wanting to forestall his climax as long as he could.

They loved each other through the night, sharing the excitement of each other's touches and kisses. Afterward they remained coupled until she felt the gradual softening of him within her, and he looked down at her.

"My sweetest love. What we have is more important than anything else in the world to me," he whispered, which was his way of telling her Elaine meant nothing to him.

As the days went by, Tamara could almost feel the tension building to explosive proportions. One afternoon when Elaine was in her room resting, Tamara was arranging flowers for a centerpiece. She heard Mark and his father arguing loudly on the terrace.

"Have you gone senile? She is young enough to be your daughter," Mark accused.

"The difference in our ages is not important. After all, age is mostly a mental attitude," Thomas replied gruffly. "We have a great deal in common and have agreed to do everything together. She makes me feel young again. She has given me much that I missed in life."

Mark gave an angry laugh. "You are in your second childhood."

"Have you forgotten so quickly what it is like to fall in love? Love is not reserved for the young, you know. What makes you think you have a priority on it?"

"If it is love, 'tis a one-way affair, I assure you."

"She loves me," Thomas Schofield insisted. "And I need her. I could not live without her. But I know you. You do not think it possible for anyone to love me."

"You old fool! Elaine has tried for years to catch a rich husband. In time you will see she is nothing but a brazen whore. She can be charming and sweet when she wants something, and she wants the Schofield money, money that I have worked very hard to help accumulate."

"I started the company. If it weren't for me, you would have nothing," the older man exploded.

There was silence for a moment. Tamara held her breath.

Mark started shouting, cursing his father. "Back in London she threw herself at me. I know her. I took her to bed often enough."

Tamara dropped the flower in her hand and ran to the terrace. She saw Thomas swing and hit Mark, who reeled backward. When he recovered his balance, he rubbed his chin. His lip was cut and bleeding. He pulled a handkerchief from his pocket and dabbed the blood.

Tamara was afraid Mark would hit his father back, and wedged herself between them pleadingly. "Stop it! Please stop."

Both ignored her.

"If you were not my father, you would pay for that," Mark said.

"Umph! You might be the one to live to regret your words," Thomas Schofield snarled. "All I have done for you. I cannot understand why you object to my marriage . . . to my finding happiness." He faltered. His hand flew up to his chest. His face twisted as if he was in pain. He recovered his composure with obvious effort.

Mark's lip began to swell. He held the handkerchief up to his chin to wipe the blood away. "I do not object to your marrying again. If you had found someone . . . Dammit! 'Tis the woman you chose that I object to."

"I did not choose your wife. What makes you think you have the right to choose or judge mine?"

Mark shrugged his shoulders. "What point is there in arguing?" he asked, stalking away, still dabbing the red-stained handkerchief to his lip.

In the weeks that followed, Mark and his father avoided each other. Elaine complained and fussed about everything—the heat, the bugs, and the food—so that it was no surprise, and almost a relief to Tamara that a month and a half after Thomas Schofield came home, he announced he and his wife were returning to England.

"Elaine does not like it here. She feels like an intruder."

"I am sorry you feel that way, Elaine," Tamara said truthfully. "We will be moving in a few weeks when our home is completed. Please stay. Maybe you will be happier when you and Mr. Schofield are alone in your home."

"We have decided to live in England," snapped Thomas. "Elaine's family and friends are there."

59

In the beginning of September Thomas and Elaine Schofield left Jamaica for England.

"Why don't you come back for the winter?" Tamara asked as they departed. "It is lovely here in January and February."

"I doubt it," was Thomas' only reply.

Tamara's heart was heavy, for all her efforts to reconcile Mark and his father had failed. She strongly suspected that Elaine, having a strong influence over Thomas Schofield, played a part in the unsuccessful attempts to reunite father and son.

Tamara and Mark concentrated on the completion of Montjoy, its furnishings and landscaping, and by November moved in. The home with thick stone walls possessed a cool, airy, informal atmosphere, and its owners basked in its relaxed serenity. The library contained a large stone fireplace, and evenings they sat and gazed into the flames of a fire lit to take away the coolness of the mountain breezes.

Dodie and Arona begged to come with them to Montjoy. At first Tamara was leery. They had been loyal houseservants employed by Thomas Schofield for many years, and she did not want to do anything to add to the problem between Mark and his father.

Mark had different ideas. "We did not ask them. They asked us. If they want to work for us and prefer to live at Montjoy, let them. We are lucky to get them. And besides, who knows whether Father will ever come back."

Gradually Tamara and Mark made friends on the island and developed a social life. There were no close neighbors, but they invited sugar planters and Queen Victoria's officials and their families to visit Montjoy. In return they were invited to balls and parties, which increased in number as Christmas approached.

Although thousands of miles away from the war-torn Southern Confederacy, Mark's and Tamara's thoughts drifted across the sea to Charleston and their friends. Tamara had written to Lila but had received no reply until the beginning of December, when Lila sent a Christmas greeting and with it a long letter.

Reports about the war had trickled in to Kingston via seamen. In July twenty thousand Confederates led by Beauregard, using his plan modeled after Napoleon's battle plan at Austerlitz, had defeated the Union near a stream called Bull Run, not far from Washington, D.C. Although the plan had gone awry, the battle turning into a rout, it shocked the overconfident North into reality and gave them a new determination to end the war once and for all.

But the war was not ended. Lila mentioned Bull Run in her letter, but only briefly. She wrote mostly about what was happening in South Carolina. In November hostilities had broken out along the seacoast. Confederate defenses collapsed. Lila described the Yankee ships coming into Port Royal Sound: "On and on they sailed across the calm waters, one by one, like soldiers on parade, moving in a circle, simultaneously shelling both Forth Walker and Fort Beauregard, two miles apart. After four hours our garrisons were abandoned, our soldiers making a hasty retreat. The South's best harbor has been lost to those dreadful Yankees!" Tamara paused in her reading of the letter. She could almost hear Lila speaking the words.

As for Charleston, Lila wrote that they felt the constant threat of invasion. Since the city was the birthplace of secession, the North strongly desired to punish it. Charlestonians were determined their city would never surrender to the enemy.

The bulk of the letter was of the hardships they were starting to feel. Shoes were difficult to find. People were beginning to wear patched clothes because of the shortage of cloth. Lila asked Mark whether he could not bring them a shipment of silks and satins. There were many handsome Confederate officers stationed in Charleston, which meant she was required to have new gowns. Many women had taken up sewing and knitting, but she had not resorted to that. A serious paper and match shortage existed. Lila complained about growing shortages of food, tea, and coffee. It was to be an austere Christmas, and she hoped they would be having a better time than she over the holidays. In the last paragraph of the letter, almost as an afterthought, Lila mentioned Oliver Bickley. General Beauregard had informed her that he had sent Oliver to Libby Prison in Richmond and from there to a Confederate camp in northern Virginia, where he was treating the sick and wounded soldiers.

When Tamara finished reading the letter, she handed it to Mark. News of the war and its hardships on their friends had a quieting, somber effect on her.

One afternoon Mark caught Tamara on her hands and knees halfway into the large closet in their bedchamber. She was hiding Christmas presents for him when she heard him enter.

"Madam, you have a magnificent posterior."

Tamara laughed, not bothering to look around. "I am searching for my pink slippers, the ones I wore at our wedding," she shouted. "I want to wear them to the Christmas ball."

"Speaking of Christmas, you have been hounding me for weeks as to what I am giving you. Come out of that blasted closet. I am prepared to give you one of your presents, now."

Tamara crawled out backward, then turned and sat on the floor, propping her back against the wall, looking up at her husband, expecting him to be holding a Christmas-wrapped gift. Tamara blinked and shrieked with laughter.

Mark was standing quite still, posing as naked as a Greek statue, looking very much like a Greek god, except for the red-and-green Christmas bow adorning his erection. He did not move except for his green eyes flashing deviltry.

"Madam, I would like to present you with this gift immediately."

Tamara roared. Downstairs, Arona was baking Christmas cookies and Dodie was sampling them. They heard the laughter filled with love, looked at each other, and smiled knowingly.

Upstairs, Tamara said, "Sir, I am happy you do not insist I wait until Christmas to receive it."

He picked her up and carried her to the bed. Falling backward on the soft comforter, he pulled her with him.

"You didn't make that bow, did you? Where did you get it?" she asked, laughing gleefully.

"Off one of those packages you have hidden for me in the closet."

"Oooooohhhh, you guff!" she shrieked, buffeting him lightly with a pillow, pulling the ribbon from his manhood.

Mark chuckled. He was in a jocular mood, and Tamara felt she would burst with joy. It struck her how much she loved him and how much he meant to her. Suffused with more happiness than she had ever known, her arms flew around the man she loved, the man who gave her so much affection, love, joy, and laughter. Her wish for Christmas was that it would never end, not knowing that within a few months their love would be put to the test.

Mark held her on top of him. "You are beautiful. I love you."

"I love you. You are my life."

Distractedly he nibbled at her earlobe, then whispered in her ear, "Take off your clothes."

Mark was on his back lying across the bed with his legs hanging over the side. He was very still as he watched Tamara undress, and when she was naked he reached out for her, taking her by the waist and lifting her up on top of him.

"Oh, love . . . love," he said softly. Tamara felt her passion sweep over her as he pulled her closer.

The first months of the war in the United States, the Northern blockade of Southern ports was ineffectual. Schofield shipping flourished. From Kingston Mark directed the mass operation of Schofield freighters sailing between England, Bermuda, Nassau, and Jamaica.

When cotton from Southern ports was landed in Nassau, it was entrusted to large jobbing houses, which received very high commissions. Mark decided to establish one of these, and toward the end of February 1862 deemed it necessary to make a trip to Nassau. Tamara accompanied him, spending her time shopping for items for their home and materials for new gowns.

Mark hired a new shipping agent for their office in Nassau, met with British and Confederate officials to discuss shipments for the South, and established the mercantile house for assuming ownership of cotton until it could be shipped to England.

When they returned to Montjoy in March, startling news awaited them. Mark turned ashen when he read Elaine's letter. A month before, his father had collapsed and died in London.

The letter was accompanied by the shocking contents of Thomas Schofield's last will and testament, made two months before his death. He bequeathed all his worldly possessions, including the Schofield Shipping Company, to his beloved wife, Elaine.

Mark stared at the will, then threw it across the room. He flew into a rage, a mixture of hurt, bitterness, hate, shock, disbelief—disbelief that his own father could do this to him. He was left practically penniless.

"May he rot in hell! The son of a bitch did it out of spite. Oh, how I loathe him, and will to my dying day!"

Tamara did everything she could to soothe him.

"Forgive him. He was not himself. I know your mother would want you to forgive him," she begged. "Please, please, darling, do not let this consume you. Forget it."

"Forget it!" He threw back his shoulders. " 'Tis a matter of pride as well as principle," he growled. "I will fight that whore through every court in England if need be. The law of primogeniture still exists."

"It must have been what he wanted."

"She coerced him."

"If that is true, she will not find it easy to enjoy her inheritance. It is difficult to live with guilt."

"Guilt hell! Her type does not suffer from a guilty conscience."

"Please, Mark, do not let this destroy our happiness."

Mark fisted his hands. Do you realize what I have for all my years of hard work? The *Lady Tamara* is mine. Thank God for that. The town house in Kensington, which I will have to put up for sale to pay the taxes and debts on this place. A little cash, no more than enough to sustain us through the year."

"With what I have, it is more than enough."

"No!"

Mark was moody and restless for weeks. He stayed away from the company office in Kingston. He refused to go to the pond or beach. He ignored Tamara completely, turning his back to her at night in bed. Tamara was at a loss as to what to do. He went unshaven and drank more and more, consuming large quantities of brandy and whiskey.

One day Tamara went to the library with a tray of food. Arona had made turtle soup, his favorite, hoping to tempt him into eating something nourishing. Tamara stood hesitantly at the door. Mark looked at her broodingly without saying a word. She felt herself blushing.

"You are so beautiful," he said softly. "You are my life, and what am I doing to you?"

He looked down at the empty bottle in his hand, stared at it moodily for a moment, then with great force flung it into the fireplace. With a loud crash the heavy glass shattered into hundreds of tiny pieces. Dead silence followed.

Tamara walked into the room and put the tray down as he continued to stare at her. "I have made a decision. I am going to run the Union blockade with the *Lady Tamara*."

Tamara whimpered and fell to her knees in front of him.

His hand slipped under her tresses at the nape of her neck.

"I can easily net close to two hundred thousand dollars each way. If I find the blockade too tight at Charleston, I will sail into New Orleans, the South's greatest port," he said, not knowing that on April 24, New Orleans, Baton Rouge, and Natchez had surrendered to Union forces.

Tamara pleaded with her eyes and her voice. "Lila said in her letter the Union's blockading fleet was stationed at Port Royal. That is not far from Charleston, and it means the blockade has become more effective since we left. Please do not go. What good is the money if you are crippled . . . or killed?"

"Nonsense! Nothing is going to happen to me." The tears he saw filling her eyes moved him. He cupped her face with his hands. "I credited you with more gumption than that, Tams. You have always been brave, my sweet. Our love should strengthen, not weaken that courage to face life's challenges."

"If something happened to you, I could not go on living. Please. I have lost so much in my life. How will I live without you even for a day?"

When she saw he was determined, she became distraught and desperate, saying things she did not mean. She rose to her feet, her voice rising with her. "You condemned your father for abandoning you and your mother by going to sea. Now you are doing the same thing to me. You are just like him," she accused emotionally.

Mark stood up and clenched his fists. "Don't ever say that!" he said harshly. "This is entirely different. It is for both of us. 'Twill only be until I make my fortune."

" 'Tis not for both of us! It is something you must prove to yourself. 'Tis something that has been festering inside you, and you would do this even if it had not been for the will. You are nothing but a vagabond looking for an excuse to go to sea again!"

Tamara had one last weapon to use, but she hesitated using it. For a week now she had suspected she was pregnant. She wondered whether he would change his mind if he thought she was carrying his child. She decided not to tell him. If she could not convince him otherwise, she would not use an innocent baby as a pawn.

Mark had made up his mind, and spent the next two weeks rounding up a crew and supplies for the *Lady Tamara*. He sent a letter to the London representative of the Confederate States of America, requesting a commission to ship arms, naval supplies, coffee, and cloth.

The Confederacy had waited anxiously, expecting help from the British. At the outset of the war the South had deliberately withheld shipments of cotton to England, believing that when the textile mills in that country needed raw cotton badly enough, England would recognize the independence of the Confederacy and enter the war. So far, that had not happened. British aid and support had not materialized. To the contrary, British sympathy seemed to be waning. She had recognized the Confederacy as a belligerent with the right to be treated according to the rules of warfare, but she did not recognize its independence as a nation. Southern hopes that British factories would be crying for cotton were also shattered. The British had a supply of cotton in 1861. When more was needed, they began to import it from India.

In an effort to discourage the British from assisting the South, President Lincoln had sent to England Charles Francis Adams, son and grandson of the former presidents. He arrived the same day England proclaimed neutrality, which, according to international law, gave her the right to trade with a belligerent.

Near the end of May the *Lady Tamara* dipped low in the water of Kingston harbor, heavy with a cargo of coffee beans for Charleston, South Carolina. Mark's plan was to run the blockade, unload the valuable cargo. He had heard that the price of coffee had soared and was expected to reach ten dollars a pound. He would take on a cargo of cotton for transfer to British ships in Bermuda and thus begin a run between Charleston and Bermuda.

Tamara had nothing more to say except that she loved him and would pray for his safe return. The night before he left Jamaica was filled with tenderness. Lying naked on their bed, arms behind his head, he observed her graceful movements as she undressed as if to implant the scene in his memory. It never ceased to amaze him how her mere presence in the same room with him evoked a feeling of possessiveness and set his blood afire.

He watched as she took the pins from her hair and brushed it in long strokes. When she came to him, impatiently he gathered her in his arms and held her tight, whispering assurances over and over that he would be back within a few months and that he would return a wealthy man. Soothingly he told her he would miss her every moment they were apart, and begged her to understand why he was going. He nipped at her ear while she begged forgiveness for the horrible things she had said. His warm breath tickled her neck. Leaving a burning trail, his lips slid to the softness of her breast, lingering before continuing down to her belly and below to the russet downy triangle, then traveling back up to her breast. Groaning appreciatively, she tilted her head back to receive and eagerly return his kisses. He could feel her lips trembling, her body shuddering with passion beneath him. Her naked nearness overwhelmed him. His heart beat frantically, as it always did when she was in his arms. He wanted to consume her, make her a part of him forever. His passion mounted along with a dull ache in his heart at the thought of leaving her. For a long moment he regretted his decision to go.

After they made sweet love, he held her close in his arms. Toward morning they made love again, but in a more urgent, desperate way and with a fervor they had never known before, saying their good-byes with each caress and every thrust of their bodies.

60

Life without Mark was unbearable. Tamara's eyes reflected her misery. Losing her appetite, she forced herself to eat after Arona's coaxing that it was for the baby's sake that she should remain healthy.

During the days and weeks following Mark's departure, Tamara could barely tolerate the loneliness. She tried to keep herself occupied by reading and sewing clothes for the baby, but it was no use. She felt as if half of herself was missing.

Mornings she took long walks along the shore, where the

waves lapped at her feet. Evenings she strolled through her gardens, lit by the tropical moon. Nowhere else was the moon as breathtaking as seen from Jamaica. With an emptiness in her heart she talked to it, seeking sympathy as she would from a person. From the time she had been forced to leave Jamaica at the age of ten until her return, she had the mistaken notion that coming back would guarantee eternal happiness. She realized now that nothing possessed the power to do that. Happiness was a lifelong quest dependent upon many factors.

Tamara's nights were especially restless. She wondered what Mark was doing, whether he missed her and was thinking of her, longing for her as she was for him. She went over and over in detail the marvelous times they had spent together. Although thousands of miles of water separated her from him, sometimes she felt as if he was strangely close, until she stretched her arm across to his side of the bed and felt its cold emptiness. Sometimes she could almost hear his laughter, feel the touch of his hands and lips upon her.

One afternoon, sitting in the garden, in a low mood, she held up the baby bib she was embroidering. Staring at it, she began to think of all she should be thankful for—her beautiful home and flowers, the view of the sea, Mark's love and his child growing inside her, and Arona and Dodie, who were a tremendous help and a constant joy. She never tired of Arona's reminiscing about Mark's childhood, and delighted in her stories of Mark's escapades. From the little things she told Tamara, Tamara got a picture of the boy growing to manhood, and the more she heard, the more she loved him.

Moreover, away from Mark, not distracted by his magnetism, she had a clearer perspective. She learned to understand his drives and knew this was something he had to do if he was to find contentment. A man's pride was a strong force. Achieving success on his own, becoming financially independent, was important for Mark's self-respect and happiness and therefore hers. She was grateful now that she had not been responsible for preventing his leaving. Had he listened to her protestations and stayed, it might have stood between them for the rest of their lives. She berated herself for the self-pity that had gripped her. Squaring her shoulders, she resolved to make the best of it until Mark's return, resigning herself to the perilous feat he had set out to accomplish.

Tamara put down her sewing and went to the library to write a letter to Mark in which she expressed all these thoughts of understanding and love. She told him about the baby, something she thought she should have done before he left. He had the right to know. When she had finished the letter, she put it aside until another day, when she would add to it until the opportunity arose for her to send it.

That opportunity came in July, almost two months after Mark's departure, when Roderick Moran came to call. He had been able to obtain a loan to purchase his own merchant ship, the *Dauntless,* establishing a trade route between Kingston and Nassau.

Tamara was so glad to see him, unthinkingly she threw herself into his arms, which closed around her.

"If you were mine, I would not leave you for a moment," he whispered in her ear. Bemused, she pulled from his embrace, laughing in an effort to treat it lightly.

They strolled through the gardens and sat by the fountains as he brought her up-to-date on his activities since last they had met. Tamara's face glowed with happiness when he handed her her first letter from Mark. Roderick had seen him in St. George, Bermuda. She ripped it open immediately. It was short. He expressed his undying love and wrote that he missed her. He advised her not to worry.

After reading the letter, she found it difficult to concentrate on her guest and wished he would leave so that she could read it again. She would send her letter with Roderick in hopes that the two men would meet again soon.

"I will be coming to Kingston about once a month. May I call on you again?"

"Yes, of course. Mark should be home soon and will be happy to see you. Won't you please stay for dinner? It will be marvelous to have someone to talk to while dining. I welcome your conversation. Tell me. What is going on in England? Have you heard any news about the Confederacy?"

In their dinner conversation Tamara asked Roderick why Mark could not establish a run such as his between Kingston and Nassau. It was much safer, and that way he could come home more frequently.

"The profits are not as great. Mark is piling up a fortune. My cargo of sugarcane and coffee beans is unloaded in Nassau and transferred to Confederate blockade-runners and vessels like Mark's willing to take the risks."

In appearance Roderick reminded Tamara of Mark. He was wearing a white captain's uniform with gold-braid trimmings. He was suntanned, but while Mark's eyes were green and sparkly, Roderick's were dark, almost black. When they caressed her, Tamara tingled all over. His mouth looked soft and sensuous. He was quiet, smiling, but never bursting into laughter like Mark. His facial expressions never betrayed his emotions. Mark's did, openly, his eyes reflecting his thoughts and moods, love, tenderness, amusement, annoyance, disgust, hate. Roderick gave Tamara the impression that he was a man of deep inner strength. As they sipped their tea, she wondered whether he had married, but concluded if he had, he would have told her.

Tamara was aware that Roderick Moran was attracted to her, but she did not realize how deeply his feelings went. He had carried a torch of love ever since she had first stepped on board the *Lady Tamara,* and now that Mark was out of the way, if only temporarily, he vowed to woo her until she was his.

Four weeks after his first visit, he called again. Tamara hoped he might become a link of communication with Mark, but he brought no letters or messages from him. He had passed her letter on to someone heading for Bermuda, but he had not seen Mark himself.

Tamara objected to the expensive gold bracelet Roderick gave her, saying she could not possibly accept it. He insisted, giving the reason that he was grateful she invited him for dinner and he could not continue to accept her hospitality unless she kept it.

Roderick was quieter than usual. Obsequiously he watched every move, every gesture, listened with interest to every word Tamara spoke. They sat on the veranda, where they had a magnificent view of the sea and the sky streaked with the deep pink of sunset. "Sometimes I wish I did not know what happened to the sun at dusk. It would be more romantic not to know, to think of it as a god going to meet a secret lover in the dark."

Roderick nodded agreement. "You wish it for the sun, but not for yourself," he mused. When it had grown dark, he announced reluctantly that it was necessary for him to return to his ship in preparation for setting sail with the midnight tide. He asked for permission to visit her when next he came to Kingston. There was complete stillness for a long moment; then he swept her into his arms. Tamara could feel the heat of his trembling body.

"You are so lovely," he said softly. And part of your charm is that you are unaware of how beautiful you are. He looked deep into her eyes. It brought a deep blush to her cheeks, as he continued his seductive words. "I have wanted you for a long time. How I have dreamed of the moment when you will be mine, when you will want me as much as I want you. That moment is not now, but it will come, Tamara."

A wave of guilt washed over her. Her body was responding. It was impossible to still the desire creeping through her body unwantedly. She had been accustomed to Mark's constant caresses and lovemaking. She had looked upon their feelings, responses, and what they did to bring pleasure to each other as being so unique as not to be known by other lovers. In reality she knew this was not true, but her romantic mind wanted to believe it. That her body could respond to any other man except Mark shocked her. Abstinence had made her hungry for a man's nourishment. Her mind told her to pull away, but her body commanded her to stay in Roderick's arms and feast on what he was offering.

"You are the most desirable woman I have ever seen."

Not trusting herself, she pulled from his grip. "You must not come here again. I welcomed you as a friend, nothing more. And . . . and selfishly I invited you with the hope that you would bring me word from Mark. I do not want to hurt you, but you must understand there can never be anything between you and me," she said unconvincingly. "I have always loved Mark, and I always will. For me there can be no other man."

She looked up into his dark eyes, searching for a response to her words.

"When I am at sea," he said quietly, almost to himself, "I look out across the waves and see your beautiful eyes the color of violets and pray they will be filled with love for me the next time I see you. I lie awake at night trying to figure out how I can make you understand how much I love you, that we are meant for each other, that I can bring you much pleasure."

Tamara's hands flew to her ears as if trying to blot out his words. "You have no right to say these things to me," she protested, secretly ashamed that the words pleased her.

"I had to say them. I have kept them inside too long."

"Roddie . . . I am carrying his child."

She saw him flinch. He had not expected her pronouncement. "And that damned fool left you!" he said in a low, disbelieving voice.

"He did not know."

"Why didn't you tell him?"

"Because I begged him not to go but I did not want the baby to influence him one way or another." A sad smile crossed her face. "I am sure it would have made no difference to him. He was determined to go. If he received my letter, he knows now."

Roderick took both her hands, kissed the inside of each wrist, then held them tightly. She saw the thumping pulse at his throat.

"We will say no more for the present. I will be back in four weeks."

Tears pushed close to the surface. Tamara knew it was because she missed Mark so desperately that she had turned to Roderick. She wanted to wrap her arms around him and beg him to stay. She knew she should tell him not to come back, but instead she said, "As long as you understand there can never be anything between us."

His soft velvety eyes burned with desire. "It will be the longest month of my life until I see you again."

There were no more letters from Mark. Each month when Roderick was in port he came to Montjoy. Tamara always asked whether he had seen Mark or if there was a letter, and the answer was always no. She gave him long love letters in which she poured out her heart. Roderick took them along to give to responsible seamen whose ports of call included Hamilton, Bermuda.

Tamara's pregnancy was showing, and concernedly Roderick inquired how she was feeling and what he could do for her. Arona always looked at Roderick suspiciously, but surprisingly held her tongue. Her disapproving expression told Tamara she did not like the idea that he came to Montjoy when Mr. Mark was away. Tamara noticed that whenever he was there, Dodie was not far away, as if protecting her.

Mark did not come to Montjoy for Christmas. Roderick did. And when he saw her time was near, he prolonged his departure from Kingston, visiting her every afternoon. He was at Montjoy when she went into labor on January 3, and he rode to Kingston for the physician while Arona, skilled in midwifery, attended her until they returned.

When she held her son in her arms for Roderick to see, he said he wished it were his. Tamara wished with all her heart it was Mark to whom she was showing their baby. She still had not heard from him, and began to lose heart. He should have been with her, not Roderick.

Tamara had recovered completely from her confinement when Roderick came in February. He brought toys for the baby and flowers for her. His eyes devoured her. "You are more beautiful than ever."

Tamara knew she was being drawn to him out of loneliness and that their relationship could not continue as it was. Either he must stop his visits or they would become lovers. When he left, she begged him not to come again, and in March he stayed away, deliberately changing his route and going to Barbados instead of Jamaica.

With mixed emotions Tamara believed she would not see him again. Admittedly feeling a loss, she was relieved and at the same time devastated. She had not realized how much his visits had meant to her and how much she had looked forward to seeing him. She had actually depended on them without her knowing it.

61

Mark had only an inkling of the danger he would face in running the Union blockade. He went into it with the opinion that nothing would happen to him, that he would not encounter Union gunboats.

The year before, after he and Tamara had left Charleston as newlyweds, both the North and South had prepared to mobilize their forces. Additional states had seceded—Virginia, Arkansas, Tennessee, and North Carolina. By the end of May the Union's blockade extended from Virginia to Texas in an attempt to prevent the South's cash crop, cotton, from being shipped out in exchange for badly needed munitions. It meant closing down Confederate harbors and river mouths with a net of armed ships extending along a coastline of over three thousand miles. The blockade could only be successful if there were warships at the entrances to the harbors. The Union lacked ships with speed, but on May 11, 1861, the blockade of Charleston Harbor began with the Union frigate *Niagara*.

Now, a year later, under cover of the dark hour of four o'clock in the morning, riding with the tide, Mark Schofield sailed toward Charleston again. When he had left Jamaica with his shipment of coffee beans, he sailed around Cuba and set his course north, making a brief stop for water and fuel supplies in Nassau. From there he sailed north-northwest. The closer he came to the coast of South Carolina, the more vigilant he became, increasing the lookout and he himself spending long hours standing on the bridge on alert for Union gunboats.

Mark heaved a sigh of relief when none had been spotted. He sighted the light placed in the spire of Saint Michael's Church to guide blockade-runners. He entered Maffitt's Channel and sailed safely past Fort Sumter, occupied now by Confederate troops. He went to the Customs House and cleared his papers with Confederate agents. Midmorning, while his cargo was being unloaded he headed for the Walker residence. Dark clouds swollen with rainwater hung heavy over the city, but it was not the threat of rain that created a dismal picture. A different mood hovered over Charleston from the last time he had been there. Bales of cotton bulged from the warehouses and overflowed along the docksides, which were no longer bustling. There were very few ships in port. He observed listless Negroes sitting or lying in a row against the storage buildings. Everything seemed to be at a standstill except the fast-moving rain clouds. Charleston was in the midst of a drought, and he was certain that if the clouds overhead dumped their moisture it would be welcome. The parched grass was like crisp straw, and flowers looked wilted.

After spending the winter months in town, the Walkers had returned to their plantation in April. Mark half-expected they would not be home when he walked up the front steps toward the entrance, but he was greeted with great fanfare by Stephen, Rosabelle, and Lila. Young Steve was stationed with the Confederate Army in Virginia. Although they put on a good act, Mark noticed subtle changes in the Walkers and in their household. They chatted and smiled as before, but with a sad, worried look in their eyes. There were fewer servants, and Mark was amused to see Lila, who had never lifted a finger before, performing tasks previously assigned to slaves.

Mark accepted their invitation to stay for dinner. As before, the table-setting was opulent. China and silver sparkled; long tapered candles in ornate silver candelabra flickered light onto the highly polished mahogany table. Mark remembered the fine dinners served in the past. While the meal was adequate, it did not compare to the vast variety of rich foods normally served. The she-crab soup was missing; there was no shad roe or any number of other dishes always included. Mark fingered the stem of his wine glass, musing to himself that conditions would never be the same as before the war.

There was one other guest for the evening meal, Lila's

friend Lieutenant Jonathan Blair, who was stationed in Charleston. He brought the Walkers the good news that Union attempts to destroy the Charleston and Savannah railroad had been foiled by Confederate forces. In a lighter vein, he made them laugh with jokes about President Lincoln. Dressed in the gray uniform of a Confederate officer, he looked quite dashing, and Lila had eyes only for him.

When they had finished eating, Stephen and Mark went to the library and talked business long into the night, agreeing that in the morning Walker cotton would be loaded on the *Lady Tamara*. Mark planned to wait until nightfall and under cover of darkness head his ship directly westward to Bermuda.

Their business concluded, the conversation turned to the war. Mark learned that the Confederate capital had moved to Richmond and that the Yankee conquerors were determined to capture it. Their plan was to isolate the Confederacy, strangle it as an anaconda squeezes its prey to death. In its deadly grip, Fort Pulaski at the mouth of the Savannah River had fallen, as well as the South's largest city, New Orleans.

Between sips of bourbon and puffs on their cigars, the two men mulled over the idea that war produces inventions and that the Civil War was producing a revolution in naval warfare, not only in the transition from sail to steam, but from wooden to ironclads. And there were rumors of experiments with torpedoes.

Stephen boasted laughingly of how the Confederates, soon after the fall of Fort Sumter, had seized the navy yard at Norfolk, Virginia. Before they evacuated it, the Yankees set fire to and scuttled the *Merrimac*, a steam warship. Stephen described to Mark how the Confederate engineers had raised the ship. The hull was cut down and slanting sides were constructed of thick pine and oak with an armor of iron covering it. The Confederates renamed it the *Virginia*.

"How effective has it been?" Mark asked curiously.

Stephen chuckled.

"Funniest looking damned thing you ever saw. It doesn't have the magnificent symmetry of the great sailing ships. When it first went into action it created a sensation. Immediately the Yankees brought out ironclads. The *Virginia* met up with one of them, the *Monitor*. It was designed by John Ericsson with a long, flat hull and a revolving turret for mounting guns.

Mark emptied his glass in one gulp.

"Sir, what was the outcome?"

"Indecisive."

"I hope I won't encounter any of them."

Mark put down his glass and rose in preparation to leave. It was almost morning when he returned to his ship.

The *Lady Tamara,* painted gray to decrease visibility, set sail with the tide at sundown, following the main channel for blockade-runners. Mark set his course due east. No Union gunboats were encountered. In Bermuda, after his cotton shipment was unloaded and bolts of muslin and cases of tools from England were loaded, he was ready to make another run to Charleston. It was at the wharf that he met his former first mate, Roderick Moran. When Roderick told him he was going to Jamaica, Mark asked him to deliver a letter to Tamara. Moran was only too willing to find an excuse to see her. Tucking the letter in his inside coat pocket, he invited Mark on a tour of his ship, after which they went to a bar and shared a bottle of whiskey.

Mark met Moran several times in the next few months in St. George, Bermuda, where the harbor was crowded with merchant ships and the bars with their crews and skippers. Each time he gave Moran a letter for Tamara and asked whether he had any news of her. He had received no letters. Moran was tight-mouthed and changed the subject to Schofield shipping.

"You could gain control of the company, Mark. You have a right."

Mark scowled. "I have no doubt on that score, but damned if I want it. I hope Elaine ruins it into nonexistence." He took a long gulp on his drink.

"From what I hear, there's a pretty good chance of that. The company is in financial straits," Moran said.

Mark gave a bitter laugh. "What you should do, Moran, is go to London and woo the woman and marry her. You'd have yourself a shipping company."

Moran laughed. "Not a bad idea."

Mark loved his wife and regretted being the cause of her unhappiness. He thought she had not sent any messages with Moran because she had not forgiven him. Each time he entered his quarters he thought of her, felt her presence. He missed the lovely sound of her voice. He could see her sitting in his tub, her hair piled on top of her head, her lovely body covered with suds.

There was much to occupy his mind, but when his ship was not in dangerous waters, his thoughts were filled with Tamara. At night, mechanically clenching the taffrail, absorbing the tang of the sea, without seeing, he broodingly focused his half-closed eyes out across the water on the dark horizon, mindless of the wind whipping through his hair. He needed Tamara. Thinking of her, he became aware of the quickening of his heart. His passion aroused to aching proportions as he recalled the heady delight, the sweet torture of their tender preludes to lovemaking, the thrilling prolonging of consummation as long as physically possible. Unknowingly he smiled as he thought of how he muffled her passionate groans with his lips.

Visions of Tamara appeared at the most unexpected moments. The longer he was parted from her, the greater the intensity of his desire. In Bermuda he succumbed and went to a house of prostitution, where his basic needs were satisfied, but he left the establishment with an empty feeling in the pit of his stomach. He wanted and needed Tamara. Absently he headed for the nearest bar, where he ordered whiskey. Tamara had ruined his desire for other women. He thought it strange that he wanted no woman except his wife, but when he stopped to think about it, he decided it was not strange at all. She was beautiful, desirable, warm and loving, responding to him passionately, going beyond her wifely duties to thrill and beguile him and keep him interested. He cherished their intimate talks and confessions. He enjoyed their quiet times and their shared joy and laughter. The love, physical and emotional, they shared was unique, predestined. He brooded whether fate had also allotted him a minimal time with her.

Mark made several safe trips back and forth between Charleston and Bermuda. They became almost routine. That he did not encounter opposition encouraged him and his crew, who shared the profits, to take on a shipment of Enfield rifles, cartridges, barrels of gunpowder, and percussion caps, for which he would obtain a small fortune.

Then, one afternoon, peering through his spyglass, Mark spotted a ship on the horizon and resigned himself to the inevitable. He judged immediately that it was a faster-moving vessel and that escape was impossible. His frown changed to a smile when he identified the approaching ship as the *Confederate*, a commerce raider notorious for having destroyed numerous Yankee whalers and vessels with valuable cargo headed for Northern ports.

It came alongside. "Ahoy there! Permission to come aboard, sir!" It was war. The *Confederate*'s captain could take no chances. When he boarded the *Lady Tamara* to ascertain her destination and cargo, friendly exchanges were made. Mark frowned when he looked across to the deck of the Confederate ship and noticed boys no more than twelve serving as powder monkeys. They seemed so young.

The *Lady Tamara* was permitted to continue on her voyage with the contraband cargo, and reached Charleston safely.

Each time Mark came to the city, he went to see the Walkers. Their spirits rose and fell according to news of the war. By August it looked as if Southern independence would be a reality, and the Walkers were cheerful. The Confederacy, which had been on the defensive, went on the offensive, and by autumn appeared close to victory.

When General Beauregard had been in Charleston in April 1861, his headquarters were located in the Charleston Hotel. When he returned in the autumn of 1862, he moved from one residence to another. When Mark arrived at the Walkers', Beauregard was staying with them, using their ballroom as his headquarters.

"How is that lovely wife of yours, Lady Tamara?"

"She is . . . all right, sir. She . . . was unhappy when I left Jamaica to run the blockade."

Beauregard smiled and nodded his head. "My poor wife, Caroline, feels the same way. She is in New Orleans waiting for me. When I left, I told her I would be gone two weeks. That was a year and a half ago." He extended his hand, gripping Mark's firmly, shaking it vigorously. "I appreciate, sir, what you are doing for the Confederacy. I will give you all the protection I can."

When Mark stopped at the Walkers' in October, he knew immediately something was wrong. Rosabelle dabbed her eyes as her husband informed Mark that they had received word their son had been killed in the bloody Battle of Antietam in Maryland. Steve had been with Lee's army of fifty-five thousand, of which twelve thousand were reported killed. McClellan's Union forces totaled eighty-five thousand and lost nearly as many as the Confederate Army.

On Christmas Day, while Roderick Moran was visiting Tamara, her confinement imminent, and on January 3, 1863, when, unknown to Mark, his son was born, he was in the middle of the Atlantic Ocean speeding toward Bermuda in an effort to escape a Union blockading squadron chasing him.

As Northern power increased at sea, the blockade became more effective and the risks increased. More Yankee gunboats prowled the coastal waters, and Northern shipyards were busy building new warships. They armed and sent south every kind of ship afloat from side-wheel ferryboats and excursion steamers to fishing schooners and whalers.

Beauregard was working sixteen hours a day planning and building the defenses of Charleston. By January 1863 he succeeded in getting completed two ironclad rams, the *Palmetto State* and the *Chicora*, gunboats equipped with underwater poles that at top speed could pierce the hull of an enemy ship.

In the beginning of March the *"Lady Tamara"* encountered its first opposition. It was close to midnight when Mark saw rockets burst in the dark sky to the north and knew it was a signal from a Union lookout barge to one of their warships in the area that the *Lady Tamara* had been spotted.

For a moment all eyes glanced skyward. The alert was sounded by the bellowing voice of the night watch, "Ship ahoy!" and the shrilling sound of the siren. As rapidly as possible, coal was shoveled on the fires to feed the furnaces in a desperate effort to build up as much steam in the boilers as possible. All sails were unfurled. It was full speed ahead as the *Lady Tamara* tried to escape the Union warship *Newport*.

The enemy inched closer. When the *Lady Tamara* was within range, she was fired upon. The first shots fell short of target. There was no question that the purpose of the warship was not to capture but to sink the enemy merchant ship. Mark decided escape was her only chance of survival. Maneuvering in a zigzag course to avoid direct confrontation, she cut an erratic path as she tried to elude the gunfire from the warship.

Most of the cannons on the *Lady Tamara* were located along port and starboard sides. Since it meant changing course to fire upon the pursuing ship, Mark believed it to be a fatal move to position the ship to make full use of them. His aim was to reach the protection of Confederate installations along the coast. He shouted to the helmsman to stay on a course due west.

Two chasers were located at the stern, and as the *Lady Tamara* sped toward the Carolina coast, slicing through the choppy waters of the Atlantic Ocean, Mark ordered them positioned and readied for firing.

"Christ, Myers," he yelled to one of the gunners. "You've got to move faster than that or we'll all have our asses blown off."

The *Newport* gained, and the *Lady Tamara* began to take

314

a hammering. The mainmast was struck and crashed across the deck.

Mark signaled to the gunners: "Aim! Load! Prime! Fire!"

The volley boomed out across the water toward the pursuing enemy ship, falling short of target by fifteen feet to starboard. A spray of water spurted from the sea. The *Lady Tamara* lurched in the repercussions. The chasers were readied again. "Aim! Load! Prime! Fire!"

As he stood on the bridge shouting commands, a vision of Tamara appeared before Mark. He thought he would never see her again. Were all his months away from her worth the wealth he had accumulated? What good would it be now if he did not live to enjoy it with her? Even if he was fortunate enough to survive, she would not forgive him. The money could not make up for the separation and the rift it had caused. Bile rose up from his stomach to burn his throat. He condemned himself unworthy of her love. He blamed himself for the loss of it. Because of his stubborn pride he had ruined their chance of a future together. A sick feeling swept through him. He regretted that his beloved would never know how much he had missed her, how much he had longed to hold her in his arms. Their life together flashed before him in a few seconds, giving him renewed determination to get out of his present predicament and return to her and never leave her again.

Wiping his sleeve across his forehead, sweated and black with coal dirt, he forced his attention back to the moment.

Suddenly the watch shouted, "Land ho!" The shore of South Carolina loomed before him. If the *Lady Tamara* could stay out of range of the *Newport* for a while longer, she could reach the safety of Charleston harbor, protected by the Confederate fortifications encircling it.

The two vessels entered the mouth of the harbor. The outline of Fort Sumter became visible. Shortly its guns opened fire on the Yankee warship. The *Palmetto State* steamed through the channel toward the *Newport*. The *Newport*, forced to give up its pursuit, changed course and headed for the open seas. Cheers went up from the *Lady Tamara*.

Like fog, gray sulfurous smoke from the now quiet chasers hovered across her deck, shielding the bleeding bodies of the wounded and dying sprawled upon it. Those still alive coughed from the irritating smoke. As once before, the *Lady Tamara* limped toward the docks of Charleston for repairs. The crew was exhausted. They had piled up more money than they had ever had before, and some of them wanted to call it quits; others were not satisfied and wanted more. Mark felt it was time to go home. He had promised Tamara he would be away only a few months. Soon it would be a year. He made up his mind that this had been his last run.

62

"I could not stay away, my darling. Don't fight me. I believe you missed me, too," Roderick said softly, his cheek pressed against Tamara's.

By April he had found it impossible to stay away. He appeared one rainy evening after the baby had been put to bed and Tamara was in the library reading. She looked up to see him watching her, his smoldering eyes saying it all. He no longer disguised his desire for her. She quivered. He stood still as she ran to him and slipped into his outstretched arms. His eyes searched hers. They remained clinging to each other for a long moment. She felt his sharp intake of breath; then hungrily he sought her lips.

Motherhood had enlarged her breasts and left a becoming roundness to her hips, over which his hands moved. His heart pounded as he felt her body press tightly to his. Her response was nearly his undoing.

Ashamed, Tamara tried without success to ignore the tremors running through her body. She knew he was battling to keep himself in check. The fiercely passionate kiss left them swaying in each other's arms. Tamara's legs felt weak, and she found it difficult to stand. Murmuring incomprehensible words of love, his lips brushed her eyelids, nose, her cheeks and throat.

Tamara grew dizzy with desire. Her conscience fought it, but it was true that she had missed him. She tried to pretend she felt nothing, but she knew she was far from immune to him. Was it possible to love two men at the same time, or was Roderick Moran merely a substitute until the man she truly loved returned to her . . . if he ever did?

She could feel her resistance draining away. To her immense relief, she was having her menstrual period and knew it would prevent her from surrendering to him that night. She did not give him the reason for her refusal, but succeeded in forestalling him, saying her greatest desire was to remain faithful to her husband. Nevertheless Roderick Moran knew he had gained ground and that he would not be waiting much longer.

"I know it is difficult for you. I know you are struggling. Do not fight me. It has been almost a year since he left you. Do you think he has remained celibate all this time? I know Mark. I am certain he has had many lovers. My dear, how long are you going to make me wait for what you know is inevitable?" he asked huskily. "Let me . . . Where is your bedroom?"

Tamara disengaged herself from his arms, shaking her head forcibly and pressed her hands over her ears. "Stop it! Stop it! Stop it!

He grabbed her and pulled her close. "Let's go to your room."

She wrenched herself away from him. "I cannot. . . . Arona . . ."

"You worry about what a servant thinks! Then come with me back to the ship."

"I cannot. . . ."

"Come to me in Kingston tomorrow."

"Tell me honestly. Do you think Mark could have been injured . . . or . . . killed?"

"I have no way of knowing. Each time I go to Nassau I make inquiries, but no one knows. My route no longer takes me to Bermuda."

"Perhaps he is in Charleston with the Walkers and cannot get out of the harbor because of the blockade."

"It is a possibility. Maybe he doesn't want to leave. Remember, Lila is there."

Moran's visit left them both shaken. Again she begged him not to come back, but at the same time wished he would. She needed adult companionship. The baby was healthy and developing nicely, but with all the attention Arona gave him, he was not enough to fill her days. She spent a great deal of time singing and talking to him, cradling him in her arms. She studied his features and each day saw more and more of Mark, his coloring, the contour of his face and head, his eyes, which had turned green with dark flecks. He was even blessed with his father's smile, Tamara thought.

She did not go to Kingston the next day. When he was not near her, she was strong in her determination to resist Moran. The nagging voice of her conscience told her time and time again it would be wrong. If she surrendered, it would be no more than an interlude until Mark returned, and when he did, what effect would it have on their lives? Could she live with her infidelity? The results could be irreparable to herself and her marriage.

Then there were times when she believed Mark would never return, that he was lost to her forever. Perhaps he had become bored with her and his settled life. Not knowing whether he was alive, dead, or simply indifferent, when Roderick was present her resolve wavered. Roderick was a handsome man and possessed great charm. He would be difficult for any woman to resist, and she was flattered by his attention. He was there, and he loved her.

The sun's heat began to fade as it descended in preparation of approaching nightfall. The breeze from the sea drifted upward along the steep mountainside and rippled through the garden, ruffling the tendrils of hair at Tamara's cheeks. She looked very feminine in a pale yellow dress with dainty white lace trim.

The water from the fountains splashed rhythmically in the circular pond as the wind spread its mist through the air. The spray increased the heavy scent of jasmine and other tropical flowers blooming in profusion.

Tamara and Roderick sat near the fountains in the blue shadows of dusk. Tamara chatted almost lightheartedly while Moran bounced the little boy on his knee until he began to squirm and she took him and rocked him in her arms.

Arona heard him and came running. "Shall I take 'im, ma'am?"

"No, Arona, he will be all right."

Arona looked at Moran defiantly. "Looks jes' like his daddy, don' he?" She turned on her heels and went inside.

When he fell asleep, Tamara put him down on the blanket spread out on the grass. He yawned in his sleep and stretched on his belly.

Tamara chuckled. "He looks so relaxed."

Roderick went to her and kissed her between the eyes. "Aye, madam. Do you sleep on your belly?" he asked intimately.

Tamara's cheeks turned a delicate shade of pink; then she burst into laughter. "No, I—"

"Well, well! What a cozy little scene," said a familiar deep voice."

63

They had not heard Mark's footsteps as he made his way across the soft grass. Roderick jerked himself to a standing position. Tamara's face drained of color, then crimsoned. She was frozen in her chair. It was as if Mark had returned from the dead. He stood before them glaring.

"So this is what has been going on in my home during my absence!"

Instead of running to him and flinging herself into his arms, the tone of his voice compelled Tamara to immobility. She waited, holding her breath as he surveyed the tranquil scene with disgust, Moran's pipe on the grass, his goblet partially filled with brandy from Mark's wine cellar, his coat draped familiarly over the back of his chair. Mark's eyes dropped to the baby, and he went stiff. His face flushed with rage. He looked at Tamara with malice-filled eyes; then he turned to Moran.

"I'll kill you, Moran!"

The thought of his wife in Moran's arms sent him into a jealous rage. He refused to listen to reason as Roderick tried to explain.

"I always knew you lusted after her, but I never thought she would become one of your victims."

"I love her, which is more than you can say truthfully."

In a rage Mark lunged for Roderick's throat. Tamara jumped up, shouting for them to stop. She ran to her husband and tried to embrace him, but viciously he thrust her aside.

"Mark," she cried, "you are making a mistake. We are not lovers. The child is yours! He is your son. If you do not believe me, just look at him."

"Slut!" He slapped her hard across the face. Her head snapped back from the force of it. "So you have become a liar as well as an adulteress."

Roderick tried to come to her defense and grabbed Mark by the collar. "If you want to strike someone, let it be me, but I warn you, if you ever hit her again, I will kill you."

Tears spilled over and ran down Tamara's cheeks, mixing

with the blood gushing from her nose. "You must believe me. This is not Roddie's child."

Mark snickered nastily. "So . . . you are like the Virgin Mary. You conceived without intercourse!"

"I was pregnant when you left me! He is your son. Can't you see by looking at him?" The commotion and shouting wakened the baby, and he began to cry. Tamara picked him up and rocked him in her arms.

Mark squinted to study him closely. "Christ, all babies look alike to me." He turned to Roderick. "Get out of my sight, Moran. That includes my home and my wife's life."

Before Tamara had a chance to say another word, Mark turned on his heel and stalked toward his horse, still tethered in the driveway. She ran after him, pleading, beseeching him to believe her. Without a backward glance he swung into his saddle and galloped away.

An eerie stillness fell around her.

"I will go after him," Roderick said, and left.

Tamara waited all night, expecting Mark to come home, but he did not. Next morning Dodie drove her to Kingston. The *Lady Tamara* was no longer in port. Tamara was told it had set sail unexpectedly during the night. The *Dauntless* was still in its berth, and Tamara went on board.

Moran was in his quarters, and when Tamara knocked he opened the door, took her hand, and pulled her inside, shutting the door behind him. Tamara looked around, noting how nice it was. But she could not help comparing it with Mark's quarters on the *Lady Tamara*, which were far more spacious and luxurious, with his personality reflected everywhere. Pain and despair gripped her heart as achingly she remembered their honeymoon.

Roderick looked dejected. He stared at the blue bruise on her cheek, then squeezed her hand reassuringly. "I have done this to you, and I am sorry beyond words."

"He's gone," she blurted.

"I know. I went to him last night . . . to try to make amends, but he is a stubborn man. He told me he was returning to Charleston and to tell you not to expect him back."

Tamara faltered, reaching out and grabbing the edge of the chair to brace herself.

"I have lost him. I will never see him again." She twisted her hands in despair.

"Forget him. You know I want you. We will give him six months. If he has not returned, I will seek him out and demand he give you a divorce. You will marry me."

Dumbfounded, Tamara shook her head back and forth emphatically. "I am sorry, but I cannot do that. I have commited myself to my husband. I want to be a faithful wife. My love for him goes beyond devotion. He saved me from a life of fear and loneliness." Her voice trembled with emotion. "My heart will always belong to him and somehow I must win him back!"

Absently Moran ran his finger over the brass spyglass on the table. "It appears to me you are pretty lonely now. You welcomed my company enough these past months," he said, with bitterness in his voice.

Losing her composure, she swung around to face him directly. "I told you not to come back! I told you it could never be more than friendship!"

Moran realized he was losing ground with Tamara. It struck him that the only way he could have her was by force, and he meant to have her. "I want you, and it's going to be now," he said calmly. "You have trifled with my affections long enough."

Tamara stiffened as his arm reached out and stopped her from leaving. He pulled her close with a jerk. His dark, handsome features looked sinister. The harder she struggled, the more determined he became. His lips crushed down hard on hers as he held her head so she could not move. His fingers dug into her tender flesh as he dragged her into the next room and roughly flung her down on the bed.

She sank her teeth into his earlobe. He winced. "Damn you, try that again and I'll bite you where you'll feel it!"

She kicked as he tried to pull up her skirt and petticoats. Becoming impatient, he ripped them away from her body. Panting hard, Tamara clawed his face and grabbed a fistful of his hair to try to pull his mouth away from her breasts which were now bare. To her chagrin, he pinned her down with his body. Her efforts to push him off failed. His hands moved all over her. One of them left her body to fumble at his trousers and release his fully engorged penis.

Tamara screamed so loud and with so much force she hurt her throat. Moran clamped his hand over her mouth. "Be still, you fool!" A shot rang out. Moran froze.

Tamara peered over his shoulder to see Dodie aiming a pistol at him. He waved it, cocked it, his finger on the trigger. "Git off 'er."

Moran complied, buttoning up his pants. Without removing his eyes from Moran, Dodie forced him into the corner with his hands in the air. Tamara crawled from the bed and tried to cover herself as best she could.

"Hol' dis gun while I ties'm up." he said to Tamara with difficulty, his cheek bulging with a wad of tobacco he'd forgotten to remove when he heard her screams.

When Dodie and Tamara returned to Montjoy, as she stepped from the carriage she reached out and hugged him. "I can never thank you enough."

Showing embarrassment at the attention thrust upon him, Dodie shifted from one leg to the other. He wiped his mouth with the back of his hand to erase the last traces of tobacco juice. "Psh," he said shyly. " 'Tweren't nothin'. Mr. Mark ordered me to protect you while he's gone, an' dats what aw been doin'."

"What happened was my fault. I encouraged Mr. Moran by welcoming him here."

Tamara had difficulty going to sleep that night, and when she did, she slept fitfully. She began to dream. A man with a black beard was standing at her bed staring down at her, the shadowed bulk of his body stenciled insidiously against the dark. Taking a closer look, she recognized Roderick. Slowly he pulled her covers away from her. The nightmare had returned.

Roderick was sneering. She was puzzled. Confusion turned to shock. In her dream she saw him as a predatory threat to herself and her marriage. This was not the Roderick she knew. He reached down and grabbed her breasts, groping as she slid across the bed in an attempt to escape him. He caught her wrists and pulled her back. She pleaded and begged. She called out for Mark to rescue her, but Mark was far away. Roderick did not utter a word. He struck her across the face to still her struggles. He moved in slow motion as he ripped off her nightgown and threw himself on top of her. In her dream as she screamed he plunged his hard shaft into her unprepared body, tearing her open. Blood coursed down her legs. A scream pierced the quiet night. Hers. She screamed and screamed. Far away, someone called her name. "Lady Tamara. Lady Tamara." Someone held her, shook her. Drenched in perspiration, dazedly she opened her eyes. Arona was sitting on the edge of the bed trying to comfort her.

64

After his hasty departure from Jamaica, Mark sailed to Nassau, where he headed for the most exclusive, the most expensive establishment in town and demanded from the madam a bosomy redhead. He paid for her services for three days, along with several bottles of whiskey. He would get Tamara out of his blood if it was the last thing he ever did. The whore was asked to do everything short of masochism, for which he had no taste.

When he sobered up, he took on a full crew and a shipment of badly needed medical supplies. He had learned in Nassau that Charleston remained in the hands of the Confederacy, but was under siege. The Union's grip tightened. The swiftest blockade-runners dared not attempt to get in or out.

In the taverns of Nassau while waiting for their ships to depart, seamen and military men discussed the city most of them had entered. "You're crazy if you head yer ship fer Charleston," the seamen warned Mark. "Would be committin' suicide."

Mark shrugged indifference, but took their advice. He left Nassau in the middle of the night, his destination was Mobile, Alabama, on the coast of the Gulf of Mexico, east of New Orleans, a Confederate city still considered safe for blockade-runners.

As the *Lady Tamara* steamed through the Gulf of Mexico, Mark tried not to dwell upon the painful scene at his home. Unable to stay away from his wife a moment longer, he had sailed home. When he had reached Kingston, so eager was he to take her in his arms, his steed could not travel fast enough to reach Montjoy. Memories of their amorous lovemaking had stirred his desires. The closer he got, the more intense the gnawing ache of passion. His body was aflame when he dismounted and tethered his horse. Suspecting Tamara would be in the garden, he had headed there first, only to find her with Moran . . . and the child. The urge to strike out and kill had been followed by sickening despair. Since then, however hard he tried, he found it impossible not to think of Tamara. She was not only his wife, but his lover, his mistress, his true

323

love. She had come to him pure, untouched, afraid of men. He had nurtured her natural instincts with his patience, affection, and love until he had won her. It was he who had encouraged her not to repress her desires, to abandon herself to him. He had taught her the pleasures of love and how to reach the ultimate height of passion with him, no one else. She was his. She belonged to him alone. He had wanted her to be the mother of *his* children. Now it was too late. And love was like money, not fully appreciated until it was lost.

Sitting in the leather chair in his salon with a glass of bourbon in his hand, he groaned aloud. His left hand flew up and briskly rubbed across his face in an effort to blot out the scene that pained him agonizingly. Tamara and Moran. He was crushed to the marrow of his bones by her betrayal. It was almost more than he could endure. He drained his glass. What she had done was irreparable. When a wife was unfaithful to her husband, it could not be undone.

He leaned forward, resting his arms on his thighs, his head drooping, his fingers curled around the empty glass. He was feeling wretched. He had written letter after letter and had given them to Moran, but had received none from her in all the time he had been gone. That alone should have told him she had not forgiven him for leaving, but to turn to Moran! Even if she were angry, it never occurred to him that his beloved would be anything but faithful to him. There were many women he could never trust, but Tamara—he had trusted Tamara. He had been too sure of her.

In his self-castigation he told himself his wealth meant nothing to him except a bitter reminder that in accumulating it he had lost the one thing that meant more to him than all the money in the world. Why, then, was he risking his neck again? Because he thought he could lose himself in the danger of it.

He refilled his glass to the brim and downed it in long gulps. The more he drank, the more doubts set in, doubts about Roderick Moran and the scene at Montjoy as it appeared on the surface. Whenever the two men had met, Moran had told him he was passing Mark's letters on to someone going to Jamaica or that he had sent them with the mail steamer. He told Mark he had not seen Tamara.

"Dammit, Tamara was incapable of deception," he said aloud with a slurred tongue. "I've known her since she was a child. She would not lie."

He slouched back in his chair and stretched his long legs

out in front of him. His fingers brushed back his hair. "Then it must be Moran."

Mark was sober when the *Lady Tamara* slipped into Mobile Bay. The medical supplies for the Confederate Army were unloaded. In a short time the ship was steaming out of the harbor, and as it entered the Gulf of Mexico, indecision gripped him. Should he set his course homeward toward Jamaica or east-southeast to Nassau?

65

Mark sailed to Nassau. He made preparations for another shipment of medicines for Mobile. Since many of his men refused to return to the dangerous zone of the Gulf of Mexico swarming with Union gunboats, he posted notices for positions open on board the *Lady Tamara*. He preferred English or Irish seamen but would consider other Europeans. He went to the Anchor Pub, a popular bar for sailors looking for work, located near the wharf. The first night he signed on two, the second night one, but he was still shorthanded. On the third night when he entered the noisy, smoke-filled barroom he noticed the tables were all occupied. Several ships had come into port that day. He scanned the bar—and spotted Roderick Moran.

Mark hesitated. He had the option to turn and leave or to remain, either ignoring or confronting him. He reached a quick decision and headed for Moran, who was leaning on his elbows on the bar with a drink in front of him. Mark grabbed his collar. Moran had been drinking heavily and turned limply. With a jerk Mark pulled on his collar and gestured with a side nod of his head.

"Outside."

Moran's head wobbled as he tried to focus on his assailant.

"Outside," Mark repeated. "If necessary, I intend to drag the truth from you."

Moran protested noisily. "Keep your damn hands off me. I am no longer in your employ."

The bartender threatened to call the bobbies if they did not leave quietly. He wanted no fighting in his respectable establishment.

Moran, in compliance with the bartender's demands, slid from his wooden stool and went outside with Mark. They emerged from the pub to face each other on the sidewalk, followed by seamen on liberty, always eager for excitement when in port. Mark and Roderick were followed, then surrounded by bar patrons who prodded them on, hoping for a fight.

Mark ignored them. "Moran, when was the baby born?" he demanded to know.

Moran swayed. "You're some father. Don't even know when your brat was born."

Mark lifted a fist as if to punch him. He shoved him instead, then grabbed the lapels of his coat and shook him. For a moment it appeared as if the crowd would get what it wanted.

"Deck 'im," yelled one of the seamen.

Mark relinquished his grip as he tried to keep his anger under control. Moran steadied himself. "The beginning of January. I was there with her. Where the hell were you?"

"You know damned well where I was." Mark paused to figure out when conception had taken place—almost two months before he left Jamaica. Then there was no question. The child was his.

"You son of a bitch, you knew. You saw me a number of times. Why didn't you tell me? Why didn't she tell me?"

Moran shrugged his shoulders. "Why should I?"

"What happened to all those letters I gave you to pass on to the mail steamer here in Nassau?"

At first Moran balked at answering, ignoring the question as if he had not heard it. Mark's threatening fist persuaded him.

"I gave her the first one, destroyed the others."

"Did she give you any letters for me?"

Moran nodded.

"And you destroyed them?"

Moran nodded.

"Exactly what I suspected. She never gave in to you, did she, as you led me to believe? You don't have to answer that. It is perfectly clear to me now. I should have known Tamara was incapable of duplicity, which is what you were demanding of her. You always wanted what was mine, didn't you?"

Moran had sobered in a hurry. He straightened his collar and brushed the dust from his uniform. "You had everything—money, ships, women. Was it so unnatural for me to envy you?"

326

"I thought we were friends—until recently."

Moran smirked. Mark took a step closer. He lowered his voice. "The night I found you at Montjoy—you came to me on my ship and told me Tamara said I should never come back. She was finished with me and never wanted to see me again. Was that the truth?"

Moran did not answer. Mark grabbed him by the throat. Hoots and cheers went up from the bystanders. "Kill 'im," chanted several sailors. Mark's hands tightened around his throat.

"It was a lie," Moran said in a monotone resignedly. "She told me to go after you and bring you back. The next morning she went to Kingston looking for you, but you were gone. You are a thick-headed fool."

The flesh between Mark's eyes formed a deep crevice. He stared in disbelief. When the full meaning of Moran's words reached him, he shoved him with all his force. Moran reeled, then fell backward to the sidewalk. Mark didn't want to fight him. It was a gesture that he never wanted to see him again, that he should stay out of his life. He wanted the truth, and now he had it. He turned to leave. Moran, sprawled on the pavement, called after him. "I just might follow your suggestion and marry your stepmother."

Mark quickened his pace to get away from him. At dawn he set sail for Mobile, vowing that after he delivered his cargo he would sail home to Tamara.

66

Life at Montjoy settled into a routine revolving around the baby, who was now six months old. In the letter Tamara had written to Mark informing him she was going to have a baby, she had asked him what his preferences were in names. She had waited, but since there was no reply, she chose her father's name. Her son was christened Robert Mark Schofield.

When Tamara recovered from Roderick's attack and Mark's sudden appearance and abrupt departure, she considered going after him. She thought she would start looking for her husband by going to Nassau first. If she could not find him there, she would go to Bermuda, and if not there she would attempt to reach Charleston. But it could be an endless search, during which time she would be away from her child. Even if she did find Mark, he might refuse to listen to her. After sleepless nights and much deliberation, she rejected the idea, deciding instead to remain at Montjoy and pray for his return.

A year ago she would have thought it inconceivable to live such a long time without him. However poorly, she had managed to do so. She had Robert to fill the emptiness in her life, and she would plunge into work. She toyed with the idea of turning Montjoy into a coffee plantation again. She sought advice and was told the old trees could be cut down and saplings planted without difficulty. She also considered replanting the old citrus grove. She knew what the other planters would say. It was no job for a woman, even with a capable overseer.

Two letters arrived from London. One was addressed to Tamara, the other to Mark, a large brown envelope similar to two others that had been delivered since he left. The first came a few days after he had departed on his first trip to Charleston with the shipment of coffee beans. Because it was addressed to him, Tamara had put it in his desk drawer in the library to await his return. A second had been delivered, and now a third.

Tamara went to the library and tossed it on top of the desk. She sat down and ripped open the letter addressed to her. It was from her Uncle Arthur. She was concerned that something dreadful must have happened for him to write after all this time, but as she read the letter, she learned that that was not the case. He wrote that he was relieved when informed of her whereabouts by the family solicitor, to whom she had written. After conducting an investigation of Mark, he was forced to conclude that she had married well.

He and Lady Alma were well. Beverly and Valerie had given birth to daughters within three weeks of each other. They were eighteen months old now. Lady Alma had become a doting grandmother. He mentioned that Lord Darrington had married and Lord Lyndenhurst had died.

Tamara's uncle wrote that one day when he was attending the House of Lords a member by the name of Foxcomb had approached him and inquired about her. "I told him you were married and living in Jamaica. Whereupon he bowed and left."

Tamara's hand dropped to her lap. She gazed into space, remembering Lord Foxcomb, Foxcomb Manor, and Lady

Pamela. She wondered whether her health had deteriorated. She thought about what would have happened had she returned to Foxcomb Manor with Sir Richard. Tamara sighed, then continued reading the letter. Her Uncle Arthur asked her to write to him to let him know she was all right. He had never meant her harm and only had her welfare in mind. He was her only living relative, and she should not cut him off.

Tamara agreed. She decided she would answer her uncle's letter. She walked to the desk and saw the brown envelope addressed to Mark. She fingered it, and thinking it might be important, opened it and the others. Each envelope contained a check from a London bank in a very large sum. The bank's explanation was that the checks represented interest on a substantial trust fund Thomas Schofield had established for his son, Mark. There was a letter from his solicitor explaining the trust. Tamara put the envelopes back in the desk drawer until she could decide what to do about them.

The next afternoon when she put Robert to bed for his nap, studying him closely, patting him until he was asleep, she wondered whether he would ever see his father. To Tamara he was the most precocious, the most beautiful child that had ever been born. It saddened her that his father was not present.

With a heavy heart Tamara went to the kitchen. Arona was baking coconut cookies and offered her some. Tamara took one and nibbled on it. "It is delicious, Arona."

"T'ank you, ma'am."

Tamara unthinkingly twisted the gold wedding band on her left hand. The servant looked at her hesitantly. "You res'less today, ma'am. Somethin' aw can do fer you?"

Tamara took a deep breath. Tears appeared in the corners of her eyes. "No. Thank you, Arona. It is just that . . . that some days the ache for him is worse than others. If only I knew he was coming home for certain."

Arona looked at Tamara with a wary expression. "Aw t'ink long time if aw should tell you. Do'no if it right, but aw tells you."

"What is it, Arona?"

"Mr. Mark . . . he not Thomas Schofield's son."

Tamara took a step closer. "What did you say, Arona?"

"Mr. Mark not Thomas Schofield's son."

"How do you know this?"

"Mr. Schofield gone one year. When he come home, Mrs. Schofield expect baby. When he hears 'bout it, he go 'way an' not come home fer long, long time."

"Who . . . do you know who his father is?"

"Dead long time. Captain of Schofield ship. Came to Schofield Manor often."

"I am certain Mark is not aware of this. His mother should have told him. It would have made it easier for him to understand his father . . . I mean, Mr. Schofield."

"Yas'm. T'ink so, too, but none my business."

"Thank you for telling me, Arona."

Tamara twisted her ring again.

"You ain't had another nightmare, has you, ma'am?" Arona asked.

"No, no. I am sleeping much better."

Tamara ate another cookie. "I think I will go for a walk on the beach today."

"You go right ahead now, ma'am. Don' worry 'bout little Robert. If he wake, aw change his diaper and takes care of 'im." Knowing how Tamara was always hoping Mark would come home, Arona looked at her sheepishly. "An' if somebody come, aw tells'm where you are. 'Tain't good fer you to stay 'ere all de time."

When Robert was alseep, Tamara liked to exercise by going either for a walk or horseback riding. She always told Arona where she was going and never ventured far in case Mark came home during her absence. Walking along the beach helped Tamara to think matters through and make important decisions. The wind was brisk, the sky clear as she strolled along the water's edge, thinking about Mark. Mr. Schofield had known Mark was not his son, but he must have had some feeling for him. His trust fund made Mark a wealthy man. Could it have been that he knew the war would interfere in the shipping, that the company would be in trouble because of it? Could it have been his way of encouraging Mark to remain at home and not make the same mistakes he had made in staying away from his wife for long periods of time? He probably blamed himself for his wife's infidelity. Was he afraid Mark would make the same mistake? Tamara was deep in thought, pondering these questions. Whatever his motive, she was convinced she should find a way to inform Mark. Again she contemplated trying to find him. Since the war had interrupted the mail, she knew she could not rely on sending a letter, and she knew not where to send it. She wished that the information about the trust fund had reached Montjoy when the will arrived, before Mark left. It would not have been necessary for him to leave, and they would be together now.

Tamara's hands went up to cover her face. She had almost committed the same mistake as Mark's mother. She sighed with relief that she had not done so, that she had not given in to temptations born out of loneliness and disguised as love. Thank God she had not allowed Roderick Moran to become her lover.

The recurrence of the nightmare had left Tamara shaken. It frightened her that others would follow. She had thought that part of her life was over.

Tamara sat down on a boulder and gazed out to sea. As she thought about it, the truth converged on her threefold. She would never recover completely from her childhood tragedy. It was something that would remain in the shadows waiting to make another appearance. It had helped to mold her, had left its imprint upon her life forever, and nothing could erase it the way the tide washed away her footprints in the sand without a trace. Second, unknowingly a tragedy of a different nature had left its impact upon Mark. His mother had been unfaithful to his father and had given birth to Mark. Third, she needed Mark more than she had ever needed him before. She thought of the men who could easily have played an important role in her life—the Duke of Lyndenhurst, Lord Foxcomb, Lord Darrington, Roderick Moran. Each one was a mere episode in her life. Mark was her life.

67

As it sped through the Gulf of Mexico, the *Lady Tamara* left a trail of black puffy smoke, which dispersed across the clear blue sky. Mark was well aware of the success of the Union's blockade and the danger he was in. The blockade had turned out to be the North's most effective weapon.

In the Confederacy, practically everything needed by a nation at war had to be imported. The Yankees' blockading forces had resulted in its slow strangulation. Roanoke Island, North Carolina, was closed in February 1862, Jacksonville and St. Augustine, Florida, in March; Savannah and New Orleans in April; and Pensacola, Florida, in May.

Mobile, Alabama, remained open but was threatened by the Union's East Gulf Squadron, situated along the west coast of Florida. In order to avoid it Mark sailed farther west, following the least dangerous course rather than the established sea channel. The crew knew of the perils, and when the *Lady Tamara* slipped safely into Mobile Bay, cheers went up and echoed across the deck.

The medicines were unloaded and supplies of water, food rations, and coal were taken aboard. The ship's engines were kept going, and at dawn the following morning she set sail at high tide, her gray color blending in with the color of the night sea and sky.

Luck ran out. A high-speed Union torpedo-ram appeared out of nowhere. A superior vessel built for speed rather than carrying cargo, it outclassed the *Lady Tamara*. Mark was certain the ram carried explosives suspended from a long rod fastened at the prow beneath the water's surface. It was steaming full speed toward the *Lady Tamara*.

The ram struck her full force at stern. There followed an explosion. Then another. And another. Water gushed through a large gap in the hull. A boiler exploded. The ship was on fire. Orange flames and black smoke shot skyward, then, whipped by the wind, spread across the deck. Mark made a feeble attempt at retaliation. One round of shots was fired from starboard cannons; then he ordered the abandonment of his ship.

"Stand by to evacuate! Lower the longboat!"

Crewmen, firemen, engineers, coal heavers dived into the water and made a desperate attempt to swim away from the sinking ship to avoid being pulled down by the force of it. Mark waited until the last moment. He removed his heavy boots, jacket, and shirt so they would not weigh him down. He dived deep into the shark-infested waters.

Mark came up to watch his stricken ship. With a feeling of total helplessness he knew there was nothing he could do to save it. The ship sank beneath the surface of the water. To him it had been more than a ship. It had been his home, his refuge for many years, and the place where he had fallen in love with Tamara and where they had spent their honeymoon. His loss was indescribable.

He was wearing trousers and was bare from the waist up. The sun had made its appearance and beat down on him. Before long he realized he should have kept his shirt. Losing track of time, he had no idea how long he was adrift. It seemed an eternity. His lips were swollen, his face and back raw from the hot rays of the sun. He prayed for clouds, an overcast sky, nightfall. All feeling left his body except the pain in his arms, which were clasped around a floating object. Tired and weak, he was about to give up, to unfold his arms and float free. He saw something move—dark, triangular-shaped. What was it? No doubt the fin of a shark. If he was to die, he preferred drowning to being torn apart.

He had no idea what happened to the longboat. It had disappeared from sight. Debris from the ship floated on the surface of the heavy salt water around him. He could not tell whether humans were clinging to it or not. He called out, then listened. He called out again, but there was no answer. He heard nothing but the slapping of the waves. Never before had he felt so alone, so helpless. For the first time in his life, which he believed was about to end, he wondered whether there was any significance to life except to be born and to die.

Mark took a deep breath and let go. Immediately panic engulfed him and he grabbed for the wood, part of a three-foot-wide beam. He struggled and with the little strength he had left slipped his body across it, then collapsed. He was aware of a rocking motion, of water lapping around him. A heavenly feeling of floating on clouds washed over him.

"Hang on! Hang on!" a voice said from deep within. Tamara's face appeared before his blurred vision. It was she who was telling him not to give up. He no longer felt the pain in his arms and shoulders. He was completely numb. Oblivion descended over him.

The next thing he knew, he was being pulled from the water. A man's voice penetrated through his semiconsciousness. "He was clinging to a wooden beam. Lucky we spotted him. Roll him over on his stomach."

Water gushed from Mark's mouth. He vomited. Someone stripped off his pants and wrapped a blanket around him. He shivered from the sunburn. Total consciousness returned, but he kept his eyes closed, listening to the men standing around him on the deck. The Southern drawl was missing. The accent was clearly New England. He opened his eyes to appraise his new enemy.

Mark was given a swig of whiskey. In a weakened condition, as he lay stretched on the deck he pieced together fragments of what had happened. He was told he had been rescued by the Union cruiser *Salem*. He knew he was a prisoner.

68

"If I never see another turnip, it will be too soon!" Mark grumbled.

"Beats stah'vin," retorted the rebel prisoner sitting next to him, scraping the last of his rations from his tin plate and dipping a hard biscuit into the juice at the bottom.

"I have developed a loathing for them—along with sweet potatoes and salt pork," Mark complained as he sat on the ground in the fever-ridden prison camp in New Orleans.

His fellow prisoner chuckled mirthlessly. "What do you expect? The menu from New Orleans' finest French restaurant? Or do you prefer the rice and molasses we had yes'taday? At least it fills tha emptiness in the belly."

After Mark was pulled from the sea by members of the crew on board the *Salem,* he was taken below deck. He suffered from exposure, particularly sunburn, and remained in a state of semidelirium throughout the night. By morning he had regained full consciousness. He was feverish. The blisters on his shoulders looked like sponges. Lying in his bunk in sick bay, he studied the movement of the vessel and was certain it was traveling westward. That could mean only one destination, New Orleans, occupied by Union troops since Admiral David Farragut's victory two years earlier.

Mark had now been at the camp for a month. Each day seemed to be hotter and more humid than the day before. Sitting in the much-cherished shade of an elm, he put his empty plate aside. Perspiration bubbled on his brow. In the sweltering heat, he could feel the moisture collecting on the nape of his neck and trickling down his back. Absently, he watched a Union corporal approaching and was told to follow him. Taken to the officer in charge of the prisoners, he stood silent, waiting for him to speak. A fan moving slowly close to the ceiling did little to cool the room.

As Mark waited in his dirty prison garb, he noted the clean, meticulously uniformed officer. He hated the sour stench of himself, which was worse in the closed room. He had tried to keep himself clean, but water was limited and he had been forced to wear the same clothes since his arrival.

His face had been too sunburned to shave. His beard grew thick and dark.

The blue-coated officer smashed the stub of his cheroot in the ashtray on his desk. "Don't know exactly what to do about you," the officer said, studying the papers before him. "You sure you have no papers of identification or citizenship?"

"No, sir. I lost everything when my ship went down. I told you before, I am a subject of the crown. My home is Jamaica."

"Yes. Yes. You told me that. And we are well aware of the activities of the *Lady Tamara*." The officer frowned in displeasure and cleared his throat. "According to a cartel signed by the North and the South, prisoners are to be exchanged on a ration basis, private for private, general for general, sixty privates for a general." The officer smirked. "In what category do I put you? Our General Grant has been objecting to the release of prisoners who go right back into combat again."

The officer leaned back, causing his swivel chair to make a cracking noise. He folded his hands at the back of his head and looked Mark straight in the eye.

"Are those your intentions? To get another ship and start all over again? What are your plans if I release you?" he queried.

"Sir, I want to go home to Jamaica."

The officer looked at him skeptically. "Saying it and doing it are two different things." He sat forward, the swivel chair creaking back into place. He folded the portfolio in front of him. "That will do for now."

Mark turned to leave and then faced the officer again. "Sir, do I have your permission to send a letter to my wife?"

The officer was silent for a moment, then sighed, leaning back in his chair again. "Write your letter. I'll see it gets mailed. We'll read it first, though."

Mark nodded. "I will need paper and ink, sir."

"Ask the corporal on the way out."

Mark pulled an old crate under the elm in the prison yard and wrote a long letter to Tamara. After he informed her that he was a prisoner in a Union camp in New Orleans, he poured out his heart to her, and when he was finished he sighed and stretched out on the ground and brooded. Thinking of Tamara had brought on a sharp pang of wanting her.

Mark was joined in the shade by other prisoners searching for the coolest spot. Each day the number of prisoners hovering in the yard grew smaller, as more and more came down with dysentery. A rebel prisoner, James Huguenin, nicknamed Hughy, not more than eighteen, sat next to him. Mark glanced around the prison yard and without looking at Hughy commented, "Not as many soldiers on duty today. Are they getting sick too, Hughy?"

"They're at the funeral. Ovah'heard'm talkin' 'bout it," Hughy replied in a drawl.

"Whose funeral?" Mark asked.

"Mrs. Beauregard's."

Mark thought for a moment. "General Beauregard's wife?"

"Yep. Ain't it a crime? He can't even come home for his wife's funeral. Union Army is swarming the city like bees. Would arrest 'im fer sure."

"But why are Union soldiers attending Mrs. Beauregard's funeral?"

"Suh, they ain't attendin', they's guardin' with bayonets, I heard tell. They's afraid of demonstrations. The people of New Orleans hates their Yankee captors. No tellin' what they's liable to do. The cortege is bein' taken to the levee, where Mrs. Beauregard's casket will be put on a boat to carry it to the family burial grounds."

Mark turned pensive. He thought of General Beauregard, proud, gallant, stubborn, a man he had learned to admire and respect. He wondered whether the general had received word of his wife's death. He was being called upon to make almost inhuman sacrifices for the cause of the Confederacy.

Mark crossed his legs and leaned back against the tree trunk. He glanced about the overcrowded, rat-infested compound baking in the hot sun. It consisted of eight clapboard barracks. A separate building of brick and stone surrounded by shade trees housed the Union soldiers. The stench was hardly bearable. He cursed and blamed his stupid pride for the predicament he was in.

About a hundred of the prisoners were from Iowa, members of the same regiment. Most of the others came from Louisiana, Alabama, and Georgia.

Mark took a deep breath and turned his head toward the prisoner next to him. "Where you from, Hughy?"

"Macon, Georgia, suh."

"Can you draw a map?"

"No, suh. Why?"

"It doesn't look as if I am to be released soon. I have to get out of here and find my way to Charleston. I need a map. If you could make a rough sketch, I would be grateful."

"Need paper."

"Here." Mark handed Hughy a sheet of paper he had left from writing his letter to Tamara.

Hughy hesitated. "Take me with you."

"It is too risky. You could get shot!"

Hughy threw down the paper and pen stubbornly. "Well, damnation, so could you."

"All right. All right." Mark flapped his hand, motioning impatiently. Hughy proceeded to make a crude drawing showing the shortest route from New Orleans to Charleston by way of Macon, Georgia.

Mark kept an eye open for the Union sentinel as the blond-haired youth explained the map. Youth. Mark noted he was far older than his years, aged by the experiences of war and imprisonment. When he had volunteered to join the Confederate Army, he was obese, having been coddled by his mother, who encouraged him to eat her rich foods and pastries. The pudginess had disappeared, and since his capture, his cheeks were sunken. The trousers of his tattered, dirty Confederate-gray uniform hung loosely. He had found a piece of twine to slip through the belt loops to hold them up.

"If we could reach the railroad heah," he said, pointing to a spot on his map, "we'd have it made—if it hasn't fallen into the hands of the cursed Yankees."

Later that night they discussed the possibility of escape.

"This might be the best night. There is no moon. Not many soldiers are on duty because of Mrs. Beauregard's funeral," Hughy suggested eagerly.

"It is too soon. I need more time to think it through, study the routine of the sentinels. Usually there is only one on patrol."

Hoping to be freed, Mark bided his time. Months dragged by. In the beginning of August he made his move. Observing only one sentry on night patrol in the compound, he and Hughy waited until three in the morning. It was a black night with no moon to betray their movements as they hid, waiting to strike.

The guard paraded back and forth. Back and forth. He turned his back. Mark sprang like a panther.

69

On the night of Mark's attempt to escape prison, Tamara sat at the desk in the library at Montjoy, frowning as she went over the account books. She had gone ahead with plans for clearing the old coffee trees and planting saplings. She had hired an overseer, Avery Southworth, a white-haired man approaching sixty who had a wide range of experience in the cultivation of coffee. He in turn had hired ten Negro workers and had purchased two mules. The old trees were pulled out, old sheds torn down, and new ones constructed.

Economic conditions in Jamaica fluctuated from one year to the next. Tamara worried that she had made a serious mistake in investing in coffee. It seemed to be the wrong time. Prices of both sugar and coffee had slumped, and exports were low because of the Civil War in America and the effectiveness of the Union blockade. In Jamaica, Kingston particularly, the black laboring class suffered severely. Unemployment was high, wages low. Imported-food prices were high because of the American war. Heavy flooding had caused widespread damage to food crops, followed by droughts, which resulted in higher prices for domestic foods.

Tamara closed the ledgers and put them in the desk drawer. She went to bed and the next morning galloped her horse along the shore, mulling over whether she should continue with the project or not.

When she returned to the house, Arona announced there was a gentleman waiting to see her in the library.

"Who is it?"

Arona shrugged her shoulders and shook her head. "Nebba see 'im before."

When Tamara entered the library, the tall man was standing by the window looking out at the view. He leaned over and put his hat and cane on the windowsill. When he turned, Tamara gasped.

"Lord Foxcomb!"

Sir Richard turned to gaze into the violet eyes of the woman he had tried but found impossible to forget. For a

338

moment they stared at each other; then Tamara flew into his open arms.

"Sir, I have thought of you many times."

"And I, you . . . more than you can imagine." Holding her at arm's length, he took in her loveliness. "You have grown more beautiful."

"Thank you, sir. Will you not be seated? Would you like refreshment . . . a drink, perhaps?"

"No, thank you. You are all the refreshment I need for the moment." He patted the couch where he sat. "Come sit beside me so I can look at you."

Tamara sat down, a respectable distance between them. "What brings you to Jamaica, sir?"

Lord Foxcomb smiled sheepishly. "You."

"Me?" Tamara's voice rose excitedly. "You came all this distance just to see me?"

"I came to the Bahamas and Barbados to purchase property, but I confess I used it partly as an excuse to look you up."

"I am very glad you did. How long can you stay?"

"My ship departs for London day after tomorrow."

"You will stay here, of course."

"No. No. I have my compartment aboard ship."

"I will not hear of it! I shall send my servant Dodie to the ship for your luggage immediately."

Sir Richard chuckled. "If you insist, then. My servant is there. I will send a note and a list of my needs."

While Sir Richard wrote instructions for his servant, Tamara excused herself to tell Arona and Dodie she would be having a guest. When all was settled, she led him into her gardens. She was very proud of her flowers and landscaping, and delighted in showing them to all her visitors.

Tamara could not keep her eyes from him. He was not a handsome man, but he was strikingly attractive, wearing expensive, perfectly tailored clothes. There had been a time when she shrank from him out of fear, as she had reacted to most men. The fear had not only disappeared; she felt herself drawn to him.

Sir Richard paused and looked around the garden as if he were searching for something. "Ah . . . there it is."

"What?"

"The bed of white roses. I knew you would have one. I have not forgotten how much you admired the ones at Foxcomb Manor, and I have gone to great lengths to make it the most beautiful bed on the estate."

Tamara did not have a chance to reply, for Robert came running with a ball in his hand, followed by Arona, who remained in the background. Robert was nineteen months old, walking and learning new words every day.

"Mama. Ball."

"Well, well, who is this fine-looking young man?"

Tamara smiled proudly. "This is my son, Robert Mark Schofield."

Sir Richard bowed from the waist. Robert mimicked him, which caused amusement to light the nobleman's eyes before they turned serious. "He should be my son."

Ironically he was the second man who had spoken those words, first Roderick Moran and now Lord Foxcomb, Tamara mused silently.

"Where is the boy's father?"

"He is running the Union blockade in the War Between the States."

Lord Foxcomb scowled. "A dangerous business."

Arona called for Robert. At first the child balked, but encouraged by his mother, he ran to the servant, and Tamara and Lord Foxcomb sat down by the fountains.

Before he spoke, his lordship captured Tamara's eyes with his and held them. "Lady Pamela died several months ago."

"I am sorry," Tamara responded softly, pressing her hands tightly together in her lap.

His eyes were riveted to hers. "You know why I am here. I want to take you back with me to Foxcomb Manor. I want you to be my wife."

Tamara stared at him, her pearly teeth biting down hard on her dry lower lip. She surprised herself by not rejecting him immediately. She remembered his kindness, his concern for her welfare, and felt gratitude and . . . tenderness—but not love.

Lord Foxcomb broke into her thoughts. "It appears your husband has deserted you. Will you consider my proposal?"

Tamara did not reply. Encouraged by her silence, he smiled. "At least you have not turned me down completely."

"Please. I . . . I need time to think."

He reached out and took her hand. "Of course. Then let us talk about something else which concerns you. With your husband away, I am worried about your safety. You are quite isolated here. Upon arrival in Kingston, I heard reports of trouble among the Negro working class."

"Yes. There is a great deal of unemployment. They have

suffered many hardships since emancipation. For those who do work, their treatment by the planters has not improved a great deal. I fear the Negroes in the United States are heading for the same kind of suffering, now that they have been emancipated."

A worried look crossed Lord Foxcomb's face. "I am concerned about what is happening *here*. I fear for you. I smell rebellion in the air, Tamara."

Tamara was unperturbed. "Oh, I do not think so."

"I do not wish to alarm you, my dear, but the reports make me feel very uneasy. I have been told the planters have resorted to importing workers from India. Is that true?"

"Yes, that is true, and they are taking jobs away from the Negroes. I have hired only Negroes."

The time of Lord Foxcomb's visit flew swiftly. After dinner on the patio, Tamara showed him the coffee mountain and the newly planted citrus groves. The next day they went riding along a trail through the mountain, and later in the day went sailing. He was very attentive in a gentlemanly fashion, taking her arm or holding her hand to assist her at every opportunity.

On the night before his departure, when she went to her room to change for dinner, she sat on the bed, hers and Mark's, where they had shared many intimate moments. Her hand rubbed across the satin spread thoughtfully as she glanced about the room, her eyes resting on mementos of Mark, one of his pipes on the chiffonier, his clothing hanging in his armoire just as they were when he left.

Tamara could hear Sir Richard pacing in his room. Tension had been building between them, each knowing that the time was approaching when she would have to make her decision. Unable to sleep, she had given the prospect of going with him a great deal of thought. Foxcomb Manor was the most magnificent estate she had ever seen. The question was, could she be happy there? She was sure Sir Richard would be good to her, do everything in his power to make her happy. He loved her. Why would he come thousands of miles if he did not? It was true she did not love him in a deep, passionate way, but what had her deep, passionate love for Mark brought her? A few months of bliss followed by years of loneliness. Sir Richard would take her to London, Paris, Rome, wherever she wished to go.

It would mean divorce, something almost unheard-of. She

was stunned that she would even consider it. She had cause. Desertion. Hadn't she waited faithfully long enough? It would serve Mark right to come home and find her gone.

70

In the pitch-dark New Orleans compound Mark knocked the sentry unconscious. Hughy grabbed his rifle. The two prisoners jumped the fence and stalked away from captivity.

Mark had been in New Orleans several times before the war. He had an idea of the general direction to follow. Sticking to side streets to avoid Union soldiers, by dawn they were well out of town, heading into open country through the state of Louisiana. They encountered no sign of the enemy. At the hottest part of the day they sought shelter beneath a large tree, rested, and ate biscuits they had saved from the meal the previous night. They rested until it was dark, and then began their journey again, establishing a pattern they would follow day after day.

At nightfall they cased a farm for food. Finding a beat-up iron pot, they filled it with eggs they stole from the hen house. When well away from the farm, they lit a fire and cooked the eggs. Hughy had pulled several large carrots from the vegetable patch, which they crunched as they made their way northeast, fording streams, walking across darkened fields.

In the morning they stopped at a plantation house and asked for food. The woman, obviously alone, was at first reluctant, appearing at the door with a rifle in her hand. Hughy did the talking, and when she heard his Southern accent and the story of their escape, she invited them in and fed them.

The Union had not penetrated the area, and as they plodded across the quiet countryside, they relaxed their guard. Toward noon they came to a stream. They swam, bathed, and refreshed themselves. They washed their clothes and hung them in the sun to dry, then stretched out in the shade to sleep.

By late afternoon they took up their march again. At dusk they spotted the small, weather-worn home of a sharecropper. A hound ran toward them barking a warning not to come any closer. Hughy talked to the dog, scratched his neck to win him over. When Hughy stopped scratching, the dog nudged his arm with his nose. Yapping, it tagged alongside.

A man sat on a wobbly plank rocker on the front porch. He stopped rocking. Blindness had sharpened his other senses, and even before the dog barked he could hear the footsteps of the strangers. He was barefoot and shabbily dressed in overalls and the remnants of a Confederate Army shirt. A red-striped cat purred on his lap until it saw the dog, then leaped to the porch and climbed the old apple tree nearby.

"Who's there?" he shouted with alarm in his voice, although the two men were close to the porch. From the peculiar stare, Mark knew he was blind.

"Ella!" the man called.

Hughy spoke, introducing himself and Mark. "Don't be scared. We ain't Yankees."

The man's wife, Ella, dashed through the door, wearing a faded cotton print dress. She was thin and haggard-looking. Nervously wiping her hands down the sides of her dress, she stopped when she saw Hughy and Mark. "What do you want?"

"We're just passing through, ma'am. Escaped the Yankees. Was wondering whether you could spare a bite of food," Hughy explained.

Jasper and Ella relaxed visibly.

"Sit down on the stoop and I'll bring you what I have," Ella said, soon returning with two bowls of cabbage soup and biscuits. " 'Tain't much, but it's all we got," she apologized.

"This is fine," Mark assured her.

As the hungry men devoured the soup, Ella put Jasper's corncob pipe in her mouth, held a match to it, and puffed until she was sure it was lit. She handed it to her husband.

"Any news from Charleston, ma'am?" Mark asked between spoonfuls of the tasty soup.

"Fort Sumter was bombarded last year this time, through August and September. There was a lull, then the second attack came in October through to December. Lasted forty-one days."

"For godsakes!" gushed from Hughy's mouth. "How'n hell could they hold out?" he asked in amazement.

Mark stopped eating. "That was last year," he said impatiently. "What has happened since?"

The woman looked annoyed at his interruption. "That's

what I'm getting at. This summer the fort was under siege during May, June, and nearly all of July."

"Jesus!" escaped from Hughy.

"In between the three principal bombardments there was occasional firin' and smaller bombardments. The fort is only a mass of ruins," she continued.

"Any news of Charleston itself?" Mark asked pensively, scratching his bearded chin.

"Last we heard, Charleston was still holdin' out," Jasper answered, puffing on his pipe.

Ella stiffened her back proudly. "They'll never surrender."

"Do you know whether General Beauregard is still in Charleston?" Mark asked.

"Last we heard, he had been sent to Virginny," said Ella.

The floorboards creaked as Jasper resumed his rocking. "Suppose ya heard about the battle up north last summer, at Gettysburg, Pennsylvania. That's where ah lost my eyesight." Contempt crossed his square-jawed face. "Ah was with one of Longstreet's brigades." He paused, remembering the scene well. "After three days of fightin' the two armies suffered fifty thousand casualties. Our wounded and dyin' lay uncared for." Jasper rocked faster. "An Lee—mah heart bled for General Lee that day. 'All this has been my fault,' the General moaned, retreating back into Virginny."

Ella pulled a handkerchief from her apron pocket. "That same day Vicksburg surrendered to the Union's General Grant."

Mark looked at her as she fretted, her eyes welling with grief and tears.

"Our two sons were killed at Vicksburg," Jasper said softly. "We's all that's left of our family."

Mark and Hughy listened intently, enveloped in pity.

The war news was disheartening. Mark began to question the advisability of heading for Charleston. By the time he reached it, it might be in Yankee hands—but where else could he go?

As the two men made their way toward Georgia, the peaceful countryside belied the turmoil raging through the South. They rested in a stable and "borrowed" two horses tethered to a post outside a tavern in a small town they came to. In the passing days, they continued the same routine. Morning and evening they were on the move, and rested the hottest part of each day. They slept beneath trees or in barns, either stealing or asking for food.

After fourteen days they reached the railroad and followed

the tracks, riding their stolen horses for hours with no sign of a train. Toward evening their excitement grew as they heard a train approaching. Hiding in bushes, they waited until they were certain it was in control of the Confederates. They saw the gray uniforms. Confederate troops were being transported into Georgia in cattle cars. Mark and Hughy leaped up, grabbing outstretched hands that caught them and pulled them into the moving car.

They identified themselves. The soldiers resumed their conversation. News of the war was not good. They talked about Chattanooga, Tennessee, a strategic railroad center that had fallen into enemy hands. At Spotsylvania twelve thousand men had fallen in twelve days of bitter fighting. Grant was trying to take Richmond, the Confederate capital.

The railroad car swayed its passengers rhythmically, its wheels churning on shiny rails. Mark sat with his back against the side of the car, listening to the steady rumble beneath him. He did not say it aloud, but to himself he wondered how much longer the South could fight. The defeats the soldiers spoke of had happened the year before, in 1863. The year had definitely been the turning point in the war.

"Hey, you guys! Don't be so glum," said one of the soldiers above the voices of the others. "What about General Lee's big victory at Chancellorsville?"

"Yeah," said another morosely, "but what a price to pay. We lost Stonewall Jackson."

"Don't worry, fellas. Lee's going to come up with a big victory," said another confidently.

One of the rebels put his harmonica to his mouth and began to play. The soldiers joined in, singing sentimental ballads about their women at home. "Aura Lea." "Lorena." Mark, like most of the men in the boxcar, thought about and longed for the woman he loved. Her haunting vision was with him night and day. The train was taking him a long way around to reach her, but at each grinding turn of the wheels he felt he was one step closer.

The train slowed at Macon but did not stop. Mark and Hugh prepared to jump. They bid farewell to their new-found friends and wished them luck.

Clasping the hand of a corporal, Mark shook it firmly. The corporal looked at him directly. "Atlanta's under siege since July 22. We're goin' to help Hardee and Hood beat Sherman. Why don't you join us? We need all the help we can get."

The idea caught on among the soldiers surrounding Hughy and Mark. "Yeah, yeah," they agreed. As Mark and Hughy hesitated, rifles were shoved into their hands. They were being patted on the back. Caught like a branch in a raging flood stream, Mark was helplessly carried along. He found it impossible to jump off the train. He and Hughy remained with the troops on the Macon & Western Railroad headed for Atlanta.

The soldiers began to sing again, the more lively "The Yellow Rose of Texas." Their favorites, which they sang over and over, were "All Quiet Along the Potomac" and "Dixie."

Mark had heard the songs so often he knew the words. He joined in the singing, then stopped and glanced around. What the hell am I doing here? he asked himself. I am in the midst of an unbelievably horrible war, brother killing brother, American fighting American. It is not even my country.

At first Mark had gotten involved for all the selfish reasons. To gain a fortune was uppermost in his mind. Deplorably he had used a war to satisfy his greed for wealth. That and his driving pride and determination to prove to himself and his wife he was an independent man had brought him to the South.

Mark had no obligation to the Confederacy, and yet he was drawn to it. He stretched his legs out in front of him on the straw-covered floor and crossed his arms on his chest. Now he understood how Pulaski, Von Steuben, Lafayette, and De Kalb had felt—all foreigners who had helped Americans fight for independence in 1776. Pulaski had been killed right there in Georgia, in the siege of Savannah, and De Kalb in the battle of Camden, South Carolina. They had given their lives for a cause, but he had no cause. He could get himself killed, and for what? A lost cause. He certainly did not believe in slavery. Damnation, why, then, was he with the Confederate troops heading into battle? He searched into his soul for the answer. It was because he liked the people, admired their spirit, was sympathetic toward them. To have left the troops in Macon would have been like turning his back on a starving child with bloated belly and tormented eyes. He felt a need to contribute, to do whatever he could in their noble, dying hour.

That need could get him killed. He was not afraid of dying. He had come close to it many times. But . . . he did not want to die. He wanted to live to be with Tamara. Tamara. What of Tamara and his son if he should be killed? In his marriage vows before God he had promised to protect her. He had made a vow to himself to do everything in his power to make her happy. And damnation, look what he had done!

A muscle twitched in his cheek. Tamara. He hungered for the tender touch of her lips.

The wheels of the train churned round and round. Mark noticed a rebel looking at him suspiciously.

"You ain't a spy, are you?"

Mark laughed. The soldier, no more than a lad, persisted.

"You ain't related to that bastard Yankee General John Schofield who's aidin' Sherman in trying to take Atlanta?"

"No. Never heard of him," Mark said firmly, trying to assure the young soldier. So now he would be fighting a Schofield.

The train chugged slowly through rich countryside, fields of vegetables, watermelons, grove after grove of peach trees heavy with fruit, pastures dotted with sheep and cattle. No army would starve here. It could live off the land.

Approaching Atlanta from the south, the train stopped when it came upon General Hood's bedraggled, retreating army. The troop train was too late. Atlanta had fallen. Eager to hear firsthand accounts, the men on the train mingled with the battle-weary troops. The road beside the train was congested with wagon upon wagon, each piled with a few precious belongings of the occupants, refugees, young children, old men and women, sick, leaving Atlanta by any means they could find.

"What the hell is going on?" Mark asked one of Hood's lieutenants.

"That son of a bitch Sherman has taken Atlanta and has plunked himself down in its midst. He wants to use it to rest his army. Ordered all Atlanta citizens to evacuate their homes. God! They don't know where to go."

Mark and Hughy looked at each other. Mark felt sick inside. When he had seen the misery of the Crimean War, he swore never to know the evils of war again. And here he was. Hughy pulled on his arm. "Come on. We're goin' home to Macon."

The Huguenins lived in a clapboard house at the edge of Macon, next to the blacksmith shop. The family consisted of Hughy, his parents, and two sisters, ages eleven and fourteen. They greeted Hughy with heartfelt tears and joyful smiles. They welcomed Mark and listened attentively as the tale of the two men unfolded.

Patrick Huguenin, Hughy's father, was the town's blacksmith, an occupation Hughy planned to follow when the war was over. Patrick was a big, muscular man. He had volunteered when the war started and was sent to Manassas, where he received a serious leg injury and was forced to go home. Ordinarily a jovial man, he brooded about his helplessness. He could no longer serve the Confederacy, and his business was just about nil, most of the horses having been taken off to war along with the men.

Hughy's mother was a tiny woman with fiery red hair inherited from her Irish ancestors. Kate looked at her son warily. "You're home for good now, aren't you?"

"Mom, you don't think I can sit here while the war's still goin' on, do you?" he asked impatiently. "I'll stay a couple of days, then report to the nearest Confederate unit."

The Huguenins insisted Mark stay the night and get a good night's sleep. In the morning they fed him, lent him what money they could spare, along with a horse. Hughy and Mark shook hands, then Mark was on his way to Charleston, not knowing what he would find there.

71

A month had gone by since Tamara made her decision. When she had joined Lord Foxcomb for dinner in the dining room, she recognized the hungry look in his eyes. Afterward in the moonlit garden her muscles tightened as he stood very close to her, watching her silently, pleadingly, then reaching out and touching her shoulder, bared by her fashionable gown. She held her breath, all too aware of what he was about to ask her.

The feel of her soft flesh had inflamed him. He was unable to resist pulling her into his arms and bringing his lips down on hers. At first Tamara struggled, tried to pull away, turning her body this way and that, feeling his hard arousal pressing against her. Her rejection made him feel as if he was being robbed of what was rightfully his. His grip tightened until she thought she could not breathe. Unthinkingly her arms slipped up around his neck and her mouth opened to the pressure of his. At her response he turned gentle, his lips softening on hers. His hand slipped up her back until his fingers found the bare flesh of her shoulders. Before she knew what was happening, he maneuvered her to a secluded part of the garden beneath the low branches of a shade tree. His hand found its way beneath the soft folds of her low neckline and caressed one breast, then the other. Only then did she realize his full intentions. Old fears struck. She succeeded in pulling herself from his arms.

"I . . . am . . . sorry," she stammered lamely.

"Come with me. Please. I love you."

Shaken by her body's responses and his words, Tamara dropped her head, unable to speak. Sir Richard took a step closer. "Can I not persuade you?" He waited an eternity for her answer.

Tamara shook her head, and when she looked up, her eyes were filled with tears. "I will wait for him forever if need be."

Lord Foxcomb stiffened. Silently he studied the expression on her face. "Just as I have waited for you. . . . But I cannot wait forever . . . I need an heir. Tamara, I want you to be my wife, mistress of Foxcomb Manor . . . mother of my son, my heir."

"I am sorry. I cannot . . ." Tamara found it difficult to continue.

He persisted in holding her eyes. "There is a lovely lady in London who would . . . accept my proposal. If there is no hope . . . You must understand. I am desperate for a son."

Tamara nodded.

He waited another moment before speaking. "I will leave early in the morning."

"I will see you then. And . . . I want you to know that I wish you much happiness and . . . many sons."

Upon Lord Foxcomb's departure early the following morning, Tamara had fled to the sanctuary of the shore. A solitary figure on the beach, she walked briskly, determined to rid herself of the frustrations gripping her. When she became exhausted and out of breath, she sat down beneath a palm tree and leaned back against its arched trunk. The rhythmic splashing of waves was part of the tranquillity of the shore, and she relaxed. She drew in a deep breath, gazing out across the turquoise sea with heart-filled despair.

"Oh, my beloved. Come home to me. I need you. Your son needs you."

Tamara closed her eyes and reminisced about their voyage to Charleston and how she had fallen in love, or more accurately, how she had become aware of her love, for she had loved him all her life. She chuckled aloud when she thought about the night she had gone to Mark's bedroom at the Walkers'. How innocent she was. What a gentleman he had been. She relived the first sweet time he had made love to her. Her recollections brought her to an afternoon they had spent together on the beach. She could almost see him, almost hear his voice and laughter. They had run along the shore seeking the seclusion of the cove. She remembered his deep, throaty voice, the way he had looked at her, how it had made her heart turn over. She recalled how he had held her so lovingly in his arms. She had trembled at the touch of his caressing hands as they slipped beneath her petticoats, touching her bare thighs as he removed her confining lace-trimmed silk underdrawers. There was so much love between them, doing what they both wanted with sweet abandonment. Afterward they swam and made love again.

The memories spawned longings—but also hope, hope that Mark still loved her and was coming home. Stirring from her revery, Tamara opened her eyes, and her mind returned to the present. She had stayed on the beach longer than she planned. Robert would be awake, and she wanted to go to him.

Several days later a crate arrived with two German-shepherd puppies.

"Aren't they adorable!" Tamara exclaimed, clasping her hands. The accompanying note said, "Treat them with kindness and they will love you and protect you with their lives—as I would have done." It was signed "Richard."

"What shall we name them?" she asked Arona and Dodie. "I know. Sir and Herr."

"Hee, hee," was Dodie's response. "One's a she."

Tamara laughed. "All right. We will call then Hansel and Gretel."

The dogs were a godsend. They adored Robert, becoming very protective. As they grew, they became good watchdogs. Reports of raids and looting spread across the island. Several wives and daughters of planters had been brutally raped. Hanzel and Gretel gave warning of any strangers approaching.

Whenever she rode or walked on the beach, Tamara carried her pistol with her. She asked the overseer, Avery Southworth, to move into the house, and supplied him with a gun.

As economic conditions and unemployment went from bad to worse, the threat of violence against whites increased. The young coffee trees at Montjoy had not begun to bear fruit, but other coffee plantations were suffering. Sacks of coffee beans were piled in warehouses, awaiting shipment.

With the reports and the threat of violence, fear of being ravished returned to Tamara. Nightmares and phantoms became regular visitors in the night to plague her nerves. She kept a lamp burning and read late, until she could hardly keep her eyes open. In the morning when it was time to get up, she could have slept.

All across Jamaica mass meetings were held to urge the British government and the colonial assembly to take action. The government failed to respond to the problems.

Dodie came back from Kingston stammering the news that an uprising had broken out at Morant Bay. Sugar plantations were plundered and buildings burned.

"Has the government done nothing to stop it?" Tamara asked anxiously, wondering whether she should take Robert and leave.

"Troops was sent. Marital law declared."

"Anybody killed?" asked Arona.

"In Kingston they say ovah fifty peoples killed or wounded at Morant Bay."

Nobody at Montjoy slept that night except Robert, who was innocent of what was going on. Tamara waited for the dogs to bark, but everything was quiet. Twice during the early hours of the morning, fearing someone might have killed them, she checked to be sure they were all right.

Early in the morning she sent Mr. Southworth to Kingston to learn the latest developments. Tamara breathed easier when he returned and reported that the uprising had been confined, that 439 rioters were to be executed and 600 flogged.

Feeling safer, Tamara resumed her rides. One afternoon she returned to the house to find Arona quite excited, waving an envelope. Her heart leaped. It was a letter from Mark. She ripped it open and hastily read the first paragraph. Arona waited anxiously, shifting from one foot to the other.

"He is alive and well, Arona!"

Tamara read the next paragraph. "But he is a prisoner in a Union camp in New Orleans."

"What dis *Union* mean? What he do they arrest 'im?"

"There is a war, Arona. The one side, the Northern part of the United States, is called the Union," she answered, impatient to read the rest of the letter. It was very personal and affecting. Tears clouded her vision. She dug into her pocket for a handkerchief and dabbed them from her eyes so she could see to read. When she came to the end, she looked at Arona. "He will come home as soon as he is free to do so."

The two women embraced, half-laughing, half-crying.

72

The warm September sun pressed down on Charleston. Heat wavered upward from the dusty streets. Mark's weary horse, it's coat shiny with perspiration, trod slowly down Meeting Street, its hooves trampling the grass that grew in the street. Flowerbeds looked neglected, overgrown with weeds and untrimmed shrubbery. Leaves were coated with dust.

Mark passed leveled buildings, one after another, remaining evidence of a destructive fire that had swept through the city in 1861. The structures had not been rebuilt. The men were off to war. He paused to stare at Saint Michael's Church. It had been painted black so as not to be a glaring target for the enemy. There were few people on the streets, mostly women and children. Charleston had become a city of war wives, widows, and orphans.

Mark reined in his horse in front of the Walker residence on Legare Street. The wrought-iron gates, discolored by dust and bird droppings, were closed. He dismounted and unlatched them, relieved they were not locked. He walked through, leading his mount up the leaf-strewn driveway. He tethered the horse and climbed the marble steps, banging the tarnished brass knocker on the front door.

The place looked deserted. The windows were shuttered. No one was in sight. Nothing moved. There were no sounds. He tried the doorknob. As he expected, it was locked.

Realizing the Walkers had probably gone to Jessamine, their plantation west of Charleston, he sat on the top step in the shade of the marble columns, rested his arms across his thighs, and pondered his next move. Where could he go? He could force an entry and remain, sure the Walkers would not mind. He could make his way to their plantation. He had never been there, but there must be someone who could direct him. One thing was certain. He could not leave Charleston by sailing out of the harbor.

Mark looked down at himself. His boots were scuffed and

covered with dirt, the soles worn through. His shirt was threadbare. A bare knee protruded from his soiled and badly worn trousers. His hair and whiskers were untrimmed. He was a sore sight.

Mark turned at a noise behind him. The front door opened and an elderly Negro limped across the piazza, aiming a pistol at him.

"Git goin'." The Negro waved the pistol.

"Moses?"

The Negro faltered, looking Mark up and down.

Cautiously Mark stood up. "I am looking for the Walkers. I am a friend of theirs. Don't you remember me? Mr. Schofield."

The elderly servant squinted, hobbling to the edge of the piazza. He smiled with relief when he recognized Mark, glancing back toward the window.

Lila and Rosabelle came running.

"Sorry, Mark. We did not recognize you," said Mrs. Walker while Lila hugged and kissed him.

Looking down at himself, he cringed. "I wonder why!" He pushed Lila away. "Please, ladies. Do not come closer. You will die from the stench. I need a bath and change of clothing badly. I apologize for my appearance."

"Fiddlesticks," retorted Lila, giving him another peck on the cheek. "We are living here alone and scared to death. Now you have come to protect us," Lila gushed.

"Where is your father?"

"He is over at Sumter helping to defend our city," she answered bravely.

As Mark sank down into a tub of hot water, he closed his eyes drowsily and sighed from the sheer enjoyment of it. He felt himself drifting into much-needed sleep. In an effort to keep his weary eyes open, he shook his head vigorously and splashed his face.

He thought of the two women downstairs, their anxious eyes, the faded gowns. Somberness had replaced joviality.

When he joined them in the library, he was happy to see them smile, and he laughed. He was wearing one of Stephen's suits, which was too short in the sleeves and trousers and too wide at the waist. Lila brought a tray of peaches, apples, and sliced cheese. Mrs. Walker poured him a glass of brandy.

Mark told them of his capture and escape from prison. He looked at Rosabelle. "I was in the camp in New Orleans when Beauregard's wife died. Six thousand turned out to view the cortege."

"Pierre was heartbroken. It was impossible for him to go home for the funeral."

Lila peeled a peach, put it in a saucer, and handed it to Mark. "It was very difficult for the general, Mark. He is the most chivalrous man I know. Always the perfect gentleman, and he has sacrificed so much," she said.

"All of you have." Mark emptied his snifter of deep-red blackberry brandy.

"The only thing we mind sacrificing is . . . our only son," Rosabelle said, her voice shaking. "The South's greatest loss is her sons. What have we done to them?"

Absently Lila played with the folds of her dress. She had changed, Mark mused to himself. No one would ever be the same—he, Tamara, the South, the North. He looked at Lila, studied her thoughtfully. She was pale. A worried look persisted on her face. She was distracted.

"How have you been, Lila?"

Briefly the familiar smile appeared, showing dimples. The smile faded too quickly. "My fiancé is over there, too—at Sumter—and we do not know when another attack will come."

"Your fiancé!"

Lila nodded.

"Have I met him? Is he the young officer I met here the last time I dined with you?"

"Yes. Lieutenant Blair. Jonathan Blair."

"Well! I did not realize congratulations and best wishes were in order."

Lila smiled weakly and rose from her chair. "Yes, Mark. We are planning to be married as soon as the war is over. I did not want to wait, but he insisted." She stiffened her shoulders defiantly. "I do hope it will be over soon."

Lila—the coquettish, spoiled belle, the selfish, pampered girl—had disappeared. In her place Mark saw a mature woman possessed of an inner strength, a reservoir of courage that had failed to show itself until needed. The shallow girl had changed into a lovely, courageous woman, a woman who would be tested before long, he thought.

Mark's feelings were a jumble of contradictions. He admired the new Lila, but he was not sure he did not regret losing the old. He had always found her coquettish ways delightful. She had been a joy to be around. He had been tempted to capitulate to her charms. Looking back, he was glad now that she had the experiences of a carefree youth, that she had lived during Charleston's age of gilded elegance, which would be no more. Her life had not prepared her for the hardships she was suffering, and he marveled that she was able to cope so magnificently.

An ache resurged and tore into Mark as he thought of Tamara and his son, whom he had seen only once, and then only briefly. How old was he now? In a few months he would be two.

"Tamara and I have a son, you know."

Rosabelle brightened. "No. We did not know. How wonderful! And how tragic . . . that you are away from them."

Mark rose and poured himself more brandy. He drank, then smacked his lips contemplatively. "Fool that I am, I have made Tamara and my son victims of this war," he accused himself.

"Tamara has what it takes," Lila said. "She has strength, determination, and understanding. She will be all right, Mark."

Mark gulped his brandy and shook his head. A sound close to a sob escaped his throat. "You do not know. I worry about her. She suffered a traumatic experience as a child. She was . . . witness to the murder of her mother and father."

"Oh, my! She never told me," Lila said.

"She seemed to have recovered from it. We were so happy. The future was ours . . . then I left her when she needed me." Mark squirmed, then pushed himself up from his chair. "I sent her a letter from New Orleans, but I have no way of knowing whether she received it . . . and if she did, what her reaction was." He dared not think that Tamara might reject him. Frustrated he began to pace back and forth across the room. A fierce look entered his eyes. "I must go home! How the devil can I get out of here?"

"It is impossible, Mark. There are no ships leaving or entering the harbor. Union gunboats are right offshore. Stay with us until there is a way out," advised Rosabelle. "We do not have much left, but you are welcome to share what we have. Please. It will be a comfort to have a man in the house."

Mark looked drawn. He was exhausted. "Tamara is my life. If I lose her . . ." Claustrophobia struck him. He felt confined, shut in, with a desperate need to get out. "There must be some means by which I can get out of Charleston," he moaned heavily, resignedly, sitting down in his chair.

73

Mark's body ached for a soft bed. It had been a long time since he had enjoyed the luxury of a pillow and clean sheets. He slept late. By the time he appeared in the dining room, Lila and Rosabelle had eaten breakfast and were drinking a second cup of tea, a luxury they rewarded themselves to boost their morale.

Moses served him eggs and sausage. "Moses, you took care of my horse last night?"

"Yas, sah. Watered an' fed'm."

Mark looked at Rosabelle. "I don't know whether to walk or ride to the wharf. I have several errands to do."

"It is a lovely morning. If you walk, I will go with you," Lila said.

Mark glanced at her and smiled. "You are welcome to come with me—if you are not ashamed to see me dressed this way," he answered, looking down at her father's ill-fitting coat and pants. "I plan to stop at that tailor on King Street."

Lila did most of the talking. She looked beautiful even though her white dress was shabby and discolored. She hooked her hand over Mark's arm as they walked down Legare Street. When they reached the wharves, they stood silently, looking at the scene. Scattered piles of cotton bales and bags of rice were waiting to be shipped. Warehouses were deserted, some of them having been hit by shells. Stranded ships lulled in the harbor.

All was quiet at Fort Sumter. The Confederate flag waved proudly in the morning breeze sweeping in from the sea. They turned and left the Battery. Along King Street, high embankments of earthwork defenses hid the fronts of some of the houses facing the harbor. Residences along East Battery were damaged from the bombardments. The lowest part of the city was shelled the hardest. Cannons pointed out to the harbor, to be used to withstand a Union invasion from the sea.

Lila and Mark stopped at the Carolina Bank, where he withdrew a large amount from his account and was given Confederate currency. They went to T. M. Bristoll on King

Street for boots and shoes. The selection was poor, the stock low, and the prices exorbitant. Mark was fortunate to find a pair of leather shoes in his size, though not in the style he preferred. The shoemaker agreed to make him a pair of boots.

The tailor shop was next. Shelves once filled with bolts of the finest cloth made were practically empty, and what was available was very expensive. The shortage of material narrowed Mark's choice, but he ordered two suits and several shirts to be made.

When they came to Sell & Foster Millinery Shop, Mark stopped. "Let's go in."

"Why?"

"You will see."

"The young lady needs a new bonnet," he told the clerk. He was pleased to see Lila's response. A smile broke out on her face and a sparkle entered her eyes. She tried on one bonnet after another and posed for Mark.

"What do you think?" she asked, turning her head this way and that, coquettishly displaying a trace of the old Lila.

"I like the white straw," Mark commented.

"But it is *three hundred dollars!*" she whispered.

"Do you like it?" Their eyes met.

"Yes, of course, but ..."

"Miss, wrap this one."

"Oh, Mark. Thank you, thank you. I love it. I sincerely do!"

"Nothing like a new bonnet to lift a woman's spirits."

Lila batted her lashes. "Mark, you know so much about women."

Mark took Lila to lunch at the new Fehrenback's on Meeting Street, the old having been in the path of the 1861 fire. After they had eaten, Mark led Lila to a jeweler's, saying, "Help me select a piece of jewelry for Tamara." They looked at rings, necklaces, pins, trying to decide what Tamara would like. Mark finally chose a gold bracelet and had it engraved.

He purchased a box of expensive cigars at the tobacco shop. They stopped at the hardware store. Mark could not believe the prices. Items considered necessities before the war had become expensive luxuries. How could people afford them? No wonder the shops were empty.

When they passed the bakery, Mark pulled on Lila's arm. "Come on. That homemade bread smells too good to resist.

"Three dollars! For a loaf of bread!" he protested to the baker.

"Yes, sah. Heah's a smallah loaf foah two dollars," he said, holding up the tiny loaf.

"Never mind. I'll take the larger one."

Their purchases included two large cans of tea and two pounds of coffee, for which he paid ten dollars a pound.

"We will have a feast," Lila exclaimed excitedly, clutching his arm as they headed homeward.

A week later Stephen Walker came home from Fort Sumter. Mark observed him closely as he hugged and kissed his wife and daughter. He had aged. Wearing the Confederate uniform of a lieutenant colonel, he was haggard-looking, his back bent, his vitality spent. The ravages of war showed on his face. His flesh hung loose on cheeks and chin that had once been plump, but he had not lost his gentlemanly bearing. He shook Mark's hand firmly. "Glad you are here, Mark. I was worried about my women living alone."

"Daddy, have you seen Jonathan?" Lila asked.

"Yes. He is fine and sends his love."

As Stephen sat in his wing-back chair in the drawing room, Rosabelle removed his boots, propped his legs up on a stool, then handed him a glass of bourbon.

Mark, being around the two women for a week, was anxious to talk to a man. "How is it over there, sir? I viewed the fort from the wharf today. It looks like a heap of rubble."

Stephen looked at Mark, hesitant in his reply. "It has been practically leveled, but we're rebuilding it. Casements were wrecked, but the Union failed to destroy the three-gun battery on the channel front."

Mark shook his head. "How can it hold out, sir?"

Stephen looked affronted by the question. "Sumter has been pounded to rubble, but there is absolutely no thought of surrender."

"The Union knows that."

"You are damned right they know it." Stephen unbuttoned his shirt at the collar. "Did you hear about their ironclad, the *Keokuk?*"

"No, sir, I didn't."

"We sank it about thirteen hundred yards off the southern tip of Morris Island. We could see its turrets at low tide. Under instructions from Beauregard, workmen were taken to the wreck at night to try to retrieve its two large cannons, which we certainly could use."

"Impossible," commented Mark.

"Frankly, I didn't think they could do it either." Stephen

went on with the account. "The men worked in the dark, soaked to the skin by the constantly lashing rough waters." He chuckled hollowly. "The Union vessels patrolling nearby had no idea what was going on."

Mark listened intently, handing Stephen a cigar, then lighting one for himself.

"The mechanics worked two weeks, using sledges, crowbars, chisels," Stephen continued.

Mark leaned forward in his chair. "Did they succeed?" he asked, anxious to hear the outcome.

"By God, how they managed it I will never be able to tell you, Mark, but they did. Each gun weighed sixteen thousand pounds. They brought them to Charleston. One is mounted on the wall at Fort Sumter, the other on Battery Bee on Sullivan's Island."

Rosabelle walked to the back of her husband's chair, reached over to rub his neck. "How long will you be home?" she asked, massaging his constricted shoulder muscles.

"My dearest, they sent me home to get a good rest. I will go back in a few days."

"Don't you think you should go to bed?" she asked.

"Yes, in a little while."

"When can Jonathan come home?" Lila asked impatiently.

"I do not know, my dear." Seeing her pout, he tried to brighten her spirits. "You must be patient. Times will be better. You will see."

Stephen waited until the two women retired before he spoke frankly to Mark.

"Mark, it doesn't look good," he announced, peering over the rim of his bourbon glass. "We are doomed. Sherman is in Atlanta with an army of sixty-two thousand ready to move." He glanced at Mark skeptically. "We were counting on help from your country, but it never came. We had plans to build a navy in Bristol. The bottom fell out of everything."

Mark stared into his drink thoughtfully. "What about your cotton, sir?" he asked softly.

"Haven't raised any for the last two years." Stephen cleared his throat. "When Lincoln emancipated the slaves, most of ours at Jessamine left. Those who stayed helped me raise vegetables, corn, and grain for our army. The Confederate government paid me in Confederate currency." He gave a bitter laugh. "It is of doubtful value."

Mark shook his head dejectedly. "I know. I was shocked at how much of it I used in paying for just a few purchases."

Worry entered Stephen's eyes. He drew in his breath, then

let it out slowly. "I am practically broke, Mark. When the war started, I invested heavily in Confederate bonds—bonds which will be worthless if we lose the war . . . and we are losing it."

Mark stood up, walked to Lila's harp, and plucked on a string thoughtfully. He was shocked to see his friend's confidence melt away in an unguarded moment. He turned to face him. "Do not give up hope, sir. If you lose everything, you still have your loving wife and daughter."

"But how will I support them?"

"You have your land."

"I hope I can keep it. I have no money to pay the taxes."

"I will send it to you." Mark paused, clasped his hands behind him. "Look, Stephen, is there any way I can get out of here?"

"Your only chance, which is slim and which I would advise you not to take, would be to make your way north through enemy lines to Baltimore, Philadelphia, or New York."

Stephen Walker returned to Fort Sumter. For the next few weeks nothing happened. The city held its breath, defiant, still hopeful, expectant, waiting—waiting to see what General Sherman's next move would be. In the waiting, Lila and Mark were together a great deal. In the long evenings, they bided the time playing cards and games. Lila played her harp.

In November, news reached Charleston that Lincoln had been reelected to a second term as president of the United States. Reports swept through the city that on November 3 Sherman's army had left Atlanta a burning inferno and was making its way across Georgia in a destructive path sixty miles wide, burning bridges, buildings, and stores of cotton, looting, foraging, pillaging. Railroad ties were pried loose, the rails heated and bent to look like hairpins. "Sherman's hairpins" were hung on trees all the way to Savannah. The army moved leisurely, destructively, like a swarm of locusts, eating its way, laying waste to the land.

There was nothing to stop them. They lived off the richness of the land, relishing honey, fowl, beef, Southern-baked hams, ripping down split-rail fences for firewood to roast the fowl and pork. By the time the destructive army reached Savannah, it had taken ten thousand horses and mules.

"The reports must be exaggerated," said Mark firmly.

"No, they are not exaggerated. It is all here in the Charleston newspaper," said Rosabelle.

Tension was building in Charleston. The days could not be rushed. The city was gripped with fear. In the Walker household it was like waiting for a cannonball to come flying through the window at any moment. An argument ensued between mother and daughter as to whether they should remain in Charleston or go to Jessamine. Rosabelle decided they should remain in their home in Charleston for the time being.

The Walkers and Mark were determined to make the most of Christmas. Rosabelle and Lila made garlands of pine branches and rhododendron leaves. Mark bought gifts in an attempt to cheer them, careful not to select anything too personal for Lila. He had discovered that Lila had not changed completely from her old ways. He noticed her yearning eyes upon him, aware she sought him out more and more. They were often alone. He suspected she groomed and kept herself looking as inviting as she could for his benefit. As she played the soothing music of the harp, her eyes drifted seductively to his. Her lips became a temptation, evoking his male needs. If only Pansy were still available, he thought, but she was no longer there. All the former household slaves had left, except the faithful elderly Moses and Verbena.

The waiting was getting on everyone's nerves. Mark's disposition turned sour.

Stephen came home Christmas Eve with the horrifying news that "Attila of the West," General Sherman, was in control of Savannah. Its fall had a demoralizing effect throughout the city and in the mansion on Legare Street. What would be Sherman's next move? Would he move up the coast to Charleston? Would Charleston suffer the same fate as Atlanta? What more could they do to save their magnificent city from the ravages of war?

A special effort was made to be convivial, but the evening meal was somber, until Lila pursed her lips and jumped up.

"Fiddlesticks! It is Christmas! Let's forget the nasty war for a day. Let's drink a toast." Lila held up her wineglass.

"To what?" Rosabelle asked forlornly.

"To tomorrow. And Christmas."

"You are right," her father said. "Each of us must consider his blessings."

They waited while Moses replenished their wineglasses, then all stood up and clicked their glasses, briefly pretending all was well.

Lila grasped Mark's hand and pulled him away from the

361

table. "Let's go to the widow's walk." Mark looked back at the Walkers but did not protest as Lila tugged at his hand.

From the rooftop Charleston looked deceptively safe and at peace. The city was dark, the only lights coming from the Union ships, which used calcium lights to illuminate the waters between Morris Island and Fort Sumter to keep an eye on Confederate ships that might approach. Fort Sumter looked like the wounded hulk of a monster floating in the harbor.

Mark recalled the night he had kissed Tamara in the very spot where he stood now. He had been stunned by its impact. Unknowingly he smiled when the picture of her fan flying through the air appeared before him. He never did buy her another. He made a mental note to do so. Lila broke his train of thought as she stepped close to him. The gentle breeze played with the dark corkscrew curls framing her face. In the dim shadows his experienced eyes saw her gown's snugness revealing her enticing feminine figure, its neckline exposing her creamy smooth shoulders, her distended nipples straining against the thin fabric.

Lila turned and stepped into Mark's arms, resting her head at the base of his neck and folding her arms around him. "Hold me close, Mark," she begged softly.

74

Mark fumed. He interpreted Lila's behavior as a direct invitation. It irritated him when a woman threw herself at him. Pursuit was a man's game, totally unfeminine. True, he needed a woman. She could satisfy his physical need. He could not do that to her or to Jonathan, and he certainly had no wish to be Lila's little diversion to forget her miseries for a while. He reached back and untwined her arms from his body.

"Lila, the situation is not pleasant for any of us, least of all for your fiancé over there," he reprimanded sternly, pointing at Fort Sumter. "I thought you had grown up, changed. Was that show of courage and maturity just a facade?"

Lila covered her face with her hands and sobbed hysterically. Mark had not realized how frightened she was. He was afraid she was breaking down in front of his eyes. He removed her hands from her face and held them. She looked up at him, the tears streaming down her face.

"We are all going to be killed," she sobbed.

"And do you think throwing yourself into my arms will save you? They are not magical wands that can make the war disappear."

"But they could make me forget for a little while. The war has been going on for almost four years. I cannot take much more. I must escape it, if only for a short time."

"I credited you with more gumption than that. You cannot escape into a make-believe world. You must face reality and all its cruelty. You must have courage for your parents' sake."

"You are more logical than I." She glanced at him warily. "The Yankees are raping women clear across Georgia. They're coming here next."

all its cruelty. You must have courage for your parents' one isolated case."

"They are *not* exaggerated!" she insisted. Lila had never met face to face with a Union soldier. Her imagination conjured up a ruthless monster wearing a dark blue uniform. He was an invisible threat worse than facing a known enemy. She shivered visibly. "Mark, I am afraid of being violated. I do not want a Yankee . . . to be the first man with me."

"I will defend your honor, Lila. Should the time come . . . if worst comes to worst, I will tell them you are my wife."

Lila lifted her head indignantly. Anger replaced fear in her eyes. His words pricked her feminine vanity. If worst comes to worse!" she mimicked. "Well, of all the . . . Sir, you would be that noble?" she asked sarcastically.

"Lila, you know I did not mean it the way it sounded." He knew Tamara was frightened of being ravished and that it was because of what she had witnessed as a child. It struck Mark that women were more afraid of being raped than most men realized. He released her hands and turned his back to look over the railing. "Lila, by now you should know there is only one woman for me, no matter what the circumstances."

"I suppose I knew it, but that was something else I did not wish to face."

He turned to look at her. "What about Jonathan? Don't you love him?"

"I am so confused. I think I do. The war . . . We have not had much time for courting. War . . . destroys certainties."

In January Jonathan came to see Lila for a few days. His blond hair had thinned, and lines of fatigue etched his handsome square-jawed face. He refused to discuss the war, saying he wanted to forget it for a while. Rosabelle and Mark found excuses to get out of the house so that the engaged couple could be alone. It was obvious to Mark by the expression in Lila's eyes that she was no longer uncertain of her love for the young Confederate officer.

Without deliberately planning it, Mark settled into a pattern in the Walker household. Rosabelle did not want to take money from him, but he insisted she use it for food purchases, otherwise he could not remain with them. He brought home some of the luxury items she could no longer afford. Tea was most welcome. Each afternoon about four o'clock they gathered in the drawing room to drink a cup of the expensive beverage.

One afternoon in February while drinking their tea, Lila and Mark heard newspaper boys shouting headlines. Mark went to Legare Street and brought back a copy of the *Mercury*. On February 1, Sherman's army, seventy thousand strong, consisting mostly of veteran troops, was on the move again. The Confederate force available to defend Charleston was 13,700 infantry and artillery.

Another item that caught Mark's attention concerned a meeting held in Virginia, attended by President Lincoln. The purpose of the meeting was to discuss peace terms. Lincoln insisted on restoration of the Union and abolition of slavery. Southerners rejected the demands. The war went on.

There was opposition to the destruction of Charleston within the Union forces. In the United States Senate, moving speeches were made to try to prevent its annihilation.

Several days later, rumors, then confirmed reports, spread through the city. Sherman had turned his route away from Charleston and was headed inland to the interior of South Carolina, stopping on February 17 in Columbia, the state's capital. Two-thirds of the city was gutted by fire.

As Sherman's army burned its way through South Carolina, it destroyed railroad lines leading to Charleston. Charleston was isolated, cut off from the interior of the state. Its harbor was surrounded by Union gunboats.

Orders reached Charleston. Fort Sumter and the city were to be evacuated immediately. Roper Hospital on Queen Street was evacuated. The children at the Charleston Orphan House were taken to Orangeburg.

On the night of February 17, at the mansion on Legare Street, Rosabelle, Lila, and Mark watched silently from the widow's walk on the rooftop. When the sun went down, the Confederate flag over Fort Sumter was lowered and the last evening gun salute boomed across the waters of Charleston harbor. For almost four years it had withstood three major and eight minor bombardments.

Mark, Lila, and Rosabelle stared without comment as transports waited. At ten o'clock, under the cloak of darkness, the entire garrison was evacuated.

Stephen came home for good. Jonathan stopped briefly before returning to his retreating regiment. Lila clung to him. He kissed her passionately and then was gone. Stephen looked at his wife and daughter helplessly. There was nothing he could do to spare them the harrowing experience of being forced from their home and city. Charleston had defied 587 days of continuous military operations against it, the most violent land and naval attacks the Union could make, but now it had to be abandoned. Teenage cadets from the Citadel joined the tired Confederate troops from Fort Sumter and surrounding fortifications as they marched to the Northeastern Railroad depot for withdrawal.

While Stephen took charge of his household to prepare it for departure to Jessamine, he prayed silently that Sherman's men had not burned it to the ground.

The furniture was covered with old threadbare sheets. "We will take the good linens and bedding with us," Rosabelle said. "It is impossible to buy silk sheets anymore."

"Remember, we have only two carriages," Stephen reminded her. "There is not enough room to take all you want to take."

The men carried two large chests to the garden. Rosabelle and Lila had filled them with family heirlooms, flat silver, silver urns, bowls, goblets, and tea sets. Moses, wearing his faded red velvet livery worn smooth at the knees and elbows, using a pick began to unearth two large azalea bushes. He was careful to keep the roots covered with the black soil.

Never a day went by that Mark did not think of Tamara. He recalled a happier night in the garden as if it were yesterday—his wedding, his lovely bride. He had known the joys of her lips at this very spot.

"Here, let me," he said, grabbing a shovel from the old servant. Spadeful after spadeful of ground was removed while the family stood by silently, watching as if he was preparing for a funeral. He dug a deep hole into which the chests were buried. The azaleas were replanted on top, the soil carefully replaced so as not to look disturbed.

When the two carriages were filled to capacity, the Walkers and Mark assembled in the drawing room, feeling an unspoken need to be together on what might be their last hour in their home. Lila picked up an ax and walked to her harp. Rosabelle screamed. "What are you doing?" she shouted.

"No dirty Yankee fingers are going to touch my harp."

Mark grabbed the tool. "Hold on, Lila. I will be right back."

"It took him longer than he expected. He rode through the city scouring it for a wagon. None was available. He just about gave up hope of finding one, when he reached the outskirts of the city. For an exorbitant price he purchased a wagon and two mules and took them back to Legare Street. Moses and Mark carried the cherished musical instrument to the wagon. There was room for other items that Rosabelle wished to take along, including a large crate of empty jars that would be needed for preserving food.

Verbena walked to the wagon carrying the nursing rocker that had been used for three generations of Walkers. She sat atop the wagon on the small rocker, her broad hips spreading out over its seat, a white turban wrapped around her head, defiantly balancing the harp in an upright position.

After Moses assisted the ladies in getting into the carriages, Rosabelle in the first, Lila in the second, he approached Stephen Walker. "Aw's stayin' heah, sah."

Stephen was puzzled. Moses had been his faithful servant for as long as he could remember. His voice cracked with emotion. "You are not coming with us, Moses?"

"Naw sah. There ain't goin' be lootin' and burnin' dis house . . . not while aw's heah."

"Moses, I appreciate what you want to do, but one man cannot stop them. You come with us," he said quietly.

In the first carriage Stephen Walker flipped the reins and joined the stream of traffic. Mark and Lila were in the second carriage, and Moses and Verbena came up behind in the mule-drawn wagon.

Stephen looked back. Mark was not sure whether he was checking to be certain they were following or whether he took one final look at his home. The February night air was cold and damp. Rosabelle drew her shawl snugly around her and moved closer to her husband.

Mark's heart went out to them. He had begun to feel like one of the family. He looked up ahead at the line of carriages, wagons, and carts leaving Charleston, a common bond existing among the strong-willed people they were transporting, people who had lived the war years with dignity and honor. For them this was a terminal time, a farewell not only to their homes and their beloved city but also to a way of life and old traditions.

As they moved slowly in the line of carriage traffic, a terrible explosion was heard and felt. The carriages vibrated and horses whinnied, bobbing their heads nervously. Several reared, wildly pawing the air with their front hooves.

"My God, have the Yankees begun to destroy the city already?" Lila asked Mark. He handed her the reins and jumped down. "I'll find out." He unfettered his horse, which was tied to the back of the wagon, and rode off. When he returned, he reported that the Northeastern Railway Depot had exploded.

Friends of the Walkers', neighbors, and strangers gathered around Mark to listen to what he had to say.

"Was anyone hurt?" someone asked.

"Yes. Looks like a hundred were killed and wounded."

"Was it the Yankees?" another asked.

"No. Damaged powder left behind by Confederate troops discharged accidentally."

Quietly the people returned to their carriages. Women wept silently. The train of carriages and wagons began to move faster. At nine o'clock the next morning they were not present to see the United States flag raised over the heap of ruins that had been Fort Sumter. Federal ironclads entered Charleston harbor. Victorious Union forces entered the city of vacant houses.

75

Spring came again. Scorning the war, its miseries, suffering, and the separation of loved ones, it burst forth blossoms and pushed seedlings up through the warm earth. Overhead, snow geese were seen and heard on their miraculous northern migration.

Four weeks earlier, Charleston had been evacuated. After leaving the city, the Walkers' small entourage had ridden in silence through the bleak countryside. When Lila stiffened and grasped Mark's arm, he looked to see what had caused her reaction. To the left of the road were the remains of a plantation house burned to the ground. The entire estate had been leveled.

"Supposing . . . ? What if . . . what if Jessamine was in the path of the advancing Union Army? Where would we go?"

Not knowing what to say, Mark put his arm around her, compelled to comfort her. He regretted he could not promise that Jessamine had not met the same fate.

Jessamine, an eleven-hundred-acre estate of mostly flat farmland, was located between Rowesville and Orangeburg. The secluded plantation house could not be seen from the main thoroughfare. Tension mounted as the two carriages, followed by the wagon, turned right onto Jessamine Lane, a broad gravel avenue shaded by a row of thirty-five oaks on each side. The carriages' occupants ducked to avoid lacy tendrils of Spanish moss hanging low from the trees. Twigs were strewn across the lane. Mark jumped down from the carriage to remove dead branches. The tired horses and mules clapped across the wooden bridge spanning the broad stream that flowed through the estate.

The animals walked a little faster. Not knowing what to expect, the Walkers and Mark held their breath. When it came into view. Stephen pulled on the reins. Mark did the same. The carriages and wagon came to a halt.

Verbena sobbed aloud. Mark let out a lungful of air. Jessamine had not been in the path of the destructive Northern army. It was magnificent. The brick mansion's four white columns gleamed in the bright sunshine. A white wrought-iron railing with grape-and-grape-leaf design enclosed the second-story gallery. Mark was moved by the home's serenity and grace.

Most of the plantation houses they had passed were constructed of wood and badly in need of paint. Except for the window frames and doors, Jessamine's red brick had withstood neglect and the elements.

The Walkers bowed their heads and silently gave thanks to God for saving their home. Then briskly Stephen flipped the reins and they proceeded to the front entrance. Before the carriages and wagon were unloaded, Mark was given a quick tour. They stepped inside to a wide entrance with a winding staircase, spacious rooms leading off to the right and left. Each luxuriously furnished room possessed a fireplace with a white-marble mantel.

Now it was spring. The yellow flowers after which the plantation was named grew in profusion. The air was filled with the fragrance of lilac-colored wisteria.

There was a great deal of work to be done on the neglected plantation. Several Negroes who had remained after emancipation had fed the chickens and livestock, but there were not enough workers for the task ahead. Sheds and outbuildings needed paint and repairs, but that would have to wait until crops were planted.

Early each morning Mark went into the fields to help with the plowing. At first he had difficulty figuring out how to hitch the plow to the mule. Then the plow did not dig deeply enough and the rows through the field were crooked. The mules stopped easily enough when he pulled on the reins and called "Whoa!" but he had trouble getting them started.

Mark was surprised at how much satisfaction he received from working the earth. He helped to plant corn, oats, barley, and tobacco.

Seeing the planting going on, several former slaves drifted back to Jessamine and asked for work. Stephen was honest with them. He told them they could live in their cabins. He would supply them with food, but he had no money to pay them wages until the crops came in. Four remained, the rest moved on.

In their determination to survive, each member of the Walker family went to work. In a truck patch, lettuce was sowed, carrots, beans, onions, red beets, and sweet potatoes planted. Stephen supervised the butchering of a pig, smoking hams and bacon, stuffing the intestines with meat for sausage. Rosabelle set hens on their nests to assure a new supply of chickens and eggs. While she weeded her herb garden and prepared to preserve food, Lila, wearing a sunbonnet, went out to pick kettles of wild strawberries to make jelly. She imagined Yankees, who committed the most debasing crimes, lurking behind trees, waiting to descend on her, not knowing that the enemy was moving north into North Carolina. When she returned to the house with a kettle of berries on each arm, she looked at her rough, stained fingers disdainfully. "How will I ever be able to play the harp again?" Then she smiled as if it really wasn't important.

Solemn jubilation, a mixture of sadness and joy, broke out when news reached Jessamine that on April 9 the war was officially over. General Lee had surrendered his badly defeated army unconditionally to Grant in Virginia. The Walkers and Mark attended services in the crowded church in Rowesville. They had lost the war, but they were glad it was ended at last. They had much to be thankful for and had hopes for the future.

Jonathan came home several days later, wearing his tattered gray uniform with cuffs of yellow. Lila was so elated at first she failed to see the lines of suffering on his face and the empty sleeve dangling from his left shoulder. When she saw it, she shrieked. His good arm slipped around her and drew her close. "Beloved, it happened in Richmond. At first I did not wish to come back to you. I did not want to tie you down to a cripple, but the more I thought about it, the more I believed that attitude was wrong—and I could not give you up. I pray it will not make any difference. My right arm is twice as strong to hold you."

Sobbing and guilt-ridden, Lila buried her head on his chest, hiding the revulsion on her face, praying he did not feel her shudder. She had always cringed at the sight of cripples. Deformities of any kind repelled her. How could she look at him when he was undressed? The sight of his stump would nauseate her. How could she allow him to come to her bed . . . to be intimate? As the questions raced through her mind, her body answered them. She trembled, not from revulsion, but desire and love, and she knew the answers to her own questions. His loss of an arm made no difference at all. If anything, it strengthened her love and admiration for him. He lifted her head, forcing her to look into his beseeching eyes.

"I love you. Please do not let this make any difference," he pleaded. "Others suffered a fate much worse than the loss of an arm. We must go on with our lives as we had planned— marriage and children." He waited agonizingly for her reply.

"It will make no difference at all, my beloved. I am grateful you are alive, and thankful your injuries are not worse."

He sighed with relief, a smile breaking out on his face. His family had been wiped out in the war. The estate in Georgia was laid to ruin. When married, he and Lila would live at Jessamine, eventually taking over its operation.

Stephen regretted he could not afford to give his daughter a large wedding. Before the war, it would have been one of the largest, most-talked-about weddings of the year. Lila understood and made but one request. She wanted to be married in Saint Michael's Church in Charleston.

Slowly the people of Charleston came back to their homes. Grateful that their city had not been ravaged, they tried to ignore the Union soldiers who were everywhere. The Walkers were relieved to find their home on Legare Street intact.

The day before Lila and Jonathan were married, the family put aside its wedding plans and joined the crowd of people going to Fort Sumter in small steamers. It was Good Friday, April 1, 1865, a warm, sunny day, exactly four years after Major Robert Anderson had surrendered the fort to the Confederacy. The harbor was filled with vessels going back and forth, taking four thousand visitors to the ruined fort.

At the noon hour, Major General Robert Anderson, United States Army, thinner, his hair silvery gray, both joy and sadness showing on his face, walked solemnly between a welcoming guard, a double line of Union soldiers and sailors, several of them Negroes. He was fifty-nine years old, but looked older.

Mark stood next to Stephen. Lila and Jonathan held hands as a short religious service was held. Rosabelle dabbed her eyes and Stephen blew his nose; many people wept openly when Anderson spoke briefly, then pulled the halyards, raising the tattered United States flag he had lowered four years before, carrying with it to the top of the flagpole a garland of roses.

The crowd listened quietly to the one-hundred-gun salute, which was followed by a speech by the Reverend Mr. Henry Ward Beecher. The war was over. It was time for healing, but that night in Washington, D.C., President Lincoln was assassinated.

Lila wore her mother's wedding dress of layers of filmy white lace skirts and cap sleeves of lacy ruffles. It was a sacred ceremony, the couple repeating the vows emotionally. When they stepped from the church, they heard the newspaper boys shouting the tragic headlines: "President Lincoln assassinated!"

Mark had been anxious to leave, but the Walkers insisted he wait until after Lila's wedding. Privately he told Stephen not to worry. He would send him money if he needed it to pay the taxes on Jessamine and the house in Charleston. Stephen put up his hand in protest, but Mark was adamant.

"It will be a loan. I made the money on the war. Why shouldn't I help you get started again?"

"What do you plan to do when you get back to Jamaica?"

"I am going to buy another ship and get started again, too. However, I'll hire a captain . . . run the operation from Kingston."

76

Tamara bent over her son every few minutes. His cheeks were red, his brow moist with fever. The child whimpered and rolled onto his side restlessly. She had cradled him during the night until he fell asleep, then put him in his bed. Arona wanted to relieve her vigil, but Tamara would not hear of it.

Thinking of Robert as a precious gift from Mark, Tamara was overprotective. Whenever he sneezed or had a runny nose, she panicked.

"You make sissy out of 'im," Dodie accused, shaking his head. "Two woman fussin' ovah'm all de time no good."

"Dodie is right, Arona," Tamara had agreed, but this time it was different. Robert had been cranky for several days. He developed a fever. Tamara feared the worst, diphtheria, malaria, the plague, scarlet fever.

At the first signs of the sky showing light, Tamara sent Dodie for the doctor. His diagnosis—teething. "A child can appear deathly ill one day and perfectly normal the next. It's recuperative powers are miraculous."

Robert proved the physician to be correct. In no time at all he was romping with Hansel and Gretel.

Tamara rode over to Schofield Manor. It was empty. She was wondering whether Elaine would ever return, when she saw a "For Sale" sign posted. In fine print at the bottom of the notice was the name of the attorney to contact.

The next morning Dodie drove Tamara to Kingston to the office of the lawyer mentioned on the sign. She introduced herself before she began to ask questions.

"Who is selling the property?"

"Elaine and Roderick Moran, husband and wife, of London, England."

"Elaine Schofield married Roderick Moran?" she asked, surprise in her voice.

"Yes, ma'am."

"Would it be possible for me to buy the property without their knowing who the purchaser is?"

"I believe that could be arranged. Mrs. Schofield, I am not betraying my client's confidence when I tell you, it is a well-known fact that the Schofield Shipping Company is bankrupt. The Morans are in desperate need of funds."

Tamara did not allow the shock she felt inside to show. "I would like to buy Schofield Manor for my husband. He grew up there."

"Yes, I know."

They discussed the price. She gave him instructions to go ahead. If Mark did not want it, he could sell it when he returned. At least he could determine who their neighbors would be.

Tamara worried constantly about Mark. News had not reached Jamaica that the American Civil War was over. She believed he was still in the prison camp in New Orleans.

As she rode back to Montjoy, she thought of Charleston. It was spring, the most beautiful time of the year. Her mind drifted back four years to the day she and Mark arrived there. Was it that long ago? The magnolia trees would be festooned in sweet-smelling pink blossoms. She could almost smell them. Spring. It was symbolic of a new beginning.

The next afternoon Tamara walked along the shore. She glanced upward along the steep cliffs to her beautiful home. Her eyes skimmed the mountain until she saw abandoned Schofield Manor partially hidden among the trees. An ache gripped her as she thought of Mr. Schofield. He must have gone through a private hell, coming home to learn his wife was carrying another man's child.

The beach was deserted. It was a warm afternoon. There was very little breeze. The sun pressed down on her back. She slowed her brisk pace. Normally she took her walk in the morning, but because of Robert's illness and restlessness she had not wanted to leave him. Idly skirting the water's edge, she let her mind float back to happier days, first as a child when she played on the beach, and later with Mark. She glanced up along the wide curve of the shore toward the secluded lagoon, their private retreat, where they had made love, sometimes leisurely, sometimes with fierce haste and abandon. She strolled the mile to reach it, stopping briefly to pick up a conch shell and hold it to her ear. Sitting down on a coral rock, she took off her shoes and lisle stockings. She lifted her dress to her knees and waded into the crystal-clear water. It refreshed her whole being. She gathered her skirt in one hand and splashed her face with the other.

Tamara looked up, the water dripping from her lashes and chin, to see a dark spot far down the beach from where she had come. The speck materialized into a man on horseback riding hard. Hooves whipped up the white coral sand. She knew at once it was Mark. He stood in the stirrups and waved.

The folds of Tamara's dress fell from her hand, swinging into place around her legs, dipping into the incoming wave that licked her bare ankles. Overhead, the vivid blue sky was cloudless. The slight breeze rippled gently through her hair. Her breathing quickened as she watched him rein his horse and dismount. He walked into the water to meet her. For a timeless instant their eyes held. Smiling disarmingly, he took in her lovely russet-gold hair glowing in the sunshine, the breeze ruffling a wispy tendril across her brow. His eyes focused on her face. Searchingly, beseechingly, he sank his eyes into the depth of hers, afraid she would not want him. What he saw made him grin. By God, she was happy to see him, was greeting him with her warm, shy smile, her eyes filled with love.

Tamara reached out and touched his thick dark beard. She could feel her heart thumping at a fast pace. Before she could recapture her breath, he was standing so close her head spun and she felt as heady as the first time he had kissed her. She blushed, and he saw it and grinned broadly.

Inwardly Mark was flooded by a wave of strong emotions. He had dreamed, prayed for this moment when she would welcome him and want him back. What a lovely creature she was, he thought. She transcended all his hopes and dreams. How he cherished her. He had a great deal to make up to her, and he intended to spend the rest of his life doing so.

His first words were, "Oh, Tamara, my sweet, precious love, to think I almost lost you. Not a day went by that I did not think of you and long for you." Then, as if he could not live another second without her in his arms, he pulled her to him. One arm went around her waist, the other hand pressed her head to his shoulder affectionately. Tenderly he nuzzled his face in her soft, fresh-scented hair.

Spellbound, Tamara closed her eyes and clung to him, allowing the deeply pleasurable sensations of being in his arms to engulf her. It was as if the half of herself that had been missing was back and she was a whole person again. She took a deep breath, savoring his sensuous masculine scent, thrilling to the comfort of his arms and the strength of his body. It was one of the most joyous moments of her life.

The slight brush of his hand across her back brought a glaze to her eyes and sent delicious ripplets of pleasure to amass in marvelous sensations between her thighs. Her knees weakened as his arms twined around her and tightened as he murmured her name over and over, giving her his heart and soul and begging forgiveness. Feeling the feverish warmth of his cheek against hers, she trembled. She struggled without success to fight back the tears of happiness.

They were oblivious of the water lapping at his boots and soaking the hem of her dress. Half-laughing, half-sobbing, as their tears blended together on their cheeks, they exchanged endearments and promises for their future together.

"My darling. You belong to me." His yearning for her was revealed in every word he spoke and every gesture he made. "Forgive me," he said softly. When she said nothing, he repeated his plea. "Please forgive me. Forgive me."

"I love you with all my heart. There is nothing to forgive."

"There is, but if you believe there is not, then that means you forgive me. How have you been? How is our son?"

Tamara nestled closer. "It has been very difficult without you. Please do not leave me," she said so softly he could barely hear.

"I promise never to leave you, no matter what the circumstances."

He held her at arm's length and looked at her directly. "I want to remain here with you, but if we travel, it will be together or not at all. I am thirty-one years old. My sea-roving days are ended."

His hand moved up and down her back. Absently his other hand toyed with the satin ribbon at her throat.

"I want to get to know my son . . . and I think 'tis time for a daughter who looks just like you . . . if that is what you want, too."

"It is what I want more than anything . . . but there is one thing I ask of you."

"What is it?"

"That you forgive your father. He loved you. If he made mistakes, they were human. I am afraid of what hatred can do to you—to us. It makes me sick inside when I think of it."

Mark's reaction was unexpected. He smiled broadly. "I loved my father. In prison I had a great deal of time to think. If there is anything to forgive, I have," he said, and laughed. "Who am I to condemn when I have treated my own family so miserably?" He brushed his finger across her cheek. "And how can I not forgive anyone when you set such an excellent example of compassion?"

There was a great deal to tell each other. She wanted to inform him of his father's trust fund and the purchase of Schofield Manor. He wanted to tell her of the loss of the *Lady Tamara* and of his life in prison and what had happened in Charleston. But it could all wait.

He kissed her below the ear as if to seal the promise he had made never to leave her. His lips left a burning trail as they slid down to her neck before he let her go. He looked at her invitingly. "It has been a long time."

"An eternity," she agreed, knowing what he had in mind, and pulling his face toward hers. "You have not kissed me properly," she admonished.

His eyes flashed the color of the surf, his smile turning into a deep, husky laugh. Their parted lips met and clung, sending molten vibrations through both of them. The kiss told it all—love, need, want. He picked her up in his arms and carried her the short distance to the seclusion of palm trees shading the coral formations.

Knowing she was still his alone, he was overcome by the need to possess her. He touched the lobe of her ear with his lips which traversed to hers, pressing them lingeringly at first, then becoming insistent, leaving them breathless.

In his embrace Tamara felt gloriously feminine. This exciting, masculine man was her husband. The awareness of his love and desire enflamed her. All the waiting, wondering, and loneliness were forgotten in the loving warmth of his arms.

He shifted, bringing her closer. "My sweet, how wonderful it is to have you in my arms again." Looking down at the woman he held with the promise of a life full of love, his voice turned urgent. "I want you here, close to me, not only now, but for the rest of my life."

He released her reluctantly to take off his fawn-colored waistcoat and spread it on the sand for them to lie upon. She felt his fingers pulling open the ribbon at her throat, unbuttoning her tufted, lace-trimmed blouse. Her body was on fire before he touched her. Their lips met, spreading flames that engulfed them in heated desire.

Their long separation ignited their desperate need for each

376